Cardington Crescent

Anne Perry

FAWCETT CREST • NEW YORK

A Fawcett Crest Book
Published by Ballantine Books
Copyright © 1987 by Anne Perry

Library of Congress Catalog Card Number: 86-27942

ISBN 0-449-21442-7

This edition published by arrangement with St. Martin's Press, Inc.

Manufactured in the United States of America

First Ballantine Books Edition: June 1988

To Ed and Peggy Wells, with thanks for their love and faith through the years.

Mrs. Peabody was hot and out of breath. It was midsum-mer; her stays imprisoned her unyieldingly and her gown, with its fashionable bustle, was far too heavy to allow her to go chasing down the pavement after a willful dog that was fast disappearing through the wrought-iron churchyard gates.

"Clarence!" Mrs. Peabody cried out furiously. "Clar-ence! Come back here at once!"

But Clarence, who was fat and middle-aged and should have known better, squirmed through the gap and shot away into the long grass and the laurel bushes on the other side of the railings. Mrs. Peabody, gasping with annoy-ance and clinging on to her broad hat with one hand, sending it rakishly over her eyes, tried with the other to force the gates open far enough to allow her extremely ample form to pass through.

The late Mr. Peabody had preferred women of generous proportions. He had said so frequently. A man's wife should reflect his position in life: dignified and substantial.

But it took more aplomb than Mrs. Peabody possessed to remain dignified while caught by one's bosom in a churchyard gate with one's hat askew and a dog yelping like a fiend a dozen yards away.

"Clarence!" she shrieked again and, drawing in her breath, gave a mighty heave, which had the opposite effect from the one desired. She let out a wail of desperation,

1

and struggled through, her bustle now alarmingly closer to her left hip.

Clarence was barking hysterically and scuffling in the laurel bushes. The ground was dry after a week without rain and he was sending up spurts of dust. But he had his prize, a very large, sodden-looking parcel wrapped in brownish paper and tied securely with twine. Under Clarence's determined efforts it was now torn in several places and beginning to come undone.

"Drop it!" Mrs. Peabody commanded. Clarence ignored her. "Drop it!" she repeated, wrinkling her nose in distaste. It was really very unpleasant; it appeared to be kitchen leavings—unusable meat. "Clarence!"

The dog ripped off a large piece of the paper, wet with blood and coming away easily. Then she saw it—skin. Human skin, pale and soft. She screamed; then as Clarence exposed more of it she screamed again, and again, and again, until her lungs were bursting and she could not find breath and the world spun round her in a red haze. She fell to the ground, unaware of Clarence, still tugging at the parcel, and passersby forcing their way through the stuck gate in alarm.

Inspector Thomas Pitt looked up from his desk, strewn with paper, glad of the interruption. "What is it?"

Police Constable Stripe stood in the doorway, his face a little pink above his stiff collar, his eyes blinking.

"I'm sorry, sir, but there's a report of a disturbance in St. Mary's churchyard in Bloomsbury. An elderly person 'avin' 'ysterics. Quite respectable, and locally known—and doesn't touch the gin. 'Usband was Temperance, 'afore 'e died. Never bin a nuisance in the past."

"Perhaps she's ill?" Pitt suggested. "Doesn't need more than a constable, does it? Maybe a doctor?"

"Well, sir." Stripe looked distressed. "Seems 'er dog ran away and found this parcel in the bushes, an' she thought it was part of a person. That's what gave 'er 'ysterics."

2

"What on earth do you mean, 'part of a person'?" Pitt demanded irritably. He liked young Wilberforce Stripe; he was normally keen and reliable. This vague story was unlike him. "What's in this parcel?"

"Well, that's it, Mr. Pitt, sir. The constable on the beat says 'e 'asn't touched it more'n necessary afore you get there, sir, but by 'is reckoning that's just what it is—a part of a woman's body. The—er . . ." He was clearly embarrassed. He did not wish to be indelicate, yet was aware that a policeman should be precise. He placed one hand across his waist and the other across his neck. "The top 'alf, sir."

Pitt stood up, papers cascading off his lap onto the floor and remaining there. In spite of his seventeen years in London, where the sumptuous and elegant heart of the Empire disported itself a stone's throw from slums that teemed with poverty so intense rotting tenements stood stacked against each other, fifteen people to a room living and dying together, he had not ceased to be shocked by the savagery of crime. He could not grasp the mass—the mind refused. But the pain of the individual still had power to move him.

"Then we'd better go and see," he replied, ignoring the disarray around him and leaving his hat on the stand where he had thrown it on arriving in the morning.

"Yes, sir." Stripe fell in behind him, following Pitt's familiar disheveled figure along the corridor, down the steps past several other constables, and into the hot and dusty street. An empty hansom clattered past them, not believing Pitt, with his coattails flapping and his tie askew, to prove a likely fare. Stripe, in uniform, was not even worth considering.

Pitt waved his arm and ran a few steps. "Cabbie!" he shouted, his anger directed not at the personal slight but against all crime in general, and this one he was going to pursue in particular.

The cabbie drew rein and looked at him with disfavor. "Yes, sir?"

"St. Mary's churchyard, Bloomsbury." Pitt scrambled in and held the door for Stripe, behind him.

"Will that be the east side or the west side?" the cabbie inquired.

"The back gate, off the avenue," Stripe put in helpfully.

"Thank you," Pitt acknowledged; then, to the cabbie, "Get on with it, man!"

The cabbie flicked the whip and made encouraging sounds, and they moved off, rapidly increasing to a trot. They rode in silence, each absorbed in his own speculations as to what they might find.

"This 'ere where you wanta be, sir?" the cabbie leaned down and asked dubiously.

"Yes." Pitt had already seen the little knot of people and the harassed constable in the middle. It was an ordinary, rather seedy suburban churchyard; dusty, grass dry with the summer heat, gravestones uneven and ornate, marble angels, and over on the right before the yew trees, a clump of dark laurels.

He climbed out, paid the driver, then crossed the pavement and spoke to the constable, who was obviously overwhelmed with relief to see him.

"What have you got?" Pitt asked dourly.

The constable jerked his elbow towards the high, spiked railings but did not turn his head. His face was pale and there was a heavy beading of sweat on his lip and across his brow. He looked wretched. "Top 'alf of a woman's body, sir." He swallowed hard. "Pretty 'orrible, it is. It was under them bushes."

"Who found it, and when?"

"A Mrs. Ernestine Peabody, out walking 'er Pekingese dog by the name o' Clarence." He glanced down at his notebook. Pitt read from it upside down; *15th June, 1887, 3:25 P.M., called to St. Mary's churchyard, woman screaming.*

"Where is she now?" Pitt asked.

"Sittin' on the seat in the church vestibule, sir. She's took pretty bad, an' I said as soon as you'd spoke to 'er she could go 'ome. It's my opinion, sir, as she won't be much use to us.''

"Probably not," Pitt agreed. "Where is this . . . parcel?"

"Where I found it, sir! I didn't touch it more'n to make sure she wasn't 'avin'—delusions, like. On the gin.''

Pitt went to the gates, heavy wrought iron and stuck fast, a little over a foot apart, wedged in the ruts of the dried mud. He squeezed through and walked along the inside of the railing till he came to the laurel bushes. He knew Stripe was immediately behind him.

The parcel was about nineteen inches square, lying where Clarence had left it, paper torn and pulled away to expose the meatlike flesh and several inches of fine-grained, white skin smeared a little with blood. There were flies beginning to gather. He did not have to touch it to see that the portion showing was part of a woman's breast.

He straightened up, feeling so sick he was afraid he was going to faint. He breathed deeply—in and out, in and out—and heard Stripe blundering away, choking and retching behind a gravestone carved with cherubs.

After a moment of staring at the dusty stones, the trodden grass, and the tiny yellow spots like pinheads on the laurel leaves, he forced himself to turn back to the dreadful parcel. There were details to note; the kind and color of the paper, the twine that wound it, the type of knots. People left their mark—tied string loosely or tightly, length or width first, made slipknots, running knots, tied at each crossover or merely looped. And there were a dozen different ways of finishing off.

He blanked from his mind what was inside it and knelt to examine it, turning it over gingerly when he had seen all he could from the top. It was thick paper, a little shiny on the inside, two layers of it. He had often seen such paper used for tying parcels of linen. It was strong and usually crackled a little if touched—only this was wet with blood and made no sound, even when he turned it. Inside the brown paper was clear, greased kitchen paper, another two layers, the sort butchers sometimes use. Whoever had wrapped this hideous thing must have imagined it would hold the blood.

The string was unusual—coarse, hairy twine, yellow rather than white, wrapped lengthways and widthways twice and knotted at each join, and finally tied with a loop and two raw ends about an inch and a half long.

He took out his notebook and wrote it down, though it was all something he would like to forget—wipe totally from his memory. If he could.

Stripe was coming back, awkwardly, embarrassed by his loss of composure. He did not know what to say.

Pitt said it for him. "There must be more. We'd better organize a search."

Stripe cleared his throat. "More . . . Yes, Mr. Pitt. But where should we start? Could be anywhere!"

"Won't be very far." Pitt stood up, knees stiff. "You don't carry that sort of thing longer than you have to. Certainly not further than you can walk. Even a lunatic doesn't get into a hansom or a public omnibus with a bundle like that under his arm. Should be within a radius of a mile at the outside."

Stripe's brows went up. "Would 'e walk a mile, sir? I wouldn't. More like five 'undred yards, if that."

"Five hundred in each direction," Pitt answered. "Somewhere five hundred yards from here." He waved his arm round the compass.

"In each . . ." Stripe's blue eyes were confused.

Pitt put the thought into words. "Must be a whole body altogether. That's about six parcels, roughly this size. He couldn't carry them all at once, unless he used a barrow. And I doubt he'd draw attention to himself by doing that. He certainly wouldn't be likely to borrow one, and who owns barrows except tradesmen and costers? But we'll check for any seen in this area, either yesterday or today."

"Yes, sir." Stripe was intensely relieved to have something to do. Anything was better than standing there helplessly while the flies buzzed round the appalling heap in the grass.

"Send a message back to the station that we need half a dozen constables. And the mortuary cart, and the surgeon."

"Yes, sir." Stripe forced himself to look down once more, perhaps because he felt somehow callous disregarding the enormity of it, walking away without some acknowledgment. It was the same instinct that makes one take off one's hat at the sight of a hearse passing in the street, even though one has no idea who is dead.

Pitt walked between the gravestones, curled and decorated, marred by weeds, and came to the graveled entrance to the church. The door was open and it was cool inside. It took a moment for his eyes to adjust to the gloom and the hazy colored splashes on the stones from the stained glass. A large woman was collapsed, half prostrate, on a wooden seat, her hat on the floor beside her, the neck of her dress undone. The sexton's wife, holding a glass of water in one hand and a bottle of ammonia smelling salts in the other, was muttering something comforting. They both looked round, startled, as Pitt's footsteps sounded on the floor. A ginger-colored Pekingese dog was asleep in the doorway in the sun and ignored him completely.

"Mrs. Peabody?"

She stared at him with a mixture of suspicion and anticipation. It was not entirely displeasing to be the epicenter of such a drama—providing, of course, that everyone understood she had no connection with it but that of an innocent woman drawn in by chance.

"I am she," she said somewhat unnecessarily.

Pitt had met many Mrs. Peabodys before, and he knew not only what she felt now but what nightmares were to come. He sat down on the bench beside her, a yard away.

"You must be extremely distressed"—he hurried on as she drew in a gasp of breath to tell him precisely how much—"so I will trouble you as little as possible. When was the last time you walked your dog past the churchyard?"

Her carefully arched eyebrows shot up into her rather sandy hairline. "I don't think you understand, young man! I am not in the habit of finding such . . . such . . ." She

7

could frame no words for the quite genuine horror that seized her.

"I'm sure," Pitt said grimly. "I assume that if it had been there the last time, your dog would have found it then."

Mrs. Peabody, in spite of her shock, was not without common sense. She saw the point immediately. "Oh. I came this way yesterday afternoon, and Clarence did not . . ." She trailed off, not liking to complete such an unnecessary remark.

"I see. Thank you. Do you know if Clarence pulled the parcel out from under the bushes, or was it already out?"

She shook her head.

It did not matter, except that had it been in the open it would probably have been noticed earlier. Almost certainly, whoever had put it there had taken the time to hide it also. There was really nothing else to ask her but her name and address.

He left them and went outside again into the heat and began to think about organizing a search. It was half past four.

By seven o'clock they had found them all. It was a grim business; going down the steps into disused areaways, sifting through refuse in rubbish cans that could be reached from the street, poking under bushes and behind railings. Parcel by parcel the rest were retrieved. The worst was in a narrow and fetid alley just over a mile from the churchyard, in the sour tenements of St. Giles. It should have provided the first clue to her identity, but as with two of the others, feral cats had discovered it first, led by scent and their ever devouring hunger. There was nothing recognizable now but long, fair hair and a crushing injury to the skull.

The long summer day did not darken till ten in the evening. Pitt trudged from door to door asking, pleading, occasionally bullying an unfortunate servant into an admission of guilt for some domestic misdemeanor—perhaps an illicit flirtation that had held them on the back steps longer than usual—but no one admitted to having seen anything remotely relevant. There had been no costermongers but those on long known and legitimate business, no residents or strangers carrying mysterious parcels, no one hurrying furtively, and no one reported missing.

Pitt was back at the police station as the sun set cherry-red over the roofs, and the gaslights came on in the fashionable thoroughfares like so many straying moons. Inside, the station smelled of closed doors, heat, the sharpness of ink, and brand new linoleum on the floor. The police surgeon was waiting for him, shirt sleeves still rolled up and stained, his waistcoat done up on the wrong buttons. He looked tired, and there was a smear of blood across his nose.

"Well?" Pitt asked wearily.

"Young woman." The man sat down without being asked. "Fair hair, fair skin. As near as one can tell, she might have been quite good-looking. She certainly wasn't any beggar. Hands were clean, no broken nails, but she'd done a bit of housework. My first guess would be a parlormaid, but it's only a guess." He sighed. "And she'd had a child, but not within the last few months."

Pitt sat down behind his desk and leaned on his elbows. "How old?"

"For God's sake, man! How do I know?" the doctor said angrily, his pity, disgust, and sheer helplessness spilling over at the only victim available. "You present me with a corpse in half a dozen pieces, like so much offal from some bloody butcher, and you want me to tell you who she was! Well, I can't!" He stood up, knocking his chair over. "She was a young woman, probably in domestic service, and some lunatic murdered her by hitting her on the back of the head and then, God knows why, cut her into pieces and left her strewn around Bloomsbury and St. Giles. You'll be damned lucky if you ever find out who she is, still less who did that to her. I sometimes wonder why you bother. Of the thousand different ways to murder people, a crack on the head might be less cruel in the long

9

run than some of the ways we ignore. Have you been in the tenements and lodging houses in St. Giles, Wapping, Mile End? The last corpse I looked at was a twelve-year-old girl. Died in childbirth—'' He stopped, his voice thick with tears he was only half embarrassed for. He glanced at Pitt savagely and strode out, slamming the door.

Pitt stood up slowly, righted the chair, and went out after him. Normally he would have walked home; it was only a couple of miles. But it was nearly eleven and he was tired and hungry and his feet hurt more than usual. He took a hansom and ignored the expense.

The front of the house was dark and he let himself in with his key. Gracie, the maid, would long have gone to bed, but he could see a light on in the kitchen and he knew Charlotte would be waiting for him. Sighing, he took off his boots with relief and walked along the corridor, feeling the coolness of the linoleum through his socks.

Charlotte was in the doorway, the gas lamp behind her shining on the auburn in her hair and catching the warm curve of her cheek. Without saying anything, she put her arms round him and held him surprisingly tightly. For a moment he was afraid something was wrong, that one of the children was ill; then he realized she would of course have seen an evening newspaper. If it had not mentioned his name, she had guessed from his lateness that he was involved.

He had not intended to tell her. In spite of all the cases she had concerned herself with, part of him still believed she should be protected from such horror. Most men felt their homes were a retreat from the harshness, and frequently the ugliness, of the outside world, a place to refresh both body and spirit before returning again to the fray. Women were part of that gentler, better place.

But Charlotte had seldom done the expected, even before she had appalled her well-bred family by marrying into the police, a descent so radical she was fortunate they had not disowned her.

10

Now she loosed herself a little and looked up at him, her face puckered with concern.

"You are on that case, aren't you, Thomas? That poor woman found in St. Mary's churchyard?"

"Yes." He kissed her gently, then again, hoping she would not talk about it. He was so tired he hurt, and there was nothing to say.

As she grew older Charlotte was learning when to keep her own counsel a little more, but this was not one of those occasions. She had read the extra edition of the newspaper with horror and pity, cooked two dinners for Pitt and had to abandon them both, and she expected at the very least that he would share with her the thoughts and some of the feelings that had possessed him during the day.

"Are you going to find out who she was?" she asked, pulling back and starting for the kitchen. "Have you eaten?"

"No, of course I haven't," he said wearily, following her. "But don't bother cooking anything now."

Her eyebrows shot up, but this time she glanced at his face and bit her tongue. Behind her on the blackened and polished range the kettle was billowing clouds of steam.

"Would you like cold mutton, pickle, and fresh bread?" she asked sweetly. "And a cup of tea?"

He smiled in spite of himself. It would be easier, and pleasanter in the long run, to surrender.

"Yes, I would." He sat down, putting his jacket over the back of the chair.

She hesitated, then decided it would be wiser to make the tea before saying anything more, but there was a little upward quirk at the corner of her mouth.

Five minutes later he had three slices of crumbly bread, a pile of homemade chutney—Charlotte was very good at chutney and marmalade—several slices of meat, and a breakfast cup full of steaming tea.

Charlotte had contained herself long enough. "Are you going to find out who she was?"

"I doubt it," he said, filling his mouth with food.

She stared at him solemnly. "Won't somebody report

11

her missing? Bloomsbury is quite a respectable area. People who have parlormaids notice if they're gone."

In spite of their six years of marriage and all the cases she had one way or another found herself involved in, she still carried with her remnants of the innocence in which she had grown up, protected from unpleasantness, imprisoned from the harshness and the excitement of the world, as young ladies of gentility should be. To begin with, Charlotte's breeding had awed Pitt and, in her blinder moments, angered him. But mostly it disappeared in all the infinitely more important things they shared: laughter at life's absurdities, tenderness, passion, and anger at the same injustices.

"Thomas?"

"My darling Charlotte, she doesn't have to have come from Bloomsbury. And even if she did, how many maids do you suppose have been dismissed, for any number of reasons, from dishonesty to having been caught in the arms of the master of the house? Others will have eloped—or been supposed to have—or lifted the family silver and disappeared into the night."

"Parlormaids aren't like that!" she protested. "Aren't you even going to ask after her?"

"We have done," he replied with a tired edge to his voice. Had she no idea how futile it was—and that he would already have done everything he could? Did she not know that much of him, after all this time?

She bent her head, looking down at the tablecloth. "I'm sorry. I suppose you'll never know."

"Probably not," he agreed, picking up his cup. "Is that a letter from Emily on the mantelpiece?"

"Yes." Emily was her younger sister, who had married as far above herself as Charlotte had descended. "She is staying with Great-aunt Vespasia in Cardington Crescent."

"I thought Great-aunt Vespasia lived in Gadstone Park."

"She does. They're all staying with Uncle Eustace March."

He grunted. There was nothing to say to that. He had a

deep admiration for the elegant, waspish Lady Vespasia Cumming-Gould, but Eustace March he had never heard of, nor did he wish to.

"She sounds very unhappy," Charlotte went on, looking at him anxiously.

"I'm sorry." He did not meet her eyes but fished for another piece of bread and the chutney dish. "But there's nothing we can do. I daresay she's bored." This time he did look up, fixing her with something approaching a glare. "And you will go nowhere near Bloomsbury, not even to visit some long lost friend, either of yours or of Emily's. Is that understood, Charlotte?"

"Yes, Thomas," she said with wide eyes. "I don't think I know anybody in Bloomsbury, anyway."

2

Emily was indeed profoundly unhappy, in spite of the fact that she looked magnificent in a shimmering aquamarine gown of daring and elegant cut and was sitting in the Marches' private box at the Savoy. On stage, in all its delicious, lyrical charm, was Messrs. Gilbert and Sullivan's opera *Iolanthe*, of which she was particularly fond. The very idea of a youth half human and half fairy, divided at the waist, normally appealed to her sense of the absurd. Tonight it passed her by.

The cause of her distress was that for several days now her husband, George, had taken no pains at all to hide the fact that he very evidently preferred Sybilla March's company to Emily's. He was perfectly civil, in an automatic kind of way, which was worse than rudeness. Rudeness would at least have meant he was sharply aware of her, not dimly, as of something blurred at the edge of his vision. It was Sybilla's presence that brought the light to his face, it was she his eyes followed, she whose words held his attention, whose wit made him laugh.

Now he was sitting behind her, and to Emily she looked as gaudy as some overblown flower, in her flame-colored gown, with her white skin and peat-water-dark eyes and all that opulent mass of hair. In spite of the hurt and the foolishness of it, Emily glanced sideways at him often enough to know that George barely looked at the stage. The hero's plight did not move him in the slightest, nor the heroine's winsome flirtations, nor the fairy Queen nor Iolanthe herself. He did smile and move his fingers gently in time to "The Peers' Song," which surely would move anyone at all, and his attention was caught for a moment's sheer pleasure in the dancing trio, with the Lord High Chancellor kicking his legs in the air with abandoned glee.

Emily could feel the misery and panic growing inside her. Everything around was color, gaiety, and sound; every face she could see was smiling—George at Sybilla, Uncle Eustace March at himself, Sybilla's husband, William, at the fantasy on stage. His youngest sister, Tassie, only nineteen, thin as her mother had been and with a shock of hair the color of sunlight on apricots, was definitely smiling at the principal tenor. Old Mrs. March, her grandmother, was twitching the corner of her tight lips upward in spite of herself; she did not care to be amused. Great-aunt Vespasia, Tassie's maternal grandmother, on the other hand, was delighted. She had a marked sense of the ridiculous and had long ago ceased to care a jot what anyone else thought of her.

That left only Jack Radley, the single nonfamily guest of the evening, currently also staying at Cardington Crescent. He was a ravishingly handsome young man with excellent connections, but unfortunately, no money worth mentioning, and a highly dubious reputation with women. He was another outsider, and for that alone Emily could have liked him, regardless of his grace or his humor. It was fairly obvious that he had been invited with a view to arranging a marriage for Tassie, the only one of the ten March daughters still unmarried. The purpose of this liaison was not yet plain, since Tassie did not appear to be fond of him and had considerably more substantial expectations than he; although his family was related to those who held power he himself had no prospects. William had said unkindly that Eustace hungered for a knighthood— and in time, perhaps, a peerage—as the ultimate accolade to his family's rise from trade to respectability. But that was surely an observation more malicious than truthful.

There was a tension between father and son, a sharpness that intruded like a sudden splinter of glass every now and then, small but surprisingly painful.

At present William was behind Emily's chair, and he was the only one she could not see.

During the interval it was he who brought her wine and a chocolate bonbon, not George; George was standing in the corner laughing at something Sybilla had said. Emily forced herself to make some sort of conversation, knowing it was a failure even as the words fell into hot silence, and the minute after she wished she had not said them. She was relieved when the curtain went up again.

"I cannot think where Mr. Gilbert gets such ridiculous plots!" Old Mrs. March drummed her fingers irritably when the final applause had died. "There is absolutely no sense in it at all!"

"There is not meant to be, Grandmama," Sybilla said with a dreamy smile.

Mrs. March stared at her over her pince-nez, the black velvet ribbon dangling down her cheek. "Someone who is foolish because nature has so designed them, I pity; someone who is foolish by intention it is beyond me to understand," she said coldly.

"That I can well believe," Jack Radley murmured behind Emily's ear. "And I'd swear Mr. Gilbert would find her equally incomprehensible—only he wouldn't care."

"My dear Lavinia, he is no more foolish than some of the romances by Madam Ouida, which I see you reading under brown paper covers."

Mrs. March's face froze, but there were pink spots in her cheeks where rouge would have been on a younger woman. She deplored the vulgarity of painting one's face; women who did that were "of a certain sort."

"You are quite mistaken, Vespasia," she snapped. "It is a pity your vanity prevents you obtaining a pair of spectacles. One of these days you will fall downstairs or otherwise make an unfortunate exhibition of yourself. William! You had better give your grandmama your arm. I don't wish to be the center of attention as we leave.'' She rose to her feet and turned to the door. ''Especially of that kind!''

''You won't be,'' Vespasia retorted. ''Not as long as Sybilla insists upon wearing scarlet.''

''Very suitable for her,'' Emily said, before she thought. She had intended it to be inaudible, but just at the precise moment everyone around them stopped speaking and her voice came clearly into the pause.

There was a touch of color in George's face, and she looked away instantly, wishing she had bitten her tongue till it bled rather than betray herself so nakedly.

''I'm so glad you like it,'' Sybilla answered quite calmly, rising also. There seemed no end to her aplomb. ''We all have colors which flatter us, and those which don't. I doubt I should look as well as you do in that shade of blue.''

That made it worse. Instead of spitting back she had been charming. Even now, George was smiling at her. Almost as if some invisible current had designed it, they were swept out of the box into the eddy of people pressing to reach the foyer, George next to Sybilla, offering his arm as if anything less would have been uncivil.

Emily found herself, hot-faced and stumbling, being pushed and jostled forward with Jack Radley's arm about her and Great-aunt Vespasia's beautiful silver head in front.

Once they reached the foyer it was inescapable that they should meet with people they knew, and be obliged to exchange opinions and inquiries as to health, and all the other chitchat of such an occasion. It swam over her head in a senseless bedlam. She nodded and smiled and agreed with everything that penetrated into her mind. Someone asked after her son, Edward, and she replied that he was at home and very well. Then George nudged her sharply, and she remembered to inquire after the family of the speaker. It all babbled on around her:

''Delightful performance!''

17

"Have you seen *Pinafore*?"

"How does that piece go again?"

"Shall you be at Henley? I do love regattas. Such a delightful thing for a hot day, don't you agree?"

"I prefer Goodwood. There is something about the races—all the silks, don't you know!"

"But my dear, what about Ascot?"

"I rather care for Wimbledon, myself."

"I haven't a *thing* to wear! I must see my dressmaker immediately—I really need an entire new wardrobe."

"Wasn't the Royal Academy too frightful this year!"

"My dear, I do agree! Perfectly tedious!"

Clumsily, she survived nearly half an hour of such greetings and comments before at last finding herself alone in her carriage with George beside her, stiff and more distant than a stranger.

"What on earth is the matter with you, Emily?" George said after they had sat in silence for ten minutes, while carriages ahead of them picked up their owners. Finally the way ahead was clear down the Strand.

Should she lie, evade the moment of commitment to the quarrel which she knew he would hate? George was tolerant, generous, of an easy nature, but he wanted emotion only at times of his own choosing, and most certainly not now, when he was full of the echoes of such civilized enjoyment.

Half of her wanted to face him, let all her scalding hurt burst out, demand he explain himself and his wounding and outrageous behavior. But just as she opened her mouth to reply, cowardice overcame her. Once she had spoken it would be too late to draw back; she would have cut off her only retreat. It was so unlike her—she was usually mistress of herself so coolly, with such measured reaction. It was part of what had first drawn him to her. Now she betrayed all that and took the easy lie, despising herself, and hating him for reducing her to it.

"I don't feel very well," she said stiffly. "I think perhaps the theater was a little hot."

"I didn't notice it." He was still annoyed. "Nor did anyone else."

It was on the tip of her tongue to point out how profoundly he had been otherwise engaged, but again she avoided the crisis.

"Then maybe I am feverish."

"Spend tomorrow in bed." There was no sympathy in his voice.

He just wants me to stay out of the way, she thought, before I become even more of a nuisance and an embarrassment to him. Tears prickled in her eyes, and she swallowed hard, painfully grateful to be in the close, sharp darkness of the carriage. She said nothing, in case her voice betrayed her, and George did not pursue the subject. They rode through the summer night, their way lit by the hundred yellow moons of the gas lamps, hearing nothing but the steady *clop-clop* of the horses' hooves and the rumble of the wheels.

When they reached Cardington Crescent the footman opened the doors, and Emily climbed down and went up the steps under the portico and in through the front door without even glancing to see if George was behind her. It was customary to attend a dinner party before the opera and a supper party afterwards, but old Mrs. March did not feel her health equal to both—although in fact there was nothing whatsoever wrong with her except age—so they had forgone the supper. Now a late meal was served in the withdrawing room, but Emily could not face the laughter, the bright lights of the chandeliers, and the probing eyes.

"If you will excuse me," Emily said to no one in particular, "it has been a delightful evening, but I am rather tired and I would prefer to retire. I wish you all a good night." Not waiting for a reply, she continued straight on to the foot of the stairs before anyone's voice held her back. It was not George, as she ached for it to be, but Jack Radley, only a pace behind her.

"Are you all right, Lady Ashworth? You look a little

pale. Shall we have something sent up to you?'' Already he was at her elbow.

''No, thank you,'' she said quickly. ''I am sure I shall be quite well when I have rested.'' She must not be seen to be rude—it was so childish. She forced herself to turn and look at him. He was smiling. He really did have the most remarkable eyes; he contrived to look intimate even when she barely knew him, and yet it was not quite enough to be intrusive. She could see quite well how he had gained his reputation with women. It would serve George right if she fell as much in love with Radley as George had with Sybilla!

''Are you sure?'' he repeated.

''Quite,'' she answered expressionlessly. ''Thank you.'' And she went up the stairs as rapidly as she could without appearing to run. She was only on the landing when she heard the conversation resume, the laughter peal again, the gay lilt of people who are still in the spell of totally carefree pleasure.

She woke to find herself alone and the sunlight streaming in through a crack in the imperfectly drawn curtains. George was not there, nor had he been. His side of the enormous bed was immaculate, the linen crisp. She had intended to have her breakfast sent up, but now her own company was worse than anyone else's, and she rang sharply for her maid, refusing morning tea and sending her off to draw a bath and set out Emily's clothes for the morning.

She put a wrap round her shoulders and knocked sharply on the dressing room door. After several moments it was opened by George, looking sleepy and rumpled, his thick hair falling loosely, his eyes wide and dark.

''Oh,'' he said, blinking at her. ''Since you weren't well I thought I'd not disturb you, so I had them make up the bed in here.'' He did not ask if she was better. He merely looked at her, at her milky skin with its faint blush and her coil of pale honey hair, came to his own conclusion, and retreated back to prepare himself for the day.

Breakfast was grim. Eustace, as always, had thrown all the dining room windows open. He was a great believer in "muscular Christianity" and all the aggressive good health that went with it. He ate pigeons in jelly with ostentatious relish, and piles of hot buttered toast and marmalade, and barricaded himself behind the *Times*, ironed and given him by the footman, which he did not offer to share with anyone. Not, of course, that any man offered his newspaper to women, but Eustace also ignored William, George, and Jack Radley.

Vespasia, to Eustace's eternal disapproval, had her own newspaper.

"There has been a murder in Bloomsbury," she observed over the raspberries.

"What has that to do with us?" Eustace did not look up; the remark was intended as a criticism. Women should not have newspapers, let alone discuss them at breakfast.

"About as much as anything else that is in here," Vespasia replied. "It is to do with people, and tragedy."

"Nonsense!" old Mrs. March snapped. "Probably some person of the criminal classes who thoroughly deserved it. Eustace, would you be good enough to pass me the *Court Circular*? I wish to know what is happening that is of some importance." She shot a look of distaste at Vespasia. "I trust no one has forgotten we have a luncheon party at the Withingtons', and that we are playing croquet at Lady Lucy Armstrong's in the afternoon?" she went on, glancing at Sybilla with a frown and a faint curl of her lip. "Lady Lucy will be full of the Eton and Harrow cricket match, of course, and we shall be obliged to listen to her boasting endlessly about her sons. And *we* shall have nothing to say at all."

Sybilla colored, a stiff, painful red. Her eyes were bright. She stared straight back at her grandmother-in-law with an expression which might have been any of a dozen things.

"We shall have to see whether it is a boy or a girl before we consider a school," she said very clearly.

William stopped, his fork halfway to his mouth, incredulous. George drew in his breath in a little hiss of surprise. Eustace lowered his paper for the first time since he had sat down, and stared at her with amazement, then slow dawning jubilation.

"Sybilla! My dear girl! Do you mean that you are . . . er . . . ?"

"Yes!" she said boldly. "I would not have told you so soon, but I am tired of Grandmother-in-law making such remarks."

"You cannot blame me!" Mrs. March defended herself sharply. "You've been twelve years about it. It is not surprising I despaired of the March name continuing. Heaven knows, poor William has had his patience strained to breaking point waiting for you to give him an heir."

William's head came round to glare at his grandmother, his cheeks burning, his eyes hot blue.

"That is absolutely none of your affair!" he said abruptly. "And I find your remarks inexpressibly vulgar." He pushed his chair back, rose, and walked from the room.

"Well, well." Eustace folded his newspaper and poured himself another cup of coffee. "Congratulations, my dear."

"Better late than never," Mrs. March conceded. "Although I doubt you will have many more, *now*."

Sybilla still looked flushed, and now thoroughly uncomfortable. For the only time since her arrival, Emily felt sorry for her.

But the emotion was short-lived. The next few days passed in the customary fashion of Society during the Season. In the mornings they rode in the park, at which Emily had taught herself to be both graceful and skilled. But she had not the outrageous flair of Sybilla, and since George was a natural horseman it seemed almost inevitable that they should more often than not end up side by side, at some distance from the others.

William never came, preferring to work at his painting, which was his profession as well as his vocation. He was gifted to the degree that his works were admired by academicians and collected by connoisseurs. Only Eustace affected to find it displeasing that his only son preferred to retire alone to the studio arranged for him in the conservatory and make use of the morning light, rather than parade on horseback for the fashionable world to admire.

When they did not ride, they drove in the carriage, went shopping, paid calls upon their more intimate friends, or visited art galleries and exhibitions.

Luncheon was usually at about two o'clock, often at someone else's house in a small party. In the afternoon they attended concerts or drove to Richmond or Hurlingham, or else made the necessary, more formal calls upon those ladies they knew only slightly, perching awkwardly around withdrawing rooms, backs stiff, and making idiotic chatter about people, gowns, and the weather. The men excused themselves from this last activity and retired to one or another of their clubs.

At four there was afternoon tea, sometimes at home, sometimes out at a garden party. Once there was a game of croquet, at which George partnered Sybilla and lost hopelessly amid peals of laughter and a sense of delight that infinitely outweighed Emily's, who won. The taste of victory was ashes in her mouth. Not even Eustace, who partnered her, seemed to notice her. All eyes were on Sybilla, dressed in cherry pink, her cheeks flushed, her eyes radiant, and laughing so easily at her own ineptitude everyone wished to laugh with her.

Again Emily drove home in bitter silence before going leaden-footed up the stairs to change for dinner and the theater.

By Sunday she could bear it no longer. They had all been to church in the morning; Eustace insisted upon it. He was the patriarch of a godly family, and must be seen to be so. Dutifully, because they were guests in his house, they went—even Jack Radley, to whom it was far from a natural inclination. He would much rather have spent his summer Sundays in a good gallop in the park, with the sun sparkling through the trees and wind in his face, scattering birds, dogs, and onlookers alike—as indeed so would George, normally. But today George seemed positively happy to sit on the hard pew next to Emily, his eyes always wandering to Sybilla.

Luncheon was spent discussing the sermon, which had been earnest and tedious, dissecting it for "deeper meaning." By the time they came to the fruit Eustace had pronounced that its real subject was the virtue of fortitude, and of bearing all affliction with a stiff upper lip. Only William was either sufficiently interested or sufficiently angry to bother to contradict him and assert that, on the contrary, it was about compassion.

"Nonsense!" Eustace said briskly. "You were always too soft, William. Always for taking the easy way out! Too many sisters, that's your trouble. Should have been a girl yourself. Courage!" He banged the table with his fist. "That's what it takes to be a man—and a Christian."

The rest of the meal was eaten in silence. The afternoon was spent reading and writing letters.

The evening was even worse. They sat around striving to make conversation suitable to the Sabbath, until Sybilla was invited to play the piano, which she did rather well and with obvious enjoyment. Everyone except Emily was drawn in, singing ballads, and occasionally, more serious solos. Sybilla had a very rich voice, a little husky with a slight catch in it.

Upstairs at last, her throat sore with the effort of not crying, Emily dismissed her maid and began to undress herself. George came in and closed the door with an unnecessarily loud noise.

"Couldn't you have made more of an effort, Emily?" he said coldly. "Your sullenness was verging on bad manners."

It was too much. The injustice of it was intolerable.

"Bad manners!" she gasped. "How *dare* you stand

there and accuse me of bad manners! You have spent the entire fortnight seducing your host's daughter-in-law in front of everyone, even the servants. And because I don't care to join in with you, you accuse me of being ill-mannered!''

The color flamed up in his face, but he stood perfectly still. "You are hysterical," he said quietly. "Perhaps you would be better alone until you can collect yourself. I shall sleep in the dressing room; the bed is still made up. I can perfectly easily tell everyone you are not feeling well and I don't wish to disturb you." His nostrils flared very slightly and a flicker of irritation crossed his face. "They won't find that hard to believe. Good night." And a moment later he was gone.

Emily stood numbed by the monstrosity of it. It was so utterly unfair, it took several moments to assimilate it. Then she threw herelf onto the bed, punched the pillow with all her strength, and burst into tears. She wept till her eyes were burning and her lungs ached, and still she felt no better—only too tired to hurt so fiercely anymore—until tomorrow.

3

Emily woke very early in the morning, even before the housemaids were up, and reviewed the situation. Last night's crisis had swept away the paralysis of indecision, the fending off of the knowledge which she knew must come with all its misery. She made a resolution. She would fight! Sybilla was not going to win simply because Emily had neither the wit nor the strength to give her a battle, however far it had gone. And she was obliged to admit, briefly and painfully, that it had probably gone all the way—witness George's alacrity in provoking an excuse to sleep in the dressing room. Even so, Emily would use every skill she possessed to win him back. And she had a great deal of skill. After all, she had won him in the first place, against considerable odds.

If she were to continue to appear as wretched as she felt, she would embarrass the rest of the household and lay herself open to a pity that would not comfortably be forgotten, even when the affair was over and she had won. Most important, it would not be in the least attractive to George; like most men he loved a gay and charming woman who had enough sense to keep her troubles to herself. An excess of emotion, especially in public, would make him acutely uncomfortable. Far from winning him away from Sybilla, it would drive him further into her arms.

Therefore, Emily would act the role of her life. She

would be so utterly charming and delightful George would find Sybilla a pale copy, a shadow, and Emily again the true substance.

For three days she kept up her charade without noticeable failure. If she felt close to weeping again she was sure no one else saw it—except perhaps Great-aunt Vespasia, who saw everything. But she did not mind that. Behind the ineffable elegance and the radical humor, Aunt Vespasia was the one person who cared for her.

However, it had proved so difficult at times she was all but overcome with the futility of it. She was bound to fail. She knew her voice sounded flat, her smile must be sickly. But since there was nothing else with any hope of success, after a moment's solitude—perhaps merely in walking from one room to another—she had renewed her effort, trying with every strength she possessed to be amusing, considerate, and courteous. She even forced herself to be civil to old Mrs. March, although she could not resist exercising her wit on her in her absence, to the rather exuberant laughter of Jack Radley.

By dinner on the third day it was becoming extremely difficult. They were all most formally dressed, Emily in pale green, Sybilla in indigo, sitting round the monstrous mahogany table in the dining room. Rust red velvet curtains, heavily swagged and draped, and too many pictures on the wall made Emily feel suffocated. It was almost unendurable to force the smile to her lips, to dredge up from a weary and fearful imagination some light and flippant remark. She pushed the food round her plate without eating and sipped more and more wine.

She must not do anything as obvious as flirting with William; that would be seen as retaliation—even by George, uninterested as he was—and certainly by everyone else. Old Mrs. March's needle eyes missed nothing. She had been a widow forty years, presiding over her domestic kingdom with a will of iron and an insatiable curiosity. Emily must be equally entertaining, equally delightful to everyone—including Sybilla—as befitted a woman of her position, even if it choked her. She was careful not to cap other people's stories, and to laugh while meeting their eyes, so as to appear sincere.

She searched for the appropriate compliment, just truthful enough to be believed, and listened with attention to Eustace's interminably boring anecdotes about his athletic exploits when younger. He was a great and vociferous believer in "a healthy mind in a healthy body" and had no time for aesthetes. His disappointment was implicit in every phrase, and watching William's tense face across the table, Emily found it increasingly hard to hold her peace and keep her expression composed in polite interest.

After the sweet, with nothing left on the table but vanilla ice, raspberry water and a little fruit, Tassie said something about a soirée she had been to, and how bored she had been, which earned her a look of disgust from her grandmother. It struck a sudden chord of memory in Emily. She looked across at Jack Radley with a tiny smile.

"They can be fearful," she agreed. "On the other hand, they can also be superb."

Tassie, who was on the same side of the table and could not see Emily's face, was unaware of her mood. "This was a large soprano singing rather badly," she explained. "And so terribly serious."

"So was the best one I've ever been to." Emily felt the memory sharper in her mind as the scene came back to her. "Charlotte and I once took Mama. It was marvelous . . ."

"Indeed?" Mrs. March said coldly. "I had no idea you were musical."

Emily continued to keep a sweet expression, ignoring the implication, and stared straight at Jack Radley. With a stinging pleasure she knew that she had his attention as deeply as she would like to have had George's, and with precisely the same nature of excitement.

"Go on!" he urged. "Whatever can be marvelous about an overweight soprano singing earnestly and badly?"

William shivered. Like Tassie, he was thin and sensitive, with vividly red hair, although his was darker and his features sharper, etched with an inner pain that had not yet touched her.

Emily recounted it exactly as it had been. "She was a large lady, very ardent, with a pink face. Her gown was beaded and fringed practically everywhere, so that it shivered when she moved. Miss Arbuthnot was playing the pianoforte for her. She was very thin, and wearing black. They huddled together for several minutes over the music, and then the soprano came forward and announced that she would sing 'Home Sweet Home,' which as you know is heavy and extremely sentimental. Afterwards, to cheer us up, she would give us Yum-Yum's delightful, lighthearted song from *The Mikado*, 'Three Little Maids.' "

"Much better," Tassie agreed. "That goes along at a lovely pace. Although she hardly sounds like my idea of Yum-Yum." And she hummed a bar or two cheerfully.

" 'Marvelous' is overstating it rather a lot," Eustace said critically. "Good song ruined."

Emily ignored him. "She faced us all," she continued, "composed her features into lines of deep emotion, and began slowly and very solemnly with a blast of sentiment—only the piano bounded away with the trills and twitters of a rollicking rhythm!"

Only Jack Radley's face registered understanding.

" 'Be it ever so hu-u-mble,' " Emily mimicked sonorously, at once savage and doleful.

"Da-di-di-dum-dum, da da dee-ee," Jack sang with delight.

"Oh no!" Tassie's eyes lit with joy, and she started to giggle. Sybilla joined in, and even Eustace smiled in spite of himself.

"They trailed off, scarlet-faced," Emily said enthusiastically. "The soprano stammered her apologies, wheeled round, and charged to the piano, where Miss Arbuthnot was fumbling wildly through sheets of music, scattering them to the floor. They gathered them all up, muttering fiercely together and wagging their fingers at each other, while we all sat and tried to pretend we had not really noticed. Nobody said anything, and Charlotte and I dared not look at each other in case we lost control. Finally they came to some agreement, new music was set up on the piano, and the soprano advanced purposefully to the front of the floor again and faced us. She took an enormous breath, her beads jangled at her throat and all but broke, and with tremendous aplomb she began a spirited rendition: 'Three Little Maids from school are we, filled to the brim with girlish glee' . . .'' She hesitated a moment, staring straight into Jack Radley's dark blue eyes. ''Unfortunately Miss Arbuthnot was crashing out the ponderous chords of 'Home, Sweet Home,' with a look of intense longing on her face.''

This time even the old lady's mouth twitched. Tassie was helpless with giggles, and everyone else chortled with pleasure.

''They struggled on for a full three minutes,'' Emily said finally, ''getting louder and louder, trying to outdo each other, till the chandeliers rattled. Charlotte and I couldn't bear it any longer. We stood up at precisely the same moment and fled through the chairs, falling over people's feet, till we collided in the doorway and almost fell outside, clasping each other. We gave way and laughed till we cried. Even Mama, when she caught up with us, didn't have the heart to be angry.''

''Oh, how that takes me back!'' Vespasia said with a broad smile, dabbing at the tears on her cheeks. ''I've been to so many ghastly soirées. Now I shall never be able to listen to an earnest soprano again without thinking of this! There are so many fearful singers I should like such a thing to happen to—it would be such a mercy for the rest of us.''

''So should I,'' Tassie agreed. ''Starting with Mr. Beamish and his songs of pure womanhood. I suppose with a little foresight it could be arranged?'' she added hopefully.

''Anastasia!'' Mrs. March said, with ice in her voice. ''You will do nothing of the sort. It would be quite irresponsible, and in the worst possible taste. I forbid you even to entertain the idea.''

But Tassie's smile remained radiant, her eyes faraway and shining.

"Who is Mr. Beamish?" Jack Radley asked curiously.

"The vicar," Eustace said frostily. "You heard his sermon on Sunday."

Great-aunt Vespasia smothered a deep gurgle in her throat and began to take the stones out of her grapes assiduously with a silver knife and fork, placing them with elegant fingers on the side of her plate.

Mrs. March waited impatiently. At last she stood up, rustling her skirts noisily and tweaking the tablecloth so the silver rattled, and George snatched at a swaying glass and caught it just as it overbalanced.

"It is time the ladies withdrew," she announced loudly, fixing first Vespasia and then Sybilla with a stony stare. She knew Tassie and Emily would not dare disobey.

Vespasia rose to her feet with the grace she had never lost; the air of moving at precisely her own speed, and the rest of the world might follow or not, as it chose. Reluctantly, the others rose also: Tassie demure; Sybilla svelte, smiling over her shoulder at the men; Emily with a sinking feeling inside her, a taste of Pyrrhic victory fast losing its savor.

"I'm sure something could be contrived," Aunt Vespasia said quietly to Tassie. "With a little imagination."

Tassie looked confused. "About what, Grandmama?"

"Mr. Beamish, of course!" Vespasia snapped. "I have longed for years to take that fatuous smile off his face."

They swept past Emily, side by side, whispering, and on into the withdrawing room. Spacious and cool in pale greens, it was one of the few rooms in the house Olivia March had been permitted to redecorate from the old lady's taste, which was dictated at a time when the weight of one's furniture indicated the worthiness and sobriety of one's life. Later, fashion had changed, and status and novelty became the criteria. But Olivia's taste flowered during the Oriental period, around the International Exhibition of 1862, and the withdrawing room was gentle, full of soft colors and with only sufficient furniture to afford comfort, quite unlike old Mrs. March's boudoir. The other downstairs sitting room was all hot rose pinks, with drapes over mantel and piano, and jardinieres, photographs, and antimacassars.

Emily followed them and took her seat, after offering token assistance to old Mrs. March. She must keep up the act every moment until she was alone in her room. Women especially notice everything; they would observe the least flicker of expression or intonation of the voice, and they would interpret it with minute understanding.

"Thank you," Mrs. March said tersely, rearranging her skirts to fall more elegantly and patting her hair. It was thick and mouse gray, elaborately coifed in a fashion common thirty years before, during the Crimean War. Emily wondered fleetingly how long it had taken the maid to dress it like that. There was not a wisp out of place, nor had there been at breakfast or luncheon. Perhaps it was a wig? She would love to have knocked it and found out.

"So kind of you," Mrs. March went on. "Too many young people have lost the consideration one would wish." She looked at no one in particular, but the tightening at the corners of her mouth betrayed an irritation that was not in the least impersonal. Emily knew Tassie was going to receive a curt lecture on the duties of a good daughter the moment they were alone, foremost among them being obedience and attention to one's betters—and doing everything possible in aiding one's family to obtain for one a suitable marriage. At the very minimum one positively did not get in the way of such efforts. And Sybilla also would come in for some grim correction.

Emily smiled warmly back at her, even if it was amusement disguised, not sympathy. "I daresay they are merely preoccupied," she said sententiously.

"They are no more preoccupied than we were!" Mrs. March retorted with a waspish glare. "We also had to make our way, you know. Being with child is an excuse for fainting and weeping, but not for sheer inconsideration. I have had seven children myself—I know what I am talking about. Not that I am not pleased. Goodness knows, it is more than time! We were beginning to despair. Such a tragedy for a woman to be barren." She glanced at Emily's slender waist with implied criticism. "She has certainly caused great disappointment to poor Eustace; he so much wanted William to have an heir. The family, you know, the family is everything, when all is said and done." She sniffed.

Emily was silent; there was nothing to say, and that curious pity came back, violently unwelcome. She did not want to remember that Sybilla also had been an outsider in this family, a failure in the one achievement that mattered to them.

Mrs. March settled a little deeper into her chair. "Better late than never, I say," she repeated. "Now she will stay at home and do her duty, fulfill herself, instead of all this ridiculous chasing of fashion. So shallow and unworthy. Now she will make William happy and create the kind of home for him he should have."

Emily was not listening. Of course, if Sybilla was pregnant it might account for at least some of her behavior. Emily could quite clearly remember her own mixture of excitement and fear when she was expecting Edward. It was a total change in her life, something that was happening to her and was irreversible. She was no longer alone; in a unique way she had become two people. But for all George's pleasure it had set a distance between them. And sharp in the middle of all of that was her fear of becoming ungainly, vulnerable, and no longer attractive to him.

If Sybilla, in her middle thirties, were facing this confusion of emotions—and perhaps also a fear of childbirth; the pain, the helplessness, the utter indignity, and even the vague possibility of death—it might well account for her selfishness now, her compulsion to draw all the masculine attention while she still felt she could, before matronliness made her awkward and eventually confined her.

But it did not excuse George! Fury choked Emily like a hot lump in her chest. All sorts of actions careered through her mind. She could go upstairs and wait until he came, and then accuse him outright of behaving like a fool, of embarrassing and insulting her and offending not only William but Uncle Eustace, because it was his house, and even all the rest of them, because they were fellow guests. She could tell him to restrict his attentions to Sybilla to those courtesies which were usual, or Emily would leave for home immediately and have nothing more to do with him until he made full apologies—and amends!

Then the rage died. A feud would bring her no happiness. George would either be cowed and obey, which she would despise—and so would he—and her victory would be bitter and of no satisfaction; or else he would be driven even further in his pursuit of Sybilla, simply to show Emily that she could not dictate to him. And the latter was far the more likely. Damn men! She gritted her teeth and swallowed hard. Damn men for their stupidity, their pigheaded perverseness—and above all for their vanity!

She could feel the lump growing larger in her throat, impossible to swallow. There was so much in George she loved: he was gentle, tolerant, generous—and he could be so much fun! Why did he have to be such a fool?

She shut her eyes, opening them again only with effort. Aunt Vespasia was staring at her. "Well, Emily," she said briskly. "I am still waiting to hear an account of your visit to Winchester. You have told me nothing."

There was no escape; she was drawn into conversation. She knew Aunt Vespasia had done it intentionally, and she did not want to let her down by being defeatist. Aunt Vespasia would never have given up and gone away into a corner to cry.

"Certainly," she said with artificial eagerness. And she plunged into a story, largely invented as she went along. She was still involved in its ramifications when the gentlemen rejoined them rather earlier than usual.

All evening she managed to keep up the charade, and when it was finally time to retire she had the small victory of having lived up to the task she had set herself. She saw the flash of approval in Aunt Vespasia's silver-gray eyes, and something in Tassie's face that could have been admiration. But only once had George looked at her, and his smile was so artificial it hurt more than a scowl, because it was as if he did not see her at all.

The sense of closeness had come from a direction she had learned to expect, but when she thought about it, not really to welcome. It was Jack Radley who joined her laughter, whose quick humor followed hers, and who at the end of the evening walked up the broad stairs with his hand at her elbow.

She stopped on the landing, almost oblivious of him, waiting for George's step but hearing instead the rustle of silk against the bannisters below her. She knew it would be Sybilla, and yet compulsion, a thread of hope, kept her looking till they came into sight, just in case it was not. George was smiling. The gas bracket on the wall shone on his dark hair and the white skin of Sybilla's shoulders.

George moved away from her as he saw Emily, the spontaneity dying out of his face and faint embarrassment taking its place. He looked back at Sybilla.

"Good night, and thank you for a most delightful evening," he said awkwardly, caught between the ease of intimacy the moment before and the faintly ridiculous formality he now finished with.

Sybilla's face was glowing; she was completely enclosed within whatever they had been saying—or doing. For her Emily did not exist, and Jack Radley was merely a shadow, part of the decor of the weekend. Words were superfluous; her smile said everything.

Emily felt sick. All her efforts had been so much waste of time. She had been an actress in an empty theater, performing only for herself—as far as George was concerned she had not been there at all. Her behavior was immaterial to him.

"Good night, Mr. Radley." She stumbled over the words, and reaching out for the handle of her bedroom door, she opened it, went in, and closed it firmly behind her. At least she could shut them out until tomorrow. She could have nine hours of solitude. If she wanted to weep no one else would know, and when she had let go of some of the confusion and pain bursting inside her, there was the refuge of sleep before the necessity of decision.

The maid knocked.

Emily sniffed hard and swallowed. "I don't need you, Millicent." Her voice was strained. "You may go to bed."

There was a moment's hesitation; then, "Very well, m'lady. Good night."

"Good night." She undressed slowly, leaving her gown over the back of the chair, then took the pins out of her hair. It was a relief not to feel the weight of it on her head.

Why? Was it something about Sybilla? Her beauty, her wit, her charm? Or was it some failure in herself? Had she changed, lost some quality that George had loved? She searched, trying to recall what she had said and done recently. How was it different from the way it had always been? In what way was she less than George wanted, or needed? She had never been cold or ill-natured, she was not extravagant, she had never been rude to his friends— and heaven knows she had been tempted! Some of them were so facile, so incredibly silly, and yet they spoke to her as if she were a child.

It was a futile exercise, and in the end she crept into bed and decided to be angry instead. It was better than weeping. Angry people fight, and sometimes fighters win!

She woke with a headache and a rush of the memory of failure. All the energy drained out of her, and she stared up at the sunlight on the plaster ceiling, finding it colorless and hard. If only it were still night and she could have more time alone. The thought of going down into the breakfast room to face all those bright smiles—the curious, the confident, the pitying—and having to pretend there was nothing wrong . . . What everyone else could see of George and Sybilla was of no importance; she knew something the others did not, something that explained it all.

She curled up smaller, hunching her knees, and hid her head under the sheet a few moments more. But the longer she stayed, the more thoughts crowded her head. Imagination raced away, giving reality to every threat, every possible misery, till she was drowned with wretchedness. Her head throbbed, her eyes stung, and it was past time she got up. Millicent had already knocked at the door twice; morning tea would be cold. The third time she had to let her in.

Emily took extra trouble with her appearance, the less she cared the more it mattered. She hated color out of a pot, but it was better than no color at all.

She was not the last down. Sybilla was absent, and Mrs. March had elected to have breakfast in bed, as had Great-aunt Vespasia.

"You look well, my dear Emily," Eustace said briskly. Of course, he was perfectly aware of the situation between George and Sybilla, but deplore it as she must, a well-bred woman bore such things discreetly and affected not to have noticed. He did not approve of Emily, but he would give her the benefit of the doubt unless she made such a charitable view impossible.

"I am, thank you." Emily forced herself to be bright, and her irritation made it easier. "I hope you slept well too?"

"Excellently." Eustace helped himself with a lavish hand from several of the chafing dishes on the massive carved oak sideboard, set his dish in his place, then went over and threw open the windows, letting in a blast of chill morning air. He breathed in deeply, and then out again. "Excellent," he said, disregarding everyone else's shivering as he took his seat at the table. "I always think good health is so important in a woman, don't you?"

Emily could think of no reason why it should be particularly, but it seemed to be largely a rhetorical question, and Eustace answered himself. "No man, especially of a good family, wants a sickly wife."

"The poor want it even less," Tassie said bluntly. "It costs a lot to be ill."

But Eustace's pontification was not to be interrupted by something so irrelevant as the poor. He waved his hand gently. "Of course it does, my dear, but then if the poor don't have children it hardly matters, does it? It is not as if it were a case of succession to a title, of the line, so to speak. Ordinary people don't need sons in the same way." He shot a sour look at William. "And preferably more than one—if you wish to see the name continue."

George cleared his throat and raised his brows, and his eyes flickered first to Sybilla, then William, and lowered to his plate again. William's face tightened sharply.

"Being sickly doesn't stop them having children," Tassie argued, spots of color in her cheeks. "I don't think health is a virtue. It is a good fortune, frequently found among those who are better off."

Eustace took a deep breath and let it out, in a noisy expression of impatience. "My dear, you are far too young to know what you are talking about. It is a subject you cannot possibly understand, nor should you. It is indelicate for a girl in your situation, or indeed any well-bred woman. Your mother would never have dreamed of it. But I'm sure Mr. Radley understands." He smiled across at Jack and received a stare of total incomprehension.

Tassie bent her head a little lower over her toast and preserves. The pinkness deepened in her face, a reflection of a mixture of frustration at being patronized and embarrassment because her father's reference to her was obviously infinitely more indelicate than anything she had meant.

But Eustace was relentless; he pursued the subject obliquely throughout breakfast. To food and health were added delicacy of upbringing, discretion, obedience, an even temper, and the appropriate skills in conversation and household management. The only attribute not touched upon was wealth, and that of course would have been vulgar. And it was a matter of some sensitivity to him; his mother was of a fine family who had squandered its means, obliging her either to reduce her style of life or marry into a family which had made its fortunes in the Industrial Revolution in the mines and mills of the North. The "Trade." She had chosen the latter, with some distaste. The former was unthinkable.

He nodded his head in satisfaction as he spoke. "When I think of my own happiness with my beloved wife, may heaven rest her, I realize how much all these things contributed to it. Such a wonderful woman! I treasure her memory—you have no notion. It was the saddest day of my life when she departed this vale of tears for a better place."

Emily glanced across at William, whose head was bent to hide his face, and accidentally caught Jack Radley's eyes, filled with amusement. He rolled them very slightly and smiled at her. It was a bright, disturbing look, and she knew without doubt that although the monumental effort she had made over the last three days might have failed with George, it had succeeded brilliantly with him. It was a bitter satisfaction, and worth nothing—unless unintentionally she should finally provoke George to jealousy.

She smiled back at him, not warmly, but with at least a shred of conspiracy.

George was drawn in, curiously enough, by Eustace. Eustace spoke to him with friendliness, seeking his opinion, expressing an admiration for him, which Emily found singularly inopportune. At the moment George was the last person in the house anyone should have consulted about married bliss. But Eustace was pursuing his own interests with Jack Radley and Tassie, and oblivious of anyone else's feelings, least of all their possible embarrassment.

Emily spent the morning writing letters to her mother, a cousin to whom she owed a reply, and to Charlotte. She told Charlotte everything about George; her pain, the sense of loss which surprised her, and the loneliness that opened up in a gray, flat vastness ahead. Then she tore it up and disposed of it in the water closet.

Luncheon was worse. They were back in the heavy, rust red dining room and everyone was present except Great-aunt Vespasia, who had chosen to visit an acquaintance in Mayfair.

"Well!" Eustace rubbed his hands and looked round at all their faces in turn. "And what do we plan for the afternoon? Tassie? Mr. Radley?"

"Tassie has errands to do for me!" Mrs. March snapped. "We do have our duty, Eustace. We cannot be forever playing and amusing ourselves. My family has a position—it has always had a position." Whether this remark was purely a piece of personal vanity or a reminder to Jack Radley that they were quite unarguably his social equals was not clear.

"And Tassie always seems to be the one keeping it up," George said with a waspishness surprising in him.

Mrs. March's eyes froze. "And why not, may I ask? She has nothing else to do. It is her function, her calling in life, George. A woman must have something to do. Would you deny her that?"

"Of course not!" George was getting cross, and Emily felt a lift of pride for him in spite of herself. "But I can think of a lot more amusing things for her to do than upholding the position of the Marches," he finished.

"I daresay!" The old lady's voice would have chipped stones—tombstones by the look on her face. "But hardly what one would wish a young lady even to hear about, much less to do. I will thank you not to injure her mind by discussing it. You'll only upset her and cause her to have ideas. Ideas are bad for young women."

"Quite," Eustace added soberly. "They cause heat in the blood, and nightmares." He took an enormous slice of chicken breast and put it on his plate. "And headaches."

George was caught between his innate good manners

and his sense of outrage; the conflict showed in his face. He glanced at Tassie.

She put her hand out and touched his arm gently. "I really don't mind going to see the vicar, George. He's awfully smug, and his teeth are wet and stick out, but he's really quite harmless—"

"Anastasia!" Eustace sat bolt upright. "That is no way to speak of Mr. Beamish. He is a very worthy man, and deserving of a great deal more respect from a girl of your age."

Tassie smiled broadly. "Yes, Papa, I am always very nice to Mr. Beamish." Then sudden honesty checked her. "Well, nearly always."

"You will go to call upon him this afternoon," Mrs. March said coldly, sucking at her teeth, "and see if you can be of assistance. There must be several of the less fortunate who need visiting."

"Yes, Grandmama," Tassie said meekly. George sighed and, for the time being, gave up.

Emily spent the afternoon with Tassie, doing good works. If one cannot enjoy oneself, one might as well benefit someone else. As it turned out it was really quite agreeable, since Emily liked Tassie more and more each time she saw her, and their visit with the vicar's wife was actually very brief. Considerably more time was taken up in the company of the curate, a large, soft-spoken young man called Mungo Hare, who had chosen to leave his native western Inverness-shire to seek his living in London. He was full of zeal and very forthright opinions, which were demonstrated by his acts rather than his words. They did indeed offer some real comfort to the bereaved and to the lonely, and Emily returned to Cardington Crescent with a sense of accomplishment. Added to this was the knowledge that Sybilla had spent the time paying afternoon calls with her grandmother-in-law, and must have been bored to distraction.

But Emily did not see George on her return, nor when

she changed for dinner. There was no sound from the dressing room except the valet coming in and then leaving, and the feeling of desolation returned.

At the dinner table it was worse. Sybilla looked marvelous in a shade of magenta no one else would have dared to wear. Her skin was flawless, with just a touch of pink on the cheekbones, and she was still as slender as a willow in spite of her condition. Her eyes were hazel; at times they seemed brown, at others, golden, like brandy in the light. Her hair was silken, black and thick as a rope.

Emily felt washed out beside her, a moth next to a butterfly. Her hair was honey fair, softer, delicate rather than rich, her eyes quite ordinary blue; her gown was very fashionable in cut, but by comparison the color was pallid. It took all the courage she possessed to force the smile to her lips, to eat something which tasted like porridge although it appeared to be sole, roasted mutton, and fruit sorbet.

Everyone else was gay, except old Mrs. March, who had never been anything so trivial. Sybilla was radiant; George could hardly take his eyes off her. Tassie looked unusually happy, and Eustace held forth with unctuous satisfaction on something or other. Emily did not listen.

Gradually the decision hardened in her mind. Passivity was not succeeding: It was time for action, and there was only one course of action that she could think of.

There was little she could begin until the gentlemen rejoined them after the meal was over. The conservatory stretched the full length of the south side of the house, and from the withdrawing room there were glass doors under pale green curtains, which opened onto palms, vines, and a walk quite out of sight beteen exotic flowers.

Emily's patience was totally exhausted. She moved to sit beside Jack Radley and took the first opportunity to engage him in conversation, which was not in the least difficult. He was only too delighted. In other circumstances she would have enjoyed it, for against her will she liked him. He was too good-looking, and he knew it, but he had wit and a sense of the absurd. She had seen it gleaming in those remarkable eyes a dozen times over the last few days. And, she thought, there was no hypocrisy in him, which in itself was enough to endear him to her after three weeks at Cardington Crescent.

"Mrs. March seemed very nervous of you," he said curiously. "When you mentioned the word 'detecting,' I thought she was going to take a fit and slide under the table." There was a shadow of laughter in his comment, and she realized just how much he disliked the old lady; a whole region of unhappiness opened a fraction to her guess. Perhaps family and circumstances were pressing him into a marriage for money. Perhaps he wanted such a union no more than the young women who were so mercilessly maneuvered by their mothers into marrying for position, so as not to be left that most pathetic of all social creatures, the unmarried woman past her prime, with neither means to support herself nor vocation to occupy her years.

"It is not my ability which alarms her," she said with the first smile she had genuinely felt. "It is the way I came by it."

"Came by it?" His eyebrows rose. "Was it something frightful?"

"Worse." Her smile increased.

"Shameful?" he pursued.

"Terribly!"

"What?" He was on the edge of outright laughter now.

She bent closer to him and held up her hand. He leaned over to listen.

"My sister married appallingly beneath her," she whispered, her lips close to his ear, "to a detective in the police!"

He shot upright and turned to face her in amazement and delight. "A detective! A real one, a peeler? Scotland Yard, and all that?"

"Yes. All that—and more."

"I don't believe it!" He was enjoying the game enormously, and there was a touch of reality in it that made it all the better.

"She did!" Emily argued. "Didn't you see Mrs. March's face? She's terrified I'll mention it. It's a disgrace to the family."

"I'll bet it is!" He chortled with delight. "Poor old Eustace—he'll never recover. Does Lady Cumming-Gould know?"

"Aunt Vespasia? Oh, yes. In fact if you doubt me, ask her. She knows Thomas quite well, and what's more, she likes him, in spite of the fact that he wears clothes that don't fit him and perfectly dreadful mufflers of most violent and unseemly colors, and his pockets are always bulging with notes and wax and matches and bits of string and heaven knows what else. And he's never met a decent barber in his life—"

"And you like him too," he interrupted happily. "You like him very much."

"Oh, yes, I do. But he's still a policeman, and he gets involved in some very gruesome murders." The memory of them sobered her for a moment; he saw it in her face, and immediately took her mood.

"You know about them?" Now he was truly intrigued. She had his total attention, and she found it exhilarating.

"Certainly I do! Charlotte and I are very close. I've even helped sometimes."

His bright eyes clouded with skepticism.

"I have!" she protested. It was something she was obscurely proud of: it had, really, something to do with life outside the suffocation of drawing rooms. "I practically solved some of them—at least, Charlotte and I did together."

He was not sure whether to believe her or not, but there was no criticism in his face; his wide gaze was quite genuine. Were she a few years younger she could have lost herself in that look. Even now she was going to make the best of it. She stood up with a little twitch of her skirt.

"If you don't believe me . . ."

He was at her side immediately. "You? Investigating murders?" His voice was just short of incredulous, inviting her to convince him.

She accepted, walking half a step ahead of him towards the conservatory doors and the hanging vines and sweet smell of earth. Inside it was hot and motionless among the lilies, dim as a tropical night.

"We had one where the corpse turned up on the driving seat of a hansom cab," she said deliberately. It was quite true. "After a performance of *The Mikado*."*

"Now you are joking," he protested.

"No, I'm not!" She turned her widest, most innocent look on him. "The widow identified it. It was Lord Augustus Fitzroy Hammond. He was buried in the family plot with all due ceremony." She tried to keep her face straight and stare back into his eyes, with those incredible eyelashes. "He turned up again in the family pew in church."

"Emily, you're preposterous!" He was standing very close to her, and for the moment, George was not paramount in her mind. She knew she was beginning to smile, in spite of the fact that it was perfectly true. "We buried him again," she said with a hint of a giggle. "It was all very difficult, and rather disgusting."

"That's absurd. I don't believe you!"

"Oh it was—I swear! Very awkward indeed. You can't expect Society to turn up to the same person's funeral twice in as many weeks. It isn't decent."

"It isn't true."

"It is! I swear it! We had four corpses before we'd finished—at least I think it was four."

"And all of Lord Augustus whatever?" He was trying to control his laughter.

"Of course not—don't be ridiculous!" she protested. She was so close to him she could smell the warmth of his skin and the faint pungency of soap.

"Emily!" He bent and kissed her slowly, intimately, as

Resurrection Row.

if they had all the time in the world. Emily let herself go, stretching her arms up round his neck and answering him.

"I shouldn't do this," she said frankly after a few moments. But it was a factual remark, not a reproach.

"Probably not," he agreed, touching her hair gently, then her cheek. "Tell me the truth, Emily."

"What?" she whispered.

"Did you really find four corpses?" He kissed her again.

"Four or five," she murmured. "And we caught the murderer as well. Ask Aunt Vespasia—if you've the nerve. She was there."

"I just might."

She disengaged herself with a shadow of reluctance—it had been nicer than it should have been—and began her way back past the flowers and the vines to the withdrawing room.

Mrs. March was holding forth on the chivalry of the pre-Raphaelite painters, their meticulousness of detail and delicacy of color, and William was listening, his face pinched and pained. It was not that he disapproved, but that she totally misunderstood what he believed to be the concept. She missed the passion and caught only the sentimentality.

Tassie and Sybilla were so positioned that they were obliged either to listen or to be openly rude, and long habit precluded the latter. Eustace, on the other hand, was master of the house and owed no such courtesy. He sat with his back to the group and discoursed upon the moral obligations of position, and George had on his face his look of polite interest which masked complete absence of attention; he was gazing towards the conservatory doors. He must have seen Emily and Jack Radley.

Emily felt a sudden, rather alarming sense of excitement; it was a crisis provoked at last!

She walked a fraction ahead of Jack but was still conscious of him close behind her, of his warmth and the gentleness of his touch. She sat down next to Great-aunt Vespasia and pretended to listen to Eustace.

The rest of the evening passed in a similar vein, and Emily hardly noticed the time until twenty-five minutes to midnight. She was returning to the withdrawing room from the bathroom upstairs, passing the morning room door, when she heard voices in soft, fierce conversation.

". . . you're a coward!" It was Sybilla, her voice husky with anger and contempt. "Don't tell me—"

"You may believe what you like!" The answer cut her off.

Emily stopped, almost falling over as hope and fear choked each other and left her shaking. It was George, and he was furious. She knew that tone precisely; he had had the same welling up of temper when his jockey was thrashed at the race track. It had been half his own fault then, and he knew it. Now he was lashing out at Sybilla, and her voice came back thick with fury.

The door of the boudoir swung open and Eustace stood with his hand on it. Any moment he would turn and see Emily listening. She moved on swiftly, head high, straining to catch the last words from the morning room. But the voices were too strident, too clashing to distinguish the words.

"Ah, Emily." Eustace swiveled round. "Time to retire, I think. You must be tired." It was a statement, not a question. Eustace considered it part of his prerogative to decide when everyone wished to go to bed, as he had always done for his family when they all lived here. He had decided almost everything and believed it his privilege and his duty. Before she died, Olivia March had obeyed him sweetly—and then gone her own way with such discretion he was totally unaware of it. Many of his best ideas had been hers, but they had been given him in such a way he thought them his own, and he therefore defended them to the death and put every last one into practice.

Emily had no will to argue tonight. She returned to the withdrawing room, wished everyone good sleep, and went gratefully to her room. She had undressed, dismissing her maid with instructions for the morning, and was about to get into bed when there was a knock on the dressing-room door.

She froze. It could only be George. Half of her was terrified and wanted to keep silent, pretend she was already asleep. She stared at the knob as if it would turn on its own and let him in.

The knock came again, harder. It might be her only opportunity, and if she turned him away she would lose it forever.

"Come in."

Slowly, the door opened. George stood in the archway, looking tired and uncomfortable. His face was flushed—Emily knew why immediately. Sybilla had made a scene, and George hated scenes. Without thinking, she knew what to do. Above all, it would be disastrous to confront him. The last thing he wanted now was another emotional woman.

"Hello," she said with a very small smile, pretending this was not an important occasion, a meeting that might turn their lives and all that mattered to her.

He came in tentatively, followed by old Mrs. March's spaniel, which to her fury had taken such a liking to him that it had abandoned its mistress. He was unsure what to say, fearful lest she were only biding her time before launching at him with an accusation, a justified charge he could not defend himself against.

She turned away to make it easier, as though it were all perfectly ordinary. She struggled for something to say that would not touch on all that was painful between them.

"I really quite enjoyed my afternoon with Tassie," she began casually. "The vicar is terribly tedious, and so is his wife. I can see why Eustace likes them. They have a lot in common, similar views on the simplicity of virtue"—she pulled a face—"and the virtue of simplicity. Especially in women and children, which they believe to be roughly the same. But the curate was charming."

George sat down on the stool before the dressing table, and she watched him with a tiny lift of pleasure. It meant he intended to stay, at least for a few minutes.

"I'm glad," he said with an awkward smile, fishing for something to continue with. It was ridiculous; a month ago they spoke as easily as old friends—they would have laughed at the vicar together. Now he looked at her, his eyes wide and searching, but only for a moment. Then he looked away again, not daring to press too hard, afraid of a rebuff. "I've always liked Tassie. She's so much more like the Cumming-Gould side of the family than the Marches. I suppose William is, too, for that matter."

"That can only be good," Emily said sincerely.

"You'd have liked Aunt Olivia," he went on. "She was only thirty-eight when she died. Uncle Eustace was devastated."

"After eleven children in fifteen years, I should imagine she was, too," Emily said tartly. "But I don't suppose Eustace thought of that."

"I shouldn't think so."

She turned to him and smiled, suddenly glad he had never even implicitly expected such a thing of her. For a moment the old warmth was back, tentative, uncertain, but there; then, before she could take too much for granted and be disappointed, she looked away again.

"I've always thought visiting the poor was probably more offensive to them than leaving them decently alone," she went on. "But I think Tassie really did some good. She seems so very honest."

"She is." He bit his lip. "Although she's not yet in Charlotte's class, thank heaven. But perhaps that's only a matter of time; she doesn't have as many opinions yet." He stood up, wary lest he overstay and risk the precious fragment regained between them. He hesitated, and for a moment the indecision flickered on his face. Dare he bend and kiss her, or was it too soon? Yes—yes, it was still too fragile, Sybilla too recent. He reached out and touched her shoulder and then withdrew his hand. "Good night, Emily."

She looked at him solemnly. If he came back it must be on her terms, or it would only happen again, and she would not willingly suffer that. "Good night, George," she replied gently. "Sleep well."

He went out slowly, the dog pattering after him, and the door clicked shut. She curled up on the bed and hugged her knees, feeling tears of relief prickle in her eyes and run smoothly and painlessly down her cheeks. It was not over, but the terrible helplessness was gone. She knew what to do. She sniffed fiercely, reaching for a handkerchief, and blew her nose hard. It was loud and unladylike—distinctly a sound of triumph.

4

Emily slept well for the first time in weeks and woke late, with the sun filling the room and Millicent rapping on the door.

"Come in," she said hazily. George was still in the dressing room; there was no need to think of privacy. "Come in, Millie."

The door opened and Millicent swept in, balancing the tray on one hand while closing the door behind her. She then carried the tray to the dresser and put it down.

"What a mess there is in that there upstairs pantry, m'lady," she said, pouring the tea carefully. "Never seen anything like it. One moment everybody's there; the next, kettle's filling the 'ole place wi' steam and not a soul to take it off. Such a fuss, all 'cause 'is lordship likes coffee instead o' tea—although I don't know 'ow 'e can drink it first thing. Anyhow, Albert took it to 'im quarter of an hour since an' saw 'e 'd got that little dog of Mrs. March's lying up there, too. Taken a proper fancy to 'is lordship, it 'as. Makes the old lady ever so cross." She came over and held out the cup.

Emily sat up, took it, and began to sip. It tasted hot and clean. Already the day felt promising.

"What'd you fancy to wear this morning, m'lady?" Millicent drew the curtains briskly. " 'Ow about the apricot muslin? Right pretty shade, that is. And not everyone as can get away with it. Makes some look sallow."

Emily smiled. Millicent had obviously made up her mind.

"Good idea," she agreed. "Is it warm outside?"

"It will be, m'lady. And if you're going calling this afternoon, what about the lavender?" Millicent was full of ideas. "And the white wi' the black velvet trim this evening. Very fashionable, that is, and ever such a good swish to it when you walk."

Emily conceded, finished the tea, and got up to begin her morning toilette. Today everything had an air of victory about it.

When she was ready and Millicent had gone, she went to the dressing room door and knocked. There was no answer. She hesitated, on the point of knocking again, but suddenly becoming self-conscious. What was there to say except good morning? She should not behave like a simpering bride! She would only embarrass George and make herself ridiculous. Far better to be natural. Anyway, he had not answered; no doubt he was already downstairs.

But there was no sign of him in the breakfast room. Eustace was as usual, moon-faced and beaming with good health. He had thrown the windows open, as was his habit, regardless of the fact that the room faced west and was decidedly chilly. His plate was piled high in front of him with sausages, eggs, deviled kidneys, and potato. His napkin was tucked in his waistcoat, and round him on the table were a rack of crisp toast, a dish of butter, the silver cruet of condiments, and the milk, sugar, and silver Queen Anne coffeepot.

Old Mrs. March was taking breakfast in bed, as usual. Other than that, everyone was present except George—and Sybilla.

Emily's heart sank and all her happiness was cut off like a candle flame someone has pinched. Her hand felt numb on the back of the chair as she pulled it out, and when she went to lift the device for slicing the top off the boiled egg the parlormaid placed in front of her, she fumbled and had to steady herself. She had not dreamed it—George *had* quarreled with Sybilla. The nightmare was over. Of course, things would not be repaired between them instantly. It would take a little while, maybe even two or three weeks. But she could manage that—easily.

"Good morning, my dear," Eustace said in exactly the same tone he used every day. "I trust you are well?" It was not a question, merely an acknowledgment of her arrival. He did not wish to hear about women's indispositions; they were both uninteresting and indelicate—especially in the morning, when one wished to eat.

"Very," Emily said aggressively. "I hope you are also?" The question was totally unnecessary in view of the abundance upon his plate.

"Most certainly I am." His eyes widened under his short, rounded eyebrows. He let his breath out through his nose with a slight sound, and his glance flickered over the rest of the table: Vespasia eating a boiled egg delicately and silently; Tassie looking as pale as her freckles and flaming hair would allow, shadows under her eyes; Jack Radley staring at Emily, brow furrowed, two spots of color on his cheeks; and William, his whole body tight, his face pinched, and his hands gripping his fork as if it were a life belt someone might jerk away from him. "I am in excellent health," Eustace reiterated with a note of accusation.

"I'm so glad." Emily was determined to have the last word. She could not fight Sybilla and she did not want to fight George. Eustace would serve very well.

Eustace turned to Tassie. "And what do you intend to do with the day, my dear?" Before she could reply, he continued. "Compassion is most desirable in a young woman. Indeed, your dear mother, may the Lord rest her, was always about such things." He reached for the toast and buttered a pile absently. "But you have other duties as well—to your guests, for a start. You must make them feel welcome. Of course, your home is primarily an island of peace and morality where the shadows of the world do not penetrate. But it should also be a place of comfortable entertainment, seemly laughter, and uplifting conversation.'' He disregarded Tassie's growing discomfort as if he were totally unaware of it, as indeed perhaps he was. Emily loathed him for his sheer blindness.

''I think you should take Mr. Radley for a carriage ride,'' he went on, as if the idea had suddenly occurred to him. ''It is excellent weather for such a thing. I am sure your grandmother Vespasia will be happy to accompany you.''

''You are nothing of the kind!'' Vespasia snapped. ''I have my own calls to make this afternoon. Tassie is welcome to come with me, if she likes, but I shall not go with her. No doubt she would find Mr. Carlisle of interest—as would Mr. Radley, if he cares to come as well.''

Eustace frowned. ''Mr. Carlisle? Is he not that most unsuitable person who occupies himself in political agitations?''

Tassie's head came up in immediate interest. ''Oh?''

Eustace glared at her.

Vespasia did not quibble over the description, but her cool, dove gray eyes met Emily's for an instant with a flash of memory, images of excitement, of appalling poverty and murder, and Emily found herself blushing hotly as the much closer thought of yesterday evening in the conservatory returned. She had begun by telling Jack Radley of precisely that same affair in which she had met Somerset Carlisle.*

''Most unsuitable,'' Eustace said irritably. ''There are better ways of serving the unfortunate than making an exhibition of oneself trying to undermine government and alter the whole foundation of society. The man is quite irresponsible, and you should know better than to involve yourself with him, Mama-in-law.''

''Sounds fascinating.'' Jack Radley looked away from Emily for the first time and towards Vespasia. ''Which

Resurrection Row.

54

particular foundation is he working on at the moment, Lady Cumming-Gould?''

"Suffrage for women," Vespasia replied immediately.

"Ridiculous!" Eustace snorted. "Dangerous, time-wasting nonsense! Give women the vote and heaven only knows what kind of Parliament we'd have. Full of hotheads, and revolutionaries, I shouldn't wonder—and incompetents. The man is a threat to all that makes England decent, all that has created the Empire. We raise great men precisely because our women preserve the sanctity of the home and the family.''

"Stuff and nonsense," Vespasia said smartly. "If women are as decent as you suppose them, they will vote for members who will uphold exactly what you value so much.''

Eustace was thoroughly angry. He controlled himself with a visible effort. "My dear, good woman," he said between his teeth, "it is not your decency that is in question, it is your sense." He took a deep breath. "The fairer sex are designed by God to be wives and mothers; to comfort, to nurture and uplift. It is a high and noble calling. But they do not have the minds or the fortitude of temperament to govern, and to imagine they have is to fly against nature.''

"Eustace, I told Olivia when she married you that you were a fool," Vespasia replied. "And over the years you have given me less and less reason to revise my opinion." She dabbed her lips delicately with her napkin and stood up. "If you think I am an unsuitable chaperone for Tassie, why don't you ask Sybilla to accompany her. Presuming she gets out of her bed in time." And without even glancing behind her she swept from the room, the parlor-maid opening the doors and closing them behind her.

Eustace's face was scarlet. He had been insulted in his own domain, the one place in the world where he was the absolute authority and should have been inviolable.

"Anastasia! Either your sister-in-law or your grandmother March will accompany you." He swung round. "You, Emily, will not. You are scarcely better than your great-aunt. Such of your past behavior that I know of has been deplorable, but that is George's problem. I will not have you misguiding Tassie."

"I wouldn't dream of it," Emily snapped back with a blinding smile. "I'm sure Sybilla is much better suited to be an example to Tassie as to how a decent and modest woman should behave than I could ever be."

Tassie choked into her handkerchief; Jack Radley tried frantically to find something to occupy himself with looking at, and failed. William, white to the lips, rose awkwardly, dropping his napkin and rattling his cup in its saucer.

"I'm going to work," he said brusquely, "while the light is so good." Without waiting for comment he left.

Emily was sorry: by allowing her temper to reveal her own pain she had also hurt William. He must be feeling somewhat the same as she was; confused, rejected, terribly alone, and above all, humiliated. But to seek him out and apologize now would only make it worse. There was nothing to do but pretend not to have noticed.

She forced down enough of her breakfast to make it appear she was quite normal. Then she excused herself and went determinedly upstairs to find George and demand he exercise at least discretion, even if he could not or would not exercise morality.

She knocked briskly on the dressing room door and waited. There was no answer. She knocked again, then when nothing happened, turned the handle and went in.

The curtains were open and the room full of sunlight. George was still in bed, the sheets rumpled, the morning coffee tray sitting on the table, obviously used. In fact, there was an empty saucer on the floor near the foot of the bed where he must have shared his coffee with the old lady's spaniel.

"George!" Emily said angrily. She did not even wish to think what he had been doing all night that he was still asleep at nearly ten in the morning. "George?" She was standing beside the bed now, staring down at him. He looked very white, and his eyes were sunken as though he had slept badly, if at all. In fact he looked ill.

"George?" Now she was undeniably frightened. She put out her hand and touched him.

He did not move. There was not even a flutter of the eyelids.

"George!" She was shouting, which was ridiculous. He must be able to hear her; she was shaking him roughly enough to waken anyone.

But he was motionless. Even his chest did not seem to rise and fall.

Appalled, her mind already guessing at the impossible and terrified of it, she ran to the door, wanting to cry out for someone—but whom?

Aunt Vespasia! Of course. Aunt Vespasia was the only one she could trust, the only one who cared for her. She flew down the stairs and across the hall, almost pitching into a startled housemaid, and threw open the morning room door. Vespasia was writing letters.

"Aunt Vespasia!" Her voice was shaking, and was far louder than she had intended. "Aunt Vespasia, George is ill! I can't wake him! I think—" She took a choking breath. She could not form the words that would make it real.

Vespasia turned from the rosewood desk where her paper and envelopes were spread, her face grave.

"Perhaps we had better go and see," she said quietly, laying the pen down and rising from the chair. "Come, my dear."

Heart pounding, scarcely able to swallow for dread of what she would find this time, Emily followed her back up the stairs to the landing with its peony-patterned curtains and bamboo jardiniere full of ferns. Vespasia tapped smartly on the dressing room door and, without waiting, opened it and walked over to the bed.

George was exactly as Emily had left him, except that now she saw the white stiffness of his face more clearly and wondered how she could ever have deceived herself into imagining he was alive.

Vespasia touched his neck gently with the backs of her fingers. After a moment she turned to Emily, her face weary, her eyes brimming with sorrow.

"There is nothing we can do, my dear. I think, from my very little knowledge, it was his heart. I daresay he felt little beyond a moment. You had better go to my room, and I will send my maid to help you while Millicent gets you a stiff brandy. I must go and tell the household."

Emily said nothing. She knew George was dead, and yet she could not grasp it—it was too big. She had experienced death before; her own sister had been murdered by the Cater Street Hangman.* Everyone was used to loss: smallpox, typhus, cholera, scarlet fever, tuberculosis, all were commonplace, and too frequently bringers of death—as was childbirth. But it was always someone else. There had been no warning of this—George had been so *alive!*

"Come." Vespasia put her arm round Emily's shoulder and without Emily's realizing it she was walking along the landing again past the ferns and into Vespasia's room, where her lady's maid was making the bed.

"Lord Ashworth is dead," Vespasia said frankly. "He appears to have had a heart attack. Will you stay with Lady Ashworth, please, Digby. I will send someone up with a stiff brandy, and inform the household."

The maid was an elderly North Country woman, bright of face, broad of hip. In a lifetime of service she had seen many bereavements and suffered a few of her own. She made only the briefest of replies before taking Emily gently by the arm, sitting her on the chaise longue with her feet up, and patting her hand in a fashion which at any other time would have annoyed her profoundly. Now it was human contact and absurdly reassuring, a memory of safety more real than the sunlight in the room, the elabo-

The Cater Street Hangman.

rate Japanese silk screen with its cherry blossom, the lacquer table.

Vespasia left the room and went downstairs slowly. She was filled with grief—most of all for Emily, of whom she was deeply fond, but also for herself. She had known George since he was born. She had watched him through childhood and youth, and she knew both his virtues and his faults. She did not condone all he did by any means, but he was generous, tolerant, quick to praise others, and within his own parameters, honest. The obsession with Sybilla was an aberration, a piece of stupid self-indulgence which she did not forgive.

But none of that altered the fact that she had loved him, and she felt a profound sorrow that he should have been robbed of life so young, barely yet half her own age.

She opened the breakfast room door. Eustace was still at the table with Jack Radley.

"Eustace, I must speak with you immediately."

"Indeed." He was still nursing his affront and his face was cold. He made no move to stand up.

Vespasia fixed Jack Radley with a glance, and he saw that there was something deeply wrong. He rose, excused himself, and left, closing the door behind him.

"I would be obliged, Mama-in-law, if you would be more courteous to Mr. Radley," Eustace said with ice in his voice. "It is very possible he may marry Anastasia—"

"That is extremely unlikely," Vespasia cut him off. "But that is far from important at the moment. I am afraid George is dead."

Eustace swung round, his face blank. "I beg your pardon?"

"George is dead," she repeated. "He appears to have had a heart attack. I have left Emily in my room with my maid. I think you had better call the doctor."

He drew breath to say something, but found it inadequate. The normally ruddy color had vanished from his face.

Vespasia rang the bell, and as soon as the butler appeared she spoke to him, disregarding Eustace.

"Lord Ashworth has had a heart attack in the night, Martin, and he is dead. Lady Ashworth is in my room. Will you send someone up with a stiff brandy. And call the doctor—discreetly, of course. There is no need to put the house into an uproar. I myself will inform the family."

"Yes, my lady," he said gravely. "May I say how extremely sorry I am, and I am sure the rest of the staff will wish me to say the same on their behalf."

"Thank you, Martin."

He bowed his head and left.

Eustace stood up awkwardly, as if he were suddenly rheumatic.

"I will tell Mama. It will come as a terrible shock to her. I don't suppose there's anything that can be done for Emily, poor creature?"

"I expect I shall send for Charlotte," Vespasia answered. "I admit, I feel most distressed myself."

"Of course you do." Eustace softened a fraction. After all, she was well over seventy. But there was another thought uppermost in his mind. "I really don't think we need to send for her sister. I gather she is a rather unfortunate creature, whose presence would be anything but helpful. Why not send for her mother? Or better yet, take her back to her mother, as soon as she feels well enough to travel. Surely that would be the kindest thing to do."

"Possibly," Vespasia said very dryly. "But Caroline is on the Continent, so for the time being I shall send for Charlotte." She fixed him with such a glare the protest died on his lips. "I shall dispatch my carriage for her this afternoon."

Vespasia left the room and went back upstairs. There was one more duty to perform, which was bound to be arduous. And because, in spite of the young woman's inexcusable behavior over the last few weeks, she was fond of Sybilla, she wanted to tell her herself rather than let her hear from the servants—or worst still, from Eustace.

She knocked on the bedroom door and opened it without waiting for a reply. The breakfast tray, finished with, sat on the side table. Sybilla was propped up in the large bed, lace-edged shawl thrown carelessly round her, peach satin nightgown sliding a little off one pale shoulder, and her black hair coiled at the nape of her neck and falling over her shoulder and down her bosom. Even at a moment such as this, Vespasia was struck by what a beautiful woman she was. It was a little overpowering.

"Sybilla," she said quietly, entering and sitting down on the edge of the bed uninvited. "I am sorry, my dear, but I have some very sad news for you."

Sybilla's eyes opened wider with fear, and she sat upright. "William—"

"No. George."

"What . . . ?" Sybilla was obviously surprised, confused. Her first thought had been for William, and she had not adjusted whatever threat had been in her mind. "What has happened?"

Vespasia reached forward and took the white hand that was closest to her, holding it hard. "George is dead, my dear. I am afraid he had a heart attack some time early this morning. There is nothing you can do, except to behave with the discretion you have so singularly failed to display so far—for Emily's sake, and William's, at least, if not for your own."

"Dead?" Sybilla whispered, as if she did not understand. "He can't be! He was so . . . so healthy! Not George—"

"I am afraid there is no doubt." Vespasia shook her head. "Now, I suggest you have your maid draw you a bath, get dressed, and remain in your room until you feel you have composed yourself sufficiently to face the family. Then come down and offer your assistance in whatever way it may be useful. I assure you, it is the best way in the world of overcoming your own distress."

Sybilla smiled so slightly it was barely a shadow. "Is that what you are doing, Aunt Vespasia?"

''I suppose so.'' Vespasia turned away, not wishing to betray the pain that was so close beneath the surface. ''That should surely recommend it to you.''

She heard the slither of sheets as Sybilla got up, and then a minute later the movement of the bellpull. It would ring in the servants' hall and in her maid's room, and wherever the girl was, she would come.

''I must go and tell William,'' Vespasia continued, trying to think what else there was to do. ''And no doubt there will be arrangements, letters and so on.''

Sybilla started to say something; it was going to be about Emily. But her nerve failed her before the sentence was complete enough to be spoken aloud, and Vespasia did not press her.

The doctor came a little before noon, and Eustace met him and conducted him to the dressing room, where George was still precisely as Emily and Vespasia had found him. He was left alone, but for a footman to attend to any requirements he might have, such as hot water or towels. Eustace had no wish to be present for such a distressing matter, and he awaited the doctor's remarks in the morning room with Vespasia. Emily and Sybilla were still in their respective rooms; Tassie had returned from the dressmaker and was in tears in the withdrawing room. Old Mrs. March was in the hot pink boudoir, which was her special preserve, being comforted by Jack Radley, whose attention she demanded. William was in the conservatory, the corner specially cleared for him to use as a studio. He had returned to his painting, pointing out that there was no purpose to be served by his sitting wringing his hands in the boudoir, and he found it more relief to his feelings to be alone and struggling with brush and color to translate some of his emotions into vision. He had two pictures in progress, one a landscape commissioned by a patron, the other a portrait of Sybilla for his own pleasure. Today he was working on the landscape; spring trees, full of April sunlight and sudden, stabbing cold. It was a mood evoking the frailty of happiness and the eternal imminence of pain.

The morning room door opened and the doctor returned. He had a deeply lined face, but they were all agreeable lines, marks of mobility and good nature. At the moment he looked profoundly unhappy. He closed the door behind him and turned from Eustace to Vespasia and back again.

"It was his heart, as you supposed," he said gravely. "The only shred of comfort I can give you is that it must have been very quick—a matter of moments."

"That is indeed a comfort," Eustace acknowledged. "I am most obliged. I shall say so to Lady Ashworth. Thank you, Treves."

But the doctor did not move. "Did Lord Ashworth have a dog, a small spaniel?"

"For heaven's sake, what on earth does that matter?" Eustace was astounded by the triviality of the question at such a time.

"Did he?" the doctor repeated.

"No, my mother has. Why?"

"I am afraid the dog is also dead, Mr. March."

"Well, that really hardly matters, does it?" Now Eustace was annoyed. "I'll have one of the footmen dispose of it." With an effort, he remembered his position, and thus his manners. "I'm obliged. Now if you will do whatever is necessary, we will make arrangements for the funeral."

"That will not be possible, Mr. March."

"What do you mean, 'not possible'?" Eustace demanded, the pink mounting up his cheeks. "Of course it's possible! Just do it, man!"

Vespasia looked at the doctor's grim face.

"What is it, Dr. Treves?" she said quietly. "Why do you mention the dog? And how do you know about it? The servants did not call you to see a dead dog."

"No, my lady." He sighed deeply, the lines of his face dragging downward in acute distress. "The dog was under the foot of the bed. It died of a heart attack also, I should judge at about the same time as Lord Ashworth. It appears he fed it a little of his morning coffee from the tray served him, and drank some himself. In both cases, a very short while before death.''

The color fled from Eustace's face. He swayed a little. "Good God, man! What on earth do you mean?''

Vespasia sank very slowly into the chair behind her. She knew what the doctor was going to say, and all its darkness was already crowding in upon her mind.

"I mean, sir, that Lord Ashworth died of a poison that was in his morning coffee.''

"Nonsense!" Eustace said furiously. "Absolute nonsense! The very idea is preposterous! Poor George had a heart attack—and—and the dog must have got upset—death, and all that—and it died as well. Coincidence! Just a—wretched coincidence.''

"No, sir.''

"Of course it is!" Eustace spluttered. "Of course. Why on earth would Lord Ashworth take poison, for heaven's sake? You didn't know the man, or you wouldn't suggest such a damnable thing. And he certainly wouldn't try it out on the dog first! George loved animals. The damn creature was devoted to him. Irritated my mother. It's her dog, but it preferred George. He wouldn't dream of hurting it. Bloody silly thing to say. And I assure you, he had no reason whatever to take his own life. He was a man of''—he gulped, glaring at Treves—"every possible happiness. Wealth, position, a fine wife and son.''

Treves opened his mouth to attempt again, but Vespasia interrupted him.

"I believe, Eustace, that Dr. Treves is not suggesting that George took the poison knowingly.''

"Don't be idiotic!" Eustace snapped, losing his self-control entirely. "Nobody commits suicide by accident! And no one in this household has any poison anyway.''

"Digitalis," Treves put in with quiet weariness. "Quite a common medicine for heart complaints. I understand from the lady's maid that Mrs. March herself still has

some, but it is perfectly possible to distill it from foxgloves, if one wishes.''

Eustace collected himself again and his eyebrows rose in
superb sarcasm. ''And Lord Ashworth crept out at six
o'clock in the morning, picked foxgloves in the garden,
and distilled some digitalis?'' he inquired heavily. ''Did he
do this in the kitchen with the scullery maids, or in the
upstairs pantry with the lady's maids and the footmen?
Then, if I understand your implication correctly, he went
back to his bedroom, waited till his coffee came, accidentally poisoned the dog, then poisoned himself? You are a
raving fool, Treves! A blithering and incompetent ass!
Write a death certificate and get out!''

Vespasia felt unaccountably sorry for Eustace. He was
not going to be able to cope. He had never been as strong
as he imagined—perhaps that was why he was so insuffer-
ably pompous.

''Eustace,'' she said quietly and firmly, ''Dr. Treves is
not suggesting that George took it accidentally. As you
observe, it is absurd. The inevitable conclusion is that
someone else put it in his coffee while it was in the
pantry—it would not be difficult, since everyone else takes
tea. And poor George had no idea it was poisoned, either,
when he gave it to the dog, or when he drank it himself.''

Eustace swung round and stared at her, suddenly hot
with fear. His voice was hoarse and came with a squeak.
''But that would be . . . murder!''

''Yes, sir,'' Treves agreed softly. ''I am afraid it would.
I have no alternative but to inform the police.''

Eustace gulped and let out his breath in a long sigh of
pain. The struggle was obvious in his face, but he found
no resolution.

''Of course,'' Vespasia acknowledged. ''Perhaps, if you
would be so kind, you will call an Inspector Thomas Pitt.
He is experienced and—and discreet.''

''If you wish, my lady,'' Treves agreed. ''I really am
very sorry.''

''Thank you. The butler will show you the telephone.

Now, I must make arrangements to have Lady Ashworth's sister come to be with her.''

"Good." Treves nodded. "For the best, as long as she is a sensible woman. Hysterics won't help. How is Lady Ashworth? If you wish me to call on her . . . ?''

"Not yet—perhaps tomorrow. Her sister is extremely sensible. I shouldn't think she's ever had hysterics in her life, and she's certainly had cause."

"Good. Then I'll call again tomorrow. Thank you, Lady Cumming-Gould." He bowed his head very slightly.

Emily would have to know; telling her would be most painful. First Vespasia would see old Mrs. March. She would be outraged. And that was about the only gossamer-thin thread of perverse satisfaction in all that had happened: Mrs. March would have something other to do than embarrass Tassie.

She was in her boudoir. The downstairs sitting room was reserved for ladies—or it had been, in the days when she ruled the house, as well as her daughters, two nieces, and an impoverished and thus dependent female cousin. She had clung on to her dominion of this strategically placed, octagonal room, renewing the suffocating pink decor, keeping the drapes on the mantelpiece and the pianoforte, the banks of photographs of every conceivable family group, and keeping the numerous surfaces ornamented with dried flower arrangements, wax fruit, a stuffed owl under glass, and multitudinous pieces of embroidery, doilies, runners, and antimacassars. There was even an aspidistra in the jardiniere.

Now she was sitting here with her feet up on the pink chaise longue; if she had remained in her bedroom she would have been too far from the center of the house and might have missed something. Vespasia closed the door behind her and sat down on the overstuffed sofa opposite.

"Shall I send for a fresh dish of tea?" Mrs. March asked, eyeing her critically. "You look extremely peaked—quite ten years older."

"I shall not have time to drink it," Vespasia answered. "I have some extremely disturbing news to give you."

"You can still take a dish of tea," Mrs. March snapped. "You can drink and talk at the same time—you always have. Your face is decidedly pinched. You always favored George, regardless of his conduct. This must come very hard to you."

"It does," Vespasia replied curtly. She did not want to discuss her pain, least of all with Lavinia March, whom she had disliked for forty years. "However, when I have told you I shall have to tell others, prepare them for what must happen."

"For goodness sake, stop talking in circles!" Mrs. March said sharply. "You are ridiculously self-important, Vespasia. This is Eustace's house and he is quite capable of dealing with the arrangements. And as for Emily, of course, whatever you wish to do about her is your affair, but personally, I think the sooner she is sent back to her mother the better."

"On the contrary, I shall send for her sister this afternoon. But rather before that, I fancy, we shall have her brother-in-law here."

Mrs. March's eyebrows rose; they were round and a little heavy, like Eustace's, only her eyes were black.

"Has your bereavement robbed you of your wits, Vespasia? You will not have a vulgar policeman in my house. The fact that he is related to Emily is unfortunate, but it is not a burden we are called upon to bear."

"It will be the least of them," Vespasia said baldly. "George was murdered."

Mrs. March stared at her for several seconds in silence. Then she reached for the flowered porcelain bell on the table and rang it instantly.

"I shall have your maid attend you. You had better lie down with a tisanne and some salts. You have taken leave of your senses. Let us hope it is temporary. You should take a companion. I always said you spent too much time alone; you are a prey to unfortunate influences, but I am sure you are more sinned against than sinning. It is all most unfortunate. If the doctor is still in the house, I'll send him up to you.'' She rang the bell again so furiously she was in danger of cracking it. ''Where on earth is that stupid maid? Can no one come when they are told?''

''For heaven's sake, put it down and stop that racket!'' Vespasia ordered. ''Treves says George was poisoned with digitalis.''

''Nonsense! Or if he was, then he took his own life in a fit of despair. Everyone can see he is in love with Sybilla.''

''He was infatuated with her,'' Vespasia corrected almost without thinking. It was only a matter of fact, and almost irrelevant now. ''It is not at all the same thing. Men like George don't kill themselves over women, you should know that. He could have had Sybilla if he wanted her, and probably did.''

''Don't be coarse, Vespasia! Vulgarity is quite uncalled for!''

''He also killed the dog,'' Vespasia added.

''What are you talking about? What dog? Who killed a dog?''

''Whoever killed George.''

''What dog? What has a dog to do with it?''

''Your dog, I'm afraid. The little spaniel. I'm sorry.''

''That proves you're talking nonsense. George would never kill my dog. He was extremely fond of it—in fact he practically took it from me!''

''That is my point, Lavinia; someone else killed them both. Martin has sent for the police.''

Before Mrs. March could find a retort to that the door opened and a white-faced footman appeared.

''Yes, ma'am?''

Vespasia stood up. ''I do not require anything, thank you. Perhaps you had better bring a fresh dish of tea for Mrs. March.'' She walked past him and and across the hallway to the stairs.

*   *   *

Emily woke up from a sleep so deep, at first she was confused and could not remember where she was. The room was very Oriental, full of whites and greens, with bamboo-patterned wallpaper and brocade curtains with chrysanthemums. The sun was off the windows, and yet the air was full of light.

Then she remembered it was afternoon—Cardington Crescent—she and George were staying with Uncle Eustace. . . . It all came back in an icy wave engulfing her: George was dead.

She lay and stared at the ceiling without seeing, her eyes fixed on the scrolls of the plasterwork; it could as well have been waves of the sea or summer leaves on a branch.

"Emily."

She did not answer. What was there to say to anyone?

"Emily." The voice was insistent.

She sat up. Perhaps replying would provide a diversion, an escape from her thoughts. She could forget for a few moments.

Aunt Vespasia was standing in front of her, Vespasia's maid a little behind. She must have been there all the time—Emily could remember seeing her white cap and apron and her black dress last thing before she closed her eyes. She had brought her a drink—bitter—it must have had laudanum in it. That was why she had slept when she had thought it impossible.

"Emily!"

"Yes, Aunt Vespasia?"

Vespasia sat down on the bed and put her hand over Emily's on top of the smooth, embroidered edge of the sheet. It looked very thin and frail, an old hand, blue-veined and spotted with age. In fact, Vespasia looked old; there were hollows of shock round her eyes, and the fine-grained skin that had for so long been blemishless was somehow shadowed.

"I have sent for Charlotte to come and be with you." Vespasia was talking to her. Emily made an effort to

69

listen, to understand. "I have sent my carriage for her, and I hope she will be here by this evening."

"Thank you," Emily murmured automatically. It would be better to have Charlotte here, she supposed. It did not seem to matter a lot. Nobody could change anything, and she did not want to be forced into doing things, making decisions, feeling.

Vespasia's grip was tighter on her hand. It hurt. "Before that, my dear, Thomas will be here," Vespasia went on.

"Thomas?" Emily repeated with a frown. "You shouldn't have sent for Thomas! They'll never let him in—they'll be rude to him! Why on earth did you send for Thomas?" She stared. Had Aunt Vespasia been so shaken by grief she had lost all her common sense? Thomas was a policeman—in the eyes of the Marches little better than one of the less desirable tradesmen, on a level with other such necessary evils as a ratcatcher or cleaner of drains. She felt a sudden rush of pity for her, and anger that Aunt Vespasia, whom she admired so much, should be reduced to foolishness—and in the Marches' house of all places. She gripped her hand tightly. "Aunt Vespasia . . . ."

"My dear." Vespasia's voice was very soft, as if she found it difficult to speak, and her eyes, with their magnificent hooded lids, were full of tears. "My dear, George was murdered. He can hardly have known it, or felt pain, but it is indisputable. I have sent for Thomas in his office as policeman. I pray that it will be he who comes."

Murdered! She formed the word with her lips, but her voice made no sound. George? Poor George! But why should anybody want to—

Then the answers came flooding in wave after wave of horror: Sybilla, because he had rejected her in whatever quarrel Emily had half overheard last night; or William, in jealousy—that would be so easily understandable. . . .

Or worst of all, Jack Radley. If he had some insane idea, after the ridiculous scene in the conservatory, that Emily meant something more than a stupid flirtation—that she could possibly— That thought was obscene, hideous. She would be responsible for deluding him, for encouraging the man to murder George!

She closed her eyes, as if she could shut out the thought with darkness. But it persisted, ugly and violently real, and the hot tears trickling down her face washed nothing away, even when she bent her head on Vespasia's shoulder and felt her arms tighen round her and at last let herself go in the weeping she had held within too long.

5

Pitt returned along the hot, dusty street amid the clatter of hooves, the hiss of wheels, and the shouting of a dozen different sorts of vendors of everything from flowers, bootlaces, and matches to the collection of rags and bones. Nine- or ten-year-old boys shouted where they swept a footpath between the horse droppings so gentlemen might pass from one pavement to another without soiling their boots and ladies might keep the hems of their skirts clean.

Constable Stripe was waiting at the station entrance. "Mr. Pitt, sir, we've bin looking all over the place for you! I told 'em as you'd bin to find that magsman."

Pitt caught his alarm. "What is it? Have you turned up something in the Bloomsbury case?"

Stripe's face was pale. "No, sir. This is much worse, in a manner o' speaking. I'm that sorry, sir. Truly I am."

Pitt was assailed by a sudden, terrible coldness—Charlotte!

"What?" he shouted, grasping Stripe so fiercely the constable winced in spite of himself. But he did not look away, nor did anger show for even an instant, which frightened Pitt even more—so much so that his throat dried up and he could make no sound.

"There's bin a murder at Cardington Crescent, sir," Stripe said carefully, making no move to shake off Pitt's viselike fingers. "A Lord Ashworth is dead. And Lady Ves—Ves— Lady Cumming-Gould especially asked if you'd be the one as goes. An' to tell you as she'd already sent 'er own carriage for Miss Charlotte, sir. An' I'm awful sorry, Mr. Pitt, sir.''

Relief flooded through Pitt like a hot tide, almost making him sick; then he felt shame for his selfishness, and lastly an overwhelmingly pity for Emily. He looked at Stripe's earnest face and found it extraordinarily good.

He loosened his fingers. "Thank you, Stripe. Very thoughtful of you to tell me yourself. Lord Ashworth is—was my brother-in-law." It sounded absurd. Lord Ashworth his brother-in-law! Stripe had astounding good manners not to laugh outright. "My wife's sister married—"

"Yes, sir," Stripe agreed hastily. "They did insist as it was you. And there's an 'ansom waiting."

"Then we'd better go." He followed Stripe along the footpath a dozen yards beyond the station doorway, where a hansom cab was drawn in to the curb, horse standing head down, the reins loose. Stripe opened the door and Pitt climbed in, Stripe following immediately behind after directing the driver where to go.

It was not a long journey and Pitt had little time to think. His mind was in turmoil, all rationality drowned in grief for Emily and a surprising sense of loss for himself. He had liked George; there was an openness about him, a generosity of thought, a pleasure in life. Who on earth would want to kill George? A chance attack in the street he could have understood, even a quarrel in some gentleman's club or at a sporting game which had gotten out of hand. But this was in a town house with his own family!

Why was the cab going so slowly? It was taking forever, and yet when they were there he was not ready.

"Mr. Pitt, sir?" Stripe prompted.

"Yes." He climbed out and stood on the hot pavement in front of the magnificent facade of Cardington Crescent; the Georgian windows perfectly proportioned, three panes across, four down, the ashlar stone, the simple architraves and the handsome door. It looked like everything that was comfortable and centuries secure. It made it worse: there was nothing left inviolable anymore.

Stripe was standing beside him, waiting for him to move.

"Yes," he repeated. He payed the cabbie and walked up to the front door, to Stripe's acute discomfort. Police went to the tradesmen's entrance. But that was something Pitt had always refused to do, though Stripe did not know that yet. He had only dealt with the criminal world of the tenements and rookeries, rat-infested labyrinths of the slums like St. Giles, a stone's throw from Bloomsbury, or the petty bourgeoisie, clerks and shopkeepers, artisans grasping after respectability but boasting only one street entrance all the same.

Pitt pulled the bell, and a moment later the butler stood in the doorway, grave and calm. Of course. Vespasia would have told him that Pitt never went to the back. He regarded Pitt's height, his unruly hair, the bulging pockets, and reached his conclusion immediately.

"Inspector Pitt? Please come in, and if you will wait in the morning room, Mr. March will see you, sir."

"Thank you. But I will have Constable Stripe go to the servants' hall and begin inquiries there, if you don't mind."

The butler hesitated for a moment, but realized the inevitability of it. "I will accompany him," he said carefully, making sure they both realized that the servants were his responsibility and he intended to discharge it to the full.

"Of course," Pitt agreed with a nod.

"Then if you will come this way." He turned and led Pitt across the fine, rather ornate hallway and into a heavily furnished room; masculine, hide-covered armchairs by a rosewood desk, Japanese lacquer tables in startling reds and blacks, and an array of Indian weapons, relics of some ancestor's service to queen and Empire, displayed haphazardly on the walls opposite a Chinese silk screen.

Here, rather awkwardly, the butler hesitated, confused as to how he should deal with a policeman in the front of the house, and eventually left him without saying anything further. He must retrieve Stripe from the entrance and conduct him to the servants' hall, making sure he did not frighten any of the younger girls, who were no more than thirteen or fourteen, and that the staff acquitted themselves honorably and in no way spoke out of turn.

Pitt remained standing. The room was like many he had seen before, typical of its station and period, except that it contained an unusual clash of styles, as if there were at least three distinct personalities whose wills had met in the decisions of taste: at a guess, a robust, opinionated man, a woman of some cultural daring, and a lover of tradition and family heritage.

The door opened again and Eustace March came in. He was a vigorous, florid man in his mid fifties, at this moment torn by profoundly conflicting emotions and forced into a role he was unused to.

"Good afternoon, er—"

"Pitt."

"Good afternoon, Pitt. Tragedy in the house. Doctor's a fool. Shouldn't have sent for you. Entirely domestic matter. Nephew of mine, sort of cousin by marriage to be precise, great-nephew of my mother-in-law—" He caught Pitt's eye and his face colored. "But I suppose you know that. Anyway, poor man is dead." He drew in his breath and continued rapidly. "I regret to say it, but he had got himself into a hopeless situation in his marriage—seems he sank into a fit of depression and took his own life. Very dreadful. Family's a bit eccentric. But you wouldn't know the rest of them—"

"I knew George," Pitt said coolly. "I always found him eminently sensible. And Lady Cumming-Gould is the sanest woman I ever met."

The blood mounted even higher in Eustace's mottled cheeks. "Possibly!" he snapped. "But then, you and I move in very different circles, Mr. Pitt. What is sane in yours may not be regarded so favorably in mine."

Pitt could feel an unprofessional anger rising inside him, which he had sworn not to allow. He was used to rudeness; it ought not to matter. And yet his feelings were raw, because it was George who was dead. All the more impor-

tant that he behave irreproachably, that he not give Eustace
March an excuse to have him removed from the case—or
worse, permit his own emotions to so cloud his judgment
that he fail to discover the truth and disclose it with as
much gentleness as possible. Investigation, any investigation, uncovered so much more than the principle crime;
there was a multitude of other, smaller sins, painful secrets, silly and shameful things the knowledge of which
maimed what used to be love and crippled trust that might
otherwise have endured all sorts of wounds.

Eustace was staring at him, waiting for a reaction, his
face flushed with impatience.

Pitt sighed. "Can you tell me, sir, what is likely to have
caused Lord Ashworth such distress or despair that on
waking up this particular morning he immediately took his
own life? By the way, how did he do it?"

"Good God, didn't that idiot Treves tell you?"

"I haven't seen him yet, sir."

"Ah, no, of course not. Digitalis—that's a heart medicine my mother has. And he said some rubbish about
foxgloves in the garden. I don't even know if they're in
flower now. And I don't suppose he does either. The
man's incompetent!"

"Digitalis comes from the leaves," Pitt pointed out. "It
is frequently prescribed for congestive heart failure and
irregularity of heartbeat."

"Oh—ah!" Eustace sank suddenly into one of the hide-
covered chairs. "For heaven's sake, man, sit down!" he
said irritably. "Dreadful business. Most distressing. I hope
for the sake of the ladies you will be as discreet as you
can. My mother and Lady Cumming-Gould are both considerably advanced in years, and consequently delicate.
And of course, Lady Ashworth is distraught. We were all
extremely fond of George."

Pitt stared at him, not knowing how to break through the
barricade of pretense. He had had to do it many times
before—most people were reluctant to admit the presence of
murder—but it was different now when the people were so

close to him. Somewhere upstairs in this house Emily was sitting numb with grief.

"What tormented Lord Ashworth so irreparably he took his own life?" he repeated, watching Eustace's face.

Eustace sat motionless for a long time, light and shadow passing over his features, a monumental struggle waging itself within his mind.

Pitt waited. Truth or lie, it might be more revealing if he allowed it to mature, even if it laid bare only some fear in Eustace himself.

"I'm sorry to have to say this," Eustace began at last, "but I'm afraid it was Emily's behavior, and . . . and the fact that George had fallen very deeply—and I may say, hopelessly—in love with another woman." He shook his head to signify his deprecation of such folly. "Emily's behavior has been . . . unfortunate, to say the least of it. But do not let us speak ill of her in her bereavement," he added, suddenly realizing his charity ought to extend to her also.

Pitt could not imagine George killing himself over any love affair. It was simply not in his nature to be so intense about an emotional involvement. Pitt remembered his courtship of Emily; it had been full of romance and delight. No anguish, no quarrels, no giving way to obsessive or fancied jealousies.

"What happened last night that precipitated such despair?" he pursued, trying to keep the contempt and the disbelief out of his voice.

Eustace had prepared for this. He gave a rather shaky nod and pursed his lips. "I was afraid you would press me about that. I prefer to say nothing. Let it suffice that she showed her favors most flagrantly, where all the household might be aware of her, to a young gentleman guest staying here on my youngest daughter's account."

Pitt's eyebrows rose. "If Emily did it in front of everyone else in the house, it can hardly have been very serious."

Eustace's lips tightened and his nostrils flared as he breathed. He kept his patience with difficulty. "It was my mother, and poor George himself, who were witness to it, I grieve to say. You will have to accept my word, Mr.—er, Pitt, that in Society married women do not disappear into the conservatory with gentlemen of doubtful reputation and return some considerable time later with their gowns in disarray and a smirk on their faces."

For only an instant Pitt thought that that was precisely what they did do. Then anger for Emily swept away anything so trivial.

"Mr. March, if gentlemen were to kill themselves every time a wife had a mild flirtation with someone else agreeable, London would be up to its waist in corpses, and the entire aristocracy would have died out centuries ago. In fact, they would never have made it past the Crusades."

"I am sure in your station in life, especially in your trade, that you cannot help a certain vulgarity of mind," Eustace said coldly. "But please restrain yourself from expressing it in my house, particularly in our time of bereavement. There is really nothing for you to do here, beyond satisfying yourself that no one has attacked poor George—which is perfectly obvious to the veriest fool! He took a dose of my mother's heart medicine in his morning coffee. Possibly he only meant to cause unconsciousness and give us all a fright—bring Emily back to her senses. . . ." He trailed off, aware of Pitt's monumental disbelief and floundering for a better solution. He seemed to have forgotten that he had said Jack Radley was here for Tassie, contradicting himself by branding him as of ill reputation. Or perhaps it was all right to marry a girl to such a man, simply not to allow him near your wife. The moral contortions of Society were still unclear to Pitt.

At another time Pitt might almost have been sorry for Eustace. His mental acrobatics were absurd, and yet how often he had seen them before. But this time his patience was worn raw. He stood up. "Thank you, Mr. March. I'll see the doctor now, and then I'll go up and see poor George. When I've done that, I'll want to see the rest of the household, if I may."

"Not necessary at all!" Eustace said quickly, scrambling to his feet. "Only cause quite pointless distress. Emily is a new widow, man! My mother is elderly and has had a severe shock; my daughter is only nineteen, and most naturally delicate in her sensibilities, as a girl should be. And Lady Cumming-Gould is considerably more advanced in years than she realizes."

Pitt hid a bitter smile. He was quite sure Great-aunt Vespasia knew better than Eustace precisely how old she was, and she was certainly braver.

"Emily is my sister-in-law," he said quietly. "I should have called upon her whatever the circumstances of George's death. But first I'll see the doctor, if you please."

Eustace left without speaking again. He resented the position he had been placed in; his house had been invaded and he had lost control of events. It was a unique and frightening occurrence—he was taking orders from a policeman, here in his own morning room! Damn Emily! She had brought all this upon them with her vulgar jealousy.

Treves came in so soon he must have been waiting close at hand. He looked tired. Pitt had not met him before, but liked him instantly; there was both humor and pity in the weary lines of his face.

"Inspector Pitt?" he said with a raised eyebrow. "Treves." He held out his hand.

Pitt took it briefly. "Could it have been suicide?"

"Rubbish!" Treves replied dourly. "Men like George Ashworth don't steal poison and take it in their coffee at seven o'clock on a sunny morning in someone else's house— and certainly not over a love affair. If he'd ever have done it at all—which I doubt—it would have been in a fit of despair over a gambling debt he couldn't pay, and he'd have blown his brains out with a gun. Gentlemanly thing to do. And he damn surely wouldn't poison a nice little spaniel at the same time."

"Spaniel? Mr. March said nothing about a spaniel."

"He wouldn't. He's still trying to convince himself it's suicide."

Pitt sighed. "Then we'd better go up and see the body. The police surgeon will look at it later, but you can probably tell me all I need to know."

"Enormous dose of digitalis," Treves answered, walking towards the door. "Coffee would disguise it. I daresay your constable in the kitchen will have found that out. Poor fellow must have died very quickly. I suppose if you have to kill someone, short of a bullet through the head this would be about the most merciful and the most efficient way of doing it. I daresay you'll find the old lady's entire supply is gone."

"She had a lot?" Pitt asked, following him across the hall and up the wide, shallow stairs to the landing and into the dressing room. He noted sadly that George apparently had been sleeping in a separate room from Emily. He knew perfectly well it was the custom among many people of affluence for husband and wife each to have their own bedroom, but he would not have cared for it. To wake in the night and know always that Charlotte was there beside him was one of the sweetest roots deep at the core of his life, an ever waiting retreat from ugliness, a warmth from which to go forth into the coldness of any day, even the most violent, the weariest and the most tragic.

But there was no time now to contemplate the difference in lives and how much or little it might mean. Treves was standing beside the bed and the sheet-covered body. Wordlessly he pulled the cover back, and Pitt stared down at the waxy, pale face. They were George's features—the straight nose, broad brow—but the dark eyes were closed, and there was a blueness around the sockets. Everything was the right shape, exactly as he remembered him, and yet it did not seem to be George. Death was very real. Looking at him one could not imagine that the soul was present.

"No injury," he said quietly. George was not really there, this was only a shell, but it seemed callous to speak in a normal voice in its presence.

"None at all," Treves replied. "There was no struggle.

Nothing but a man drinking coffee that had enough digitalis in it to give him a massive heart attack—and an unfortunate little dog getting a treat, and dying as well.''

"Which means it wasn't suicide." Pitt sighed. "George would never have killed the dog. It wasn't even his. Stripe will get the details from the servants, find out where the coffee was, who could have reached it. I expect George was the only person to take coffee at that hour. Most people take tea. I'll have to see the family."

"Nasty," Treves said sympathetically. "Domestic murder is one of the tragedies of our human condition. God knows what we do to each other in what is fondly imagined to be the sanctuary of our homes, and is too often a purgatory." He opened the door onto the landing again. "The old lady is a selfish and autocratic old besom—don't let her fool you she is in delicate health. There's nothing the matter with her except old age."

"Then why the digitalis?"

Treves shrugged. "She didn't get it from me. She's the sort who affects vapors and palpitations when her family thwarts her; it's about the only hold she has over young Tassie. Without obedience dominion is empty, so she persuaded one of the other doctors in the area to prescribe it for her. She seldom misses an opportunity to tell me how he saved her life—implying I would have let her die." He smiled grimly.

Pitt remembered other dowagers he had met who ruled their families with relentless threats of imminent collapse. Charlotte's grandmother was a fearsome old lady who could cast a gloom on almost any family proceedings with a catalogue of the ingratitude she suffered at their hands.

"Perhaps I'd better see her next," he remarked, offering his hand to the doctor. "Thank you."

Treves shook it with a firm grip. "Good luck," he said shortly, and his face conveyed his disbelief in it.

Pitt dispatched a note about digitalis to Stripe in the servants' hall, and set about the next duty. He asked the footman to take him to Mrs. March.

She was still downstairs in the hot-pink boudoir, and in spite of the extremely pleasant early afternoon there was a fire burning strongly in the grate, making the room stuffy— quite unlike the rest of the house, where the windows were thrown open.

She was lying on the chaise longue, a tray of tea on a rosewood table beside her, also an ornate glass bottle of smelling salts. She clutched a handkerchief to her cheek as if she were about to burst into weeping.

The room was crowded with furniture and drapery, and Pitt found it almost robbed him of breath, closing in on him. But the old woman's eyes over her fat hand, shining with rings, were as cold as chips of stone.

"I presume you are the policeman," she said with distaste.

"Yes, ma'am." She did not offer him a seat, and he did not invite rebuff by taking one unasked.

"I suppose you'll be poking your nose into everybody's affairs, and asking a lot of impertinent questions," she went on, eyeing his wild hair and bulging pockets.

He disliked her immediately, and George's white face was too recent a vision for his usual self-control.

"I hope also to ask some pertinent ones," he answered. "I intend to discover who murdered George." He used the word *murder* deliberately, turning its harshness on his tongue.

Her eyes narrowed. "Well, you'll be a fool if you can't do that! But then I daresay you are a fool."

He stared back at her without a flicker. "I presume there has been no intruder in the house overnight, ma'am?"

She snorted. "Certainly not!" Her little mouth turned down at the corners in contempt. "But a burglar would hardly use poison, would he."

"No, ma'am. The only possible conclusion is that it was someone in the house, and it's extremely unlikely to be a servant. Which leaves the family, or your guests. Will you be kind enough to tell me something about those presently in the house?"

"You don't need to go through them all." She sniffed and pulled a face. The room was stifling, the cloudless sun hot on the windows, but she did not seem to notice. "There is only my immediate family: Lord Ashworth, he was a cousin; Lady Ashworth, whom I have heard tell is somehow connected with you." She let this incredible piece of intelligence fall into the hot air and remained silent for several seconds. Then, as Pitt made no remark, she finished tartly, "And a Mr. Jack Radley, a person of some disappointment—to my son, anyway. Although I could have told him."

Pitt took the bait. "Told him what, ma'am?"

Her eyes gleamed with satisfaction.

Pitt felt the sweat trickle down his skin, but it would not be acceptable to take off his jacket in her boudoir.

"Immoral," the old lady said baldly. "No money, and too handsome by half. Mr. March thought he would be a suitable match for Anastasia. Nonsense! She doesn't need to marry good blood, she's got plenty of her own. Not that you'd know anything about that." She stared up at him, cricking her neck to see him but determined not to let him sit down. He was an inferior, and he must be made to remember it; it was not for the likes of policemen to sit themselves on the good furniture in the front of the house. By such license had begun the whole erosion of every value that now afflicted the nation. If this man had to sit, let him do it in the servants' hall. "Anyway," she went on, "a man like Radley doesn't pick a plain-Jane like Anastasia. All that orange-colored hair and skin full of speckles—doesn't come from our side of the family! And thin as a washboard. Hardly a woman at all. A man like that is out to marry for money, for something fashionable to be seen with in public. Something handsome to bed. Ha! I shock you!"

Pitt remained totally straight-faced. "Not at all, ma'am. I'm sure you are right. There are many men like that, and many women who are much the same. Except, of course, they also like a title, where it is to be had."

The old lady glared at him, wishing to snub his insolence, but he had made the point she desired, and at the moment that need was stronger.

"Hum-ha! Well—Mr. Radley and Emily Ashworth are an excellent pair. Came together like two magnets, and poor George was the victim. There—I've done your job for you. Now go away. I'm tired and I feel ill. I have had a severe shock today. If you had the slightest idea how to behave you would . . ." She trailed off, not sure what he would do.

Pitt bowed. "You are bearing up magnificently, ma'am."

She glared at him, sure there was sarcasm there but unable to pinpoint it exactly enough to retaliate. His face was almost offensively innocent. Wretched creature.

"Ha," she said grudgingly. "You may go."

For the first time he smiled. "Thank you, ma'am. Gracious of you."

In the large hall he found a footman waiting for him.

"Lady Cumming-Gould is in the breakfast room, sir. She would like to see you," the footman said anxiously. "This way, sir."

With a slight nod, Pitt followed him to the door, knocked, and went in. The room was heavily furnished; bright sunlight picked out the massive sideboard and large breakfast table. The windows were open and a chatter of birds drifted in from the garden.

Vespasia was sitting at the foot of the table—Olivia's place when she had been alive. She looked tired; there was a stoop to her shoulders that he had never seen before, even in the weariest days when she had been fighting to get the child poverty bill through Parliament. The relief in her eyes when she saw him was so intense, it gave him a lurch of pain that he could do nothing to make it easier for her. Indeed, he feared already that he was going to make it worse.

She straightened up with an effort. "Good afternoon, Thomas. I am pleased it was possible for you to take this—case—yourself."

For once he could think of nothing to say. Grief was too strong for the few words he could find, and yet to speak purely as a policeman would be appalling.

"For heaven's sake, sit down," she ordered. "I am in no mood to break my neck looking up at you. I am sure you have already seen Eustace March, and his mother."

"Yes." He sat down obediently opposite her across the heavy polished table.

"What did they say?" she asked bluntly. There was no time for gentle skirting round the truth, simply because it was unpleasant.

"Mr. March tried to convince me it was suicide because George had fallen in love with another woman—"

"Rubbish!" Vespasia interrupted tartly. "He was infatuated with Sybilla. He behaved like a fool, but I think by last night he had realized that. Emily handled it perfectly. She had every bit as much sense as I could have hoped."

Pitt glanced down for a moment, then up again. "Mrs. March said that Emily was having an affair with the other guest, Jack Radley."

"Spiteful old besom!" Vespasia said in exasperation. "Emily's husband was behaving like an ass with another woman, and without the slightest discretion, an affliction which Lavinia has had to put up with herself, and failed to resolve. Of course Emily made it appear she was developing an interest in another man. What woman with spirit wouldn't?"

Pitt did not comment on Lavinia March; the pain of the dilemma was known to both of them. A man could divorce his wife for adultery; a woman had no such privilege. She must learn to live with it the best she could. With this death the fears engendered by suspicion had begun to grow, to warp thought, to seize and enlarge every ugly trait.

"Who is Sybilla?" he asked, because he had to.

"Eustace's daughter-in-law," Vespasia answered wearily. "William March is Eustace's only son—my grandson." She said it as if the idea surprised her. "Olivia had ten daughters, seven of whom lived. They are all married except Tassie. Eustace wanted to marry her to Jack Radley. That's why he is here—to be inspected, so to speak.''

"I assume he does not meet with your approval?"

Her finely arched eyebrows rose and there was a gleam of humor in her eyes, too slight to reach her mouth. ''Not for Tassie. She doesn't love him, nor he her. But he's pleasing enough, as long as one is sensible and doesn't expect too much. He has one redeeming feature: I cannot imagine he will ever be a bore, and that is more than one can say of most socially acceptable young men.''

"Who else is there in the house?" He dreaded the answer, because if there had been any other outsider he knew Mrs. March would already have told him. No matter how she disapproved of Emily, she would never choose her for a cause of suicide had there been any other answer available. It reflected too badly on the family.

''No one,'' Vespasia said very quietly. ''Lavinia, Eustace, and Tassie live here; William and Sybilla were visiting for the Season. George and Emily were to be here for a month, and Jack Radley and I are here for three weeks.''

He could think of nothing to say. George's murderer had to be one of the eight. He could not believe it was Vespasia herself—and please God it was not Emily!

"I had better go and see them. How is Emily?"

For the first time Vespasia could not look at him; she bent her head and hid her face in her hands. He knew she was weeping and he longed to comfort her. They had shared many emotions in the past: anger, pity, hope, defeat. Now they shared grief. But he was still a policeman whose father had been a gamekeeper, and she was the daughter of an earl. He dared not touch her, and the more he cared for her the more deeply it would hurt him if he trespassed and she were to rebuff him.

He stood helpless and awkward, watching an old lady racked with grief and the beginning of terrible fears.

Anyway, what could he say? That he would somehow

alter things, hide the truth if it were too ugly? She would not believe him, or want him to do that. She would not expect him to betray himself, nor would she have done so in his place.

Then instinct overrode reason and he reached forward his hand and touched her shoulder gently. She was extraordinarily thin, for all her height when she stood; her bones felt fragile. There was a faint smell of lavender in the air.

Then he turned and went out of the room.

In the hall there was a girl of perhaps twenty, her hair the brilliant color of marmalade, her face pale under its dapple of freckles. She had hardly a shred of the beauty with which Vespasia had dazzled a generation, but she was just as thin, and there was perhaps an echo of the high cheekbones, the hooded eyelids. She was staring at Pitt with a mixture of horror and curiosity.

"Miss March?" he inquired.

"Yes, I'm Tassie March—Anastasia. You must be Emily's policeman." It was a statement, and phrased like that it was surprisingly painful.

"May I speak with you, Miss March?"

She gave a little shiver; her revulsion was not for him—her eyes were too direct—but for the situation. There had been a murder in her home, and a policeman must question her.

"Of course." She turned and led the way through the dining room to the withdrawing room, cool and silver-green, utterly different from the suffocating boudoir. If that was the old lady's taste, this must have been Olivia's, and for some reason Eustace had permitted it to remain.

Tassie offered him a seat and sat down herself on one of the green sofas, unconsciously placing her feet together and holding her hands as she had been taught.

"I suppose I should be honest," she observed, looking at the pale muslin of her dress. "What do you want to know?"

Now that it came to the moment, there was very little to

ask her, but if she was like most well-bred young ladies she was confined to the house a great deal of the time with little to do, and she might be extremely observant. He debated whether to treat her delicately, obliquely, or frankly. Then he looked at the steady, slate-blue eyes and thought she was probably more like her mother's family than her father's.

"Do you think George was in love with your sister-in-law?" he said without preamble.

Her eyebrows shot up, but she retained her composure with an aplomb worthy of an older woman.

"No. But he thought he was," she replied. "He would have got over it. I understand that sort of thing happens from time to time. One just has to put up with it, which Emily did superbly. I don't think I should have been so composed—not if I loved someone. But Emily is terribly sensible, far more than most women, and infinitely more than most men. And George was—" She swallowed, and her eyes filled with tears. "George was very nice, really. I beg your pardon." She sniffed.

Pitt fished in his breast pocket and brought out his only clean handkerchief. He passed it to her.

She took it and blew her nose fiercely. "Thank you."

"I know he was," he agreed, filling the silence before it became an obstacle between them. "What about Mr. Radley?"

She looked up with a watery smile. "I think he's quite tolerable. In fact, as long as I don't have to marry him, I daresay I should like him well enough. He makes me laugh—or he did." Her face fell.

"But you don't wish to marry him?"

"Not in the slightest."

"Does he wish to marry you?"

"I shouldn't think so. He doesn't love me, if that is what you mean. But I will have some money, and I don't think he has any."

"How very candid you are." She was almost worse than Charlotte, and he found himself wishing he could protect her from all the anguish that was bound to come.

"One should not lie to the police in matters of importance," she said quite sincerely. "I was really very fond of George, and I like Emily, too."

"Someone in this house murdered him."

"Yes. Martin told me so—he's the butler. It seems impossible. I've known them all for years—except Mr. Radley, and why on earth should he kill George?"

"Might he have imagined Emily would marry him if George were dead?"

She stared at him. "Not unless he is a lunatic!" Then she turned it over in her mind, realizing the only other possibilities. "But I suppose he could be. You can see very little indeed of some people in their faces, watching them do all the usual things everyone does, eating their dinner, making silly conversation, laughing a bit, playing games, writing letters. There is a way of doing all these things, and you are taught it as a child, like the steps of a dance. It doesn't have to mean anything at all. You can be any kind of person underneath it. It's sort of uniform."

"How perceptive you are. You are like your grandmother."

"Grandmother Vespasia?" she asked guardedly.

"Of course."

"Thank you." She breathed out in relief. "I am not in the least like the Marches. Have you solved anything?"

"Not so far."

"Oh. Is that all? I should like to go and see how Emily is."

"Please do. I shall find your brother, if I can."

"He'll be in the conservatory, at the far end. He has a studio there." She stood up, and courtesy bade him stand also.

"Painting?"

"He's an artist. He's very good. He's had several things in the Royal Academy." There was pride in her voice.

"Thank you. I shall go and find him." As soon as she had gone he turned to the row of French doors and the vines and lilies beyond. The conservatory felt humid and full of heavy growth and smelled of lush flowers and hot, perfumed air. The afternoon sun beat on the windows till it was like an equatorial jungle. In the winter a giant furnace maintained the temperature, and a pond the dampness.

William March was precisely where Tassie had said he would be, standing in front of his easel, brush in his hand, the sunlight making a fire of his hair. His thin face was tense, utterly absorbed in the image on his canvas; a country scene full of glancing sunlight and fragile, almost insubstantial trees, as though not only the spring but the garden itself might vanish. Pitt hardly needed his occasional work recovering stolen art to know that it was good.

William did not hear him till he was a yard away. "Good afternoon, Mr. March. Forgive me for interrupting you, but I must ask you certain questions about Lord Ashworth's death."

At first William was startled, simply because his concentration had precluded his awareness of anyone else; then he put down the brush and faced Pitt bleakly.

"Of course. What do you want to know?"

Thoughts were teeming in Pitt's head, but looking at the clever, vulnerable face, the delicate mouth, the quicksilver dreamer's eyes, he abandoned them as clumsy, even brutal. What was there left to say?

"I am sure you must realize that Lord Ashworth was murdered," he began tentatively.

"I suppose so," William agreed with obvious reluctance. "I have tried to think of a way in which it could conceivably be an accident. I failed."

"You did not consider suicide?" Pitt said curiously, remembering Eustace's determined attempts.

"George wouldn't kill himself." William turned away and looked at the canvas on his easel. "He wasn't that kind of man. . . ." His voice trailed off, and his face looked even thinner, pinched with a sorrow that seemed to run right through him.

It was precisely what Pitt knew to be true. There was

infinitely less hypocrisy, less self-regard in William than in his father. Pitt found himself liking him.

"Yes, that is what I thought," he agreed.

For a moment William was silent, then recognition lit his face.

"Of course—I forgot. You're Emily's brother-in-law, aren't you?" he said, so quietly his words were almost lost. "I'm sorry. It's all very . . ." He searched for an expression of what he felt, but it eluded him. "Very hard."

"I am afraid it won't get better," Pitt said honestly. "I'm forced to believe someone in this house killed him."

"I suppose so. But I can't tell you who—or why." William picked up his brush again and began to work, touching a muted raw sienna into the shadows of a tree.

But Pitt was not ready to be dismissed. "What do you know of Mr. Radley?"

"Very little. Father wants to marry him to Tassie because he thinks Jack's family might get him a peerage. We have a lot of money, you know—from trade. Father wants to become respectable."

"Indeed." Pitt was startled by his frankness. There was no attempt to protect his father's weakness, no family defense. "And might they?"

"I should think so. Tassie's a good catch. Jack's not likely to do better—aristocratic heiresses can afford a title, and the Americans won't settle for anything less. Or to be accurate, their mothers won't." He went on working in the shadows, looking at the Vandyck brown, discounting it, and squeezing out burnt umber.

"What about Emily?" Pitt asked. "Doesn't she have more money than Miss March?"

William's hand stopped in midair. "Yes, she will have, now that George is dead." He winced as he said it. "But Jack has too much experience of women, if even half his reputation is deserved, to believe from a couple of evenings' flirtation that Emily would consider marrying him—especially with George behaving like such a fool. Emily was only retaliating. You may not be aware of it, Mr. Pitt, but in Society married women have little else to do but gossip, dress up in the latest fashions, and flirt with other men. It is their only source of entertainment. Not even an idiot takes it seriously. My wife is very beautiful, and has flirted as long as I have known her.''

Pitt stared at him but could see no additional pain, no new anger or awareness of fear as he said it. "I see."

"No, you don't," William said dryly. "I don't suppose you've ever been bored in your life."

"No," Pitt admitted. There had never been time; poverty and ambition do not allow it.

"You are fortunate—at least, in that respect."

Pitt looked at the canvas again. "Neither have you," he said with conviction.

For the first time William smiled, a sudden flash; then it was gone again as quickly, replaced by the knowledge of tragedy.

"Thank you, Mr. March." Pitt stepped back. "I shan't disturb you any longer, for the moment."

William did not reply. He was working again.

Downstairs, Stripe was also finding things difficult; he was not any more welcome in the servants' hall than Pitt had been in the withdrawing room. The cook looked at him with acute disfavor. It was the hour after luncheon, when she should have been able to take a little time off before beginning to think of dinner, and she wished to sit with her feet up and gossip with the housekeeper and the visiting lady's maids. There was always scandal to exchange, and today especially she was overburdened with the need to express her emotions. She was a large, capable woman with pride in her job, but spending all day on her feet was more than anyone should be asked to bear.

"Hurts me veins something terrible!" she confided to the housekeeper, a rotund woman of her own age. "Wouldn't tell them flipperty parlormaids that, though! Gets above themselves far too easily as it is. Not the discipline there was in *my* young days. *I* know how a house ought to be run.''

"Everything's going downhill," the housekeeper agreed. "And now we've got the police in the 'ouse. I ask you, whatever next?''

"Notice, that's what." The cook shook her head. " 'Alf the girls givin' notice, you mark my words, Mrs. Tobias.''

"You're right, Mrs. Mardle, you're right and no mistake,'' the housekeeper agreed sagely.

They were in the housekeeper's sitting room. Stripe was still in the servants' hall, where they ate and had such companionship as their duties allowed time for. He was uncomfortable, because it was a world he was unused to and he was an intruder. It was immaculately clean; the floor was scrubbed by the thirteen-year-old scullery maid every morning before six A.M. The dressers and cupboards were massed with china, any one service worth a year of his wages. There were jars of pickles and preserves, bins of flour, sugar, oatmeal and other dry stores, and in the scullery he could see piles of vegetables. There was a vast black-leaded cooking range with its bank of ovens, and beside it scuttles of coke and coal. Of course, the boiling coppers, sinks, washboards, and mangles would all be in the laundry room, and the airing racks drawn up to the ceiling by pulleys, full of clean linen.

Now, in this warm, delicious-smelling kitchen, he was standing in the middle of the floor with an array of maids and footmen in front of him; all stiffly to attention, immaculate, men in livery, girls in black stuff dresses and crisp, snowdrift caps and aprons, the parlormaids' trimmed with lace many middle-class ladies would have been glad to own. Stripe thought by far the handsomest of them was the lady's maid of the household, Lettie Taylor, but she seemed to regard him with even more disdain than the others. The visiting ladies had naturally brought their own staff, and they were also present, except Digby, Lady Cumming-Gould's maid. She had been elected to remain with the new widow, perhaps because she was the oldest, and considered the most sensible.

Somewhat uncomfortable under their hostile gaze, Stripe licked his pencil, asked the questions he was obliged to, and noted down their answers in his book. It all told him nothing except that the trays were set the night before and left in the upstairs pantry, where the kettles were brought and the tea made freshly—or in Lord Ashworth's case, the coffee—each morning. On this particular occasion there had been an unusual turmoil and the pantry had been filled with steam, and apparently unattended, for some minutes. Anyone could, at least in theory, have slipped in and poisoned the coffee.

He asked for a private room and was shown the butler's pantry, which actually was a sitting room for the butler's personal use. There he interviewed each member of the staff alone. He asked—with commendable subtlety, he thought—for any information they might have about relationships within the family, comings and goings; and learned precisely nothing that his own guess could not have told him. He began to wonder if they identified with their masters or mistresses so closely that it was their own honor they defended, their own status in the small community that existed in this house.

Finally, on being handed Pitt's note regarding the digitalis, he asked Lettie to take him upstairs and show him Mrs. March's room and her medicine cabinet, and any other medicine cabinet in the house.

She put her hands up to tuck her hair in more tidily, then smoothed her apron over her slim hips. To Stripe, blushing a little at the thought and terrified lest it should show in his face, she was the prettiest, most pleasing woman he had ever seen. He found himself hoping this investigation would take a long time—several weeks at the least.

He followed her obediently up the back stairs, watching the tilt of her head and the swish of her skirt and finding he was daydreaming when they came to the pantry. She had spoken to him twice before he pulled his attention to the subject at hand and looked round at the tables where the trays were laid.

"Where was Lord Ashworth's tray with the coffee?" he asked, clearing his throat painfully.

"Aren't you listening to me?" she said, shaking her head. "I just told you, it was there." She pointed to the end of the table nearest the door.

"Was that usual? I mean . . ." Her eyes were the color of the sky above the river on a summer day. He coughed hard and began again. "I mean, did you put them in the same places each morning, miss?"

"That one, yes," she replied, apparently unaware of his gaze. "Because it was coffee, and the others were tea."

"Tell me again what happens every morning." He knew what she had already said, but he wanted to listen to her again and he could think of no more relevant questions.

Dutifully she repeated the story, and he noted it down again.

"Thank you, miss," he said politely, closing his notebook and putting it in his pocket. "Now, would you show me Mrs. March's medicine cupboard, if you please."

She looked a little pale, forgetting her general umbrage at having the police in the house at this sudden reminder of death.

"Yes, of course I will." She led the way through the upstairs baize door onto the main landing and along to old Mrs. March's room. She knocked on the door, and when there was no answer, opened it and went in.

The room was like no other Stripe had ever imagined, let alone seen. It was as pink and white as an apple blossom. Everywhere he looked there were frills: laces, doilies, ribbons, photographs with satin bindings, a suffocating sea of pillows, pink velvet curtains drawn and swagged to reveal white net ruching beneath.

Stripe was robbed of words; the air seemed motionless and hot, and it clogged his lungs. Awkwardly, in case he left a large footprint in it, he tiptoed across the pink carpet behind Lettie to the ornate cupboard painted pink and white, where she opened a little drawer and looked into it, her face grave.

Stripe stood behind her, smelling a slight flower perfume from her hair, and peeked down at the little space packed with bottles, twists of paper, and cardboard pillboxes.

"Is the digitalis there?" he asked, breaking the silence.

"No, Mr. Stripe," she said very quietly, her hand trembling above the drawer. "I know what all these are, and the digitalis is gone."

She was frightened, and he wanted to reassure her, promise he would look after her himself, personally see that no one ever hurt her. But that would offend her so much the very idea was painful to him. She would be outraged by his temerity. Doubtless she already had admirers—that thought, too, was extraordinarily unpleasant. He pulled his wits together.

"Are you sure?" he asked in a businesslike manner. "Could it be in another drawer, or on the bedside table?" He looked round the cloying room. There could be an entire apothecary's shop hidden in all these billowing frills and folds.

"No," Lettie said decidedly, her voice high. "I have tidied this room this morning. The digitalis is gone, Mr. Stripe. I—" She shivered.

"Yes?" he said hopefully.

"Nothing."

"Thank you, miss." He began back towards the doorway, still careful not to knock anything. "Then I think that'll be all for the moment. I'd better send a message to Mr. Pitt."

She took a deep breath. "Mr. Stripe?"

"Yes, miss?" He stopped and turned to face her, aware of the blood burning up his cheeks.

She was trying to hide her fear, but it was there in her eyes, dark and shivery. "Mr. Stripe, is it true Lord Ashworth was murdered?"

"We think so, miss. But don't you worry, we'll take

good care o' you. An' we'll find whoever did it, be sure."
Now he had said it. He waited for her reaction.

Relief flooded into her face; then she remembered herself, her position, and her loyalties. She drew herself up and lifted her chin very high. "Of course," she said with dignity. "Thank you, Mr. Stripe. Now if there's nothing else, I'll be about my business."

"Yes, miss," he said regretfully, and allowed her to guide him downstairs again to resume his own duties in the butler's pantry.

Pitt saw Sybilla March also, and the moment she walked into the room he understood why George had behaved with such abandon. She was a beautiful woman, vivid and sensuous. There was a warmth about her face, a grace in her movement utterly different from the cool elegance of fashion. And yet, for all the curves of her body, the fragility in the slenderness of her neck, the smallness of her wrists, made her also seem vulnerable and robbed him of the anger he had wanted to feel.

She sat down on the green sofa exactly where Tassie had been an hour earlier. "I don't know anything, Mr. Pitt," she said before he had time to ask. Her eyes were shadowed, as if she had been weeping, and there was a tightness about her which he thought was fear. But there had been a murder in the house, and whoever had committed it was still here. Only a fool would not be afraid.

"You may not appreciate the value of what you know, Mrs. March," he said as he sat down. "I imagine anyone had the opportunity to put the digitalis in Lord Ashworth's coffee. We shall have to approach it from the point of discovering who might wish to."

She said nothing. The white hands in her lap were clenched so tightly the knuckles were shining.

He found it unexpectedly difficult to go on. He did not want to be brutal, and yet skirting round the subjects that were painful would be useless, and would only prolong the distress.

"Was Lord Ashworth in love with you?" he said bluntly.

Her head jerked up, eyes wide, as if she had been startled by the question, and yet she must have known it was inevitable. There was a long silence before she replied—so long, Pitt was about to ask again.

"I don't know," she said in a husky voice. "What does a man mean when he says 'I love you'? Perhaps there are as many answers as there are men."

It was a reply he had not foreseen at all. He had expected a blushing admission, or a defiant one, or even a denial. But a philosophical answer that was a question itself left him confused.

"Did you love him?" he asked, far more brashly than he had planned.

Her mouth moved in the slightest of smiles, and he suspected there was an infinity of meaning in it he would never grasp. "No. But I liked him very much."

"Did your husband know the true nature of your regard for Lord Ashworth?" He was floundering now, and he was acutely aware of it.

"Yes," she admitted. "But William was not jealous, if that is what you imagine. We mix in Society a great deal. George was not the first man to have found me attractive."

That Pitt was obliged to believe. But whether William was jealous or not was another matter. How far had the affair gone, and did William know its extent? Was he either ignorant of it, or truly a complacent husband? Or was there nothing to mind?

There was certainly no point in asking Sybilla.

"Thank you, Mrs. March," he said formally.

Now he could no longer put it off. He must go and see Emily, face her grief.

He stood up and excused himself, leaving Sybilla alone in the green withdrawing room.

In the hall he found a footman and requested to be taken to see Emily. The man was reluctant at first, having more respect for grief than the necessities of investigation. But common sense overcame him, and he led the way up the broad stairs to the landing, with its jardinieres of ferns, and knocked on Vespasia's bedroom door.

It was opened by a middle-aged maid with a plain, wise face, at the moment creased with pity. She stared up at Pitt grimly, quite prepared to stand her ground and defy him. She would protect Emily at any cost, and Pitt could see it in the shape of her shoulders and the square planting of her feet.

"I'm Thomas Pitt," he said loudly enough for Emily, beyond the door, to hear him. "My wife is Lady Ashworth's sister. She will be here soon, but I must speak to Lady Ashworth first."

The maid hesitated, looked him up and down with a measured gaze, and made up her mind. "Very well. I suppose you'd best come in." She stood aside.

Emily was sitting up on the bed, fully dressed in a gown of dark blue—she had nothing black with her. Her hair was loose at the back of her neck and she was almost as pale as the pillows behind her. Her eyes were cavernous with shock.

He sat down on the bed and took her hand, holding it in both of his. It felt limp and small as a child's. There was no point in saying he was sorry. She must know that, must see it in his face and feel it in his touch.

"Where's Charlotte?" she asked shakily.

"Coming. Aunt Vespasia sent her carriage; she'll be here soon. But I have to ask you some questions. I wish I didn't, but wishing doesn't change things."

"I know." She sniffed, and the tears escaped her will and ran down her cheeks. "Dear heaven, do you think I don't know!"

Pitt could feel the maid behind his shoulder, alert and defensive, ready to drive him out the moment he threatened Emily, and he loved her for it.

"Emily, George was deliberately killed by someone in this house. You know I have to find out who."

She stared at him. Perhaps part of her mind had understood that already, or at least rejected all the other possibilities, but she had not actually faced it as bluntly as that. "That means—the family, or Jack Radley!"

"I know. Of course it is conceivable we could turn up a reason among the servants, but I don't believe it."

"Don't be ridiculous, Thomas! Why on earth would one of Uncle Eustace's servants murder George? They hardly even knew of him a month ago. Anyway, why would any servant murder anyone in the house? It's a nice thought, but it's stupid."

"Then it is one of the eight of you," he said, watching her face.

She breathed out slowly. "Eight? Thomas! Not *me*! You can't—" She was so white he thought she was going to faint, even lying against the pillows as she was.

He gripped her hand harder. "No, of course I don't. Nor do I think it was Aunt Vespasia. But I have to find out who did, and that involves finding out the truth about a lot of things."

She said nothing. Behind him he could hear the maid winding her hands in her apron. Silently he blessed the woman again, and Vespasia for providing her.

"Emily—could Jack Radley have imagined that you might one day marry him, were you free to?"

"No . . ." Her voice faded away and her eyes left his, then came back. "Not from anything I said. I—I flirted a little—a very little. That's all."

He thought that was less than the truth, but it did not matter now. "Is there anything else?" he persisted.

"No!" Then she realized that he was no longer thinking only of Jack Radley but of anyone. "I don't know. I can't think why anyone should want to kill George. Couldn't it possibly have been an accident, Thomas?"

"No."

She looked down at her hand, still in his. "Could it have been meant for someone else, and not George?"

"Who? Does anyone else have coffee first thing in the morning?"

Her voice was hardly even a whisper. "No."

There was no need to pursue the conclusion; she understood as well as he did.

"What about William March, Emily? Could he have been jealous enough to kill George over his attentions to Sybilla?"

"I don't think so," she said honestly. "He showed no sign of even having noticed, much less caring. I think all he minds about is his painting. But anyway . . ." Her fingers curled round his, responding to his grip. "Thomas, I swear I heard George and Sybilla quarreling last night, and when George came up, before he went to bed, he came to see me and—" She struggled for a moment to keep mastery of herself. "And he let me know that it was over with Sybilla. Not—not directly, of course. That would have been admitting there was something— But we understood one another."

"He quarreled with Sybilla?"

"Yes."

There was no point in asking her if the quarrel had been violent enough to prompt murder: she could not answer, nor would it mean anything if she did.

He stood up, letting her hand go gently. "If you think of anything at all, please send for me. I can't leave it go."

"I know that. I'll tell you."

He smiled at her very slightly, to blunt the edge of what he had said and to try to throw the frailest of lines across the gulf between the policeman and the man.

She swallowed hard, and the corners of her mouth lifted in an answering shadowy smile.

It was an hour later when the bedroom door opened again and Charlotte came in. She said nothing at all, but came and sat on the bed, reached out her hand to Emily, and slipped her arms round her and let her weep as she needed to, holding her close and rocking a little back and forth, murmuring old, meaningless words of comfort from childhood.

6

When at last Emily lay back against the pillows her face was drawn, her eyes puffy, with dark shadows below them, and her usually pretty hair straggled in untidy wisps. The sight of her brought home to Charlotte the reality of death and fear far more violently than all the words imaginable, or excessive weeping. People weep for many things.

She began with the painful, practical help she knew was the only way to move to any real healing. She rang the bell by the bed.

"I don't want anything," Emily said numbly.

"Yes, you do." Charlotte was firm. "You want a cup of tea, and so do I."

"I don't. If I take anything I shall be sick."

"No, you won't. But if you go on crying you will. It's enough for now. We have things to do."

Suddenly Emily was furious; all her shock and fear exploded in resentment because Charlotte was still safe, wrapped up in her own marriage, and this was just one more adventure for her. She was sitting on the bed with a businesslike complacency in her face, and Emily hated her for it. George had been carried away, white and cold, only an hour ago, and Charlotte was busy! She should have been shattered and frozen inside, as Emily was.

"My husband was murdered this morning," she said in a tight, hard voice. "If all you can do is exercise your curiosity and self-importance, then I'd feel a lot better if you'd go back home and get on with your housework, or whatever it is you do when you haven't got anyone else's life to meddle in."

For a moment Charlotte felt as if she had been slapped. The blood burned in her face, and her eyes stung. The retort stopped on her lips only because she could find no words for it. Then she took a deep breath and remembered Emily's pain. Emily was younger; all the protective feelings of childhood came back in a tumble of images, always Emily the smallest, the last to achieve any milestone to maturity. Emily had envied her, admired her, and tried desperately to keep up, just as she herself was always a step behind Sarah.

"Who murdered George?" she asked aloud.

"I don't know!" Emily's voice rose dangerously.

"Then don't you think we had better find out—very quickly, before whoever it is makes it look even more as though you did?"

Emily gasped, and her face looked even grayer than before.

At that moment the door opened and Digby came in. As soon as she saw Charlotte her expression hardened.

But Charlotte had not forgotten all her early years in her parents' home, when she was accustomed to having a lady's maid, and the habit returned automatically.

"Will you be kind enough to bring us a tray of tea," she said to Digby. "And perhaps something sweet to eat with it."

"I don't want anything," Emily repeated.

"Well, I do." Charlotte forced the outline of a smile to her lips and nodded a dismissal to Digby, who retired obediently, but obviously she deferred judgment upon Charlotte.

Charlotte sat down facing Emily. "Do you want me to tell you again how deeply I grieve for you, how sorry I am, how horrified?"

Emily looked at her grudgingly. "No, thank you, there would hardly be any point."

"Then help me to learn at least enough of the truth to prevent another tragedy. Because if you think someone who would murder George would then be averse to seeing that you were blamed for it, you are dreaming."

"I didn't do it," Emily whispered.

Charlotte controlled herself with a difficulty so sharp for a moment the breath caught in her chest with a stab and tears prickled in her eyes.

"I know," she said with a quiver in her voice, and she coughed to try to cover it up. "Have you any idea who did? What about this Sybilla? Could they have quarreled? Or her husband—you didn't tell me his name. Or did she have another lover?"

She saw concentration overtake anger in Emily's face, then grief again, and unrestrained tears. Charlotte waited, forcing herself not to lean forward and put her arms round her. Emily did not need sympathy now, she needed practical help.

"Yes," Emily said at last. "They quarreled last night, just before we went to bed." She blew her nose fiercely, and again a second time, and stuffed the handkerchief under the pillow and reached for another. Charlotte passed her own.

The door opened and Digby came in with a tray bearing a flowered china teapot, a dish of warm, crumbly scones, and butter and strawberry jam. She set it down carefully.

"Shall I pour, ma'am?" she asked with guarded eyes.

Charlotte accepted. "Yes, please. And if you can find some handkerchiefs, bring them."

"Yes, ma'am." Digby's face relaxed. Perhaps Charlotte was not as bad as she feared.

Charlotte passed Emily a steaming cup, and buttered a scone and spread jam on it. "Eat it," she advised. "Slowly. And chew it well. We are both going to need all our strength."

Emily took it obediently. "His name is William," she continued, answering the question as soon as Digby was out the door. "And I suppose he could have killed George, but he didn't seem to care about Sybilla. I don't even know whether he really noticed how far it had gone. Maybe Sybilla always behaves like that.''

''Do you know?'' Charlotte hated the question, but it would hover on the edge of their minds until it was answered.

Emily hesitated only a moment. ''I can guess. But it was over! He came into my room before he went to bed, and we talked.'' She took a shivery breath, but this time she did not lose control. ''It was going to be all right, if—if he hadn't been killed.''

''So it could have been Sybilla.'' Charlotte made it a statement rather than a matter open to doubt. ''Is she that kind of woman? Has she enough vanity, enough hate?''

Emily's eyes widened. ''I don't know.''

''Don't be silly! She was trying to take George away from you—you know everything about her that you possibly can! Now *think*, Emily.''

There were several minutes of silence while Emily sipped her tea and ate two scones, surprising herself.

''I don't know,'' she said again, at last. ''I really don't. I'm not sure whether she loved him, or just found him fun and enjoyed the attention. It might be that if it wasn't George it would have been someone else.''

Charlotte did not find that in the least helpful, but she realized that it was all Emily could give. She left it for a moment.

''Who else is there?''

''Nobody,'' Emily said quietly. ''It doesn't make any sense.'' She looked up, eyes wide and hollow, too hurt to think.

Charlotte reached out and touched her gently. ''All right. I'll judge for myself.'' She took another scone and ate it absently.

Emily sat up a little, her shoulders stiff, pulling the thin fabric of her wrap round her. It was almost as though she expected some kind of a blow and was tensed to ward it off.

"I really don't know what George felt for Sybilla." She stared down at the embroidered hem of the sheet between her fingers. "For that matter, I'm not as sure as I used to be precisely what he felt for me, even before we came here. Perhaps I didn't know him so very well. It's funny, when I look back on Cater Street and all the things that happened there towards the end—I thought I'd never make all those mistakes myself, like Sarah, and Mama. Taking things for granted, assuming you know someone, just because you see them every day coming and going in the house, even sleep in the same bed with them sometimes, touch them . . ." She hesitated a moment, grasping her self-control hard. "Assume that you know them, that you understand. But perhaps that's exactly what I did. I assumed a lot of things about George, and maybe I was wrong." She waited without looking up.

Charlotte knew she was half hoping for a contradiction, and yet she would not have believed one had it been offered.

"We never do know anyone else completely," she said instead. "And nor should we—it would be an intrusion. And I daresay, at times it would be painful and destructive. And perhaps boring. How long would you stay in love with someone you could look through like glass, and see everything? One has to have mystery somewhere ahead left to explore, or why go on?" She crept a hand forward and took Emily's gently. "I'd hate Thomas to know everything I thought or did—some of the weak and selfish things. I'd rather fight them on my own, and then forget them. I couldn't do that if he knew—I'd wonder at all the wrong times if he remembered. He'd never find it so easy to forgive me if he knew some of the thoughts in my mind. And there are some things about people it is better not to know, just because if you did, you couldn't ever completely dismiss them."

Emily looked up, her face angry. "You think I flirted with Jack Radley, that I led him to expect something!"

"Emily, I never even heard of him until just now."

Charlotte met her eyes frankly. "You are accusing your-self, either because Thomas has said something, or you think he will, or because there is a thread of truth in it."

"You're damnably pious about it!" Emily suddenly lost her temper again and snatched her hand away. "You sit there as if you'd never flirted in your life! What about General Ballantyne?* You lied to him just to do your detecting—and he adored you! You used that! I never treated anyone like that!"

Charlotte burned at the memory, but there was no time for the self-indulgence of guilt or explanation now. Not that there was an explanation—the charge was true. Emily's anger hurt, but Charlotte understood, even though her feelings made her want to lash back that it was unfair, and had nothing to do with the problem now. But more power-ful than that superficial abrasion was the deep hurt for Emily, the knowledge of a loss more profound than she had ever felt herself. Sometimes when Pitt had followed thieves into the dark alleys of the rookeries, Charlotte had feared for his life till she was cold and sick. But it had never been a reality, something that did not finally end in the overwhelming warmth of his arms and the certainty that, until next time, it was all a mirage, a nightmare vanished with the day. There would be no sunlit awaken-ing for Emily.

"Some people are incredibly vain," she said aloud. "Could Mr. Radley have imagined you might offer him more than friendship?"

"Not unless he's a complete fool," Emily said less harshly. She seemed about to say something more, then lost the words.

"Then we are left with William and Sybilla, or someone else in the family who has a reason we haven't even guessed at."

Emily sighed. "It doesn't make much sense, does it? There must be something very important—and very ugly—

*Death in the Devil's Acre.

107

that I don't know. Something I haven't even imagined. It makes me wonder how much of my safe and pretty life was all a lie.''

Charlotte had met no one on her arrival except Great-aunt Vespasia, and her only briefly. She knew she was going to be given the dressing room where George had slept, partly because it was immediately next to Emily, but also because no one else intended to give up their own accommodations for her. George's body was laid out, silent and white-wrapped, in one of the old nurserymaids' rooms in the servants' wing. Charlotte dreaded lying in the same bed that George had died in only a few hours ago, and yet there was no alternative. The only way in which she could bear it would be in refusing to allow the thought into her mind.

Her few dark clothes suitable for summer mourning had already been unpacked for her. She blushed as she remembered how worn they were, how plain the underwear, even mended in places, and her dresses adapted from last year to look a little less unfashionable. She had only two pair of boots, and neither of them was really new. At another time she would have been angry at the embarrassment of it, and stayed away rather than cause Emily to be ashamed for her. Now there was no time for such petty emotions. She must change from traveling clothes, wash her face and do her hair, and present herself for the evening meal, which was bound to be appallingly grim, perhaps even hostile. But someone in this house was guilty of murder.

On the way downstairs for dinner she had reached the lowest step, past the dark paneling and rows of muddy oil paintings of Marches of the past, when she came almost face to face with an elderly woman in fierce black, jet beads glinting in the gaslight on her neck and bosom. Her gray-white hair was screwed back in a fashion more than twenty years out of date. Her cold blue marble eyes fixed Charlotte with immovable distaste.

"I presume you are Emily's sister?" She looked her up

and down briefly. "Vespasia said she sent for you—although I do think she might have informed us first and invited an opinion before taking matters into her own hands! But perhaps it is just as well you are here. You may be of some use—I'm sure I don't know what to do for Emily. We've never had anything like this in the family." She regarded Charlotte's gown and the toes of her boots, which showed beneath the hem. They were not of the quality she was accustomed to. Even the maids had one new pair every season, whether they needed them or not, for the sake of appearances. Charlotte's had obviously seen several seasons already.

"What's your name?" she demanded. "I daresay I've been told, but I forget."

"Charlotte Pitt," Charlotte answered her coldly, her eyebrows raised in question as to who the asker might be herself.

The old lady stared at her irritably. "I am Mrs. March. I presume you are"—she hesitated almost imperceptibly and glanced again at Charlotte's boots—"coming in to dinner?"

Charlotte swallowed the retort that rose to her lips—this was not the time for self-indulgent rudeness—and forced herself to assume an expression far meeker than she felt. She accepted as though it had been an invitation. "Thank you."

"Well, you are early!" the old lady snapped. "Don't you have a timepiece?"

Charlotte felt her cheeks burn; she understood with a passion how so many girls marry anyone who will have them, simply to leave home and put away forever the specter of living out the rest of their lives at the beck and call of an overbearing mother. There must have been a million loveless marriages contracted for just such reasons. Please heaven they did not contract such a mother-in-law instead!

She swallowed hard. "I thought I might have the opportunity of meeting the family first," she replied quietly. "They are all strangers to me."

"Quite!" the old lady agreed meaningfully. "I am going to my boudoir. I daresay you will find someone in the withdrawing room." And with that she walked off, leaving Charlotte to find her own way through the dining room, set for the meal but as yet unoccupied, and through the double doors into the cool, green withdrawing room beyond.

Already there, standing in the middle of the carpet, was a girl of about nineteen, very thin under her muslin dress, her vivid red hair piled untidily, her wide, delicate mouth grave. She smiled as soon as she saw Charlotte.

"You must be Emily's sister," she said immediately. "I'm so glad you've come." She looked down, then up again, ruefully. "Because I don't know what to do—even what to say—"

Neither do I, Charlotte thought painfully. Everything sounds banal and insincere. But that was no excuse; even clumsy help was better than ignoring grief, running away as if it were a disease and you were afraid of being contaminated.

"I'm Anastasia March," the girl went on. "But please call me Tassie."

"I'm Charlotte Pitt."

"Yes, I know. Grandmama said you'd be coming." She pulled a little face. Charlotte had already been given Grandmama's opinion of that.

Further conversation was prevented by the doors opening again and William and Sybilla March coming in; she first, dressed in glittering black, lace around the smooth, white throat; he a step behind. Charlotte could see instantly how George had been fascinated with her. She had a vibrancy even in repose that Emily did not, an air of mystery and intensity that would intrigue many men. She did not need to do anything—it was there in her face, the dark, wide eyes, the curve of her mouth, the richness of her figure. Charlotte could well imagine how hard Emily had had to work, how unceasing her charm, how tight her self-control, to win George's attention back again. No wonder Jack Radley had been drawn! But how careless had Emily been, with her mind solely on George? Could she have given away far more than she intended, and been too preoccupied to notice how seriously he had taken her advances?

And William March, the so slightly complacent husband—his face was anything but uncaring. His features were sensitive, ascetic; thin nose, chiseled mouth. Yet there was passion of some sort within him, even if it was more complex than simple adoration or a fire in the blood. He might despise both of those, and yet be just as much their victim.

Her contemplation was cut off by Eustace March himself sweeping in, immaculately dressed, his round eyes flicking from one to another, seeing who was absent, assuring himself that all was as he wished it. His gaze stopped on Charlotte. He seemed already to have made up his mind how he was going to treat her, and his smile was unctuous and confident.

"I am Eustace March. Most fortunate you were able to come, my dear Mrs. Pitt. Very fitting. Poor Emily needs someone who knows her. We shall do our best, of course, but we cannot be the same as her own family. Most suitable that you should be here." His eyes flicked towards Sybilla, and he gave a slight, satisfied smile. "Most suitable," he repeated.

The door opened again and the only unrelated guest came in, the one who troubled Charlotte the most. Jack Radley. As soon as she saw him standing elegantly just inside the arch of the lintel, she understood more of the problem than she had before, and felt the coldness grow inside her. It was not so much that he was handsome—although his eyes were amazing—as that he had a grace and a vitality that demanded a woman's attention. No doubt he was totally aware of the fact; his charm was his primary asset, and he had sufficient intelligence to make the best possible use of it. Meeting his gaze across the short space of the green carpet, she could understand only too well how Emily had used him as a foil against which to win George's attention again. A flirtation with the man might be enormous fun, and all too believable. Only it might prove more addictive than she had foreseen—and far harder to end than to begin. Perhaps after the heady excitement of a forbidden romance, the exhilaration of the game superbly played, George, familiar and predictable, would be a prize less worth the winning. Might Emily, perhaps without acknowledging it, have been willing to continue the affair? And had Jack Radley seen it as his chance at last for a wife prettier and far, far richer than Tassie March?

It was an ugly thought, but now that it was in her brain it was ineradicable without another solution to force it out, to disprove it beyond the smallest doubt.

She glanced at Eustace, standing with his feet a little apart, solid and satisfied, his hands clasped behind his back. Whatever nervousness he might feel was under control. He must have convinced himself he was in charge again. He was the patriarch leading his family through a crisis; everyone would look to him, and he would rise to the occasion. Women would lean on him, confide in him, rest on his strength; men would admire him, envy him. After all, death is a part of life. It must be dealt with with courage and decorum—and he had not been overfond of George.

She looked next at Tassie, as unlike her father as it was possible to be. She was painfully slender where he was thick, broad-boned; vivid and alive where he was innately immovable, settled and sure.

Did he really want to marry Tassie to Jack Radley in order to purchase himself the ultimate respectability of a title through the Radley family connections, as Emily had said in her letters? Looking at him now it seemed eminently likely. Although again, it could be no more than the desire of any good father to see his daughter escape the prison of home, to find another man to provide her with an establishment of her own when he no longer could, and with the social status of wife, and that goal and haven of all women, a family.

Was it what Tassie wanted?

Charlotte cast her mind back to the time when she had been taken with other young women of her age to parties, balls, and soirées in desperate hope of catching the right husband. If one were well-born enough to "come out," it was a disaster to finish the Season unbetrothed, the mark of social failure. No one married unless the arrangement were suitable, the proposed partner acceptable to one's family. Very seldom did one know the person, except in the most perfunctory way; it was impossible to spend time alone together or to speak of anything but trivialities. And once a betrothal was announced it was rarely broken, and only with difficulty and subsequent speculation of scandal.

But perhaps anything was better than life in perpetual bondage, first to old Mrs. March and then to Eustace. He looked robust enough to live another thirty years.

The introductions had been effected and she had barely noticed. Now Eustace was chunnering on about his emotions, rocking slightly back and forth and holding his strong, square, and immaculately manicured hands together.

"We offer you our condolences, my dear Mrs. Pitt. It grieves me that there is nothing we can do to be of comfort to you." He was making a statement of fact, distancing himself and his family from the affair. He did not mean to become any further involved, and he was making sure Charlotte understood.

But Charlotte was here to investigate and she had no compunction at all. She might feel profound pity, perhaps even for Eustace, before all this was over; but she could not afford such tenderness now, when Emily was on the edge of such danger. They hanged women as easily as men for committing murder, and that thought drove all others from her mind.

She smiled sweetly up at Eustace. "I am sure you underestimate yourself, Mr. March. From Emily's letters I believe you are a man of the greatest ability, who would rise to assume natural leadership in a crisis. Just the sort of man any woman would turn to when the situation overwhelms her.'' She saw the blood rise in his face till he was scarlet to the eyes. She was describing him precisely as he wished to be seen—at any time but this! "And of course your loyalty to your family is beyond anyone to question," she finished.

Eustace drew a shuddering breath, and let it out with a splutter.

Tassie stared aghast, not seeing the irony, and Sybilla sneezed repeatedly into a lace handkerchief.

"Good evening, Charlotte," Aunt Vespasia said from the doorway, her eyes for an instant catching some of their old fire. "I had no idea Emily had written so well of Eustace. How charming."

Some flicker of movement made Charlotte turn, and she caught a glimpse of black hatred on William's face that was so swiftly removed she was half convinced it was a trick of the light, a reflection of the gas lamp in his eyes. Tassie moved a step closer to him as if to touch her fingers to his arm, but changed her mind.

"Family loyalty is a wonderful thing," Sybilla remarked with an expression that could have meant anything at all, except what it said. "I expect a tragedy like this will show us where our true friends really are."

"I am sure," Charlotte agreed, looking at no one, "we shall discover depths in each other we had not dreamed of."

Eustace choked, Jack Radley's eyes opened so wide he seemed transfixed, and old Mrs. March threw the door open so violently it jarred against the wall and bruised the paper.

Dinner was grim, conducted mostly in silence, since Mrs. March chose to freeze any conversation at birth by staring fixedly at whoever spoke. Afterwards she declared that in view of the day's events it would be suitable if everyone retired early. She glowered at Eustace and then at Jack Radley so they could not possibly escape her meaning; then she rose and commanded the ladies to follow her. They trooped obediently to sit for an insufferable hour in the pink boudoir before excusing themselves and going upstairs.

Emily had gone back to her own room, because naturally Vespasia required hers for herself. Lying hot and tangled in George's bed in the dressing room, Charlotte was acutely aware of her, wondering if she should get up and go to her, or if it was one of those times when Emily needed to be alone, to work through the stages of her grief as she must.

She woke for the final time a little late to find the air heavy and humid and the room full of white, flat light. There was a maid standing in the doorway with a tray in her hands. A hideous flood of memory swamped Charlotte, not only of where she was and that George was dead, but that he had had poisoned coffee on his morning tray. For a moment the thought of sitting here in this same bed and drinking tea was intolerable. She opened her mouth to say something angry, then saw that it was the short, sensible figure of Digby, and the protest died.

"Good morning, ma'am." Digby set the tray down and drew the curtains. "I'll draw you a bath. It'll be good for you." She did not allow any question into her tone. It was clearly an order, possibly originating with Great-aunt Vespasia.

Charlotte sat up, blinking. Her eyes were gritty, her head ached, and she longed for the luxury of hot, clean-tasting tea. "Have you seen Lady Ashworth this morning?" she asked.

"No, ma'am. The mistress gave her some laudanum last night and said I was to leave her till ten at the soonest and then take her breakfast in. No doubt you'll be wanting to take yours downstairs with the family." Again it was not a question. In fact, it was the last thing Charlotte felt like, but it was clearly a matter of duty. And she could certainly be of no service to Emily lying here in bed.

Breakfast was another almost silent meal taken in a room sharply chilly, since Eustace had preceded them and thrown all the windows open, and no one dared to close them while he was still there, plowing his way with unabated appetite through porridge, bacon, kedgeree, muffins, and toast and marmalade.

Afterwards Charlotte excused herself and went to the morning room, where she wrote letters for Emily, informing various more distant members of the family of George's death. That at least would save Emily some pain.

By eleven she had completed all she could think of, and Emily was still not down, so she decided to begin her pursuit in earnest.

She had intended to speak to William, to see if she could form a clearer impression of him and confirm in her own mind what that extraordinary expression she had glimpsed the evening before might have been. She learned from the parlormaid that he was likely to be in his painting studio at the far end of the conservatory, and that the police were in the house again—not the inspector who had been the day before, but the constable—and the whole kitchen was set on its ears by his probing and prying into all sorts that was none of his affair. Cook was beside herself, and the scullery maid was in tears; the bootboy's eyes were bulging out like organ stops, the housekeeper had never been so insulted in all her life, and the in-between-maid was giving notice.

However, she did not get as far as the studio, because just inside the entrance of the conservatory she met with Sybilla, standing silent and motionless staring at a camellia bush. Charlotte gathered her wits and availed herself of this opportunity instead.

"One could almost imagine oneself out of England altogether," she observed pleasantly.

Sybilla was jerked out of her reverie and struggled to

find a civil reply to such a banal remark. "Indeed one could."

There were lilies blooming a few feet away; their succulent flesh reminded Charlotte of bloodless faces. She did not know how long they would be alone there. She must use the time, and she fancied Sybilla was too intelligent for any oblique approach to succeed. Surprise just might.

"Was George in love with you?" she asked candidly.

Sybilla stood frozen for so long Charlotte could hear the condensation dripping from the top leaves near the roof onto the ones below. The fact that she did not instantly deny it was important in itself. Was she debating the truth with herself, or merely the safety of answering? Surely they must all know by now that it was murder, and have expected the question.

"I don't know," she said at last. "I am tempted to say, Mrs. Pitt, that it is a private matter, and none of your concern. But I suppose that since Emily is your sister, you cannot help caring." She swung round to face Charlotte, her eyes wide, her smile vulnerable and curiously bitter. "I cannot answer for him, and I am sure you don't expect me to repeat everything he said to me. But Emily was jealous, that is undoubted. She also carried it superbly."

Looking at her, Charlotte was aware of intense emotions inside her, of the capability for passion and for pain. She could not possibly dislike her as she had intended.

"I apologize for asking," she said brittlely. "I know it sounds gauche."

"Yes," Sybilla agreed dryly, "but you don't have to explain." There was no anger visible in Sybilla's face, only a tightness, a consciousness of both irony and tragedy.

Charlotte was furious with herself and entangled in confusion. This woman had taken Emily's husband—whether intentionally or not, in front of the whole house—and perhaps directly caused his death. She wanted to hate her with an unfettered, clean violence. Yet she could so easily imagine herself with similar feelings, and she was unable to sustain rage against anyone the moment she comprehended the capacity for pain. It ruined her judgment and tied her tongue.

"Thank you." The words came out clumsily; it was not at all what she had meant for this interview. But she must try to salvage something out of it. "Do you know Mr. Radley well?"

"Not very," Sybilla replied with a faint smile. "Papa-in-law wishes him to marry poor Tassie, and he is here for everyone to come discreetly to some arrangement. Although there is not much discreet about Jack—nor, I gather, has there ever been."

"Is Tassie in love with him?" She felt a stab of shame for Emily. If she were, and being engineered into a marriage while Jack Radley quite openly humiliated her by displaying his attraction to Emily, then how she must have suffered. Were there any possibility of mistake, Charlotte would have supposed the poison intended for Emily.

Sybilla was smiling slightly. She reached out and touched the camellia petals. "Now I suppose they will go brown," she remarked. "They do if you touch them. No she wasn't, in fact. I don't think she wanted to marry him at all. She's something of a romantic."

In that one phrase she summed up a host of things: a world of both regret and contempt for girlish innocence, a wry affection for Tassie, and the knowledge that Charlotte must be of a lower social class than herself to ask such a question at all. People like the Marches married for family reasons—to accumulate more wealth, to consolidate trade empires or ally with competitors, above all to breed strong sons to continue the name—never for emotional fancies like falling in love. It passed too quickly and left too little behind. What was falling in love anyway? The curve of a cheek, the arch of a brow, a trick of grace or flattery, a moment of sharing.

But it was hard to commit oneself to such an intimate and permanent tie without something of the magic, even if it was very often an illusion. And sometimes it was real! Most of the time Charlotte took Thomas for granted, like a profound friendship, but there were many moments when her heart beat in her throat and she still knew him in a crowded street among hundreds by the way he stood, or recognized his step with a lift of excitement.

"And Mr. Radley, I take it, is a realist?" she said aloud.

"Oh, I think so," Sybilla agreed, looking back at Charlotte and biting her lip very slightly. "I don't think circumstances have allowed him a choice."

Charlotte opened her mouth to ask if he might not have become obsessed with Emily all the same, then realized that the question was anything but helpful. Tassie March might inherit a pleasing sum from both her grandparents, but it would pale beside the Ashworth fortune that would now be Emily's alone. Why look for a motive of love of any degree when that of money was so apt?

They were at the doorway of the conservatory, and there was nothing more to say. Charlotte excused herself and escaped inside. She had learned nothing that she had not already surmised, except that instinctively she felt an empathy for Sybilla March which threw all her budding theories into turmoil again.

Luncheon yielded nothing but platitudes. Afterwards, Charlotte spent an hour with Emily, ever on the brink of pressing her for answers and, seeing her white face, changing her mind. Instead she went to find William March, who was still painting in the conservatory. She knew perfectly well that she was interrupting him and he would hate it, but there was no time to nurse her own sensibilities.

She found him in the studio that had been cleared for him beyond the lilies and vines. He stood with the angular grace of someone who uses his body and is unaware of being observed. There was nothing posed about him: his elbows stuck out, his head was to one side, and his feet were apart. Yet his balance was perfect. The top window was open and there was a whispering of wind in the leaves like water through pebbles on a shore. He did not hear

Charlotte's approach, and she was almost beside him when she spoke. Ordinarily she would have felt a crassness that would chill her stomach to speak to him, but after talking with Sybilla she was even more conscious of the danger in which Emily stood. To any unbiased observer she must look guilty. There was only her word that George had quarreled with Sybilla, whereas everyone had seen George's affair—and had seen Emily accept attention from Jack Radley. If there was a reason anyone else in the family was involved, she had not yet found it.

"Good afternoon, Mr. March," she said with forced cheerfulness. She felt like a fool and a philistine.

He was startled and the brush jerked in his hand, but she had chosen a moment when it was still far from the canvas. He turned to look at her coldly. His eyes were surprisingly dark gray, and deep-set under the red brows.

"Good afternoon, Mrs. Pitt. Are you lost?" It was plain to the point of rudeness. He resented being disturbed and still more being placed where he was obliged to conduct a pointless conversation with a woman he did not know.

She lost any hope of fooling him. "No, I came here on purpose, because I wished to talk with you. I realize I am preventing your work."

He was surprised; he had expected some silly excuse. He still held the brush in the air and his face was tight with concentration. "Indeed?"

She looked past him at the picture. It was far cleverer than she had foreseen; there was a shivering in the leaves—an impression more than an outline—and just beyond the brightness of sunlight there was ice, wind that cut the skin, a sense of isolation and pain. It was as much the tail end of winter, with sudden frost that kills, as it was a herald of spring, and she felt it in the mind as well as the eye.

"It's very fine," she said sincerely. She thought it was far too good for someone who merely wanted a representation of his possessions and would be blind to the artist's voice illuminating it like flame. "You should exhibit it before you hand it over. It has the cruelties of nature, as well as the loveliness."

He flinched as though she had hurt him. "That's what Emily said." His voice was quiet; it was more a reflection to himself than a remark to her. "Poor Emily."

"Did you know George well?" She plunged straight in, watching his eyes and the curious, chiseled mouth. But she saw no alteration but sadness, no evasion.

"No," he said quietly. "He was a cousin, so naturally I have met him from time to time, but I cannot say I knew him." He smiled very slightly. "We had few interests in common, but that is not to say I disliked him. On the contrary, I found him very agreeable. He was almost always good-natured, and harmless."

"Emily thought he was in love with Mrs. March." She was franker than she might have been with someone else, but he seemed too intelligent to dupe and too perceptive to misunderstand her.

He stared at the painting. "In love?" He turned the phrase over in his mind. "I suppose that is as good a term as any—it covers almost whatever you like. It was an adventure, something daring and different. Sybilla is never a bore—she has too much unknown in her." He began to wipe the paint off his brush, not looking at Charlotte. "But he would have forgotten her after he left here. Emily is a clever woman, she knew how to wait. George was childish, that's all."

Charlotte had known George for seven years, and what William March said was precisely true, and he had seen it as clearly as she.

"But someone killed him," she persisted.

His hands stopped moving. "Yes, I know. But I don't believe it was Emily, and it certainly wasn't Sybilla." He hesitated, still watching the spread-out hairs of the brush. "I would consider Jack Radley, if I were you. Emily is now a young and titled widow with a considerable fortune, and a most attractive woman. She has already shown him some favor, and he might be vain enough to fancy it could increase."

"That would be vile!"

He looked up at her, his eyes bright. "Yes. But vileness exists. It seems we can think of nothing so appalling that someone somewhere hasn't thought of it too—and done it." His mouth twitched, and with difficulty he controlled it. "I'm sorry, Mrs. Pitt. I beg your pardon. I did not wish to offend you."

"You haven't, Mr. March. As I am sure you could not have forgotten, my husband is a policeman."

He swung round, letting the brush drop, and stared at her as if part of him wanted to laugh at the joke on Society. "You must have great courage. Were your family horrified?"

She had been too much in love to take a great deal of notice of anyone else's feelings, but that seemed a peculiarly insensitive thing to say now to this man, whose wife had responded so fully and so publicly to George. Instead, she told him the easiest lie.

"They were so pleased with Emily marrying Lord Ashworth they tolerated me really quite well."

But mention of George and Emily only brought back the sharp contrast with Emily's present loss. "I'm so sorry," he said quietly, and turned back to the cruel, sensitive painting.

She was dismissed, and this time she accepted it, walking slowly back through the jungle of growth to the rest of the house.

In the afternoon they were visited by the pink-faced curate. He made an embarrassed and rather abrupt apology for the vicar who, apparently, was unable to come in person due to some emergency, the nature of which was unclear.

"Indeed!" Vespasia said with unconcealed skepticism. "How unfortunate."

The curate was a large young man of obvious West

Highland origin. With the bluntness of youth, and perhaps some judgment of his own, he made no effort to embellish the excuse. Charlotte warmed to him immediately and was not surprised to observe that Tassie also seemed to find him agreeable.

"And when do we expect this crisis to pass?" Mrs. March inquired coldly.

"When our reputation is restored and we are not the seat of scandal anymore," Tassie said instantly, and blushed as soon as the words were out.

The curate took a deep breath, bit his lip, and colored as well.

"Anastasia!" Mrs. March's voice cracked like a whip. "You will excuse yourself to your room if you cannot guard your tongue from uncharitableness, let alone impertinence. No doubt Mr. Beamish has his reasons for not calling upon us to give us his comfort in person."

"I expect Mr. Hare will do rather better anyway," Vespasia murmured to no one in particular. "I find the vicar peculiarly tedious."

"That is beside the point!" Mrs. March snapped. "It is not the vicar's function to be amusing. I always felt you did not understand religion, Vespasia. You never knew how to behave in church. You have had a tendency to laugh in the wrong places as long as I have known you."

"That is because I have a sense of the absurd, and you have not," Vespasia replied. She turned to Mungo Hare, balanced on the edge of one of the hard-backed, withdrawing room chairs and trying to compose his face to display the appropriate mixture of piety and solicitude. "Mr. Hare," she continued, "please convey to Mr. Beamish that we understand his reasons quite perfectly, and that we are very satisfied that you should take his place."

Tassie sneezed, or that is what it sounded like. Mrs. March made a clicking noise with her tongue, excessively irritated that Vespasia should have contrived to insult the vicar more effectively than she herself had. How dare the wretched, cowardly little man send a curate in his place to call upon the Marches? And Charlotte remembered with renewed vividness why she had liked Aunt Vespasia from the day they had met.

Mungo Hare duly unburdened himself of the condolences and the spiritual encouragement he had been charged with; then Tassie accompanied him upstairs to repeat it all to Emily, who had chosen to spend the afternoon alone.

Charlotte meant to go up later and see if she could tap Emily's memory for some observation, however minor, which would betray a weakness, a lie, anything which could be pursued. But as she was crossing the hall Eustace emerged from the morning room, straightening his jacket and coughing loudly, thus making it impossible for her to pretend she had not seen him.

"Ah, Mrs. Pitt," he said with affected surprise, his round little eyes very wide. "I should like to talk with you. Perhaps the boudoir? Mrs. March has gone to change for dinner, and I know it is presently unoccupied." He was behind her, hands wide, almost as if he would physically shepherd her in the direction he wished her to go. Short of being unexplainably rude, she could not refuse.

Charlotte found the room one of the ugliest she had ever seen. It exemplified the worst taste of the last fifty years, and she felt suffocated by everything it symbolized as much as by the sheer weight of the furniture, the hot color, and the wealth of ornaments and drapings. It seemed to be expressive of a prudery that was vulgar in its very consciousness of the things it sought to cover—an opulence that was lacking in any real richness. It was difficult to keep the distaste from showing in her face.

For once Eustace did not fling open the windows in his customary manner, and it was the only time when she would willingly have done it for him. He seemed too preoccupied with the burden of framing his thoughts.

"Mrs. Pitt. I hope you find yourself as comfortable as may be, in these tragic circumstances?"

"Quite, thank you, Mr. March." She was confused.

Surely he had not brought her to this room to ask her in private such a trivial question?

"Good, good." He rubbed his hands together and remained looking at her. "Of course, you do not know us very well. Nor perhaps anyone like us. No, no you wouldn't. We must seem alien to you. I should explain, so that we do not add confusion as well to your natural grief for your sister. If I can help you at all, in the least way, my dear . . . ?"

Charlotte opened her mouth to say that she was no more confused than anyone else would be, but he hurried on, drowning her protest.

"You must excuse Lady Cumming-Gould her eccentricities. She was a great beauty once, you know, and so she was allowed to get away with being outrageous, and I'm afraid she has never grown beyond it. Indeed, I think with age she has become more so—I know my dear mother finds her quite trying at times." He rubbed his hands and smiled experimentally, searching Charlotte's face to see how she responded to this information. "But we must all exercise forbearance!" he went on quickly, sensing disapproval. "That is part of being a family—so important! Cornerstone of the country. Loyalty, continuity, one generation to the next—that's what civilization is all about. Marks us from the savages, eh?"

Charlotte opened her mouth to argue that in her opinion savages had an excellent dynastic sense, and were intensely conservative, which was precisely why they remained savages instead of inventing and exploring things new. But again Eustace carried on regardless before she could begin.

"And of course from your point of view poor Sybilla must seem most cruel and ill-behaved, because you will naturally take Emily's part. But you know there was far more to it than that. Oh dear, yes. I am afraid it was George who pursued, you know—quite definitely George. And dear Sybilla is so used to admiration she failed to discourage him appropriately. It was ill-judged of her, of course. I feel obliged to tell her so, directly. And George should have been far more discreet—''

''He shouldn't have done it at all!'' Charlotte interrupted hotly.

''Ah, my dear!'' Eustace's face was lit with a smile of patience and condescension. He wagged his head a little. ''Let us not be unrealistic. One expects girls of Tassie's age to have romantic illusions, and heaven forfend I should wound her susceptibilities at so tender a stage in her life, when she is just on the brink of betrothal. But a married woman of Emily's years must come to terms with the nature of men. A truly feminine woman has forgiveness in her nature for our foibles and weaknesses, as indeed we men have for the frailties of women.'' He smiled at her, and for a moment his hand hovered warmly over hers and she was intensely aware of him.

Charlotte was furious. There was something about him that brought back in a rush every patronizing word she had ever heard. She ached to wipe the complacence off his moon face.

''You mean that if Emily had lain with Mr. Radley, for example, George would have forgiven her?'' she asked sarcastically, pulling her hand away.

She had succeeded. Eustace was genuinely shocked. She had preempted a subject he would not have put words to himself. The blood drained from his skin, then rushed back in a tide of color. ''Really!'' he spluttered. ''I appreciate that you have had a grave shock, and perhaps you are afraid for Emily, understandably. But my dear Mrs. Pitt, there is no call for vulgarity! I shall do you the favor of putting from my mind that I ever heard you so forget yourself as to make such a vile suggestion. We shall agree never to refer to it again. You strike at the very root of all that is fine and decent in life. If women were to behave in that way, why, good God!—a man wouldn't know if his son were his own! The home would be desecrated, the very fabric of Society would fall apart. The idea does not bear thinking of!''

Charlotte found herself blushing, although as much from anger as embarrassment. Perhaps she was being ridiculous, and the movement of his hand really had been no more than sympathy.

"I did not suggest it, Mr. March!" she protested, raising her chin and staring at him. "I merely meant that perhaps Emily expected as high a standard from George as she was prepared to adhere to herself."

"I see you are very inexperienced, Mrs. Pitt, and somewhat romantic." Eustace shook his head knowingly, but his expression eased out into a smile again. "Women are quite different from men, my dear, quite different! We have our corresponding virtues of intellect, manliness and courage." Unconsciously he flexed the muscles of his arm. "A man's brain is a far more powerful thing than a woman's." His eyes roamed gently and with pleasure over her neck and bosom. "Think what we have achieved for humanity, in every way. But if a woman does not have modesty, patience and chastity, a sweet disposition, what is she? Indeed, what is the whole world without the influence of our wives and mothers? A sea of barbarism, Mrs. Pitt—that is what it is." He stared at her, and she met his gaze unflinchingly.

"Was that what you wished to say to me, Mr. March?" she asked.

"Ah, no, er . . ." He seemed thrown off balance and blinked rapidly; he had lost the thread of his thought entirely, and she gave him no assistance.

"I merely wished to make sure that you were comfortable," he said at last. "We must present a united face to the world. You are one of us, my dear, through poor Emily. We must do what is best for the family. It is not a time for selfishness. I am sure you understand that."

"Oh, absolutely, Mr. March," she agreed, staring solemnly at him. "I shall not forget my family loyalties, you may be assured."

He smiled with a gust of relief, apparently forgetting that Thomas Pitt was her most immediate relative. "Excellent. Of course you will not. Now I must leave you time to change for dinner, and perhaps to visit poor Emily. I am sure you will be an enormous help to her. Ha!''

After dinner the ladies withdrew from the dining room, to be followed quite soon by the gentlemen. Conversation was stilted, because Emily had joined them for the first time since George's death and no one knew what to say. To speak of the murder seemed needlessly cruel, and yet to converse as if it had not happened deformed all other subjects into such artificiality as to be grotesque. Consequently Charlotte rose at a little after nine and excused herself, saying she wished to retire early and was sure they would understand. Emily went with her, much to everyone's relief. Charlotte imagined she could hear the sigh of exhaled breath as she closed the door behind them, and people sank a little more easily into their chairs

She woke in the night, thinking she had heard Emily moving about next door, and she was anxious in case her sister was too distressed to sleep. Perhaps she should go to her.

She sat up and was about to reach for a shawl when she realized the noise was from a different direction, more towards the stairs. Why should Emily go downstairs at this time of night?

She slipped out of bed and, without fumbling for slippers, went to the door, opened it, and crept out and along to the main landing. She had put her head round the corner before she saw what it was in the gaslight at the head of the stairs; she froze as if the breath had been snatched from her and her skin doused in cold water.

Tassie March was coming up the stairs, her face calm and weary, but with a serenity unlike anything Charlotte had seen in her before. The restlessness was gone, all the tension released. Her hands were held out in front of her, sleeves crumpled, smears of blood on the cuffs, and a dark stain near the hem of her skirt.

She reached the top of the stairs just as Charlotte realized her own position and shrank back into the shadows. Tassie passed on tiptoe less than a yard away from her, still with that unhurried smile, leaving a heavy, sickly, and quite unmistakable odor behind her. No one who had smelled fresh blood could ever forget it.

Charlotte went back to her room, shivering uncontrollably, and was sick.

7

Emily woke early the next morning. It was the day of George's funeral. She felt cold immediately, and the white light on the ceiling was bleak, without warmth or color in it. She was filled with the kind of misery that is edged with anger and intolerable loneliness. This would make it all final. Not, of course, that it was not final anyway. George was dead, there was no going back or recapturing anything of the past warmth, except in memory. But a funeral, a burial, made it certain in the mind, took the immediacy out of it, and relegated the man to the past.

She hunched up under the blankets, but there was no comfort in it. It was too early to get up, and anyway she did not want to see other people. They would be full of their own business, making a show of it, thinking what hat to wear, how to behave, how they looked. And above all they would be watching her, suspiciously. Most of them believed she had killed George, deliberately crept into old Mrs. March's room, stolen her digitalis, and slipped it into the coffeepot.

Except one. One of them would know she had not— because that one had. And that person was prepared to see her suspected, perhaps charged—even tried, and . . . She let her thoughts continue, even though it was stupid, self-inflicted pain. And yet she went on, visualizing the courtroom, herself in drab prison dress, hair screwed back, face white and hollow-eyed, the jury that could not look at her, the odd women among the spectators whose eyes reflected pity—perhaps who had suffered the same rejection, or felt they had. Then the verdict, and the judge with a face like stone, reaching for the black cap.

There she stopped. After that it was too frightening. In her imagination she could smell rope and damp, inky darkness. It was not just a morbid thought; it could be real, with no warm bed, no relieved awakening.

She sat up and threw off the bedclothes, then reached for the bell. It was a long, flat five minutes before Digby knocked and came in, her hair a little hastily pinned up and her apron tied unevenly. She looked nervous but determined.

"Good morning, m'lady. Would you like a cup of tea straightaway, or shall I draw your bath?"

"Draw the bath," Emily replied. There was no need to discuss what she would wear; it could only be the formal black barathea with black hat and black veil which she had sent for. Not a fashionable, flattering veil that lent mystery, but a widow's weeds, hiding the face, disguising the ravages of grief.

Digby disappeared and came back a few minutes later, sleeves rolled up, a tentative smile hovering uncertainly on her lips. "It's a fine day, m'lady. At least you won't get rained on."

Emily really did not care, but perhaps it was a minor blessing. Standing at a graveside with water trickling down her neck, wetting her feet, and making the edges of her skirts heavy and sodden would add a physical dimension to the bleakness that consumed her mind. It might even have been welcome; it was easier to think of frozen feet and wet ankles than of George lying white and rigid inside the closed coffin, being lowered into the ground and covered up, gone for the rest of her life. He had been so warm, so important, always at the foundation of her thoughts for so many years. Even when he was not with her, the sure knowledge that he would be there in a little while was a safety she had never considered losing.

Suddenly the tears came, catching her by surprise; all the sniffing and swallowing did not control them. She sat down again and covered her face with her hands.

Quite unexpectedly she found Digby's arms round her and her head resting against Digby's stiff, sloping shoulder. Digby said nothing; she just gently rocked Emily back and forth, stroking her hair, as if she were a very young child. It was so natural, Emily felt no embarrassment, and when the pain inside her eased and the relief of tiredness came over her, she let go, and went to her bath without the need to explain or reassert in any way that she was the mistress and Digby the maid. There were no questions or answers. Digby knew precisely what was needed, and the silence was one of understanding.

She took breakfast alone with Charlotte. She did not wish to see anyone else, except perhaps Aunt Vespasia, but she did not appear.

"She did not say so," Charlotte said quietly as they took a thin slice of toast each and spread them with butter, then poured themselves cups of hot, weak tea from the flowered pot, "but I think she is busy massing a sort of defense."

Emily did not ask what she meant; they both knew the ranks were closing against the police, against intrusion and scandal—and that meant against Emily also. If she were guilty it could all be over in a few days. No more investigation. They could grieve in decency for the appropriate time and resume their lives again.

Charlotte smiled bleakly. "I don't think even Mrs. March will give her tongue full rein with Aunt Vespasia there. I feel there is not much love lost between them."

"I wish I could think it was Mrs. March who killed George," Emily said thoughtfully. "I've been trying to scrape up any kind of reason why she should."

"Did you succeed?"

"No."

"Nor I. But there must be an enormous amount that we don't know." Charlotte's face was dark and tense, as if she was afraid. "Emily, I woke up in the night and I thought I heard you walking around."

"I'm sorry—"

"No, it wasn't you! It was coming from the stairs, so I got up to follow, but when I got the landing I saw it was Tassie. She was coming up and she walked past me to her bedroom. I saw her quite clearly. Emily, her sleeves were smeared with blood, and there were splashes down the front of her skirt and at the hem. She was smiling! There was a sort of peace about her. Her eyes were shining and wide open, but she didn't even see me. I kept back in the small passage to the dressing room, and she walked so close I could have touched her." She felt a little sick again as the smell came back, nauseating and sweet.

Emily was dazed—this was unbelievable. She offered the only explanation she could conceive of. "You had a nightmare."

"No, I didn't," Charlotte insisted. "It was real." Her face was tight and miserable but she did not waver. "I thought I might have been dreaming, with everything that's happened, so I went down to the laundry room this morning and found the dress soaking in one of the coppers."

"And was it covered in blood?"

Charlotte shook her head no more than an inch. "No, it was washed out. But then it would be; she'd hardly leave it like that for the maids to find, would she."

"But it doesn't make sense," Emily still protested. "Whose blood? Why? Nobody's been murdered that way"— she swallowed—"that we know of."

Another hideous memory stirred in Charlotte's mind, of parcels in a graveyard, but she refused to allow it to take shape. "Do you think she could be mad?" she said wretchedly. It seemed the only explanation left—and one must be found, for Emily's sake.

"I suppose so," Emily said reluctantly. "But I'm sure George didn't know—unless he'd just found out. Which could be a reason for old Mrs. March to have killed him."

"Do you think so?" Charlotte pursed her lips. "Would George ever have told anyone?"

"Yes! If she were dangerous—which she must be, if it was human blood."

Charlotte said nothing, but she looked increasingly unhappy.

Emily knew why: she liked Tassie also. There was something in her that was immediately appealing, frankness, humor and generosity. But she had seen her coming up the stairs with blood bright on her sleeves and staining her dress. She shivered. Please God, it mustn't be Tassie.

"It doesn't have to be her," Charlotte said quietly. "I suppose there could be some other explanation. An animal? An accident in the street? We don't know anything. I just find it too hard to believe Tassie is . . . Anyway, if the family knew they'd lock her up in an asylum, for her own sake."

"Perhaps they didn't know how bad she was," Emily said quietly. "Maybe she has suddenly got worse."

"But there is still Jack Radley," Charlotte argued. "You can't forget him. Or Sybilla. And William has to be an obvious choice. It could even be Eustace. I don't know why, but maybe George found out something about him. After all, this is his house. Perhaps he's doing something very wrong, or has a secret in his past that he couldn't afford to have known."

Emily looked up. "Such as what?"

"I don't know. Maybe an illegitimate child—or a love affair with someone wildly inappropriate."

Emily's fair eyebrows shot up. "Eustace? A love affair? That taxes the imagination! Can you visualize Eustace in love?"

"No," Charlotte admitted. "But I wasn't thinking of love so much as lust. The most unlikely people can feel that, even pompous and unctuous middle-aged men like Eustace. And anyway, it doesn't have to be recent. It could have been something that happened years ago, even when Tassie's mother was alive. And there are other, even

134

worse possibilities. People have the strangest obsessions, you know. Maybe she found that out.''

"You mean something truly disgusting?" Emily said slowly. "Like a child? Or another man? Do you suppose Olivia could have found out, and he killed her?''

"Oh . . ." Charlotte let out her breath with a sigh. "Actually I hadn't thought of anything quite like that. Rather, a servant, or a farm girl. I heard of a highly respectable man who only liked big, dirty scrubwomen.''

"That's rubbish!" Emily scoffed, taking another slice of thin toast and biting into it without any enjoyment.

"No, it isn't, and one wouldn't want it known.''

"No one would believe it, would they? Not to the point where it was worth murdering to keep them quiet.''

"Maybe. And certainly, if he killed Olivia it would be.''

"But unless he did kill Olivia—and I don't believe that—George wouldn't have told anyone. He wouldn't want it known any more than Eustace would. After all, Eustace is family.'' She swallowed the toast like a lump in her throat. "And George was rather conventional about things like that.''

"That's true,'' Charlotte said more gently. "But perhaps he didn't trust George not to tell his friends, as a joke. George did not always think before he spoke. Or he might even have brought pressure on him to stop.''

"He wouldn't!''

"Maybe not, but perhaps Eustace could not be sure enough of it.'' She shook her head. "But all I'm saying is that we don't know. There could be all kinds of things.''

Emily sat still. "Well, we'd better find at least one piece of evidence about some of them for Constable Stripe—and soon.''

"I know.'' Charlotte bit her lip. "I'm trying.''

The service was to be held in the local church, which had also been the last resting place of the Ashworths since the family had acquired its first town house in the parish, nearly two hundred years ago.

Naturally Emily had informed her own household. That had been the most difficult of all the letters to write, and the only one with which Charlotte could not help her. How does one say to a five-year-old son that his father has been murdered? She knew he could not read her letter now; it would be his nanny, large, comfortable Mrs. Stevenson, who would try to explain to him, help him to understand death and allow his mind to grasp it slowly through the confusion of great and terrible emotions round him. Emily knew, too, that the gentle woman would try to comfort him, so he did not feel betrayed because his father had left him so soon, nor guilty that in some indefinable way it was his fault.

Emily's letter would be for later on, when he was older, something he would keep and reread in quieter moments. He would find by the time he was a young man that he knew it by heart. So she had written it only once, letting her own loss and wholehearted grief come through. Inelegance of style would matter little; insincerity would clang like a false note with louder and harsher echoes through the years.

Today, of course, Edward would be there, small, cold and frightened but performing the rites expected of him. He was now Lord Ashworth: he must sit in the church, upright and well-behaved, and follow his father's coffin to its grave, and mourn as was seemly.

Edward would come from home with Mrs. Stevenson and afterwards return with her. Charlotte and Emily would return to Cardington Crescent; the peculiar circumstances of murder made that necessary. They rode with Aunt Vespasia and Eustace in the family carriage, for this occasion draped in black and pulled by black horses. The hearse, of course, was provided by the undertaker and was draped and plumed as always.

Mrs. March and Tassie came next in the second-best barouche. Both Charlotte and Emily stared at Tassie, but she wore a veil, and beneath it her expression was invisible. It could have been one of sorrow and awe as everyone presumed, or it could equally easily have been remnants of the strange happiness Charlotte had seen in her on the stairs—or complete forgetfulness of it and whatever ghastly episode had preceded it. One could not even guess.

There was some argument as to where Jack Radley should ride; in the end, with great unease, Mrs. March took him with her, and William and Sybilla went in their own vehicle.

They alighted at the lych-gate one by one, and walked up the narrow earth and gravel path towards the old smoke-darkened, stone-towered church. The gravestones on either side were worn and green-rimed with age, inscriptions long since softened into blurred edges till one had to peer to distinguish them. Far towards the yew hedges and the long grass there were white ones, like new teeth. Here and there a bunch of flowers, laid by someone who still cared.

Charlotte took Emily's arm and walked close to her. She could feel her shaking and she seemed thinner, smaller than she had thought. She could not forget for a moment that she was the elder sister. This was oddly like Sarah's funeral*—only the two of them left—but Emily was far less vulnerable then. Then there had been boundless optimism under the sorrow, a sureness of herself that lay like a wide certainty underneath the surface grief and fear and was strong enough to outlast it.

This was different. Emily had not only lost George, the first man she had loved and committed herself to, but she had lost the confidence in her own judgment. Even her courage was a barer thing; not instinctive, but fought for—a broken-nailed, desperate clinging.

Charlotte's fingers tightened and Emily reached for her hand. Mr. Beamish, the vicar, was waiting at the door, a thin, fixed smile on his face. His cheeks were red and his white hair fluffed, as if he had run his hands through it

*The Cater Street Hangman.

137

nervously. Now, as he recognized Emily, he stepped forward, extended his arm, and then hesitated and dropped it again. He murmured something indistinguishable that fell away in a downward cadence. To Charlotte it sounded like a bad psalm. Behind him his maiden sister shook her head fractionally and gave a little sniff. She touched her handkerchief delicately to her cheek.

They were embarrassed. Rumor, supposition, had reached them. They did not know whether to treat Emily as a bereaved aristocrat to whom it was their social and religious duty to extend every pity, or a murderess, a scarlet woman, a creature they should shun, as a good Christian example, and before they themselves were contaminated by her double sin.

Charlotte returned their stare without smiling. Part of her knew a moment's empathy for their predicament, but a much larger part despised them; she was aware it showed in her expression. Her feelings always did.

Inside the church Mrs. Stevenson, somber and gentle, was holding Edward by the hand. His face was pale and looked so like Emily's it was painful. He let go of Mrs. Stevenson's hand and came to her, awkwardly at first, conscious of a new gravity; then as she put her arms round him he relaxed and sniffed fiercely, before straightening up again and walking beside her.

Mungo Hare was standing in the aisle beside the March family pew at the front. He was a large man with a fair, open face and blunt features. He held his head up and his eyes looked at Emily squarely.

"Are you all right, Lady Ashworth?" he said quietly. "I've put a glass of water on the ledge there, if you need it. It'll not be a long service."

"Thank you, Mr. Hare," Emily said absently. "That is most thoughtful of you." She slid into the pew with Edward, leaving Charlotte to follow her, then Aunt Vespasia and Eustace. She could hear Mrs. March clattering irritably in the pew behind and banging the hymnbook.

She resented not being at the front, and she intended to make her displeasure known.

Tassie sat beside her, head down, hands folded in her lap. It was incredible to think of her as she had been last night; calm, blood-smeared, tiptoeing along the landing. The curate passed beside her and spoke to the old lady.

"Good morning, Mistress March. If I can be of any service to you, or offer you any comfort—"

"I doubt it, young man," she said tersely, "except to keep my granddaughter sufficiently occupied in good works that she doesn't run off and marry unsuitably, and end up getting murdered for her money!"

"That would be rather pointless," Tassie murmured. "You wouldn't leave me any if I did that."

"If anyone murdered you it would be for your tongue!" the old lady snapped at her. "Kindly remember you are in church, and don't be flippant."

"Good morning, Miss March." The curate bowed his head.

"Good morning, Mr. Hare," Tassie said demurely. "Thank you for your concern. I expect Grandmama would be grateful if you called upon her."

"I'd rather have Mr. Beamish," the old lady interrupted. "He's a good deal nearer to death than you are. He understands bereavement, loss, seeing one's own blood caught up in unholy passions, to fall victim to its rages, and pay its price."

The curate gasped, and turned it into a sneeze.

"Indeed?" Vespasia said from the row in front, without turning her head. "If that is so then you know a great deal about Beamish that I do not."

Tassie was making a curious little gurgling noise into her handkerchief, and the curate moved on to speak to William and Sybilla. Charlotte dared not twist around to observe.

The service was somber and intoned in the curious singsong voice of formalized grief. At moments, though, there was something vaguely comforting about it, perhaps

139

no more than an expression of darker emotions that had been suppressed till now. This was an acknowledgment of what was unspeakable in the house; here was death and its physical corruption given name, instead of closed into the mind and forbidden the tongue, but always waiting just beyond, behind the spoken word. Even the organ notes shivered through the ear and held an eternal quality, so that one could hear them long into the next note. They seemed to come from the whole fabric of the church and die away into it again. The stonework and the jewel windows and the pipes were all one with the sound.

Emily stood straight and silent, and under her veil it was impossible to see her face. Charlotte could only guess her feelings. Between them Edward was stiff and upright, but he pressed very close to Emily and his free hand was clenched hard.

The last organ notes faded into the high arches of stone, and they turned slowly to face the worst. Six men in black, all expression wiped from their faces, lifted the coffin and walked in step, carrying it sedately out into the hard sunlight. Two by two the congregation followed, led by Emily and Edward.

The grave was a neat-edged hole in the damp earth. The Ashworths had never cared for a family crypt or mausoleum, preferring to spend their money on the living, but of course there would be a marble headstone, perhaps carved and gilded in time. Now all that seemed irrelevant, even vulgar.

Beamish, still pink-faced, his thick white hair ruffled by the wind till it looked like a pie frill round his head, was beginning to recite the familiar words. He was happy with these because they gave him no option, no room to have to invent his own, but still he avoided Emily. He glanced once at Aunt Vespasia and tried to smile, but she looked so drained and frail it died on his lips. He continued waveringly, his mind fogged with dawning suspicion.

Charlotte looked round at the faces. One of them here had killed George. Had it been a moment of passion, perhaps now turned to terror or remorse? Or did whoever it was feel justified, perhaps released from some danger? Or was the murderer grasping at a reward?

The most obvious suspect was Jack Radley. Could he have imagined Emily would . . . what? Marry him? Surely that was the only answer. If he were capable of thinking she would accept him at all, then merely to be her lover would hardly merit killing George. If Emily were a widow she would almost certainly be a rich one, and at thirty, with a young child, a very vulnerable one.

Charlotte had also worn a light veil, partly for decorum, but more to give her the opportunity to watch people without their being aware of it. Now she looked across the grass and the turned earth with its open hole at Jack Radley on the far side. He was standing with his hands folded, very sober, his face suitably grave. But his suit was fashionably cut, his tie elegant, and she imagined she could see the shadow of his eyelashes on his cheek as he lowered his gaze. Had he the monumental vanity to think he could kill George and then take his place? Had envy given way to temptation, and then a slow-forming plan, and had at last opportunity turned it into act?

She saw nothing on his face; he could have been a choirboy standing there. But then, if he were guilty of such a plan he was without conscience, and she should not expect to find any reflection of guilt in his face.

Eustace's features were composed in pious rectitude and showed nothing but his sense of the occasion and his own part in it. Whatever else was in him, there was no guilt, and absolutely no fear. If he had committed murder it was without remorse. What could possibly, even to his mind, justify that?

That left the last, and the other most obvious, suspects: William and Sybilla. They stood side by side, and yet in only the barest and most literal sense were they together. William looked straight ahead of him over the grave, past Eustace and the figure of Beamish to the yew trees, perpetual guardians of death, skirting the burial yard from the living city, sheltering darkness in their needle leaves and dense, heavy wood. Nothing grew under them, and their fruit was poison.

Such knowledge could have been passing behind William's silver-gray eyes as he stood listening. There was pain in his mouth, and the flesh of his cheeks was pinched. Charlotte felt pain watching him, as though his fair skin were a layer thinner than other people's, and the wounds of nature reached the nerves beneath more readily. Perhaps that was necessary, to paint the shadows and the sweeping light in the sky as he did. All the skill in the world cannot interpret what has not first been felt.

Had that delicate, creative hand also stolen the digitalis and emptied it into the coffeepot for George to drink—and die? Why? The answer was glaring: because George had wooed Sybilla, and won her.

Automatically Charlotte's gaze moved to Sybilla herself. She was a beautiful woman, and dressed in reliefless black she looked better than anyone else here. The white skin of her neck was perfect, almost luminous as pearl, her jaw slender. Her upper face was masked by her veil, and Charlotte had been watching her for several minutes, trying to read something into it, when she noticed the tears bright on her skin and the faint lines of strain, the tight muscles in her throat. She glanced downwards. The black-gloved hands were clenched and the lace was ripped off the handkerchief. Even as she looked the fingers unknotted, picking at the cambric, tearing fragments of the cotton off and letting them fall, little snowflakes of broken lace. Grief? Or guilt? For having seduced another woman's husband, or for having murdered him when he tired of her?

Suddenly Charlotte felt a cold grip clutch at her, deep in the pit of her stomach. Was Sybilla's guilt the belief that she had driven Emily to murder? How much had George loved her? There was only Emily's word about the reconciliation. What had really happened that evening in her bedroom when George had come in? Was Emily now remembering the truth, or only what her pride and her pain told her to remember?

No! That was nonsense . . . treacherous . . . weak . . . Get rid of the thought! Refuse to have it. But how do you refuse to have a thought? The more you try to reject it the stronger its hold on you, the more it consumes your mind.

"Aunt Vespasia!"

But Vespasia was unaware of her; her mind and heart were absorbed in a bright width of memory, nursery days and youth, old confidences and small pleasures shared, foolish hopes, unfettered dreams—all crumpled now into one hard, cold box, so close she might have stretched out her thin hand and touched it.

Then the coffin was lowered into the ground, and Beamish scattered something on the lid where it lay a little crooked deep in the hole. It looked ill-fitting. What did it matter? George would not care. All of him that was real had gone, gone somewhere bright and warm, leaving the fears of earth behind.

Emily bent and picked up a handful of pebbles and threw them in with a clatter. She started to say something, but her voice failed.

Charlotte took her arm and they turned away, keeping Edward between them.

They rode home in silence. Emily had said good-bye to Edward and left him with Mrs. Stevenson to go back to his own home, his nursery, safe and familiar. In her mind she was already alone.

She had not killed George. Someone else had crept into the pantry and slipped the digitalis into the coffeepot. But why? It was the last act at the end of a long succession of events and emotions. Perhaps many people had contributed, each a word, a small addition; but was it Emily herself who had given the major part?

It would be nice to think that George knew some secret that was worth killing to keep; it would drive out the dark thoughts that intruded more and more. There were three real suspects: William, Sybilla, and Jack Radley. And all of them had the same reason—George's infatuation with Sybilla.

Emily had to be part of it. If she had been warm enough, interesting enough, generous, tactful, gay, witty, then George would never have felt more than a passing attraction to Sybilla. Nothing that mattered, nothing that hurt Emily or William, and nothing that Sybilla would be desperate over losing.

Was she? Had she been so much in love with George? Aunt Vespasia had said Sybilla had had many admirers, and William had never before shown jealousy. She was discreet, and however far it had gone, it was her secret. And even with George there had been nothing that anyone could be sure was more than they saw in the open. She had accepted his admiration, even encouraged it. But had she actually taken him into her bed? The thought hurt deeply; it was a betrayal of all her own most intimate and precious moments, but to try and skirt round it was idiotic. Emily did not know the answer, and there was no reason to imagine that William did.

No, it was far more likely to be a game for Sybilla, a compliment to her vanity, and perhaps a ripple of danger made it more fun.

If William were suddenly jealous, then the one thing he would guard would be his vanity. He had remained complacent all these years. He would not now make a spectacle, a laughingstock of himself by attacking George. There might be sympathy for the cuckolded husband but there was also laughter, a pity profoundly scarred with cruelty, relief that it was someone else. There were ribald jokes, slurs against manhood—and that was the ultimate insult, the unbearable thing that robbed the stuff of life but denied the peace of death. The victim was still sentient and raw to all the awareness of his loss. He would never have brought that upon himself, never—not in hot temper nor in cold revenge.

No. She did not believe William had killed George. It would only bring upon him the very thing every man found intolerable.

Sybilla?

George was charming, fun, generous, but only if she were totally hysterical would she fall so in love with a man she could not marry that a quarrel would turn her into a murderess. She had had other affairs. They must all have ended one way or another. Surely she knew how to conclude it gracefully, how to sense the coming of the break, see the signs, and be the first to cool. She was not eighteen, and far from inexperienced.

Could this affair really have been so radically different? Why should it? Emily could think of no reason.

That left Jack Radley, and the answer to that was the ugly thought she had been trying to avoid all the time. She had encouraged him, and she had enjoyed it. In spite of the misery inside her, the pain over George, she had liked Jack, enjoyed flirting with him, and had felt justified.

Justified! Perhaps—as far as George was concerned. Sauce for the goose was sauce for the gander. But what about Jack himself? To begin with, she had hardly bothered to look at him as a person, but simply as an opportunity. He was extraordinarily charming, with outward warmth and virility. She had heard that he had very little money, but she had been uninterested; it made no difference to her.

But did it? If she had bothered to look more closely would she have seen a man in his mid-thirties, of good birth but with no money and no prospects, other than those he could make for himself with his wits? Might she have seen a weak man, grown accustomed to a very gracious style of living, envious of his financial betters and suddenly tempted by a pretty woman; a woman publicly ignored by her husband, vulnerable because she understood the conventions with her mind but not her heart?

Just how far had she encouraged him? Could she possibly have led him to imagine she would marry him if she were free to? Surely he realized her attention was merely a ruse to win George back. Even less than that—a by-product of her being charming rather than create a scene which could only drive George further away!

Perhaps not. Perhaps Jack Radley was even farther from families like the Ashworths or the Marches than she was—perhaps financial restriction and mounting ambition had eroded all other feelings.

She had judged him the sort of man too vain, too fond of his own pleasures and far too aware of his own interests to fall in love. Physical attraction was a different matter, but not to be taken seriously, never to be allowed to jeopardize the things of lasting importance, like means and status. Even the middle classes understood the necessities. One did not throw away everything on a whim. Certainly a man who had survived to thirty-five on his charm and wit knew a great deal better than to give in to romanticism or appetite.

Or did he? People did fall in love; some of the least likely were vulnerable. Had she really been so utterly delightful that he had thrown all sense to the winds—and in a fit of passion murdered George?

No. It would be a calculated greed. And he had chosen his moment so impetuously because somehow he also had heard the row between George and Sybilla and known that his opportunity was slipping away. Another day and it could be gone.

The carriage was passing in the dappled sunlight through an avenue of birch trees, and the wind in the leaves sounded like the rustle of skirts, black bombazine on the graveyard walk, the clink of jet beads round fat necks. She shivered. It was cold inside; the white silk handkerchief in her hand reminded her of lilies, and death.

Was she at heart responsible? She had not wished it, but neither had she cared. The moral guilt would remain, whatever the police discovered. And the social stigma too.

The fact that she had done no more than be attentive would be forgotten. Society would remember her as the woman whose lover had murdered her husband.

And the money?

She had already received a quick note from the lawyer, a condolence merely, but she knew there was a great deal of money. Some of it was in trust for Edward, but she herself would still have a very considerable amount—enough to keep Jack Radley in very fine style indeed. And of course, she would have the houses.

The thought was frightening; a cold, clammy sickness gripped like a hand at her stomach. If he had murdered George then she must share the responsibility. If he was discovered she would be a social outcast at best—at worst she would be hanged with him.

If he were not discovered the suspicion would remain over her forever. She would spend the rest of her life with other people wondering and whispering about her. And she might be the only other person who would know without the worm of doubt that she was innocent—and he was guilty.

Could he afford to let her live, with the danger she might one day somehow prove it was he? She would have to try, for her own honor. Surely she would one day also have an "accident," or maybe even "commit suicide." The draft through the carriage window brought out goose pimples on her skin.

Luncheon was a chill, formal affair, as a funeral meal should be. Emily bore it with as much dignity as she could, but afterwards she excused herself and went not to her bedroom where Charlotte or Vespasia could find her, but beyond. She wanted time to think without interruption, and she did not want anyone pressing her with questions.

Anywhere in the main house there was the risk of running into one of the others, forcing her either to make some obvious excuse to leave or else to find conversation, knowing what they were thinking of her and going through the charade of forced politeness.

She went up the stairs, and then up the second, narrower flight to what had been the children's floor a generation ago, where their games and their crying would not disturb the rest of the house. She passed their bedrooms—closed off now—the nurserymaid's room, the night nursery—empty except for two sheet-covered cribs and a chest of drawers painted pink and white—and at the very end of the corridor came at last into the big main day nursery.

It was like a world apart, trapped in amber a decade ago when Tassie, the last child, had left it. The curtains were wide, and sunlight caught the walls with gold, showing the faded patches and the rime of dust on the tops of the pictures: little girls in crisp pinafores and a boy in a sailor suit. It must have been William, face softer in childhood, bones not yet formed, mouth hesitant in a half smile. In the sepia tint, without the red of his hair, he looked oddly different. In his young face there was something sharply reminiscent of the picture she had seen of Olivia.

The little girls were different, but all but one had Eustace's round face, round eyebrows, and confident stare. The exception was Tassie, thinner, more candid, more like William, except for her mouth and the bow in her hair.

There was a dappled rocking horse by the window, its bridle broken, saddle worn. A frilled ottoman in patched pink was covered with a row of dolls, all sitting to attention, obviously tidied by the unloving hand of a maid. A box of tin soldiers was closed neatly and piled next to colored bricks, a dollhouse with a front that opened up, two music boxes, and a kaleidoscope.

She sat down on the big nursery chair and caught sight of her own black skirt spread across the pink. She hated black. In the sunlight it looked dusty and old, as if she were wearing something that had died. She would be expected to keep to it for at least a year.

Ridiculous. George would not have wanted it. He liked gay colors, soft colors, especially pale greens. He had always loved her in pale greens, like shaded rivers or young leaves in spring.

Stop it! It was an unnecessary hurt to keep on thinking of George, turning it over and over. It was too soon. Perhaps in a year she would be able to remember only the good things. She would be used to being alone by then, and the rough edges would have worn off the wound. The healing would begin.

The room was warm and full of light, and the chair was very comfortable. She closed her eyes and leaned back, her face to the sun. It was totally silent up here; the rest of the house need not have existed. She could be anywhere, their quarreling and spite, the whispers, the fear and the malice a hundred miles away in another city. There were the smells of dust and old toys, the cotton of dolls' dresses, the wood of the horse, the sharp, bitter smell of lead and tin boxes and toy soldiers. It was all vaguely pleasing, perhaps because it was different, half a memory from a simpler, infinitely safer time of her own life.

She was half asleep when the voice broke in, quite quietly but so startling that she felt as if she had been struck.

"Couldn't you bear us anymore? I don't blame you. No one knows what to say, but they go on saying it anyway. And the old woman is like something out of a Greek play. I came up here to find you because I was afraid you weren't well."

Her eyes flew open and she stared up, squinting in the sun. Jack Radley was standing gracefully, leaning a little against the doorway. He had changed out of his funereal black and was in a pleasant brown. She could think of nothing at all to answer him. The words froze in her brain.

He moved forward and sat on a nursery stool at her feet. The sun made a halo out of the edge of his hair and cast the shadow of his eyelashes on his cheek. It all reminded her of the conservatory, and her conscience wrenched at her again. George had been alive then. . . .

She found an answer at last. "I'm not in the mood for

conversation. I don't feel like forcing myself to be polite anymore, with everyone trying—very clumsily—not to mention murder, while at the same time making it perfectly clear they think it was me.''

''Then I shall avoid the subject,'' he replied without a qualm, looking at her with exactly the same warm candor she had seen in him that night he had kissed her so intimately. It brought back very precisely the taste of his mouth, the smell of his skin, and the thick, soft, texture of his hair under her fingers. Her guilt was overwhelming.

''Don't be ridiculous!'' she snapped with unreasonable fury. Normally she could have exchanged harmless banter indefinitely, but the knack had abandoned her. She did not want to talk to Jack Radley at all, about anything. She could not get out of her mind the thoughts she feared he might have with regard to her, the idea that she could have been so attracted to him that when George was dead she would be prepared to think of marrying anyone else—let alone a man who might have murdered him!

''I'm sorry,'' he said quietly. ''I know it's impossible not to think. I suppose you can't even put it out of thought for half an hour.''

She looked at him reluctantly. He was smiling and looked so agreeable and innocent here amid these childish things she felt bizarre thinking of murder. And yet the knowledge would not be banished. It was true! Someone had murdered George. She had not done it; she found it hard to think it was Sybilla—she had nothing to gain and so much to lose—and impossible to think it was William. She would love to think it was old Mrs. March, but she could rake up no possible reason. And of course there was the abominable picture of Tassie creeping up the stairs in the night, tired and smelling of blood. Could she have killed George in a fit of madness? But even madness has some reason!

Or even at a very wild extreme, Eustace, to hide Tassie's affliction? Perhaps she had done something else dreadful before. Could it be to conceal that? But that did not make sense. If Eustace knew Tassie was mad he would hardly seek to marry her to anyone; he would have her locked away, for all their sakes.

Surely it had to be Jack Radley, sitting here two feet away from her, the sun shining on his hair, his shirt dazzling white. She could smell the clean cotton just as she could smell the dust and the sun's heat on the chair and the tin soldiers.

She avoided his eyes, afraid he would see the fear in her own. If he did see her thoughts and understand them, how would he feel? Hurt, because he cared what she thought of him? Because it was unjust, and he had hoped for better? Angry, because she misjudged him? Or because his plans were failing? How angry? Angry enough to strike out at her?

Or worse, far worse, fearful that she would betray him, become a danger to his safety?

Now she dared not look up. What if he saw all that in her eyes? If he had killed George, then he would now have to kill her too. But he would be caught!

Not if he made it look like suicide. The Marches would be only too glad to accept it and dismiss the whole matter and send the police away, and Thomas would have to go, to accept the obvious. The family would not question it or make an issue—far from it! They would be grateful.

Charlotte would never believe it, of course. But who would take any notice of her? There would be nothing she could do. And even if she could, it would hardly help Emily.

She was sitting in the nursery in the silence and the sun. It was so bright it dazzled her. She felt a little dizzy and the chair was suddenly very hard under her. It seemed to be tilting. This was ridiculous, she must not faint! She was alone here with him, out of hearing of everyone. If he killed her here it could be days before anyone found her— weeks! Not till a maid came again to do a little perfunctory dusting. They would think she had run away—admitting her guilt.

"Emily, are you all right?" His voice sounded anxious. She felt his hand warm on her arm, very strong, tight.

She wanted to pull away violently. A sweat of terror broke out on her skin, wetting the black cloth of her dress and trickling cold down her back. If she tore away from him he would know she was afraid, and he would know why. She would not be able to get up and run away before he could catch her. It was possible she would reach the door behind him, and race along the passage to the steep stairs. It would be so easy to push her, a headlong fall. She could already see her own crumpled body at the foot, hear his voice with the explanation. So simple, so sorry. Another tragic accident—she was beside herself with grief and guilt.

There was only one way: pretend innocence, convince him she had no suspicions, no ideas, no fear of him.

She swallowed hard and gritted her teeth. She forced herself to look up at him, meet his eyes without flinching, speak without biting her tongue or fumbling.

"Yes—yes, thank you. I just felt dizzy for a moment. It's warmer in here than I expected."

"I'll open the window." He stood up as he said it, reaching for the catch, and lifted the heavy sash. That was it! A fall out of the window! They were three stories up; she would hit the hard walk outside once and that would be the end. Who would hear her if she screamed? No one, up here. That was precisely why it was the nursery, so the cries of the children should not disturb anyone. But if she stayed seated he would find her hard to pick up, a dead-weight. It was a little, a very little, but there was nothing she could do but take it a step at a time, searching for the next one.

"Yes. Yes, perhaps that would help," she agreed.

He turned round, facing her, silhouetted against the sun and the blue dazzle of the leaves and the sky through the window. He walked over and leaned forward a little, taking her hand. He was warm, and she felt with a shudder how strong. She could not possibly get out of the chair now. He was standing almost above her, imprisoning her.

"Emily?" He looked at her face—in fact, he was staring. "Emily, are you afraid of them?"

She was so frightened her body ached and the sweat ran down her back and between her breasts.

"Afraid?" She feigned innocence, trying to look as though she were not sure what he meant.

"Don't pretend with me." He was still holding her hand. "Eustace and that fearful old woman are hell-bent on having you blamed for murder. But that's only so they can get the matter hushed up and the police out of the house. Surely Pitt knows that. Isn't he your brother-in-law? And I have the opinion that your sister will not let any accusations against you go by without doing her best to tear them to bits, let the pieces fall where they may."

Did he have any idea what she was thinking? Could he smell her fear? Surely he would know it was immediate and physical, nothing so remote as the Marches' suspicions. It was an obvious, compelling step from that to the knowledge that she thought he had killed George, and why.

"I find it very uncomfortable," she said with a dry little swallow, her face hot. "Of course, it isn't pleasant to have people, even someone like Mrs. March, imagine such a thing of you. But I know it's because she's afraid for her own."

"Her own?" He sounded surprised, but she did not look at him.

"I think it would be better if I did not discuss it," she said quietly. "But there are certain things . . . in the family—"

"Who? Tassie?" There was disbelief in his voice now.

"Really, Mr. Radley, I would very much rather not talk about it. I don't suppose it was anything to do with her, but Mrs. March may be very anxious." She made her move at last, praying he would step back and allow her to stand. She was weak with relief when he did.

"But you think it was Tassie?" he pressed on, but she refused to look at him. Carefully, breath tight in her throat, she moved past him towards the door.

"No—probably because I don't want to. I don't want to think it of anyone, but I cannot avoid it." She was in the night nursery now, and he was close behind her. "There was as good a reason for William to have done it as for me." It was a miserable thing to say, but all she could think of was escaping, reaching the stairs and getting down them to the main landing where there would be people.

"Of course." He was still beside her, very close, ready to catch her if she felt faint again. "If he cared. I never saw any sign that he did. And George was certainly not the first man to be besotted with Sybilla, you know."

"I can imagine, but that doesn't mean he didn't mind!" She was walking rapidly now, too rapidly. The thought of safety only yards away was too sweet; relief welled up inside her, tightening her throat. She must just get down the stairs ahead of him, where he could not push or trip her. She wanted to run, to make sure of it now.

Then with almost unbearable horror she felt his hand close over her elbow. She wanted to wrench away, call out, scream. But there might be no one else, even beyond that flight of steps. Then she would have betrayed her fear and be left alone with him. She froze.

"Emily," he said urgently. "Be careful!"

Was it a threat? At last she looked at him, almost involuntarily. But she had to know.

"Be careful of William," he said earnestly. "If it was William, and he realizes you know, he might hurt you—even if only by trying to incriminate you somehow."

"I will. In fact I shall try not to discuss it, if I can."

He laughed without pleasure. "I mean it, Emily."

"Thank you." She gulped and all but choked. They were at the top of the stairs. She could not stay here; he would know she expected him to push her—and that knowledge would be enough to bring it about. He could not dare let her live, and he would never have a better chance than this. A simple slip of the foot and she would pitch down, breaking her back, or her neck. Her feet were already on the second step. She forced herself, shaking, knees weak— the third, the fourth. He was behind her; it was too narrow to come beside. The seventh step, the eighth—she tried not to hurry. With every second she was nearer. At last she was at the bottom—safe! For now.

She took an enormous breath, scuffed her shoes with the clumsiness of relief, and hurried across the landing towards the main stairs.

8

Pitt attended the funeral, but at such a discreet distance that he was sure none of the family saw him. Afterwards he followed them back to Cardington Crescent and this time entered through the kitchen, taking Stripe with him. They had gone over and over the meager evidence, pursued the few threads of conversations overheard, impressions formed, hoping to surprise an unguarded revelation, but nothing had stayed in his mind sharper than the rest, nothing led him more clearly through the maze.

He left Stripe to question the servants one more time, on the chance that in repetition a fragment would be remembered, that some flash of new recollection would rise to the surface of the mind.

He wanted to see Charlotte. No absorption in this case, the Bloomsbury one, or any other, could drown out the loneliness in the evenings when he returned home, often close to midnight, and found only the night-light burning in the hall, the kitchen empty and tidy, everything put away but for the supper Gracie had carefully prepared and left on the table for him.

Every night he ate silently by the remains of the fire in the stove; then he took his boots off and tiptoed up the stairs, looking in first at the small, motionless forms of Jemima and Daniel in the nursery before going on to his own bed. He was tired enough to sleep within a few minutes, but he woke in the morning aware of an in-

156

completeness, and sometimes he was actually physically cold.

In the mornings Gracie reported to him the events of the previous day that she considered important, but it was a shy, bare account—nothing like Charlotte's, full of opinion, detail, and drama. He used to think her incessant talking through breakfast an intrusion, one of the penalties men invariably pay for marriage. But without it he found himself unable to concentrate on the newspaper and taking little pleasure in it.

Now he inquired of the footman where she was, and was shown into the overcrowded boudoir, close as a hothouse, and requested to wait. It was less than five minutes before Charlotte came in and, pushing the door closed sharply behind her, threw her arms round him and clung to him fiercely. She made no sound, but he could feel that she was weeping, a tired, slow letting go of tears.

Presently he kissed her—her hair, her brow, her cheek—then he passed her his only decent handkerchief, waiting while she blew her nose savagely, twice.

"How are the children?" she asked, swallowing and looking up at him. "Has Daniel cut that tooth yet? I thought he was getting a bit feverish—"

"He's perfectly all right," he assured her. "You've only been gone a couple of days."

But she was not satisfied. "What about the tooth? Are you sure he isn't feverish?"

"Yes, I'm quite sure. Gracie says he's fine, and eating all his meals."

"He won't eat cabbage. She knows that."

"May I have my handkerchief back? It's the only one I've got."

"I'll get you one of—of George's. Why haven't you got any handkerchiefs? Isn't Gracie doing the laundry?"

"Of course she is. I just forgot."

"She should put it in your pocket for you. Are you all right, Thomas?"

"Yes. Thank you."

"I'm glad." But her voice was doubtful. She sniffed, and then changed her mind and blew her nose again. "I suppose you don't know anything about George yet. I don't. The more I watch the less I seem to see."

He put his hand on her shoulder gently, feeling her warm beneath his touch.

"We will," he said with more conviction than he had any grounds for. "It's too soon yet. How is Emily?"

"Feeling ill, and frightened. I—I think she found letting Edward go back with Mrs. Stevenson the hardest thing. He's so awfully young—he doesn't understand. But he will, soon. He'll—"

"Let's solve today's problems first," he interrupted. "We'll help with Edward after—"

"Yes, of course." She swallowed again and unconsciously rubbed her hands over her skirt. "We must know more about the Marches. It was one of them, or . . . or Jack Radley."

"Why do you hesitate before you mention him?"

She looked down, avoiding his eyes. "I suppose—" She stopped.

"Are you afraid Emily encouraged him?" he asked, hating to say it. But if he did not it would still hang between them; they knew each other too well to lie, even by silence.

"No!" But she knew he did not believe her. It was the answer of loyalty, not conviction. "I don't know," she added, trying to find something closer to the truth. "I don't think she meant to." She took a deep breath. "How are you getting on with the Bloomsbury case? You must be busy with that as well."

"I'm not." He felt a heaviness as he said it. He had no hope of solving that, and no solution would show anything more than a common tragedy he was incapable of preventing again. It was only the grotesqueness of the corpse that marked it in the public mind.

She was looking at him; puzzlement gave way to understanding. "Isn't there anything? Can't you even find out who she was?"

"Not yet. But we're still trying. She could have come from anywhere in a dozen directions. If she was a parlormaid dismissed for immoral conduct, or even because the master of the house made advances to her and the mistress found out, then she could have taken to the streets to earn a living, and been killed by a customer, a pimp, a thief—anyone."

"Poor woman," Charlotte said softly. "Then it's hopeless."

"Probably. But we'll keep on a little longer."

She stared at him fiercely. "But this isn't hopeless here! Whoever killed George is one of us in this house right now. It's Jack Radley, or one of the Marches." She frowned, fighting with herself for a moment and then coming to some decision. "Thomas, I have something very—very ugly to tell you." And without stopping to watch his face or allow interruption, she recounted exactly what she had seen at the head of the stairs in the middle of the night.

He was confused. Had she been dreaming? She had certainly had enough cause for nightmare in the last few days. Even if she had been awake and really gone to the landing, might not the abrupt arousal from sleep, the flickering of the dim gas night-light, have misled her vision, caused her to imagine blood where there were only shadows?

Now she was staring at him, waiting, looking in his face for an answering horror.

He tried to mask doubt with amazement. "Nobody's been stabbed," he said aloud.

"I know that!" Now she was angry, because she was frightened, and she knew he disbelieved her. "But why does anyone creep up the stairs in the small hours reeking of blood? If it was innocent, why has nothing been said? She was perfectly normal this morning. And she wasn't distressed, Thomas! I swear she was happy!"

"Say nothing," he warned. "We won't learn anything by attacking openly. If you are right, then there is something very evil indeed in this house—in this family. For God's sake, Charlotte, be careful." He took her by the shoulders. "Perhaps Emily'd better go home, and you go with her."

"No!" She resisted him, pulling away, her head coming up. "If we don't find out who it is, and prove it, Emily could be hanged, or at best have the doubt stain her all her life, have people remember and whisper to each other that she might have killed her husband. And even if that were bearable for Emily, it's not for Edward!"

"I'll find out without you," he began grimly, but her face was tight and her eyes hot.

"Maybe. But I can watch and listen in a way you never can, not in this house. Emily is my sister, and I'm going to stay. It would be wrong to run away, and you wouldn't argue with me about that. And you wouldn't run."

He weighed it for a moment. What would happen if he tried to order her home? She would not go; her loyalty to Emily at this moment was greater, rightly so. All his emotion strained backwards, wanting, demanding that she run from the danger; his reason knew it was cowardice, fear for his own pain should anything happen to her. But if he failed to solve this crime, if Emily were hanged, then he would have lost all in his relationship with Charlotte that gave it fire and value.

"All right," he said at last. "But for the love of heaven, be careful! Someone in this house is murderous—maybe more than one!"

"I know," she said very quietly. "I know, Thomas."

Later in the afternoon, Eustace sent for Pitt to come to him in the morning room. He was standing, hands in his pockets, in front of the unlit fireplace, still in the clothes he had worn at the funeral.

"Well, Mr. Pitt?" he began as soon as the door was

closed. "How are you proceeding? Have you learned anything of value?"

Pitt was unprepared to commit himself, least of all to say anything about Charlotte's story of Tassie on the stairs.

"A great deal," he replied levelly. "But I am not yet sure as to its value."

"No arrest?" Eustace persisted, his face brightening and his broad shoulders relaxing, making the well-cut jacket sit more evenly without the tensions in the weave. "You don't surprise me. Domestic tragedy. Told you so in the first place. I daresay a nursing home can be found. There will be no shortage of means, and she can be made very comfortable. Best for all of us. Nothing proved. Not possible. No blame attached to you, my dear fellow. Invidious position for you."

So he was already preparing to have the case closed and all investigation effectively prevented. It would be so easy for the Marches to protect themselves by blaming Emily. They had barely waited till the body was in the ground before beginning, with a small lie here or there, a very discreet conspiracy, for the sake of them all. They might even convince themselves—all but one—that it really had been Emily who murdered George, in a fit of jealousy. And that one would be the keenest of all, whether they betrayed it or not, to have Emily disposed of quietly and the guilt forever apportioned, the case closed.

Worse than that was the wisp of suspicion nagging at the back of his mind that it was not impossible that it had been Emily. He would not say so to Charlotte, and he felt a sting of guilt for the thought. But no one else had mentioned the supposed reconciliation, and without that she had one of the oldest and best motives in the human condition: that of the woman ridiculed and then betrayed. She had been witness to so much of the aftermath of murder, through Charlotte and himself, perhaps the idea was closer in the shadows of her thought than they knew.

"Most unfortunate," Eustace repeated with increasing satisfaction. "No doubt you did all you could."

The unctuousness of it, the assumption of his blindness, his willingness to comply, was insulting.

"I have barely begun," Pitt said harshly. "I shall discover a great deal more; in fact I shall not rest until I have proof as to who murdered George."

"For heaven's sake, why?" Eustace protested, eyes wide at such nonsensical behavior. "You can only cause needless pain, to your own wife not least. Have a little compassion, man, a little sensitivity!"

"I don't know that it was Emily!" Pitt glared at him, feeling angry and helpless and wishing he could beat that appalling certainty out of Eustace. He was standing there squarely in front of the dead fireplace, with all his comfortable possessions round him, disposing of Emily's life as if she were a household pet that had become troublesome. "There's no proof!" he said loudly.

"Then you can't expect to find it, can you?" Eustace was eminently reasonable, his eyes wide. "Don't blame yourself. I daresay you are perfectly efficient, but you cannot work miracles. Let us deal with it without scandal— for Emily's sake, and for the child's."

"His name is Edward!" Pitt was furious and he could feel himself losing the control which was the core of any intelligent pursuit of truth, but he scrambled after it in vain, his voice rising. "Why do you believe it was Emily? Have you some evidence you've not given me?"

"My dear chap!" Eustace rocked back and forth gently, hands still in his pockets. "George was having an affair with Sybilla! Emily knew it, and could not control her jealousy. Surely you realize that?"

"That is an excellent motive." Pitt lowered his voice with an effort. "For Emily, and for Mr. William March. I can see no difference, unless you believe Emily's story that she and George were reconciled, in which case the motive is stronger for Mr. March!"

Eustace smiled broadly, his composure quite undisturbed. "Not at all, my dear fellow. First of all, I for one do not believe the story of a reconciliation. Wishful thinking, or very natural fear. But even so, the position for Emily is quite different from that for William. Emily wanted George—indeed, needed him.'' He nodded once or twice. ''If a husband has affairs a woman has no choice but to accept it as best she may. A wise woman will pretend not to know—that way she does not have to do anything at all. Her home and her family are not jeopardized by a little foolishness. Without her husband she has nothing. Where would she go, what would she do?'' He shrugged. ''She would be outcast from Society and without a penny to bless herself, let alone to feed and clothe herself and her children.

''On the other hand, for a man it is quite different. I may as well tell you, Sybilla has behaved indiscreetly on other occasions, and poor William resolved not to put up with it any longer. Added to which, she had given him no family, which, although I daresay it is an affliction the poor woman cannot help, it is an affliction nonetheless. He wished to divorce her and take a more suitable wife, who would fulfill a wife's role for him and be the fount of family joy. He was very pleased Sybilla had at last provided the justification he needed so as not to seem in anyone's eyes to be unjust, or to cast her aside because she is barren.''

Pitt was staggered. It was something he had not even imagined. ''William was going to divorce Sybilla?'' he repeated stupidly. ''No one said so.''

''Ah, no.'' Eustace's smile grew even more confidential and he leaned forward a little, taking his hands out of his pockets and placing one on the back of the chair to maintain his balance. ''I daresay that was the quarrel Emily thought she overheard. Now that Sybilla is going to have a child at last, that naturally changes things. For the child's sake, William has forgiven her and will take her back. And of course she is very grateful and repentant. I imagine her behavior in future will be all that can be desired.'' His face shone with eminent satisfaction.

Pitt was speechless. He had no idea whether it was true,

but he knew from his slight knowledge of the divorce laws that what Eustace said was correct: a man might divorce his wife and put her out on the street for adultery, but a woman could do nothing whatsoever by law. Adultery was beside the point, as long as it was he who committed it, and not she.

"I see you understand," Eustace was saying, the words passing over Pitt's head like the rattle of water. "Very wise. Least said the better. Treated you to a confidence. Know you won't repeat it. Trust your discretion. Matters like that are between a man and his wife." He spread his hands wide, palms up in a confidential gesture from one man of reason to another. "Just told you so you would understand. Poor William has had a lot to put up with, but he should be at the beginning of happiness now. Tragedy poor Emily couldn't have kept her head—another few days and all would have been well. Tragedy." He sniffed. "But you can rest assured we shall look after her; she'll have the best of care."

"I'm not leaving," Pitt said, feeling foolish. He must look ridiculous in this sedate room, with its collection of family relics, and Eustace himself as solid as the hide chairs. Pitt had a tumble of hair, his tie was crooked and his coat hung askew, and he had two of George's handkerchiefs in his pocket. Eustace's boots were polished by the bootboy every day; Pitt's were patched on the soles and cleaned by Gracie, when she remembered and had the time. "I'm not finished," he said again.

"As you wish." Eustace was disappointed, but not concerned. "Carry out whatever you think is necessary. Make it look fitting, by all means. Don't want to lose you your job. I'm sure the kitchen will give you dinner, if you like. And your fellow, Stripe, of course."

Stripe was delighted to have dinner in the kitchen, not because he had any hope at all that he would learn something of value to the case, but because Lettie Taylor was also there, neat and pretty as a cottage garden, and in

Stripe's opinion, every bit as pleasing. He kept his eyes deliberately on his plate, longing to look at her but furiously self-conscious. He was not accustomed to eating in such formal, even hierarchical, company. The butler sat at the head of the table like the father of a large family, and the housekeeper at the foot, as a mother would. The butler presided as if it were a function of great importance, and strict ritual was observed. The junior footmen and youngest maids did not speak at all unless they were spoken to. The lady's maids, resident and visiting, seemed to be a class apart, both by the house servants' reckoning and by their own. The senior footmen, kitchen maid, and parlormaid sat in the middle and volunteered a good deal of the conversation.

Table manners were quite as refined as those in the front dining room, and the discussion surely as stilted, but there was rather more of a domestic atmosphere. The food was complimented dish by dish as it was served, eaten, and cleared. The younger members' manners were corrected gently but with a parental familiarity. There were giggles, blushes, sulks, just as Stripe could remember at his own home when he was growing up. Only the standards were strange and strict: elbows at sides, all green vegetables to be eaten or there was no pudding, no peas on the knife; speaking with the mouth full was reproved instantly, uninvited opinions quashed. For him to have mentioned death would have been gross bad taste, and murder unthinkable.

Involuntarily Stripe stole a look at Lettie, prim in white lace over her black, and found she was also looking at him. Even in the gaslight her eyes were just as blue. He looked away again quickly, and was too self-conscious to eat, afraid he would push peas off his plate onto the sparkling cloth.

"Is your meal not to your taste, Mr.—er, Stripe?" the housekeeper asked coolly.

"Oh, excellent, ma'am, thank you," he answered. Then as they were still looking at him he felt something more was required, and went on. "I—I suppose my thoughts was a little taken up."

"Well, I hope you in't going to discuss them 'ere!" The cook blew down her nose in distaste. "Really! We've already 'ad Rosie in 'ysterics, and Marigold given notice and gone 'eavens knows where. I don't know what things are coming to, I swear I don't!"

"We've never had police in a house where I've been before," Sybilla's maid said stiffly. "Never. It's only my loyalty that keeps me in this house a moment longer."

"Neither have we!" Lettie answered her, so quickly the words tripped off her tongue before she had time to consider them. "But what do you want? That we should be left to be murdered in our beds with no one to protect us? I'm very *glad* they're here."

"Ha! I daresay *you* are." the housekeeper said tartly.

Lettie blushed a deep pink. "I'm sure I don't know what you mean." She looked down at her plate, and beside her one of the upstairs maids giggled, stifling it in her napkin when the butler glared at her.

Stripe felt an undeniable compulsion to defend her. How dare anyone slight her and cause her embarrassment!

"Very dignified of you, miss," he said, looking straight at her. "Understandin' adversity and takin' it calm, like. Good sense is about the best cure for times like these. Lot of 'arm avoided if there was more who showed it."

"Thank you, Mr. Stripe," Lettie said demurely. But the pinkness crept further up her cheeks, and he dared to hope it was pleasure.

The rest of the meal passed in conversation about trivialities, but when Stripe could no longer think of anything else to ask, Pitt having exhausted his duties in the front of the house, it was time to leave. He went with regret, replaced by a ridiculous elation as Lettie came down into the kitchen on some slight pretext, caught his eye and bade him good night, and then, swishing her skirt with an elegant little step, vanished up the stairs and into the hallway.

Stripe opened his mouth to reply, but it was too late. He turned and saw Pitt smiling, and knew his admiration—he would still call it that—was too plain in his face.

"Very nice," Pitt said approvingly. "And sensible."

"Er, yes, sir."

Pitt's smile widened. "But suspicious, Stripe, very suspicious. I think you had better question her a lot more—see what she knows."

"Oh no, sir! She's as— Oh." He caught Pitt's eye. "Yes, sir, I'll do that, sir. Tomorrow morning, first thing, sir."

"Good. And good luck, Stripe."

But Stripe was too full of emotion to speak.

Upstairs in the dining room, dinner was worse than even Charlotte could have imagined. Everyone was there, including Emily, looking ashen with misery. All the women wore either black or gray, except Aunt Vespasia who always refused to. She wore lavender. The first course was served in near silence. By the time they had let their soup grow cold and pushed whitefish in a sauce like glue from one side of the plate to the other, the oppression was becoming unbearable.

"Impertinent little man!" Mrs. March burst out suddenly.

Everyone froze, horrified, wondering wildly whom she was addressing.

"I beg your pardon?" Jack Radley looked up, eyebrows raised.

"The policeman—Spot, or whatever his name is," Mrs. March went on. "Asking the servants all sorts of questions about matters that are none of his business."

"Stripe," Charlotte said very quietly. It hardly mattered, but she was glad of an excuse to retaliate.

Mrs. March glared at her. "I beg your pardon?"

"Stripe," Charlotte repeated. "The policeman's name is Stripe, not Spot."

"Stripe, Spot, it's all the same. I'd have thought you'd have more important things to remember than a policeman's name." Mrs. March stared at her, her face cold, eyes like bluish-green marbles. "What are you going to do with your sister? You can't expect us to bear the burden of responsibility. God knows what she will do next!"

"That was uncalled for," Jack Radley said furiously. There was instant and icy silence, but he was unabashed. "Emily has enough grief without our indulging in vicious and uninformed speculation."

Mrs. March sniffed and cleared her throat. "Your speculation may be uninformed, Mr. Radley—although I doubt it. Mine is most certainly not. You may know Emily a great deal more intimately than I do, but you have not known her as long."

"For heaven's sake, Lavinia!" Vespasia said hoarsely. "Have you forgotten every vestige of good manners? Emily has buried her husband today, and we have guests at the table."

Two spots of scarlet stained Mrs. March's white cheeks. "I will not be criticized in my own house!" she said furiously, her voice rising to a shriek.

"Since you hardly ever leave it anymore, it would seem to be the only place available," Aunt Vespasia snapped back at her.

"I might have expected that from you!" Mrs. March swung round to glare at Vespasia and knocked over a glass of water. It rolled across the cloth and dripped water noisily down into Jack Radley's lap, soaking him to the skin, but he was too paralyzed with horror at the scene to move.

"You are perfectly accustomed to having the most vulgar people tramping through your house," Mrs. March went on, "probing and prying, and talking of obscenities and God knows what among the criminal classes."

Sybilla gasped and tore her handkerchief. Jack Radley looked at Vespasia in fascination.

"That's nonsense!" Tassie flew to her favorite grandmother's defense. "Nobody's vulgar in front of Grandmama—she wouldn't let them be! And Constable Stripe is only doing his duty."

"And if somebody hadn't murdered George, he wouldn't have any duty to do in Cardington Crescent," Eustace pointed out exasperatedly. "And don't be impertinent to your grandmother, Anastasia, or I shall require you to finish your dinner upstairs in your room.''

Temper flashed in Tassie's face, but she said nothing more. Her father had dismissed her in the past, and she knew he would do it quite easily now.

"George's death is not Aunt Vespasia's fault," Charlotte said for her. "Unless you are suggesting she killed him?"

"Hardly." Mrs. March sniffed again, a sound full of irritation and contempt. "Vespasia may be eccentric, even a little senile, but she is still one of us. She would never do such a fearful thing. And she is not your aunt."

"You've tipped your water all over our guests," Vespasia said curtly. "Poor Mr. Radley is soaked. Do look what you are doing, Lavinia."

It was so trivial and idiotic it effectively silenced Mrs. March, and there were several moments of peace while the next course was served.

Eustace drew in his breath; his chest swelled. "We have a most distasteful time ahead of us," he said looking round at each of them in turn. "Whatever our individual weaknesses, we none of us desire a *scandal*." He let the word hang in the air. Vespasia closed her eyes and sighed gently. Sybilla still sat totally mute, disregarding everyone, self-absorbed. William looked at Emily, and there was a flash of profound, almost wounding pity in his face.

"I don't see how we can avoid it, Papa," Tassie said into the silence. "If it really was murder. Personally I think it was probably some sort of accident, in spite of what Mr. Pitt says. Why on earth would anyone want to kill George?"

"You are very young, child," Mrs. March said with a curl of her lips. "And very ignorant. There are a multitude of things you do not know, and probably never will, unless you fill out a little and manage to hide all those freckles. To the rest of us it is perfectly obvious, if excessively distasteful." Again she let her fish-blue eyes rest on Emily.

Tassie opened her mouth to retaliate but closed it again.

Charlotte felt a sudden surge of anger for her. Above all things being patronized galled her soul.

"Neither do I," she said bluntly, "know of any reason why someone should have killed George."

"You would say that, wouldn't you." Mrs. March stared at her malevolently. "I always said George married badly."

Fire rushed up Charlotte's cheeks and the blood pounded in her temples. The hard, accusing look in the old woman's eyes was too plain to misunderstand. She thought Emily had murdered George and intended to see her punished for it.

She gulped air and then hiccuped loudly. Everyone was looking at her, their faces a pale sea mirrored with eyes, horrified, embarrassed, compassionate, accusing. She hiccuped again.

Next to her William leaned forward, poured her a glass of water, and passed it to her. She took it from him in silence, hiccuping once more, then drank a little and tried holding her breath, her napkin held to her lips.

"At least George's wife was his own choice." Vespasia filled the void with chipped ice. "He was encumbered with *his* family regardless of his wishes, and I think there were times when he found it distinctly a burden."

"You have no notion of loyalty, Mama-in-law!" Eustace said with a slight flaring of his nostrils and a warning note in his voice.

"None at all," she agreed. "I always felt it a spurious value to defend what is wrong merely because you are related to its perpetrators."

"Quite." Eustace avoided Charlotte's eyes and looked at Emily. "If we find that the—offender—is one of this family, we will still do our duty, painful as it may be, and see that they are locked away. But discreetly. We do not wish the innocent to be hurt as well, and there are many to consider. The family must be preserved." He flashed a smile at Sybilla. "Some people," he continued, "ignorant people, can be most unkind. They are apt to tar all of us with the same brush. And now that Sybilla is at last to bear us a child''—his tone was suddenly jubilant, and he gave William a conspiratorial glance—''we trust, the first of many, we must look to the future.''

Emily had a suffocating feeling of being crowded in. She looked at Mrs. March, who looked away, dabbing stupidly at the water she had spilled across the cloth, but it had long since soaked in. Jack Radley gave a half smile, but it died on his lips as he thought better of it.

William had eaten little and now he stopped altogether. His face was as white as the sauce on the fish. Emily already knew him well enough to be aware that he was an acutely private man, and such open discussion of so personal a subject was agonizing to him. She looked away along the table to Sybilla.

But Sybilla was gazing at William, then at Eustace, her face filled with a loathing so intense it was incredible he should be unaware of it.

Tassie picked up her wineglass, and it slipped through her fingers to crash on the table, spilling wine everywhere. Emily had no doubt whatsoever she had done it on purpose. Her eyes were wide, like pits in the bleached skin of her face.

Sybilla was the first to recover. She forced a smile that was painful, worse than the hate before because of the effort behind it. ''Never mind,'' she said huskily. ''It's a white wine—I daresay it will wash quite easily. Would you like some more?''

Tassie opened her mouth soundlessly, and closed it again.

Emily stared at William, and he looked back at her, ashen, and with a complexity of emotions she could not unravel. It could have been anything, most probably pity for her; perhaps he also believed she had murdered her husband in a frenzy of hopeless jealousy, and that was what he pitied her for. Perhaps he even felt he understood. Was it Eustace, with his complacency, his boundless energy, his virility which had ultimately exhausted Olivia, who had shadowed William's marriage for so long? Was he terrified Sybilla would die of excessive childbearing, as his mother had done? Or had he never loved Sybilla deeply anyway? Maybe he even loved someone else. Society was full of empty marriages at all levels; since marriage was the only acceptable state for a woman, one could not afford to be pernickety.

She looked at Eustace, but he was busy again with his food. He had problems to consider: keeping his family from hysteria, preventing scandal in Society, and preserving the reputation of the Marches—especially of William and Sybilla, now that the longed-for heir was to come. Emily was an embarrassment, threatening rapidly, if the old lady were to be believed, to become something far worse. He sliced a piece of meat viciously, squeaking his knife on the plate, and his face remained in deep concentration.

Emily looked across the table at Jack Radley. His eyes were candid and startlingly soft. He had been watching her already, before she looked at him. She realized how often she had seen that expression in him recently. He was attracted to her, very strongly so, and it was deeper than the triviality of a flirtation.

Oh, God! Had he killed George for her? Did he really imagine that she would marry him now?

The room swayed around her and there was a roaring sound in her ears as if she were underwater. The walls disappeared and suddenly she could not breathe. She was far too hot . . . suffocating . . .

"Emily! Emily!" The voice was booming and fuzzy, and yet very close to her. She was sitting on one of the side chairs, half reclining. It was uncomfortable and precarious. She felt as if she might slide off if she were to move. It had been Charlotte's voice. "You are perfectly all right," she said quietly. "You fainted. We expected too much of you. Mr. Radley will carry you upstairs, and I'll help you to bed."

"I will have Digby bring you up a tisanne," Aunt Vespasia added from somewhere above her in an unfocused distance.

"I don't need carrying upstairs!" Emily protested. "It would be ridiculous. And why can't Millicent bring me a tisanne—except that I don't want one."

"Millicent is upset," Vespasia replied. "She weeps at the drop of a hat, and is quite the last thing you need. I've put her to the stillroom till she can take hold of herself. And you will do as you are told and not cause yourself any more distress by fainting again."

"But Aunt Vespasia—" Before her argument was formed Charlotte's borrowed silk was replaced by black barathea, and Jack Radley put his arms round her and lifted her up. "This is quite unnecessary," she said irritably. "I am perfectly able to walk!"

He ignored her, and with Charlotte going ahead opening doors, Emily was carried out of the dining room, through the hallway, and up the stairs to her bedroom. He laid her on the bed, said nothing, but touched her arm gently and left.

"I suppose it's a little late to think of it now," Charlotte said, unbuttoning Emily's dress. "But your excess of charm to win George back was bound to attract others as well. You shouldn't really be surprised."

Emily stared at the pattern on the coverlet. She allowed Charlotte to continue with the buttons. She did not want her to go.

"I'm frightened," she said quietly. "Mrs. March thinks I killed George because he was making love with Sybilla. She as good as said so."

Charlotte did not reply for so long that finally Emily swung round and stared at her. Her face was grave, and her eyes were blurred and sad.

"That's why we have to discover exactly what did happen, painful as it will be—and difficult. I must talk to Thomas privately tomorrow and see what he has learned."

Emily said nothing. She could feel the fear growing enormous inside her, roaring into the chasm of loneliness for George; the fierce, gripping pain was like ice. The danger was closing round her. If she did not learn the truth soon she would not escape it, perhaps not ever.

*   *   *

Charlotte woke in the night, her skin crawling with horror, her body rigid under the sheets and her fists clenched. Something appalling had torn her from the dark cocoon of sleep.

Then it came again—a high, sharp scream, ripping through the silence of the house. She sat up, clutching the bedclothes as though the room were freezing, although it was midsummer. She could hear nothing, nothing at all.

She climbed out of bed slowly, her feet touching the carpet with a chill. She bumped against a chair. She was longer than usual accustoming her sight to the denseness of the curtained room. What would she find out there on the landing? Tassie? Horrific ideas of blood and the gaslight at the head of the stairs shining on knives swarmed into her imagination, and she stopped in the middle of the floor, holding her breath.

At last there was another sound, footsteps somewhere far away, and a door opening and closing. Then more steps and the confused sounds of fumbling, of people awkward with sleep.

She pulled her wrap off the chair and put it round her shoulders, then opened the door quickly. At the end of the small passage the landing itself was aglow with light. Someone had turned up the lamps. By the time she reached the head of the stairs Great-aunt Vespasia was standing beside the jardiniere with the fern in it. She looked old and very thin. Charlotte could not remember ever having seen her with her hair down before. It was like old silver scrollwork, polished too many times till it had been worn away. Now the lamplight shone through it, and it looked vaporous.

"What is it?" Charlotte's voice cracked, her throat too dry to allow the words through. "Who screamed?"

There was another sound of feet, and Tassie appeared from the stairs to the floor above. She stared at them, her face white and frightened.

"I don't know," Vespasia answered them quietly. "I heard two screams. Charlotte, have you been to Emily?"

"No." It was only a whisper. She had not even thought of Emily. She realized now that she had believed the sound came from the opposite direction, and farther away. "I don't think—"

But before she could continue Sybilla's bedroom door swung open and Jack Radley came out wearing nothing but a silk nightshirt.

Charlotte was sickened by a wave of disgust and disappointment, and in an instant the thought flew to her: how could she prevent Emily from knowing about this? She would feel betrayed a second time—however little she cared for him, he had still affected to care for her.

"There's no need to be concerned," he was saying with a slight smile, pushing his hands through his hair. "Sybilla had a nightmare."

"Indeed?" Vespasia's silver eyebrows rose in disbelief.

Charlotte collected herself. "What about?" she said sarcastically, concealing nothing of her contempt.

William opened his own bedroom door and came out onto the landing looking confused and embarrassed. His face was blurred with sleep and he blinked as though dragged from an oblivion he infinitely preferred.

"Is she all right?" he asked, turning to Jack Radley and ignoring the others.

"I think so," Jack replied. "She rang for her maid."

Vespasia walked slowly past without looking at either of them and went into Sybilla's room, pushing the door open wider. Charlotte followed, partly from some vague idea that she might help but also from a compulsion to know. If Sybilla were ever to tell the truth of what had happened it would be now, when she was still too startled to have thought of a lie.

She followed Vespasia inside and was taken aback. All her ideas were thrown into turmoil when she saw Eustace, decorously wrapped in a blue paisley dressing gown, sitting on the end of the bed, talking.

"Now, now, my dear," he said firmly. "Have your maid bring you a hot drink, and perhaps a little laudanum, and you'll sleep perfectly well. You must dismiss these things from your mind, or you will make yourself ill. They are only fancies, quite unreal. You need a good rest. No more nightmares!''

Sybilla was propped up against the pillows, but the bed was in considerable disorder, sheets tangled and blankets crooked, as if she had been thrashing around in them in her sleep. Her mass of hair was loose like a river of black satin, and her face was bloodlessly pale, her eyes wide with shock. She stared back at Eustace speechlessly, as though she barely comprehended his words.

''Perfectly all right,'' he repeated yet again. He turned and looked at Charlotte and Vespasia, half apologetically. ''Women seem to have such vivid dreams, but a tisanne and a dose of laudanum, and in the morning you will have forgotten all about it. Sleep in, my dear,'' he said again to Sybilla. ''Have your breakfast sent up.'' He stood, smiling benignly, but there was a tightness at the corners of his lips and an unusual color marking his cheeks. He looked shaken, and Charlotte could hardly blame him. It had been a terrible shriek in the depth of the night, and Jack Radley's apparent behavior was inexcusable. Perhaps it was wise for Eustace to try to convince her it was fantasy, although her tight face and burning eyes betrayed her utter disbelief.

''Put it from your mind,'' Eustace said carefully. ''Right out.''

Involuntarily Charlotte looked at the doorway. William was standing just inside, his face crumpled in anxiety, staring past his father and Vespasia to Sybilla.

She smiled at him, and there was a softness in her face Charlotte had not seen before. Charlotte knew without question that it was not something sudden, nor was William surprised to see it.

''Are you all right?'' he said quietly. The words were simple, almost banal, but there was a directness in them quite unlike Eustace's assurance. Eustace was speaking for himself; William was asking for her.

Her hands relaxed and she smiled back at him. ''Yes, thank you. I don't think it will happen again.''

"We trust it will not," Vespasia said coldly, looking back towards the landing, where Charlotte could still see Jack Radley.

"It won't!" he said a little more loudly than necessary. Looking past Vespasia into the bedroom, he met Sybilla's eyes. "But if you have any more frights . . . dreams"—he said the word heavily—"just scream again. We'll come, I promise you." And he turned and walked away, gracefully, the tails of his nightshirt round his bare legs, and disappeared into his own room without looking back.

"Good God!" Vespasia said under her breath.

"Well," Eustace began awkwardly, rubbing his hands. "Well. All had a bit of a shock. Ah." He cleared his throat. "Least said, soonest mended. We'll not refer to it again. All go back to bed and try to get a little sleep. Thank you for coming, Mrs. Pitt, most thoughtful of you, but nothing you can do now. If you need a tisanne or a glass of milk, just ring for one of the maids. Thank heaven Mama wasn't disturbed. Poor woman has more than enough to bear—er . . ." He faltered to a stop, looking at no one. "Well. Good night."

Charlotte went to Vespasia and, without giving a thought to the familiarity of it, put her arm round her, feeling with a start how thin and stiff she was under her wrap, how unprotected her bones.

"Come," she said gently. "Sybilla will be fine now, but you should have a hot drink. I'll get you one."

Vespasia did not shrug off the arm; she seemed almost to welcome it. Her own daughter was dead, now George was dead. Tassie was too young and too frightened. But she was used to servants. "I'll ring for Digby," she said automatically. "She'll get me some milk."

"No need." Charlotte walked with her across the landing. "I can heat milk, you know. I do it all the time in my own house—and I'd like to."

Vespasia's mouth lifted in the wraith of a smile. "Thank you, my dear. I should appreciate it. It has been a distressing night, and I feel no comfort in Eustace's rather san-

guine hopes. He is quite out of his depth. I am beginning
to fear that we all are."

In the morning Charlotte got up late and with a splitting
headache. Hot tea brought to her by Lettie did not help.

Lettie drew the curtains and asked if she might lay out
any particular clothes, and if she should draw a bath.

"No, thank you." Charlotte declined primarily because
she did not want to take the time. She must see how
Vespasia was, and Emily, and if she could make the
opportunity, Sybilla. There was a great deal more to last
night's events than a bad dream; there had been a look of
hatred in Sybilla's eyes, a deliberation in her voice more
than the shreds of a nightmare, however vile.

But Lettie remained in the middle of the sunlit carpet,
her hands kneading her skirt under her apron.

"I expect the inspector understands a lot of things we
don't, ma'am," she said quietly.

Charlotte's first thought was that Lettie was frightened.
In the circumstances it was hardly surprising.

"I'm sure he does." She tried to sound reassuring,
although it was the last thing she felt.

But Lettie did not move. "It must be very interesting . . ."
She hesitated. "Being married to a policeman."

"Yes." Charlotte reached for the pitcher of water and
Lettie automatically poured it for her. She began to wash.

"Is it very dangerous?" Lettie went on. "Does he get—
hurt, sometimes?"

"Sometimes it's dangerous. But he hasn't been badly
hurt. Usually it's just hard work." Charlotte reached for
the towel and Lettie handed it to her.

"Do you often wish he did something else, ma'am?"

It was an impertinent question, and for the first time
Charlotte realized Lettie was asking because it was of
some personal urgency to her. She put down the towel and
met Lettie's blue eyes with curiosity.

"I'm sorry, ma'am." Lettie blushed, and looked away.

"No, I don't," Charlotte said honestly. "It was hard to

get used to at first, but now I wouldn't have him do anything else. It is his work, and he is good at it. If you love someone, you don't want to change them from doing what they believe in. It makes no one happy. Why do you ask?''

Lettie's blush deepend. "Oh, no reason, ma'am. Just . . . just silly thoughts." She turned away and began fussing with the dress Charlotte was to wear, tweaking unnecessarily at petticoats and removing imaginary specks of dust.

Charlotte learned from Digby that Emily was still asleep. She had taken laudanum and not woken in the night. Even Sybilla's screams and the comings and goings on the landing had not disturbed her.

She expected Aunt Vespasia to have had breakfast sent up but actually met her at the top of the stairs looking ashen and hollow-eyed, holding on to the bannister, head erect, back stiff.

"Good morning, my dear," she said very quietly.

"Good morning, Aunt Vespasia." Charlotte had been intending to go to Sybilla's room, if necessary to waken her and ask her about last night. Some pretext of concern for her would have been easy enough to find. But Vespasia looked so fragile, she offered her arm, instinctively, something she would not have dreamed of doing a week ago. Vespasia took it with a tiny smile.

"There is no point in speaking to Sybilla," Vespasia said dryly as they went down. "If she had meant to say anything she would have done so last night. There is a great deal about Sybilla that I do not understand."

Charlotte let her uppermost thought find words. "I wish we could prevent Emily from finding out. I could strangle Jack Radley myself, cheerfully. He is so abysmally—cheap!''

"I admit I am disappointed," Vespasia agreed with an unhappy little shake of her head. "I had grown rather to like him. This, as you say, is quite remarkably shabby."

Breakfast was extraordinary for Eustace's absence. Not

only were all the windows still closed and the silver dishes on the sideboard untouched, but he had sent for a tray in his room. Neither was Jack Radley present; probably too ashamed to face them, Charlotte presumed. Nevertheless she was annoyed. She had wished to make him aware of her contempt.

It was after eleven when she went into the morning room to fetch some more notepaper and found Eustace sitting at the desk, silver inkwell open and a pen in his hand, but the sheet in front of him virgin white. He turned round at the sound of her step, and she saw with incredulity that his right eye was swollen and darkened with an immense bruise and there was a graze on the side of his face. She was too amazed to think what to say.

"Ah, oh . . ." He looked awkward. "Good morning, Mrs. Pitt. I—er, I had a slight, accident. Fell."

"Oh dear," she said foolishly. "I hope you are not seriously hurt. Have you sent for the doctor?"

"Not necessary! Perfectly all right." He closed the inkwell and stood up, wincing as his weight came onto his left leg. He let out his breath sharply.

"Are you sure?" she said with more concern than she felt. Her overriding emotion was curiosity. When had this extraordinary accident occurred? To sustain such injuries he must have fallen downstairs, at the very least. "I'm so sorry," she added hastily.

"Very kind of you," he answered, his eyes resting on her with appreciation for a moment. Then, as though recollecting some more pressing thought, he limped over to the door and out into the hall.

And at luncheon a totally new dimension appeared, startling Charlotte and obliging her to think far better of Eustace than she wished. Jack Radley came to the table nursing a painful right hand, and with a split and swollen lip. However, he offered no explanation at all, and no one asked him for any.

Charlotte was forced to conclude that Eustace had seen him early in the morning and thrashed him over the disgraceful affair in Sybilla's room. And, for once, she admired him for it.

Remarkably, Sybilla herself spoke to Jack Radley perfectly civilly, even agreeably, although she looked very tense. Her shoulders were tight, stiff under the thin fabric of her dress, and the very few remarks she made were distracted, her mind obviously elsewhere. Perhaps she had a share of guilt. Had she implied, however obliquely, that he might be welcome?

Charlotte tried to behave as normally as possible, mainly because she did not want Emily to know what had happened—at least, not yet. Time enough for that kind of disillusion when she was home and would not see Jack Radley again.

For now let her believe in accidents.

Emily knew nothing about the extraordinary episode in the night, and the first she observed was early in the afternoon when she came downstairs and sat in the withdrawing room staring at the sunlight on the leaves in the conservatory. She saw William briefly as he came through to his studio. He looked at her with a hollow pain she took for pity but did not speak.

Tassie had gone off on good works again with the curate, visiting the sick or some such thing. Her grandmother said it was unnecessary; in the circumstances she might be excused. But Tassie had insisted. There were certain tasks she would not forgo; apparently she had given an undertaking, and she ignored argument. Eustace had not been present to lend his weight, and for once the old lady lost the contest, retiring to her boudoir to sulk.

Charlotte was with Aunt Vespasia, leaving Emily alone to while away the afternoon. She could not be bothered to occupy herself with any of the usually acceptable feminine tasks—painting, embroidery, music. She had written all the letters that were required of her, and visiting so soon after a family death was out of the question.

Therefore she was doing nothing at all when Eustace

came in, limping noticeably. But it was not until he turned to speak to her that she saw the richly purpling bruise round his eye, now almost closed and looking acutely painful.

"Oh!" She drew in her breath sharply. "Whatever happened to you? Are you all right?" Emily stood up without thinking, as if in some way he might actually need her physical assistance.

He smiled awkwardly. "Ah, I tripped," he said without meeting her eyes. "In the dark. Nothing for you to worry about. I suppose William's in there"—he waved towards the conservatory—"fiddling about with his damn paints again. He can't seem to leave them alone for five minutes. God knows, you'd think with all this distress in the family he'd be some use, wouldn't you? But William always did run away from everything." He swiveled round, winced with pain as his injured leg took his weight, and then moved towards the conservatory doors, leaving Emily with her answer unspoken on her lips.

She sat down again, feeling even more conscious of her loneliness.

It was several minutes before she became aware of voices, fragmented by the distance, the vines and leaves, and the heavy swags of curtain between the doors. But there was no mistaking the anger in them, the sharp cutting edge of old hatred.

"If you'd damn . . . where you should, then you'd have known!" It was Eustace's voice. William's reply was indistinguishable.

". . . thought you'd have been used to it!" Eustace shouted back.

"*Your* thoughts, we all know!" This time William's answer was quite clear, ringing with unutterable disgust.

". . . imagination . . . never needed to . . . your mother!" Eustace's retaliation was disjointed, blurred by the tangle of plants.

". . . mother . . . for God's sake!" William shouted in an explosion of violence.

Emily stood up, unable to bear the intrusion she was unwittingly making into what was obviously a highly intimate matter. She hesitated between leaving by way of the dining room and fleeing to some other part of the house, or having the courage and the effrontery to interrupt the quarrel and end it, at least temporarily. She turned to the conservatory, then back to the dining room, and was startled to see Sybilla in the doorway. For the first time since she had come to Cardington Crescent the look of anguish in Sybilla's face overrode all Emily's old hatred of her and prompted a sympathy she could not have imagined even a day before.

". . . dare you! I won't . . ." William's voice rose again, thick with emotion.

Sybilla almost ran across the floor, catching her skirts on the back of a chair and tearing at them impatiently, and disappeared into the conservatory, knocking against flowers and stepping off the path into the damp loam in her haste. A moment later the voices from beyond the leaves froze and there was utter silence.

Emily took a deep breath, her stomach tight, unclenching her hands deliberately, and walked towards the dining room door. She did not wish to be here when any of them returned. She would pretend complete ignorance; it was the only possible thing.

In the main hallway she met Jack Radley. His lip was swollen and there was a line of dried blood on it, and he carried his right hand awkwardly. He smiled at her, and drew in his breath in pain as the lip cracked.

"I suppose you tripped in the dark as well?" she said icily before she could stop herself, then wished she had simply ignored him.

He licked the lip and put his hand to it tenderly, but there was still that same gentleness in his eyes.

"Is that what he said?" he mumbled. "Not at all. I had a row with Eustace and hit him—and he hit me."

"Obviously," Emily replied without quite the contempt she had intended. "I am surprised you are still here." She moved past him to go up the stairs, but he sidestepped and remained in front of her.

"If you expect me to explain myself, you'll wait in vain. It is none of your business," he said with an edge to his voice. "I don't break confidences, even for you. But I admit I expected you of all people not to jump to conclusions."

She felt a stab of shame. "I'm sorry," she said very quietly. "I've surely wished I could hit Eustace a few times myself. It looks as if you got rather the better of it."

He grinned, regardless of the blood now staining his teeth. "For what it's worth," he agreed. "Emily—"

"Yes?" Then, as he said nothing, she added, "Your face is bleeding. You had better go and wash it. And find some ointment, or it will dry and crack again."

"I know." He put his hand on her arm gently and she could feel the warmth of him through the muslin of her sleeve. "Emily, keep your courage. We will find out who killed George—I promise you."

Suddenly her throat ached abominably and she realized how deeply frightened she was, how close to weeping. Not even Thomas seemed able to help.

"Of course," she said huskily, pulling away. This was ridiculous. She did not wish him to see her weakness—above all, she did not wish him to know how very agreeable she found him, in spite of her distrust. "Thank you. I'm sure you mean well." She went hastily up the stairs, leaving him standing in the hall looking after her, and she turned onto the landing without glancing back.

9

Emily slept badly. It was a night full of enormous and ugly dreams, blood-spattered clothes, the rattle of stones on George's coffin lid, the vicar's pink face with his mouth opening and closing like a fish. And every time she woke the picture of Jack Radley came back to her, sitting on the nursery stool staring at her, the sun in his hair, and in his eyes the understanding that she knew he was guilty and there could be no escape. She woke at once sweating and chill, staring into the black void of the ceiling.

When she fell asleep again the dreams were worse, billowing one into another, swelling and bursting, then shrinking away into nothingness. Always there were faces; Uncle Eustace smug and smiling, staring at her with those round eyes that saw everything and understood nothing, not caring if she had murdered George or if it was someone else, only determined she should be blamed for it, to keep the March name clear. And Tassie, too mad to know anything. Old Mrs. March's eyes like glass marbles, blind with malice, shrieking all the time. William with a paintbrush in his hand, and Jack Radley with the sun round his head like a halo, smiling because Emily had murdered her husband for love of him, over one kiss in the conservatory.

She lurched into wakefulness and lay watching the slow light creep across the ceiling. How long had she before Thomas had no choice but to arrest her? Every second ticking away was eating her life; the remnant was slipping into eternity and she was lying here alone and useless.

What was it that had so horrified Sybilla? That had ripped the usual mask off her face to show such hatred— twice; once at dinner two days ago, and then again in the withdrawing room when she overheard the quarrel in the conservatory?

She could bear it no longer and climbed out of bed. It was already light and she could see quite easily where she was going. She put on a wrap over her nightgown and tiptoed across the room to the door. She would ask her! She would go to Sybilla's room now when she was alone and could not make some polite evasion, or claim a pressing duty, nor would anyone interrupt them.

She opened the door slowly, holding the latch so it would not fall back with a noise. There was no sound outside. She looked up and down the passage. The dawn light came in cool and gray through the windows and fell on the bamboo-patterned wallpaper opposite. A bowl of flowers glowed yellow. There was no one.

She stepped out and walked quickly towards the room she knew was Sybilla's. She had no doubt what she was going to say. She would tell Sybilla that she had seen that look in her face, and wherever her pity lay, whatever loyalties she thought she had, if she did not tell Emily what act in the past had given birth to such a depth of loathing, she would go to Thomas Pitt and let him discover it in her with pryings and questions which would be far harder. From the anger in which she left the room the night before, she was willing to threaten anything. It was too late to care about sensitivity or embarrassment now.

She found her hand was shaking as she lifted it to grasp Sybilla's doorknob and turn it slowly. Perhaps it would be locked, and she would be forced to wait till day. She could put off the inevitable answers for a few hours more. But it turned easily in her hand. Of course. Why would anyone lock doors in a house like this? It would mean having to get out of bed to let the maid in. Who wanted to do that?

Half the point of having a maid was to avoid getting up
and pulling the curtains or drawing the water yourself. If
you were going to get out of a warm bed on demand, fresh
from sleep, the whole luxury was lost.

She was inside now. It was quite light. The curtains
were yellow and the window faced the sun. Sybilla was
already awake, sitting upright against the nearest high,
carved bedpost, facing the window, her black hair in thick
tresses wound at both front and back. The thought passed
through Emily's mind that it was an odd way to wear it.

"Sybilla," she said quietly, "I'm sorry to intrude, but I
couldn't sleep. I need to talk to you. I believe you know
who murdered George, and—" She was at the end of the
bed now and she could see Sybilla more clearly. She was
sitting very awkwardly, her back rigid against the bedpost
and her head a little to one side, as if she had fallen asleep.

Emily came round the far edge of the bed and leaned
forward.

Then she saw Sybilla's face and felt the horror rising
inside her, robbing her of breath, freezing her heart. Sybilla
was staring with blind, bulging eyes out of swollen flesh,
her mouth open, tongue out; the black hair was knotted
tight round her throat and swept back round the bedpost
and tied again.

Emily opened her mouth to scream, but no sound came
at all, only a violent dry ache in her throat. She found she
had her hands to her lips, and there was blood on her
knuckles where she had bitten them. She must not faint!
She must get help! Quickly! And she must get out of
here—she must not be alone.

At first she was shaking so much her legs would not
obey her. She knocked into the corner of the bed and
bruised herself, felt for the chair to regain her balance and
nearly upset it. There was no time to be sick—someone
else might come and find her here. They blamed her
already for George's death—they would be sure to blame
her for this too.

The doorknob was stiff now; twice she turned it and her

sweaty fingers let it slip back before she pulled the door open and almost fell out into the corridor. Thank God there was no one else there, no housemaid hurrying down to clean grates or prepare the dining room. Almost running, she made her way to the dressing room where Charlotte was, and without knocking, fumbled for the handle and threw it open.

"Charlotte! Charlotte! Wake up. Wake up and listen to me—Sybilla is dead!" She could dimly make out the form of Charlotte, her hair a dark cloud on the white pillow.

"Charlotte!" She could hear her voice rising hysterically and could not help it. *"Charlotte!"*

Charlotte sat up, and her whisper came out of the cool grayness. "What is it, Emily? Are you ill?"

"No . . . no . . ." She gulped painfully. "Sybilla is dead! I think she's been murdered. I just found her . . . in her bedroom . . . strangled with her own hair!"

Charlotte glanced at the clock on the bedside table. "Emily, it's twenty past five. Are you sure you didn't have a nightmare?"

"Yes! Oh, God! They're going to blame me for this too!" And in spite of all the strength of will she thought she had, she began to weep, crumpling slowly into a little heap on the end of the bed.

Charlotte climbed out and came to her, putting her arms round her and holding her, rocking her like a child. "What happened?" she said quietly, trying to keep her voice calm. "What were you doing in Sybilla's room at this time in the morning?"

Emily understood Charlotte's urgency; she dared not indulge in misery and fear. Only thought, rational and disciplined, could help. She tried to iron out the violence in her mind and grasp the elements that mattered.

"I saw her face at dinner the night before last. For a moment, there was such a look of hatred on it as she turned to Eustace. I wanted to know why. What did she know about him, or did she fear he was going to do something? Charlotte, they are convinced I murdered

George, and they are going to make sure Thomas has no choice but to arrest me. I have to find out who did—to save myself.''

For a moment Charlotte was silent; then she stood up slowly. ''I'd better go and see, and if you're right I'll waken Aunt Vespasia. We'll have to call the police again.'' She pulled on a shawl and hugged it round herself. ''Poor William,'' she said almost under her breath.

When she had gone Emily sat curled up on the end of the bed and waited. She wanted to think, to see the pattern falling clearly, but it was too soon. She was shivering— not with cold, because the air was warm; the chill was inside, just as the darkness was. Whoever had murdered George had now murdered Sybilla, almost certainly because Sybilla knew who he—or she—was.

Was it something to do with Eustace and Tassie? Or Eustace alone? Or was it Jack Radley after all?

The door opened and Charlotte came back, her face tight and pale in the softening dawn light coming through the windows. Her hands were shaking.

''She's dead,'' she said with a gulp. ''Stay here and lock the door behind me. I'm going to tell Aunt Vespasia.''

''Wait!'' Emily stood up, and lost her balance; her legs were weak as if her knees would not lock. ''I'm coming. I'd rather come with you—anyway, you shouldn't go alone.'' She tried again, and this time her body obeyed her, and wordlessly she and Charlotte crept shoulder to shoulder along the landing, feet soundless on the carpet. The jardiniere with its splayed ferns seemed like half a tree, casting octopus shadows on the wallpaper.

They knocked at Vespasia's door and waited. There was no answer. Charlotte knocked again, then turned the handle experimentally. It was not locked. She opened it and they both slipped in, closing it behind them with a tiny click.

''Aunt Vespasia!'' Charlotte said distinctly. The room was darker than Emily's, having heavier curtains, and in the gloom they could see the big bed and Vespasia's head on the pillow, her pale silver hair in a coil over her shoulder. She looked very frail, very old.

"Aunt Vespasia," Charlotte said again.

Vespasia opened her eyes.

Charlotte moved forward into the shrouded light from the window.

"Charlotte?" Vespasia sat up a little. "What is it? Is that Emily with you?" A note of alarm sharpened her voice. "What has happened?"

"Emily remembered something she saw, an expression on Sybilla's face the other night at dinner," Charlotte began. "She thought if she understood it, it might explain things. She went to ask Sybilla."

"At dawn?" Now Vespasia was sitting upright. "And did it—explain things? Have you learned something? What did Sybilla say?"

Charlotte shut her eyes and clenched her hands hard. "Nothing. She's dead. She was strangled with her own hair round the bedpost. I don't know whether she could have done it herself or not. We'll have to call Thomas."

Vespasia was silent for so long Charlotte began to be afraid; then at last she reached up and pulled the bellpull three times. "Pass me my shawl, will you?" she asked. When Charlotte did so, she climbed stiffly out of bed, leaning on Charlotte's outstretched arm for support. "We had better lock the door. We don't want anyone else going in. And I suppose we must tell Eustace." She took a long, deep breath. "And William. I imagine at this time in the morning Thomas will be at home? Good. Then you had better write him a note and send a footman to bring him and his constable."

There was a sharp rap on the door, startling them, and before anyone answered it it opened and Digby came in looking disheveled and frightened. As soon as she saw Vespasia herself was all right the fear vanished and was replaced by concern. She pushed the straggling hair out of her eyes and prepared to be cross.

"Yes, m'lady?" she said cautiously.

"Tea, please, Digby." Vespasia replied, struggling to maintain dignity. "I would like a dish of tea. Bring enough here for all of us—you had better have some yourself. And as soon as you have put the kettle on, waken one of the footmen and tell him to get up."

Digby stared at her, round-eyed, grim-faced.

Vespasia gave her the explanation she was waiting for. "Young Mrs. March is dead. Perhaps you'd better get two footmen—one for the doctor."

"We can telephone the doctor, m'lady," Digby answered.

"Oh, yes, I forgot. I am not yet used to who has these contraptions and who has not. I presume Treves has one."

"Yes, m'lady."

"Then get one footman to send for Mr. Pitt. I'm sure he hasn't got a telephone. And bring the tea."

The next few hours moved like a feverish dream, a mixture of the grotesque and the almost offensively commonplace. How could the breakfast room look precisely the same, the sideboard laden with food, the windows thrown open? Pitt was upstairs with Treves, bending over Sybilla's corpse locked in her own hair, trying to decide whether she killed herself or someone else had crept in and tied those lethal knots. Charlotte could not keep it from her mind to wonder if that was why Jack Radley had gone in the night before, not by any amorous design—only she had wakened too soon, and raised the alarm. She knew it must have occurred to Vespasia too.

It was late when they sat down, well after ten, and everyone was at the table. Even William, ashen, hands shaking, eyes haggard, apparently preferred the noise and occupation of company to the loneliness of his room next door to Sybilla.

Emily sat rigid, her stomach knotted so hard she could not bear to eat. It would make her ill. She sipped a little hot tea and felt it burn her tongue and slide painfully down her closed throat. The sounds of crockery and talk alternately outraged and frightened her, swirling round her like so much empty rattle. It could have been the sound of carriage wheels over gravel, or geese in a yard.

Charlotte was eating because she knew she would need the strength it would give her, but the carefully coddled eggs and thin sliced toast might as well have been cold porridge in her mouth. The sunlight glittered on silver and glass and the clink of cutlery grew louder as Eustace fought his way through fish and potato, but even he found little joy in it. The linen was so white it reminded her of snowfields, glaring and cold with the dead earth underneath.

This was ridiculous. Fear was paralyzing her, solidifying like ice. She must force herself to listen to them all, to think, to make her brain respond and understand. It was all here, if only she could tear the fog from her mind and recognize it. It ought to be familiar to her now—she had seen enough murder before, the pain and the fear that led to violence. How could she be so close, and still not know it?

She looked round the table at them one by one. Old Mrs. March was tight-lipped and her fist was clenched beside her plate. Perhaps anger against the injustice of fate was the only way she could keep from being overwhelmed by the tragedy which was engulfing the family in which she had invested her whole life.

Vespasia was silent. She had shrunk; she seemed smaller than Charlotte had thought her, her wrists bonier, her skin more papery.

Tassie and Jack Radley were talking about something totally immaterial, and she knew even without listening that they were doing it to help, so that the silence would not creep in and drown them all. It did not matter what was said; anything, the weather would do. Everyone, each imprisoned in a private little island of horror, was trying to grasp back something of last week, only a tiny span of days ago, when the world had been so ordinary, so safe. They would gladly have brought back the anxieties that seemed pressing then, and so infinitely trivial now.

Charlotte had seen Pitt briefly. He had called her into

Sybilla's bedroom. At first she had drawn back, but he had told her the body was laid out quietly, the hair undone, a sheet over the terrible face.

"Please!" he had said fiercely. "I need you to come in!"

Reluctantly, shivering, she had obeyed, and he had almost pushed her through the door, arms round her. "Sit on the bed," he had ordered. "No—where Sybilla was."

She had stood rooted to the spot, pulling against him. "Why?" It was unreasonable, grotesque. "Why?"

"I need you to," he had said again. "Charlotte, please. I have to know if she could have done it herself."

"Of course she did!" She had not moved, pulling hard against his strength, and they remained frozen like that, locked in a tug-of-war in the middle of the carpet in the sun.

Pitt was getting cross, because he was helpless.

"Of course she could!" Charlotte had been shaking. "She had it round her throat; then round the bedpost. It's just like tying a scarf behind your neck, or doing up the back of a dress. She used the bedpost to make it tight enough—the carving on it tightened it again when she slipped down a bit. She must have meant to, or she wouldn't have stayed there. She'd have moved while she still had the strength. I don't suppose you black out straightaway. Let go of me, Thomas! I'm not going to sit there!"

"Don't be silly!" He had begun to lose control, because he understood what he was asking of her and he knew of no other way. "Do you want me to have to get one of the maids? I'm not asking Emily!"

She had stared at him in horror; then, seeing the desperation in his eyes, hearing the edge of it mounting in his voice, she had taken a step towards the bed, still refusing to look at the exact spot where she had seen Sybilla.

"Take the other one." He had yielded, pointing to the bedpost at the opposite side. "Sit there and reach behind your neck, round the post."

Slowly, stiffly, she had done as he ordered, stretching her arms up behind her head, reaching the post, feeling her fingers round it, pretending to tie something.

"Lower down," he had commanded.

She bent them a little lower.

"Now pull," he had said. "Make it tighter." He had taken her hands and pulled them down and away.

"I can't!" Her arms had hurt, her muscles strained. "It's too low down—I can't pull that low. Thomas, you're hurting me!"

He had let go. "That's what I thought," he had said huskily. "No woman could have pulled at it that low down behind her own neck." He had knelt on the bed beside her, put his arms round her, and buried his face in her hair, kissing her slowly, holding her tighter and tighter. There had been no need for either of them to say it. They stayed there close in the silent certainty: Sybilla had been murdered.

Charlotte's mind returned to the present, to the breakfast table and its painful charade of normality. She wanted to be gentle, comforting, but there was no time. She swallowed the last of her tea and looked round at each of them.

"We have our senses, and some intelligence," she said distinctly. "One of us murdered George, and now Sybilla. I think we had better find out who, before it gets any worse."

Mrs. March shut her eyes and grasped for Tassie's arm, her thin fingers like claws, surprisingly brown, spotted with old age. "I think I am going to faint!"

"Put your head between your knees," Vespasia said wearily.

The old woman's eyes snapped open. "Don't be ridiculous!" she snarled. "You may choose to sit at the breakfast table with your legs around your ears—it would be like you. But I do not!"

"Not very practical." Emily looked up for the first time. "I don't suppose she could."

Vespasia did not bother to lift her eyes from her plate. "I have some sal volatile, if you want it."

Eustace ignored her, staring at Charlotte. "Do you think that is wise, Mrs. Pitt?" he said without blinking. "The truth may be of a highly distressing nature, especially for you."

Charlotte knew precisely what he meant, both as to the nature of the truth he believed and how he intended it should be presented to the police.

"Oh, yes." Her voice was shaking, and she was furious with herself, but she found she could not prevent it. "I am less afraid of what might be discovered than I am of allowing it to remain hidden where it may strike again— and kill someone else."

William froze. Vespasia put her hand up to her eyes and leaned forward over the table.

"Bad blood," Mrs. March said with harsh intensity, gripping her spoon so hard it scattered sugar over the cloth. "It always tells in the end. No matter how fine the face, how pretty the manners, blood counts. George was a fool! An irresponsible, disloyal fool. Careless marriages are the cause of half the misery in the world."

"Fear," Charlotte contradicted deliberately. "I would have said it was fear that caused the most misery, fear of pain, fear of looking ridiculous, of being inadequate. And most of all, fear of loneliness—the dread that no one will love you."

"You speak for yourself, girl!" Mrs. March spat at her, turning, white-faced, her eyes blazing. "The Marches have nothing to be afraid of!"

"Don't be idiotic, Lavinia." Vespasia sat up, pushing her fallen hair off her brow. "The only people who don't know fear are the saints of God, whose vision of heaven is stronger than the flesh, and those simpletons who have not enough imagination to conceive of pain. We at this table are all terrified."

"Perhaps Mrs. March is one of the saints of God?" Jack Radley said sarcastically.

"Hold your tongue!" Mrs. March shouted. "The sooner that incompetent policeman takes you away the better. If you didn't murder poor George, then you certainly inspired Emily to do it. Either way, you are guilty and should be hanged!''

The blood fled his face, but he did not look away. There was a vacuum of silence. Somewhere across the hall a footman's steps sounded loudly till they died away beyond the baize door. Even Eustace was motionless.

Vespasia rose to her feet stiffly, as if her back hurt her. Eyes glazed, William rose also and pulled out her chair, steadying her arm.

''I assume Mr. Beamish will send Mr. Hare to console us again,'' she said quietly, and with only the slightest tremor, ''which is as well; he will be infinitely more use. If he calls I shall be in my room. I would like to see him.''

''Would you like us to send for the doctor, Grandmama?'' William found his voice with difficulty. He looked as if he were walking in a nightmare through which he had struggled all night, only to wake and find it still with him, stretching into endless, unalterable reality.

''No, thank you, my dear.'' Vespasia patted his hand, and then walked slowly from the room, keeping her balance with care.

''Excuse me.'' Charlotte set her napkin by her plate and followed Vespasia out, catching up with her in the hallway and taking her elbow all the way up the long, wide stairs. For once Vespasia did not resist her.

''Would you like me to stay with you?'' she asked at the door of the bedroom.

Vespasia looked at her steadily, her face weary and frightened. ''Do you know anything, Charlotte?''

''No,'' Charlotte said honestly. ''But if Emily is right Sybilla hated Eustace, whether for herself or for William or for Tassie, I don't know.''

Vespasia's lips tightened and her eyes looked even more wretched. ''For William, I should imagine,'' she said in barely more than a whisper. ''Eustace has never known when to hold his tongue. He is not a sensitive man.''

Charlotte hesitated, on the brink of asking if there was

anything else, but drew back from probing any more. She gave the shadow of a smile, and left her.

The idea was hardening in her, and as soon as she was sure the landing was clear, Charlotte went to Sybilla's door and tried it. The servants had naturally been told what happened, and no maid would venture in here. Pitt had moved Sybilla to the long seat by the window before, for his experiment on the bed, but perhaps he had lifted her back now, to rest in some attitude of peace, providing one did not see the face.

The door was not locked. Maybe there was no need; who would return, except in grief, and in humanity that must be allowed? Both Pitt and Treves must already have seen everything they could, and presumably gone down to the butler's pantry to consult.

She glanced round the landing once more, then turned the handle and went in. The room faced south and was full of light. There was a shape on the bed, under a sheet. She kept her eyes from it, although she knew perfectly well precisely what she would see if she were to take it off. She must control her imagination and a surprisingly sharp sense of pity, which tugged at her like a bruise of the mind. Sybilla had caused Emily dreadful pain, and yet perversely she could not loathe her as she wished, even when she was alive. She was aware of some hard knot of hurt in Sybilla also, something growing and becoming worse, more acute. She could only hate the comfortable, the unmarked, because she felt alien from them. The moment she saw the wound and believed the pain, her anger slipped away like sand through a sieve. So it had been with Sybilla, and now she intended to search for some sign of what had been the cause.

She stared round. Where to begin? Where did she keep her own private things, things that would reveal to another woman her frailties? Not the wardrobe—that would hold only clothes, and one did not leave private things in a pocket. The bedside table had a small drawer, but maids might tidy that; there was no lock on it. Still she pulled it open in case, and found only handkerchiefs, a lavender bag smelling sweet and dry, a twist of paper that had contained a headache powder, and a bottle of smelling salts. Nothing.

Next she tried the dressing table and found all the things she would have expected: brushes and combs, silk scarves for polishing hair, pins, perfumes and cosmetics. She would like one day to learn how to use them as skillfully as Sybilla had. The thought of the murdered woman's beauty was peculiarly painful, seeing these small artifices spread out so uselessly now. It was ridiculous to identify with her so much, and yet the knowledge did not dispel the feeling.

There was underwear, as she would have expected, infinitely prettier and newer than her own—probably much the same as Emily's. But there was nothing about it in which she could see any deeper meaning, no paper or article hidden underneath. She tried the jewel case, and lingered in a moment's envy for a rope of pearls and an emerald clasp. But again the bare objects told her nothing, gave her no clue as to whether they were more than the ornaments any wealthy and loved woman might have.

She stood in the center of the floor, staring round at the pictures, the curtains, the enormous four-poster. Surely there must be something.

Under the bed! She knelt down quickly and threw up the long counterpane to see. There was a trunk for clothes, and beside it, in the shadow, a small vanity case. Instantly she hauled it out, and still kneeling, tried the lid. It was locked.

"Damn!" she swore fiercely. "Damn, damn, *damn*!" She thought for a moment, peering at it. It was a very ordinary lock, small and light. There was a little tongue of metal holding the catch. If she could just move that! Where was the key? Sybilla must have had one . . .

Where did she keep her own keys? In the jewel case, of course, in the space underneath the tray for earrings. That was where she kept her own suitcase keys, not that she traveled very often these days. She scrambled to her feet, tripping over her skirt, and landed half on top of the dressing-table stool. It was there, a little brass key about an inch long, in with the gold chains.

It opened the vanity case on the floor, and with fingers fumbling with excitement Charlotte pushed back the lid and saw the pile of letters and two little white kid-bound books. One had ADDRESSES written on the front. She looked at the letters first. They were love letters from William, and after the first one she checked only the names. They were passionate, tender, written with a delicacy of wording that brought back to her mind the painting on the easel in the conservatory, full of so much more than merely wind in spring trees. There was in it all the subtlety of the turning year, of blossom and ice, and the knowledge of change.

She hated herself for doing it. They were all from William; there was nothing else, nothing from George—but then George was not a man who wrote love letters, and any other man's would surely be clumsy and inarticulate beside these.

She picked up the unmarked book. It was a diary begun some years ago in an ordinary notebook, no dates printed, no headings except those Sybilla had written herself.

Charlotte opened it at random and saw the notation, *Christmas Eve, 1886*. A few months ago. She read with horror.

William has been painting all day. I can see it is brilliant, but I wish he would not spend so much time on it, leaving me alone with the family. The old woman is still asking me when I propose to become a "real woman" and bear a family, an heir for the Marches. There are times when I hate her so much I would gladly kill her if I knew how. Perhaps I would regret it afterwards, but it could hardly be worse than the way I feel now. And Eustace sits there talking about what a waste William is—painting life instead of living it. And he looks

at me unctuously, all the time I feel as if his eyes
see through my clothes. He has such manhood!
How can I ever have been insane enough to let him
make love with me? I would give anything on earth
to have refused him—but that is a pointless thought,
we are both locked in it, and I dare not tell anyone. Tassie would be appalled, not for her father—
sometimes I think she has no love for him anyway—but for William, whom she loves so much,
and with such gentleness. More than most sisters,
I think.

Dear God! I'm so miserable I don't know what
to do. But cowardice won't help. I have always
been able to charm men. I will find a way out.

Charlotte was shaking, and in spite of the heat in the
closed room there were trickles of sweat chilling on her
body. Was that what it was all about with George? Not a
grand passion at all, not even the vanity of a beautiful
woman, but a protection from Eustace? The thought made
her feel sick.

She flicked through more pages of the little book till she
came to the end. She read the last entry.

I can hardly believe it! Nothing seems to shatter
his appetite or frighten him! I am almost driven into
thinking it was a nightmare as he tried to make us all
believe. I have to look at Jack to make myself sure.

Poor Jack. Grandmother Vespasia looks at him
with such disappointment; I think she really liked
him. He is just the sort of man I fancy she would
have led a rare dance when she was young. And
Charlotte! She is disgusted, and it shows so plainly
in her face. I imagine that is on Emily's account. I
wish I had a sister who cared for me so much. I
never before felt as if I needed one, someone to
trust, who would defend me. But I do now.

Perhaps my screaming will be enough. Please
God. Eustace did look truly horrified, just for a moment, before he thought what to say when everyone came running. I don't think he really believed I
would, until I opened my mouth.

And, so help me God—if he comes again I shall
scream again, I don't care what anyone thinks—
and I told him I would.

Now he has a black eye and Jack a split lip.

Jack must have gone to his room and thrashed him.
Dear Jack.

But what on earth can I do when he leaves?

Please, God, help me.

And there it ended. There had not been another morning
for Sybilla to write.

But why had she not told William?

Because William already had no love for his father, and
she was afraid of what he would do in rage and the depth
of his hurt and revulsion. Or perhaps because in any battle
between William and Eustace, she was afraid Eustace
would always win. No wonder she hated him.

There was a noise outside the door—not the light trip of
a housemaid, but a heavy tread. A man's step.

There was no time to escape; the footsteps stopped and
someone touched the doorknob. In a panic she threw the
vanity case back under the bed and rolled in after it,
banging against something hard, snatching her skirts after
her and pulling down the counterpane just as the door
opened and, after a moment, closed again. He was in the
room, whoever he was.

She was huddled up against the trunk, the vanity case
digging into her back, but she dared not move. She thought
of Sybilla lying stiff and cold a few feet above her on the
bed; there was only the thickness of the springs and the
mattress between them.

Who was it? He was opening and closing drawers,
searching through them. She heard the wardrobe door

squeak just as it had for her, and then the rustle of taffeta, a swish of silk. Then it closed again.

Dear heaven! Was he looking for the little book she still had in her hand? His feet were moving back this way. She would have given a lot to know who it was, but she dared not lift the counterpane even an inch to look. Whoever it was might be facing this way, and he would surely see. And then what? Haul her out and, at best, accuse her of robbing the dead—

The vanity case was digging into her, its edges bruising her back. The feet had not moved. There was a faint sound—of shifting weight, and rustling cloth—what was it?

The answer was instant. The counterpane was whipped away and she was staring, paralyzed, into Eustace's red face and round eyes.

For a long, terrible second he was as transfixed as she was. Then he spoke, his voice a parody of its usual self.

"Mrs. Pitt! Is there anything whatsoever you can say to explain yourself?"

Had he any idea what was written in Sybilla's book? She clung to it so hard her fingers were white. She tried to speak, but her throat was dry, and she was so frightened she could not move. She could not even crawl backwards, because of the trunk. If he decided to attack her, to get back the damning book—and that was surely what he had been looking for—then the only escape she had was to stay here, where he could not reach her. It was too low for his thick body to get in.

That was preposterous. She could hardly remain under the bed until someone else came to coax her out.

"Mrs. Pitt!" Eustace's face was hard now, his eyes dangerous. Yes, he had seen the little white leather book in her hand, and guessed what it was, if he did not already know. She stared back at him like a rabbit.

"Mrs. Pitt, how long do you propose to remain under the bed? I invited you to my house in order to be of comfort to your sister in her bereavement, but you force me to think you are as mentally infirm as she is!'' He held out his hand, strong and square; even now she noticed how clean it was, how perfectly manicured the nails. "And give me the book," he added with only the slightest stammer. "I will pretend I do not know you took it. It will be for the best, but I believe you should return to your own house at once. You are obviously unsuited to remain in a household such as ours.''

She did not move. If she gave him the book he would destroy it, and there would be nothing left except her word, which no one would have believed against his even before this.

"Come!" he said angrily. "You are being foolish! Get out of there!''

She reached up slowly to her neck and undid the top three buttons of her dress.

He stared at her in horrified fascination, and in spite of himself his eyes went to her bosom, always one of her handsomest assets.

"Mrs. Pitt!" he said hoarsely.

Very carefully she pushed the little white book down the front of her dress and fastened it up again. It felt uncomfortable, and no doubt looked ridiculous, but he would have to tear her bodice to take it from her, and that would be very hard indeed for him to explain.

Still looking at him, his eyes now hot and furious— perhaps he was as frightened as she was—she scrambled very awkwardly out from under the bed and stood up, rumpled and stiff, her legs shaking.

"That book does not belong to you, Mrs. Pitt," he said grimly. "Give it to me!''

"It doesn't belong to you either," she answered with as much courage as she could. He was very strong, thick-chested, broad-hipped, and he stood between her and the door. "I shall give it to the police.''

"No, you won't." He reached out and took her arm. His fingers closed right around her, immovably.

Her breath almost choked her. "Are you going to tear

my dress off to get it, Mr. March?'' She tried to make her voice light, and failed. ''That will be extremely awkward for you to explain, and I shall scream—and you won't pass this off as a nightmare!''

''And how will you account for being here in Sybilla's room?'' he asked. But he was afraid, and she smelled it in the air, felt it in the bruising pressure of his fingers.

''How will you?''

His mouth flickered in the sickest of smiles. ''I shall say I heard a sound in here and came in, and I found you going through Sybilla's jewel case—the reason for that will be painfully obvious.''

''Then I shall say the same!'' she countered. ''Only it was not the jewel case, it was the vanity case under the bed. And I shall say you found the diary, and then everyone will read what is in it!''

His hand weakened. She saw the fear deepen in his face and sweat break out through the skin of his upper lip and above his eyebrows.

''Let me go, Mr. March, or I shall call out. There must be maids around, and Aunt Vespasia is in her room across the landing.''

Slowly, an inch at a time, he took his hand away, and she waited till it was fully gone, just in case he changed his mind, before she turned and walked, legs wobbling, to the door and out onto the landing. She felt light-headed and a little sick with relief. She must find Thomas immediately.

10

Charlotte found Pitt in the butler's pantry and threw the door open, interrupting Constable Stripe in midsentence, and barely hesitating to apologize.

"Thomas! I've discovered the answer, or at least one of the answers—excuse me, Constable—in Sybilla's diary, something I never even thought of." She stopped abruptly. Now that they were both staring at her she felt vulnerable for the secret she had discovered. Not for Eustace—she would happily have seen him humiliated. But for Sybilla she felt unexplainably naked.

"What have you found?" Pitt asked anxiously, his eyes wide, seeing the fear and the flush in her face more than hearing her words. There was no triumph in her.

She glanced at Stripe—only for a moment, but he saw it, and instantly she was sorry. She swung round to turn her back to him, unbuttoned her dress just enough to pull out the diary, and handed it to Pitt.

"Christmas Eve," she said very quietly. "Read the entry for Christmas Eve, last year, and then the very last one."

He took the book and opened it, riffling through the pages till he came to December, then turned them one by one. Finally he stopped altogether, and she watched his face as he read it, the mixture of anger and disgust slowly blurring and becoming inextricably confounded with pity. He read the end.

"And he killed George over her." He looked up at Charlotte, and passed the book without explanation to Stripe. "I suppose poor Sybilla knew, or guessed."

"I wonder why he didn't look for the book when he killed her," she said with quiet unhappiness.

"Maybe he heard something," Pitt replied. "Someone else awake—even Emily coming. And he dared not wait."

Charlotte shuddered. "Are you going to arrest him?"

He hesitated, weighing the question, looking at Stripe, whose face was red and unhappy.

"No," he answered flatly. "Not yet. This isn't proof. He could deny it all, say it was Sybilla's imagination. Without any other evidence, it's only her word against his. To make it known now would hurt William, perhaps even cause more violence and more tragedy." His mouth moved in the faintest of smiles. "Let Eustace wait and worry for a while. Let's see what he does." He looked at Charlotte. "You said there was another book, with addresses?"

"Yes."

"Then we had better get that as well. It may mean nothing, but we'll check through them all, see who they are."

Charlotte went obediently back to the door. Pitt hesitated, looking at Stripe with a half smile. "Sorry, Stripe, but I shall need you for this, and it may take some time."

For a moment Stripe did not understand the reason for the apology; then his face fell and the pink crept up his cheeks.

"Yes, sir. Er . . ." His head came up. "Would there be time, sir . . . ?"

"Of course there would," Pitt agreed. "But don't waste words. Be back here in fifteen minutes."

"Yes, sir!" Stripe waited only until Charlotte and Pitt were round the corner in the corridor before he shot out, stopped the first maid he saw, which chanced to be the parlormaid, and asked her where Miss Taylor was at that moment.

He looked so urgent and impressive in his uniform that

she responded immediately, without her usual prevarication towards strangers in the house—especially of the lower orders, such as police, chimney sweeps, and the like.

"In the stillroom, sir."

"Thank you!" He turned on his heel and made his way, past the other small rooms for numerous household duties, to the stillroom, which had originally been used for the making of cordials and perfumes but was now largely for tea, coffee, and the storing of sweetmeats.

Lettie was putting a large fruitcake into a tin and she turned at the rather heavy sound of his feet. She was even prettier than last time he saw her. He had not noticed before how her hair swept off her brow, or how delicate her ears were.

"Good morning, Mr. Stripe," she said with a little sniff. "If you've come to look at this coffee, you're welcome, I'm sure, but there's no point. It's all new in—"

Stripe brought his mind to attention. "No, I didn't," he said more firmly than he would have believed. "We've got some new evidence."

She was interested in spite of herself, and frightened. She liked to tell herself she was independent, but in truth she had a strong loyalty to the household, especially Tassie, and she would have gone to great lengths to prevent any of them being hurt, especially by outsiders. She stood still, staring up at Stripe, her mind racing over what he might say and how she should answer.

She gulped. "Have you?"

He wished he could comfort her, reassure her, but he dared not—not yet.

"I'm going to 'ave to go away to look into it."

"Oh!" She looked startled, then disappointed. Then as she saw the pleasure in his face and realized she had betrayed herself, she straightened so stiffly her back was like a ramrod, and her chin so high her neck hurt. "Indeed, an' I suppose that's your duty, Mr. Stripe." She did not trust herself to go on. It was ridiculous to be upset over a policeman, of all things!

"I may be quite a time," he went on. "Might even find the solution—and not come back again."

"I hope you do. We don't want terrible things like this happening and no one caught." She moved as if to turn back to the cake tin and the rows of tea caddies, but changed her mind. She was confused, not certain whether she was angry with him or not.

Pitt's admonition was ringing in his ears. Time was sliding by. All must be won or lost now. He screwed up his courage and plunged in, staring at the Chinese flower design on the jar behind her. "So I came to say as I'd like it very much if I could call on you, personal, like."

She drew in her breath quickly, but since he was not looking at her he could not judge the reason.

"Perhaps you'd come with me for a walk in the park, when the band's playing? It can be . . ." He hesitated again and met her eyes at last. "Most pleasant," he finished, cheeks hot.

"Thank you, Mr. Stripe," she said quickly. Half of her told herself she was crazy, walking out with a policeman! What on earth would her father have said? The other half was tingling with delight—it was what she had wanted most in the world for about three days. She swallowed hard. "That sounds very agreeable."

He beamed with relief, then, collecting his composure, remembered a little dignity and stood to attention.

"Thank you, Miss Taylor. If my duties take me away I'll write you a letter and"—in a wave of triumph—"I'll call for you at three o'clock on Sunday afternoon!" And he left before she could demur.

She waited only until his footsteps had died away. Then she jammed the rest of the tea she was sorting all into one jar, and ran upstairs to tell Tassie, a remarkable amount of whose own secrets she herself shared.

Charlotte sat on the edge of her bed struggling with her growing desire to escape going down to dinner altogether. Pitt had gone with the address book to pursue the names in it and she felt a chill without him. Facing Eustace across the table would be appalling. He must surely know beyond question that she had shown the diary to Pitt, and that Pitt must be weighing whether to make it public.

And what of William? His own father, who so clearly despised him, with the wife to whom he had written such love letters! It would be unbearable. It was that which hardened in her mind the already half-made decision not to tell Emily. Let no one know who did not have to. It was not certain beyond any other possibility that Eustace had murdered George in a passion of jealousy; after all, he could hardly imagine any claim on Sybilla. If he was driven by jealousy it could only be if she had refused him in George's favor.

Then a coldness drenched her, much stronger, more sure in its grasp. Of course. Sybilla dared not look to William for protection, both because she would not wish him ever to know of her first weakness—lunacy, as she had called it—and because she was afraid for him if he and Eustace quarreled. Eustace might in malice make sure everyone else knew he had cuckolded his own son. She could imagine the old lady's face if she heard—and Tassie, who loved William with such sensitivity.

No. Far better, far wiser for Sybilla to seek her defense in George, who could be so startlingly considerate at times, when he understood the wound. He was loyal, without judgment; he would have helped her and kept silent.

Only he had done the unforeseen and become enchanted with her himself, and there had begun the unraveling of all the plan.

And then Jack—Jack had understood and helped her as well. But understood how much?

She would tell Emily nothing. Not yet.

But, dear heaven, she did not want to go through the charade of dinner! How could she excuse herself? To the company it would be easy: she had a headache, she was unwell. There would be no need to explain that; women were always getting headaches, and she had certainly had enough to justify one.

Aunt Vespasia would be concerned for her and send Digby with medicines and advice. Emily would miss her at table, and what excuse would satisfy her, or Thomas? He would not accept a headache. He would expect her to go down, and watch, and listen. That was the reason she had given him for remaining here at all. Ladies with servants might take to their beds with the vapors; working women were expected to keep on, even with fevers or consumption. He would see it for an attack of cowardice—exactly as it was. On the whole, facing Eustace was the lesser evil.

At least, she thought so until she sat down at the table, determined not to look at him, and in her very consciousness of him ended by meeting his eyes precisely when he was staring at her. She averted her gaze instantly, but it was too late. The chicken in her mouth turned to wet sawdust, her hands were clammy, and she all but dropped her fork. Surely everyone else must be looking at her, too, and wondering what on earth was the matter with her. It could only be politeness that kept them from asking. She was staring at the white ice sheet of the tablecloth, away from the dazzling facets of the chandeliers and the light on the cut glass of the cruet sets, but all her mind saw was Eustace's face.

"I think the weather is going to break," old Mrs. March said joylessly. "I hate wet summers; at least in winter one can sit by a decent fire without feeling ridiculous."

"You have a fire all through the year anyway," Vespasia replied. "That boudoir of yours would suffocate a cat!"

"I don't keep cats," Mrs. March replied instantly. "I don't like them. Insolent creatures, don't care for anyone but themselves, and there is more than enough selfishness in the world already without adding cats to it. But I did have a dog"—she shot a look of intense hatred at Emily—"until somebody killed it."

"If it hadn't preferred George to you it wouldn't have happened." Vespasia pushed her plate away in disgust. "Poor little creature."

"And if George hadn't preferred Sybilla to Emily, none of it would." Mrs. March was not to be beaten, especially not at her own table in front of strangers whom she despised, and not by Vespasia, whom she had resented for forty years.

"You said before that it was because Emily preferred Mr. Radley," Charlotte interrupted, looking at the old lady with raised eyebrows. "Have you discovered something that changed your mind?"

"I think the less you have to say the better, young woman!" Mrs. March flicked a scornful eye over her and continued eating.

"I thought perhaps you had learned something new," Charlotte murmured. Then, impelled by an inner compulsion, she looked sideways at Eustace.

It was an extraordinary expression she surprised on his face—not exactly fear—something that had superceded it, half curiosity. He was the supreme hypocrite, self-important and insensitive, plowing on in his obsession with dynasty, regardless of the trampling of subtle and private emotions. But she realized with uncomfortable surprise that he did not lack courage. He was beginning to regard her in a way quite different from the uninterested condescension which had possessed him before. She read in that one glance that she had become not only an adversary, but a woman. The passage in the diary came back to her as sharply as if it were on the tablecloth in front of her—*What manhood he has!*—and she felt her face flame. The thought was so profoundly repellent her hands shook, her fork clattering on the plate. Perhaps Sybilla had made other references, obliquely—even in detail! Her face was burning; she felt as if her dress had come undone in front of everyone, especially Eustace. He might even know what she had read, and more. He might in his own mind be repeating the words, and sharing them with her, imagining her response. She shuddered. Then, because civility demanded it, she looked up—and found Jack Radley, seated beside Emily, regarding her with concern.

"Have you discovered something?" Tassie added with distressing perspicacity.

"No!" Charlotte denied too quickly. "I don't know who it was—I don't know at all!"

"Then you're a fool," Mrs. March said viciously. "Or a liar. Or both."

"Then we are all fools or liars." William laid his napkin beside his untouched plate. Where others had pushed the food around and eaten a mouthful or two, he had not even pretended.

"We are not all fools." Eustace did not look at Charlotte, but she knew as well as if he had that he was speaking to her. "Doubtless one of us knows who killed George and Sybilla, but the rest of us have sufficient wisdom not to speculate aloud on every thought that comes into our minds. It can only cause unnecessary grief. We must remember Christian charity as well as righteous indignation."

"What in heaven's name are you talking about?" Vespasia demanded with startling anger. "Christian charity towards whom? And why? You never had an ounce of charity in you all your life. Why the sudden about-face? Are you on the other end, for once?"

Eustace looked as if he had been struck. He fumbled for a reply but found nothing that shielded him from her brilliant suspicion.

Not because she cared a lot about Eustace, but because she must defend William from the humiliation—above all, from Eustace himself—Charlotte interrupted with the first thing that came into her head.

"We all have things to hide," she said overly loud. "Foolishness, if not guilt. I have seen enough investigations to know that. Perhaps Mr. March is just beginning to learn. I'm sure he would wish to protect his family, whether he is concerned for the rest of us or not. He may believe

Emily will not retaliate, no matter what is said of her, but I don't think he misjudges me in the same way.''

Vespasia was silent. If she thought anything more she preferred not to say it now.

William looked at her with the shadow of a smile, so thin it was painful, and Jack Radley put his hand on Emily's arm.

"Indeed?" Mrs. March regarded Charlotte with a curl of her lip. "And what on earth could you say that my son would care about in the slightest?"

Charlotte forced a smile to her face. "You are inviting me to do precisely what we have just agreed would be most unfortunate—cause unnecessary distress by speculation. Is that not so, Mr. March?" She lifted her eyes and met Eustace's.

He was surprised, and a series of thoughts flashed through his mind so vividly she could trace them as if they had been pictures: alarm, temporary safety, a budding irony—a perception new to him—and finally, a reluctant admiration.

She had a hideous feeling that at that precise moment, had she wished, she might have filled the place so lately left by Sybilla, but this time she stared him out, and it was he who lowered his eyes.

Still she slept badly. She had not offered Aunt Vespasia any explanation of her extraordinary confrontation with Eustace, and she felt guilty for it. Emily was still too absorbed in her own grief and the weight of fear that haunted her to have noticed.

It was long after midnight when she heard the noise outside, very slight, as of a pebble falling. Then it came again and she was surer of it. She got out of bed and went to the window, careful to disturb the curtain as little as possible, and looked out. She could see nothing but the familiar garden in the hazy light of a half moon.

Then the noise came again; a tiny, thin *plink*. A pebble fell from above, touched the sill, and bounced out and into the void. She did not hear it land. Still she could see no one. They must be standing so close to one of the ornamental bushes that one shadow consumed them both.

An assignation for one of the housemaids? Surely not! A girl caught in such an act would lose not only her present position and the roof over her head, but her character also, which would preclude any future position as well. She would be reduced to the grim choices of a sweatshop or the streets, where she must live by thievery or prostitution. Even the hot flush of romance seldom inspired such dangerous abandon. There were better ways.

Whose window was above hers? Everyone had bedrooms on this floor—except Tassie! Tassie had kept her old childhood bedroom in the nursery wing upstairs, to leave sufficient guest rooms free.

Charlotte made up her mind instantly; any time for thought and her nerve would fail. She did not bother with underwear but grasped her warmest, plainest dark dress, climbed into it, and pulled on her boots and buttoned them, fumbling in the dark. She dared not light one of the lamps. Even with the curtains drawn the watcher outside might see it. She had no time to do more with her hair than tie it back. Then, having found her coat, she waited behind the door, straining her ears, till she heard the very faintest footfall on the landing.

She waited a moment longer, then opened the door and went out silently, closing it after her. At the head of the stairs she was just in time to see a shadow at the bottom turn and disappear, not towards the front but in the direction of the baize door and the kitchens. Of course—the front door had bolts on it which could not be fastened from the outside. In the scullery one of the servants would be blamed.

She ran down as quickly as she could, holding her skirts. She must be careful not to make a sound or get so close that Tassie might glance backwards and see her.

Was she sleepwalking? Or taken by some intermittent madness? Or quite sane, but about some dreadful business that splashed her with blood?

For a moment Charlotte hesitated. It was a delusion to say it could not be anything grotesque; horrors did happen, she knew it only too well. Before George's death Pitt had been called to a case of murder so horrific even he had come home white-lipped and sick—a woman dismembered and left in parcels round Bloomsbury and St. Giles.

She was standing rigid, alone in the hallway. Ahead of her the baize door had almost stopped swinging. Tassie must be in the scullery by now. There was no more time to decide: either she followed her and learned the truth, or she went back to bed.

The door was perfectly still. If she did not hurry she would lose Tassie. Without allowing herself to think any longer she crossed the last few steps of the hall and pushed through the door and into the servants' wing. The kitchens were deserted, smelling clean and warm; odors of scrubbed wood, flour, and, as she passed the stoves, coal dust. She could see the gleam of light on the scuttles from the streetlamp through the window. The scullery was piled with vegetables and buckets and mops. Her skirt caught against the handle of a pail and she stopped only just before it overbalanced and crashed down onto the stone floor.

The outer door ahead of her was closed; Tassie had already gone. Charlotte tried the handle and found it turned easily.

Outside the night was only a little cooler than the house. There was no breeze here in the high-walled yard. The sky was shredded with a few faint mares' tails of cloud, but the half moon shed a milky light in which she could see the back windows, the housing of the chute down into the coal cellars, several bins for rubbish, and at the far side, the gate out into the areaway and the street, and the yellow globe of a lamp above the wall. Tassie was somewhere out on the road.

Carefully lifting the latch with both hands and holding it so it would not fall, Charlotte pulled the gate open and looked outside. To the left there was nothing but the pavement; to the right, the slender figure of Tassie walking rapidly down the Crescent.

Charlotte followed, closing the gate behind her and hurrying a dozen yards before Tassie disappeared round the corner into the main avenue. Now she was free to run without fear of drawing attention to herself. There was no one else in sight, and if she delayed Tassie might be gone when she emerged into the avenue herself. Then she would never know what violent intrigue took a nineteen-year-old heiress out in the small hours of the night and brought her home reeking with blood.

But when she got to the corner and raced round it, stopping suddenly in case her feet on the cobbles were too loud and made Tassie turn, she saw no one at all along the broad sweep of the tree-lined way. Charlotte stood with the frustration boiling up inside her—and saw Tassie come out of the shadow of a sycamore fifty yards ahead, moving very quickly.

Charlotte had been too slow. She had not imagined such haste, and now if she were to keep Tassie in sight she must run, as light-footed as possible, and within the shadows as much as she could. If Tassie were to realize she was being followed, at best any chance of discovering her secret would be lost, and the worst hardly bore thinking of—a fight with a madwoman alone in the midnight streets. That blood had come from someone!

If Pitt knew about this he would be furious—he would quite probably never forgive her. The very thought of the words he would use made her cringe. But it was not his sister who faced trial and the gallows if they failed. Even a reasonable and fair-minded person would have to agree that Emily had as good a motive for murdering her husband as most women could imagine.

Tassie was still walking swiftly along the avenue, and Charlotte was only ten yards behind her now. But when she turned off without warning into a side street, narrower and poorer, Charlotte was caught by surprise. She had been lost in her thoughts and was startled back to awareness with an unpleasant realization of how close she had been to losing Tassie, and continuing alone to God knew where.

This new street was also residential, but the houses were meaner, closer together; graciousness had yielded to necessity.

They had come to the end of the street, and Tassie was still walking rapidly, as if she knew precisely where she was going. They were now in a road which was little more than an alley, close-walled and grimy, with sagging houses propped against one another, dark threatening recesses into yards, and shadows like unknown stagnant pools. There was no one else in sight but a scrawny urchin with a huge cap a few yards ahead of Tassie, walking in the same direction. Charlotte shivered, although she was warm from hurrying and the night was mild. She dared not think how afraid she was, or she would lose her nerve and turn tail, as fast as flying feet could carry her, back to the broad, clean, familiar avenue.

But Tassie seemed to be without fear; her step was quick and light and her head was high. She knew where she was going and looked forward to getting there. There was no one in sight but the urchin, Tassie, and Charlotte herself, but God knew what lurked in the doorways. Where on earth could Tassie be going in this sour maze of tenements and grimy, pinchpenny shops? She could not possibly know anyone—could she?

Charlotte's heart missed a beat and coldness rippled through her. Had George also wakened one night or, perhaps returning from Sybilla's room, seen Tassie, and followed her? Was Charlotte doing exactly what he had done? Had George discovered her abominable secret—and died for it?

Incredibly her feet did not stop; some other part of her brain seemed to be governing them and they kept on quite automatically, hurrying almost soundlessly along the dank street. She was aware now of figures slumped in doorways, of movement in the black alleyways amid the heaps of refuse. Rats, or people? Both. It was in alleys like this that Pitt's men had discovered the dismembered parts of the girl less than a month ago.

Charlotte felt sick, but the thought would not be turned away. It was the figure tiptoeing up the stairs, the blood, and the terrible serenity.

How far were they from Cardington Crescent? How many times had they turned? Tassie was still ahead of her, only ten or twelve yards; she dared not allow the distance to become greater in case Tassie turned suddenly and Charlotte lost her. She was a slight figure, almost as thin as the urchin in front of her and the other ragged shadows that swam on the edge of her vision.

It was too late to go back. Wherever Tassie went she would have to wait for her; alone she would not know how to find her way out of this slum.

One large figure took shape, detaching itself from the bulging, irregular walls. A man with broad shoulders. But far from being afraid, Tassie went towards him with a little murmur of pleasure and lifted her arms, accepting his embrace as naturally as a sweet and familiar blessing. The kiss was intimate, as easy as people who love each other with unquestioning trust, but it was swift, and the next moment Tassie disappeared into the nearest doorway, and the man after her, leaving Charlotte alone on the dark, chipped and slimy pavement. The urchin had seemingly vanished.

Now she was really frightened. She could feel the darkness coming closer, figures moving uneasily with shuffling feet, a slithering in the alleys, a settling of beams and dripping of water leaking from hidden drains. If she were robbed and killed here, not even Pitt would ever find her.

What was this place? It looked like an ordinary, mean house. What inside it drew Tassie here alone, and at midnight? She would have to wait here till she came out, then follow her again until—

There was a hand on her shoulder and her heart jumped

so violently the shriek was forced out of her in a shrill yelp that choked off in inarticulate terror.

"Wot yer be doin' 'ere, Missy?" a voice growled in her ear. Hot, rank-smelling breath. She tried to speak, but her throat was so tight the words died. The hands over her mouth were coarse and the skin had the acrid smell of dirt. "Well, Missy meddler?" The voice was so close the breath moved her hair. "Wot yer want 'ere, then? Come spyin', 'ave yer? Come ter tell tales, 'ave yer? Goin' a runnin' back for Papa ter tell 'im all abaht it, are yer? I'll give yer summin worf tellin', then!" And he yanked her savagely, bending her back and taking her off balance.

She was still shivering with fear, but anger was mounting as well, and she jabbed her elbow back sharply and at the same time trod back with her heel, putting all her weight into it. It caught the man on the instep and he howled with pained outrage.

It was just about to descend into something far uglier, when a woman's voice cut across them angrily.

"Stop it! Mr. Hodgekiss, leave her alone this minute!" A lantern shone high and bright, making Charlotte wince and close her eyes. The man spluttered and let her go, growling wordlessly in the back of his throat.

"Mrs. Pitt!" It was Tassie's voice, high with amazement. "Whatever are you doing here? Are you all right? Have you been hurt? You look terribly pale."

There was no conceivable explanation but the truth. Tassie's face when she lowered the light looked as innocent as a bowl of milk, eyes wide, dark with concern.

"I followed you," Charlotte said hesitantly. It sounded foolish now, and dangerous.

But there was no anger in Tassie's face. "Then you'd better come in." She did not wait for a reply but turned back into the house, leaving the door open.

Charlotte stood on the pavement in an agony of indecision. Part of her wanted to escape, to run as fast as her feet would carry her away from these cramped, ill-smelling streets, the yawning house in front of her, and whatever blood and madness was inside it. Another part of her knew she could not—she had no idea where she was and might as easily be running further into the slums.

She could wait no longer. It was not a decision to go in so much as a lack of the courage to bolt. She went after Tassie through the door, along a corridor so mean she could touch either side simply by extending her elbows, and up a steep stairway that creaked under her weight. Her uncertain way was lit not by gas but a wavering pool of candlelight carried only just ahead of her. She dared not imagine where she was going.

But the bedroom was desperately ordinary; thin curtains at the windows, sacking on the floor for carpet, a bare wooden table with a pitcher and bowl, and a large marital bed made tidy for the event. In it lay a girl of barely fourteen or fifteen, her face pale and tense with fear, her hair brushed off her forehead and lying in a damp tangle over her shoulders. She was obviously well into labor and in considerable pain.

On the far side of the bed stood a girl a year or two older and bearing so marked a resemblance they must have been sisters. Beside her, sleeves rolled up, ready to assist when the time should come but for now holding her hand, was Mr. Beamish's curate, Mungo Hare.

A blinding realization came to Charlotte. It was all so obvious there was no question left to ask. Somehow or other Tassie had become involved in helping to deliver the babies of the poor or abandoned. Presumably it was Mungo Hare who had introduced her to this area of need. The idea of the pink and pious Mr. Beamish organizing such a thing was absurd.

And that quick, wholehearted kiss explained itself, and also explained Tassie's compliant obedience with her grandmother's command that she should be occupied in good works. Happiness bubbled up inside Charlotte. She was so relieved she wanted to laugh aloud.

But Tassie had no time for such emotions. The girl on the bed was going into another spasm of contractions and was racked almost as much by fear as by the pain. Tassie was busy giving orders to a white-faced youth in a cloth cap, presumably the urchin who had fetched her with the stone against the window, sending him for water and as much linen as he could find that was clean, perhaps to get him out of the room. Had it not been for the girl's fear and the close possibility of death, Mungo Hare would also have been banished. Childbirth was women's business.

Charlotte could remember her own two confinements, especially the first. The awe and the pride of carrying had given way to a primitive, mouth-drying fear when the pain came and her body began its relentless cycle which would end only when there was birth—or death. And she had been a grown woman, who loved her husband and wanted her child, and had a mother and sister to attend her after the doctor had done his professional work. This girl was barely more than a child herself—Charlotte had been in the schoolroom at her age—and there was no one to help her but Tassie and a young Highland curate.

She stepped forward and sat on the bed, taking the girl's other hand.

"Hold on to me," she said with a smile. "It will only hurt worse if you fight against it. And cry out if you want to—you are entitled to, and no one will mind in the least. It will all be worth it, I promise you." It was a rash thing to say, and as soon as the words were out her mind half regretted them. Too many children were born dead, and even if it were perfect, how was this girl going to care for it?

"You're very kind, miss," the girl said between gasps. "I don't know why you should take the trouble, I don't."

"I've had two myself," Charlotte replied, holding the thin little hand more tightly and feeling it clench with another spasm of pain. "I know just how you feel. But wait till you hold your baby, you'll forget all about this." Then again she cursed her runaway tongue. What if the girl could not keep it, what if it went into adoption, or some anonymous orphanage, a charge on the parish to grow up in a workhouse, hungry and unloved?

"Me an' me sister," the girl answered her unspoken question, "we're goin' ter raise 'im—or 'er. Annie 'as a real good job cleanin' an like. Mr. 'Are got it for 'er." She gave Mungo Hare a look of trust so total it was frightening in its intensity.

Then more regular contractions cut out all conversation, and it was time for Tassie to begin her work with words of command and encouragement, and all the towels, and eventually, water. Without ever making the decision to, Charlotte helped. And at half past three in the narrow, shabby room the old miracle was fulfilled, and a perfect child was born. The girl, in a clean nightgown, exhausted, hair wet, but flushed with joy, held him in her arms and asked Charlotte timidly if she would mind if the baby were named Charlie, after her. She said quite honestly that she would count it a very great honor.

At quarter past four, as the summer dawn splashed the sky pearl above the sloping maze of roofs, gray with grime and soot, Charlotte and Tassie left the house and, with the urchin dancing a little jig, were led back to the avenue from which they could find Cardington Crescent and home. Mungo Hare did not come with them; he had said good-bye to Tassie at the corner of the alley. He had other tasks before he reported to Mr. Beamish for the ritual of the morning service.

Charlotte felt like dancing, too, except that her legs would not obey such a hectic call after the extraordinary demands that had already been made upon them. But she found herself singing some snatch of a music hall number because of its sheer joy, and after a moment Tassie joined in. Side by side they marched along the avenue in the white dawn, blood-spattered, hair wild, as the birds in the sycamores welcomed the day.

In Cardington Crescent they found the scullery door still unlocked and crept in past the piles of vegetables and the rows of pans on the wall, up the stone step into the kitchen. Another half hour and the first maids would be down to clean out the stove, renew the blacking, and get the fires going and the ovens ready for breakfast when the cook appeared. Not long after that the housemaids would be up, too, to prepare the dining room and begin the daily round.

"Haven't you ever run into anyone?" Charlotte whispered.

"No. I have had to hide in the stillroom once or twice." Tassie looked at her anxiously. "You won't tell anyone about Mungo, will you? *Please*."

"Of course not!" Charlotte was horrified that the possibility could have crossed Tassie's mind. "What do you think of me that you need to ask? Are you going to marry him?"

Tassie's chin came up. "Yes! Papa will be furious, but if he won't give me permission I shall just have to do without. I love Mungo more than anyone else in the world—except Grandmama Vespasia, and William. But that's different."

"Good!" Charlotte clasped her arm in a fierce little gesture of companionship. "If I can help, I will."

"Thank you." Tassie meant it profoundly, but there was no time for conversation now. They could not afford to linger; they were later than was safe as it was. On tiptoe Charlotte followed her along the corridor, past the house-keeper's sitting room and the butler's pantry to the baize door and the main hallway.

They were as far as the foot of the great stairway when they heard the click of the morning room door and Eustace's voice behind them.

"Mrs. Pitt, your conduct is beyond explanation. You will pack your belongings and leave my house this morning."

For an instant Charlotte and Tassie both froze, tingling with horror. Then, slowly and in unison, they turned to face him. He stood three or four yards away, just outside the morning room door, a candle in his hand dripping hot wax into its holder. He was wearing his nightshirt with a robe over it, tied round the waist, and a nightcap on his head. It was broad sunrise outside, but in here the velvet curtains had not been drawn and the flame of the candle held high was necessary to see their faces and the dark stains of the afterbirth splashed down their skirts. In spite of the dreadfulness of the moment, Charlotte could not quench in herself the infinitely more important joy, the exultant achievement in new, unblemished life.

Eustace's face blanched in the yellow candlelight and his eyes opened even wider. "Oh, my God!" he breathed, appalled. "What have you done?"

"Delivered a baby," Tassie said, with the same smile Charlotte had seen that first night on the staircase.

"You—y-you what!" Eustace was aghast.

"Delivered a baby," Tassie repeated.

"Don't be ridiculous! What baby? Whose baby?" he spluttered. "You've taken leave of your senses, girl!"

"Her name doesn't matter," Tassie answered.

"It matters very much!" Eustace's voice was rising and growing louder. "She had no business sending for you at this time of night! In fact, she had no business sending for you at all—where is her sense of propriety? An unmarried woman has no . . . no call to know about these things. It is quite improper! How can I marry you decently now— now you have been— Who is it, Anastasia? I demand to know! I shall criticize her most severely and have a few very unpleasant words to say to her husband. It is completely irresponsible—" He broke off, as a new thought struck him. "I didn't hear a carriage."

"There wasn't one," Tassie replied. "We walked. And there isn't a husband, and her name is Poppy Brown, if that helps."

"I've never heard of her—what do you mean, you walked?—there are no Browns in Cardington Crescent!"

"Are there not?" Tassie was completely indifferent. There was nothing left to be saved by tact, and she was too euphoric, too weary, and too tired of being humiliated to plead.

"No, there are not," he said with mounting anger. "I know everyone, at least by repute. It is my business to know. What is this woman's name, Anastasia? And this time you had better tell me the truth, or I shall be obliged to discipline you."

"As far as I know her name is Poppy Brown," Tassie repeated. "And I never said she lived in the Crescent. She lives at least three miles from here, maybe more, in one of the slum areas. Her brother came for me, and I couldn't find the way back there alone if I wanted to."

He was stunned into silence. They stood in the guttering candlelight at the foot of the stairs like figures in a masque. Somewhere far upstairs there was movement; a junior maid had allowed a door to swing shut unattended. Everything else was so still, the sound reverberated through the vast house.

"The sooner you are married to Jack Radley, the better," Eustace said at last. "If he'll have you, which I imagine he will—he needs your money. Let him deal with you. Give you your own children to occupy you!"

Tassie's face tightened and her hand on the bannister gripped hard. "You can't do that, Papa, he may have murdered George. You wouldn't want a murderer in the family. Think of the scandal."

The blood darkened Eustace's cheeks and the candle shook in his fingers. "Nonsense!" he said too quickly. "It was Emily who killed George. Any fool can see there is a streak of madness in her family." He shot a look of loathing at Charlotte, then turned to his daughter again. "You will marry Jack Radley as soon as it can be arranged. Now go to your room!"

"If you do that, people will say I had to marry him because I was with child," she argued. "It is indecent to marry in haste—especially a man of Jack's reputation."

"You deserve to lose your standing!" he said angrily. "You'd lose it a lot further if people knew where you'd been tonight!"

She would not give in. "But I'm your daughter. My reputation will rub off on yours. And anyway, if Emily killed George, Jack is certainly implicated—at least, people will say so.''

"What people?'' He had a point, and he knew it. "No one knows of his flirtation except the family, and we are certainly not going to tell anyone. Now, do as I tell you and go to your room.''

But she stood perfectly still, except for a tremor in her hand where it gripped the bannister.

"He may not want to marry me. Emily has far more money, and she has it now. I'll only get mine when my grandmothers die.''

"I shall see that you are properly provided for,'' he countered. "And your husband. Emily doesn't count. She will be put away quietly somewhere, in a private asylum for the insane, where she can't kill anyone else.''

Her chin came up and her face was tight and frightened. "I'm going to marry Mungo Hare, whatever you say!''

For an icy moment he was speechless. Then the torrent broke.

"You are not, my girl! You are going to marry whomever I tell you! And I say you will marry Jack Radley. And if he proves unsuitable, or unwilling, then I will find someone else. But you are most certainly not going to marry that penniless young man with no family. What in heaven's name are you thinking of, child? No daughter of mine marries a curate! An archdeacon perhaps, but not a curate! And that one hasn't even any prospects. I forbid you to meet or speak to him again! I shall talk to Beamish and see that Hare does not call at this house in future, nor will you have occasion to speak with him in church. And if you do not give me your word on it, then I shall tell Beamish that Hare has made advances towards you, and he will be defrocked. Do you understand me, Anastasia?''

Tassie was so stunned she seemed to sway.

"Now, go to your room and remain there till I tell you you may come out!'' Eustace added. He swung round to Charlotte. "And you, Mrs. Pitt, may take your leave as soon as you have packed whatever belongings you have.''

"But first I would like to speak with you, Mr. March." Charlotte had one card to play, and the decision was made without hesitation. She met his eyes levelly. "We have something to discuss."

"I—" He teetered on the edge of defying her, his mouth a thin line, his cheeks purple. But his nerve failed. "Go to your room, Anastasia!" he barked furiously.

Charlotte turned to her with a brief smile. "I'll come and see you in a few minutes," she said quietly. "Don't worry."

Tassie waited a moment, her eyes wide; then, seeing something in Charlotte's face, she let go of the bannister, turned slowly, and climbed up the stairs and disappeared onto the landing.

"Well?" Eustace demanded, but his voice had a tremor, and the belligerence in his face was artificial.

Charlotte debated for an instant whether to try subtlety or to be so direct he could not possibly mistake her. She knew her limitations, and chose the latter.

"I think you should allow Tassie to continue with her work to help the poor," she said, as calmly as she could, "and marry Mr. Hare as soon as it can be arranged without seeming hasty and causing unkind remarks."

"Out of the question." He shook his head. "Quite out of the question. He has no money, no family, and no prospects."

She did not bother to argue Mungo Hare's virtues; they would weigh little with Eustace. She struck at him where he was vulnerable.

"If you do not," she said slowly and clearly, meeting his eyes, "I shall see that your affair with your son's wife becomes public property. So far it is only with the police, and although it is disgusting, it is not a crime. But if Society were aware of it, your position would be untenable. Nearly everyone will turn a blind eye to a little discreet philandering, but seducing your son's wife in your own house—over Christmas! And then continuing to force yourself on her—"

"Stop it!" The cry was dragged out of him. "Stop it!"

"The queen would not approve," she went on mercilessly. "She is rather a prudish old lady, with an obsession about virtue, especially marital virtue and family life. There would be no peerage for you if she knew this. In fact, you would be wiped off every guest list in London."

"All right!" The surrender was strangled in his throat, his eyes beseeching. "All right! She can marry the bloody curate! For God's sake don't tell anyone about Sybilla! I didn't kill her—or George. I swear it!"

"Possibly." She would give him nothing. "The police have the diary, and as long as you are guilty of no crime against the law, there is no reason why they should ever make it known. I shall ask my husband to destroy it—after the murder is solved. For William's sake, not yours."

He swallowed hard and spoke with difficulty, hating every word. "Do you give me your word?"

"I just did. Now, if you'll excuse me I would like to go to bed; it has been a very long and arduous night. And I would like to tell Tassie the good news. She will be very happy. I think she loves Mr. Hare very much. An excellent choice. I shall not see you at breakfast—I think I will have it in bed, if you will be so kind as to order it for me. But I'll see you at luncheon, and dinner."

He made a stifled sound that she took for assent.

"Good night, Mr. March."

"Ah—aaah!" he groaned.

11

While Charlotte was enjoying breakfast in bed and telling Emily about the night's events, Pitt was reexamining the address book found in Sybilla's vanity case. By late morning he and Stripe had accounted for all entries but one. They were addresses he would expect to find any Society woman making note of: relatives, mostly elderly; a number of cousins; friends—some of whom had married and moved to other parts of the country, particularly in the winter, out of the Season, others who were merely social acquaintances with whom it was advantageous to keep up some relationship; and the usual tradesmen—two dressmakers, an herbalist, a milliner, a corsetiere, a florist, a perfumer, and others in similar occupations.

The one he could not place was a Clarabelle Mapes, at 3 Tortoise Lane. The only Tortoise Lane he knew of was a grubby little street in St. Giles, hardly an area where Sybilla March would have occasion to call. Possibly it was a charity of some sort to which she gave her support, an orphanage or workhouse. It was a matter of diligence, overly fussy and probably a waste of time—his superior was certainly of that opinion and said so witheringly—but Pitt decided to call at 3 Tortoise Lane. It was just possible Mrs. Clarabelle Mapes might know something which would add to the close but still indistinguishable picture he had of the Marches.

Much of St. Giles was too narrow to ride through and he

left his cab some half mile from Tortoise Lane and walked. The buildings were mean and gray, jettied stories overhung the streets, and there was a fetor of hot air and old sewage. Spindly clerks with stovepipe hats and shiny trousers hurried by clutching papers. A screever, wire-rimmed spectacles on his nose, shuffled aside to allow Pitt to pass. The sun was beating down from a flat, windless sky, and there was smoke strong in the air.

A one-legged man on a crutch hawked matches, a youth held a tray of bootlaces, a girl offered tiny homemade childrens' clothes. Pitt bought something from her. It was too small for his own children, but he could not bear the pain of passing her by, even though he knew dozens would—if not today, then tomorrow—and there was nothing anyone could do about it.

A coster pushed a barrow of vegetables down the middle of the street, the wheels jiggling noisily over the cobbles. The girl went to him immediately and spent all the few coins Pitt had given her, disappearing with the vegetables in her apron.

Had Eustace March really murdered George to keep secret his affair with his daughter-in-law, and then murdered her when she realized his guilt? He would like to have believed it. Almost everything about Eustace offended him; his complacence, his willing blindness to other people's need or pain, his unctuous overbearing manner, his virility and dynastic pride. But perhaps he was not wildly untypical of many socially ambitious patriarchs possessed of vigor and money. He was self-absorbed, insensitive rather than deliberately malicious. Most of the time he was convinced he was totally in the right about everything that mattered, and a lot that did not. Pitt had no awareness of a violence or fear in him that would drive him to commit a double murder, least of all in his own house.

Then there was Charlotte's lurid story of Tassie creeping up the stairs splattered with blood. And in spite of her protestations, he was still not absolutely sure she had not walked in a nightmare—the whole idea was so absurd. Perhaps in the faint gaslight of the night lamps, ordinary water splashed on a dress, or even wine, might have looked to a frightened imagination like blood. Above all, there was no one who had been stabbed. Except, of course, the horrific murder in Bloomsbury—but there was no reason to believe that had any connection with Cardington Crescent.

The other possibility, occurring to him even as he walked along the miserable streets towards Tortoise Lane, was that this Clarabelle Mapes was an abortionist, and Sybilla had procured her address for Tassie—that it was after a hasty, ill-done operation that Charlotte had seen Tassie's return in the night. And what she had mistaken for a look of joy had in fact been a grimace of pain, mixed with intense relief at being safe, back in her own house and relieved of an intolerable disgrace.

It was an unpleasant thought, and he hoped with surprising depth that this was not true. But he knew the frailties of nature well enough to accept that it was not impossible.

The other answer stemmed from George's affair with Sybilla—William as the wounded husband, in spite of Eustace's claim that he had wanted to divorce Sybilla until he knew of the child. But Pitt did not believe William March would have killed his unborn child, no matter how furious he was at his wife's infidelity. And Pitt did not yet know how far that had gone. It could have been no more than vanity and a stupid exhibition of power.

Or was the child Eustace's, and not William's at all?

No. If that were so and William knew it, surely he would have killed Eustace, not George, and perhaps felt himself justified. And there would certainly be many who, whatever their public pronouncements, would privately agree with him.

And the pregnancy predated George's arrival at Cardington Crescent, so he could not be blamed by anyone.

That left Emily and Jack Radley. They might have acted

either together or separately, for love, or greed—or both. Emily he refused to think of until there was no other possibility and it was forced upon him; and if that happened, please God Charlotte would know it for herself and he would not have to be the one to tell her.

He turned the last corner and was in Tortoise Lane. It was as shabby and squalid as the others, indistinguishable except to those who understood the labyrinth and could smell and taste in the thick air their own familiar row of crooked jetties and angled roofs. There were two grubby children of about four or five years playing with stones outside number 3. Pitt stopped and watched them for a moment. They had scratched a pattern of squares on the pavement, including about ten of the slabs, and were skidding the marker stone to a chosen one, then doing an elaborate little dance in and out of the squares, bending gracelessly on one leg to pick up the stone when they were finished.

"Do you know the lady in there?" Pitt pointed to the door of number 3.

They looked at him with confusion. "Which lady?" the bigger one asked.

"Are there a lot of ladies?"

"Yeah."

"Do you know Mrs. Mapes?"

"Mrs. Mapes," the child said soberly. "Course we do!"

"Do you live in there?" Pitt was surprised. He had already half decided it was an abortionist, and children did not fit his preconception.

"Yeah." The older child answered; the smaller child was pulling at his sleeve, frightened, and Pitt did not want to get them into trouble for the crumb of information they might be able to give him.

"Thank you." He smiled, touched the child's matted hair, and went up to the door. He knocked gently, afraid that a peremptory rap would sound like authority and perhaps elicit no answer, or at best put them on their guard.

It was opened after a very few moments by a small, thin girl who might have been anywhere between twelve and twenty. She was wearing a brown stuff dress, taken in from several sizes larger, a mobcap that held back no more than half her hair, and an outsize apron. Her hands were wet and she carried a kitchen knife. Obviously Pitt had disturbed her at her chores.

"Yeah?" she said with a lift of surprise, her eyes washed-out china blue, already tired.

"Is Mrs. Mapes at home?" Pitt inquired.

"Yeah!" The girl swallowed, put the knife in her pocket, and wiped her hands on her apron. "Yer'd better come in." Turning, she led the way through a dark, rush-matted corridor, past narrow stairs on which sat a child of about seven, nursing a baby and holding by the hand an infant just old enough to stand. But large families were common; what was less so was that so many within a few years of each other should have survived. Infant mortality was enormous.

The girl knocked on the last door, at the very end of the passage before it turned towards the huge kitchens he could see a dozen yards away.

"Come!" a throaty voice called from inside.

"Thank you." Pitt dismissed the girl and pulled on the handle. It opened easily and soundlessly into a sitting room that was almost a parody of old Mrs. March's boudoir. It was doubly startling for its contrast with the threadbare outside and the other rooms Pitt had glimpsed as he passed, and for its joke of familiarity.

The windows looked onto the blind walls of an alley rather than the March's gracious garden, but it was curtained in a similar hectic pink, faded even by this mean and dirt-filtered light. Probably the curtains had hung unmoved for years. The mantel was draped as well, although in smarter houses fashion had freed the beauty of fine wood or stone from such ornate and destructive prudery. A piano was similarly covered, and every table was bristling with photographs. Lamp shades were fringed and knotted and plastered with mottoes; Home, Sweet Home, God Sees All, and I Love You, Mother.

Seated on the largest pink armchair was a woman of ample, fiercely corseted bosom and prodigious hips, swathed with a dress that on a woman half the size would really have been quite handsome. She had stubby, fat hands with strong fingers, and on seeing Pitt they flew to her face in a gesture of surprise. Her black hair was thick, her black eyes large and shining, her nose and mouth predatory.

"Mrs. Mapes?" Pitt asked civilly.

She waved him to the pink sofa opposite her, the seat worn where countless others had sat.

"That's me," she agreed. "An' 'oo are you, sir?"

"Thomas Pitt, ma'am." He did not yet intend to tell her his office. Policemen were not welcome in places like St. Giles, and if she had some illegal occupation then she would do everything to hide it, probably successfully. He was in hostile territory, and he knew it.

She regarded him with an experienced eye, seeing immediately that he had little money; his shirt was ordinary and far from new, his boots were mended. But his jacket, in spite of its worn elbows and cuffs, had originally been of fine cut, and his speech was excellent. He had taken his lessons with the son of the estate on which his father worked and never lost the timbre or the diction. She summed him up as a gentleman on hard times, but still considerably better off than herself, and perhaps with prospects.

"Well, Mr. Pitt, wot can I do for yer? This ain't where you live, so wot you 'ere for?"

"I was given your address by a Mrs. Sybilla March."

Her black eyes narrowed. "Was yer now? Well, Mr. Pitt, me business is confidential, like. I'm sure yer understands that."

"I take it for granted, Mrs. Mapes." He was hoping that if he continued he would learn something from her, however tenuous, that he might pursue. Even a clue as to Mrs. Mapes's occupation might yield something about Sybilla he had not known. At least she had not denied the acquaintance.

"Course yer do!" she agreed heartily. "Or yer wouldn't be 'ere yerself, eh?" She laughed, a rich gurgle in her throat, and looked at him archly.

Pitt could not remember ever having been quite so revolted. He forced an answering smile that must have been sickly.

" 'Ave a cup o'tea, wiv a drop o' suffin?" she invited. " 'Ere!" She reached for a grubby bellpull. "I could do wiv one meself. An' it's only perlite ter keep yer company."

Pitt had not had time to decline when the door opened and yet another girl peered round, eyes wide, face gaunt. This one might have been fifteen.

"Yes, Mrs. Mapes, ma'am?"

"Get me a cup o' tea, Dora," Mrs. Mapes ordered. "An' you make sure Florrie is doin' the pertaters fer supper."

"Yes, Mrs. Mapes, ma'am."

"An' bring the good pot!" Mrs. Mapes called after her, then turned back to smile at Pitt. "Now wot's yer business, Mr. Pitt? Yer can trust me. I'm the soul o' discretion." She held her finger up to her nose. "Clarabelle Mapes 'ears ev'rythin' an' tells nuffin'."

He knew already that if he had hoped to trick her or intimidate her he was foredoomed to failure. She was one of life's survivors—a venturer, not a victim. Behind all the thrusting flesh and the curls and smiles she was as careful as a miser and suspicious as a dog in strange territory. He decided to appeal to her greed and at the same time see what effect surprise might have on her. Guilt he did not imagine, but there was a measure of fear deeper than mere caution that would have meaning to her.

"I'm afraid Mrs. March is dead," he said watching her closely.

But her face did not alter by a shadow or hairsbreadth of movement. "Wot a shame," she said expressionlessly, her black eyes meeting his squarely. "I 'ope as it wasn't in pain, poor thing."

"She didn't go easily," he parried.

But there was not a tremor in her. "Not many of us do." She shook her head, and the black curls bounced. "Very civil of you ter tell me, Mr. Pitt."

He pressed on. "There'll be a postmortem."

"Will there? An' wot's that?"

"The doctors will examine her body to decide exactly why she died. Cut her open if necessary." He locked his eyes on hers, trying to see inside her, to get beyond the gross, shining exterior—and failed.

" 'Ow disgustin'," she said without flinching. Her sharp, curved nose wrinkled a little but the distaste was assumed; she had seen infinitely worse—anyone who lived in St. Giles had. "Wouldn't yer think doctors'd 'ave suffin better ter do than cut up someone as is already dead? Can't 'elp 'er now, poor thing. Be better ter doctor them as is livin'—not that that's a lot o' use, often as not."

Pitt felt he was losing ground rapidly.

"They have to," he plunged on. "Something of a mystery about her death." That was literally true, even if the implication was not.

"Often is." She nodded again, and there was a rap on the door, followed by yet another girl, of about ten, bringing the awaited tea on a painted lacquer tray, chipped in several places. But in pride of place was a silver teapot, which from his experience on robbery detail Pitt judged to be genuine Georgian. The child staggered awkwardly under its weight, her spindly arms shaking. Even as she left again her eyes were fixed hopelessly on the currant cakes on the china plate.

" 'Ave a drop o' suffin ter refresh yer?" Mrs. Mapes offered when the door was closed, and fished in a cupboard beside her, twisting her huge bulk in the chair till it creaked. She brought up an unmarked green glass bottle from which she poured what from the smell could only be gin.

Pitt refused quickly. "No, thank you. Too early. I'll just have the tea."

"Often is a mystery, death," she said, finishing her

previous train of thought. "Please yerself, Mr. Pitt." And she poured a generous dollop into her own cup before adding tea, milk, and sugar. She passed a good-quality china cup across to Pitt and invited him to help himself as he wished. "But only the rich as gets doctors ter cut them up afterwards. Stupid, I calls it! As if slicin' up corpuses is goin' ter tell anyone the secrets o' life an' death!"

He gave up on the postmortem. Obviously it did not frighten her, and he was beginning to believe she had no hand in any abortion that could be traced to the March household. And yet Sybilla had kept her address, and there was no conceivable possibility of it being a social acquaintance. What did this fearsome woman do to provide for herself?

He glanced round the room. By St. Giles standards it was comfortable bordering on luxurious, and Mrs. Mapes herself all too clearly ate well. But the children he had seen looked half starved and were dressed in shabby hand-me-down clothes, ill-fitting and iller kept.

"You set a good table, Mrs. Mapes," he began cautiously. "Mr. Mapes is a fortunate man."

"There ain't no Mr. Mapes these ten years." She looked at him with brightening eyes. Then she caught sight of the neat mending on his jacket sleeves and breathed in sharply, pinching her nostrils. That was a wife's work, if ever she saw it. "Died o' the flux, 'e did. But 'e thought well o' me when 'e was 'ere."

"My mistake," Pitt said immediately. "I thought with all the children . . ."

Her eyes were hard and her hand tightened very slightly in her fat lap.

"I'm a soft'earted woman, Mr. Pitt," she said with a guarded smile. "Takes in all sorts to care fer 'em, when they ain't got nobody. Looks after 'em fer neighbors an' cousins an' the like. Always carin' fer somebody, I am. All Tortoise Lane'll tell yer that, if they're honest."

"How commendable." Pitt could not keep all the sarcasm out of his voice, although he tried; he was far from finished with Mrs. Mapes. There was the beginning of an ugly idea in his mind. "Mr. Mapes must have left you very well provided for that you have the means and the time to be so charitable."

Her chin came up, and her smile widened, showing hard, yellow-white teeth. "That's right, Mr. Pitt," she agreed. "Thought the world o' me, did Mr. Mapes."

Pitt put down his cup and remained silent for a moment, unable to think of another line of attack. She was no longer afraid and he could see it in every curve of her strong, bulging body. He could smell it in the hot air.

"Good o' yer ter come all this way ter tell me o' Mrs. March's death, Mr. Pitt." She was preparing to dismiss him. Time was short; he had no cause to search the premises, and what was he to look for even if he returned with men and a warrant?

Then a lie occurred to him that might work. Forget her fear, try the paramount urge in her character—greed.

"No more than my duty, Mrs. Mapes," he replied with only the barest faltering. Please heaven the Metropolitan Police would honor the debt he was about to contract. "Mrs. March remembered you in her will, for—services rendered. You would be that Clarabelle Mapes, wouldn't you?"

The caution fighting avarice in her face was grotesquely comical, and he waited without interruption while she sought a compromise with herself. She let out her breath in a huge, gusty sigh. Her eyes gleamed.

"Very good of 'er, I'm sure."

"You are the right person?" he persisted. "You performed some service for her?"

But she was not outmaneuvered so easily—she had already seen that trap. "Private," she said, staring at him boldly. "Between ladies, as I'm sure yer'll unnerstand, and not pry, as would be indelicate."

He allowed a look of doubt to cross his face. "I have a responsibility—"

"Yer got my haddress, or yer wouldn't be 'ere," she pointed out. "There ain't no Clarabelle Mapes 'ere but me.

I gotta be the right one, ain't I? An' I can prove 'oo I am, never you fear. Wot I done forrer ain't none o' your business. Mighta bin no more'n a kind word when she needed it.''

"In Tortoise Lane?" Pitt smiled back dourly.

"I ain't always bin in Tortoise Lane," she said, instantly regretting it. She knew she had made a mistake, and it was marked in the sudden slackness in her face, an alteration in the way she sat. "I goes out sometimes!" she said, trying to make good the damage.

"Not to Cardington Crescent, you don't." His confidence was growing, although he still had no idea towards what end. "And you've been here for some time." He looked about him. "Certainly since she wrote to you. As you pointed out, she had this house in her address book."

This time she really did pale; the color blanched from her predatory face leaving the rouge standing on her cheeks, the spot on the left cheek an inch higher than the spot on the right. She said nothing.

Pitt stood up. "I'll see the rest of the house," he announced, and went to the door before she could stop him. He opened it and went out into the dogleg of the passage, walking swiftly towards the kitchens, away from the front door. One of the girls he had seen before was on her hands and knees on the floor with a bucket of water and a brush. She moved out of the way for him.

The kitchen itself was enormous for a house of this size, two rooms knocked into one, either deliberately or by a rotten wall collapsing and being removed. The floor was wooden, scrubbed till the planks were worn uneven, nails in little islands humped above, grit driven into the cracks. Two large stoves were covered with a variety of cauldrons, and one kettle spouted steam, presumably to refresh Mrs. Mapes's teapot. Beside the stoves were scuttles of coal dust and coke refuse, close enough for the spindly-armed girls to lift them and restoke. By the far wall sank sacks of grain and potatoes and a bundle of grubby cabbages. Opposite was a huge dresser decked with dishes and pans and mugs, drawers ill-fitting, papers poking out. A ball of string, partly unwound, lay on the floor. There was a half wrapped parcel on the kitchen table, and a pair of scissors. Above them, winched to the ceiling, was an airing rail, hung with all manner of ragged clothes and linen collecting the kitchen smells.

There were three more girls working at various chores; one at the sink peeling potatoes, one stirring a cauldron of gruel on the stove, the third on her hands and knees with a dustpan. None of them could have been more than fourteen—the youngest looked more like ten or eleven. Obviously the establishment was intended to cater to a considerable number of people on a regular basis.

"How many more are there of you?" he asked before Mrs. Mapes could catch up with him. He could hear her skirt swishing and rattling behind him.

"I dunno," a white-faced girl whispered. "There's all them little ones, the babes. They comes and goes, so I dunno."

"Shush!" the oldest warned fiercely, her eyes black with fear.

Pitt did all he could to keep his expression from betraying him. Now he knew what this place was, but he was helpless to change it. And if he showed his fury, pity, or disgust, he would only make it worse. Nature fueled the need and poverty necessitated the answer.

"What do yer want in 'ere, Mr. Pitt?" Mrs. Mapes demanded from behind him, her voice shrill. "Ain't nothin' 'ere as 'as ter do wiv you!"

"No, nothing at all," he agreed grimly, without moving. There was no point at which he could even begin, let alone accomplish anything. He would do more harm by starting, and yet he was loath to leave.

" 'Ow much?" she asked.

"What?" He had no idea what she was talking about. His eyes roamed over the cauldrons: gruel, easy and cheap for the children, potatoes to fill out a stew with no meat.

" 'Ow much did Mrs. March remember me wiv?" she said impatiently. "You said as she remembered me!"

He looked at the floor and the large wooden table. They were unusually clean—that at least was something in her favor. "I don't know. I expect it will be sent to you." It would depend on what he could persuade out of his superiors. He might even forget it altogether.

"Ain't you got it?"

He did not answer. If he did he would have no excuse to remain, and there was something at the back of his mind that held him here, a sense that there was meaning, if only he could find it.

What could Sybilla March possibly have wanted with this woman? A child taken for a maidservant in trouble? It seemed the only reasonable thing. Was it worth pursuing, following to Sybilla's house and seeing if any maid there had been unaccountably absent, perhaps due to a confinement? Did it matter? Life was full of such domestic tragedies, girls who had to earn their livings and could not afford to keep a child born out of wedlock. And servants hardly ever married, precisely for that reason; they lived in their masters' houses, where there was no room for families.

Mrs. Mapes's voice grated behind him. "Then yer'd best be abaht yer business, an' leave me ter mine!"

He turned slowly, looking over the room for a last time. Then he realized what it was that held him: the parcel—the brown paper parcel on the kitchen table, half tied, next to the scissors. He had seen that paper, that curious yellow string before, tied lengthways and widthways twice, knotted at each join and tied with a loop and two raw ends. Suddenly he was ice cold, as if a breath from a charnel house had crawled over his skin. He remembered the blood and the flies, the fat woman with her bustle crooked and her bulging-eyed dog. It was too much to be a coincidence. The paper was common, but the string was unusual, the knots eccentric, characteristic, the combination surely unique. They were at least a mile and a half from Bloomsbury. What of this small parcel wrapped in the off cuts? Where was the first parcel, the larger one? He could see it nowhere in the kitchen.

"I'm going," he said aloud, surprised by the sound of his own voice. "Yes, Mrs. Mapes, I'll bring the money myself, now that I know it's you."

"When?" She smiled again, oblivious of the parcel on the table and its knots. "I wanter make sure as I'm in, like," she added in explanation, as if it could mask her eagerness.

"Tomorrow," he replied. "Sooner, if I get back to my offices in time." He must get one of these children alone and ask them about the parcels—where they went to, how often, and who carried them. But it must be away from here, where she could not overhear, or the child's life would be imperiled. "Have you got someone reliable who'll deliver a message for me, someone you trust yourself?" he asked.

She weighed the advantages against the disadvantages and decided in his favor.

"I got Nellie, she'll do it fer yer," she said grudgingly. "Wot is it?"

"Confidential," he answered. "I'll tell her outside. Then I'll be back as soon as I can. You may rest assured of that, Mrs. Mapes."

"Nellie!" she shrieked at the full power of her lungs; the blast of it shivered the china on the dresser.

There was a moment's silence, then the wail of a wakened baby somewhere upstairs, a clatter of feet, and Nellie appeared at the doorway, hair straggling, apron awry, eyes frightened. "Yes, Mrs. Mapes, ma'am?"

"Go wiv vis gennelman and do 'is errand fer 'im," Mrs. Mapes ordered. "Then come back 'ere an' get on wiv yer work. There's no food in this life fer them as does no work."

"No, Mrs. Mapes, ma'am." Nellie bobbed a half curtsy and turned to Pitt. She must have been about fifteen, although she was so thin and underdeveloped it was hard to be sure.

"Thank you, Mrs. Mapes," Pitt said, hating her as he had hated few people in his life, aware that perhaps it was only a vent for his rage against poverty itself. She was a creature of her time and place. Should he hate her for surviving? Those who died did so only because they had not her strength. And yet he still hated her.

He went past her to the corridor, along its dank, rush-matted thinness past the children still sitting on the stairs, and out of the front room into Tortoise Lane, Nellie a step behind him. He walked till he was round the corner and out of sight of number 3.

"Wot's yer errand, mister?" Nellie asked when they stopped.

"Do you often run errands for Mrs. Mapes?"

"Yes, mister. Yer can trust me. I knows me way round 'ere."

"Good. Do you take parcels for her?"

"Yes. An' I ain't never lost one. Yer can trust me, mister."

"I do trust you, Nellie," he said gently, wishing to God he could do something about her and knowing he could not. If he did, it would be misunderstood, and probably frighten and confuse her. "Did you take the big parcel from the kitchen table?"

Her eyes widened. "Mrs. Mapes told me ter, honest!"

"I'm sure she did," he said quickly. "Did you take several parcels for her about three weeks ago?"

"I ain't done nuffin wrong mister. I jus' took 'em where she said!" Now she was beginning to be frightened; his questions made no sense to her.

"I know that, Nellie," he said quietly. "Where was that? Around here, and in Bloomsbury?"

Her eyes widened. "No, mister. I took 'em to Mr. Wigge—like always."

He let out his breath slowly. "Then take me to Mr. Wigge, Nellie. Take me there now."

12

Nellie led Pitt through a maze of cramped alleys and steps till they came to a small, squalid yard stacked with old furniture—much of it mildewed and worm-eaten—bits and pieces of old crockery, and scraps of fabric that not even the ragpickers would have bothered with. At the far side, beyond the ill-balanced piles and heaps, was the entrance down to a large cellar.

"This is w'ere I brung 'em," Nellie said, looking up at Pitt anxiously. "I swear it, mister."

"Who did you give them to?" he asked, staring round and seeing no one.

"Mr. Wigge." She pointed to the steps down to the dark, gaping cellar.

"Come and show me," he requested, "please."

Reluctantly she picked her way through the rubbish to the edge of the stair, descending slowly. At the bottom she turned and knocked on the wooden door which stood open on rusted hinges. Her hands made hardly any sound.

"Mr. Wigge? Sir?"

A scrawny old man appeared almost immediately, clad in a filthy jacket, pockets torn by the weight of the junk he had piled in them over the years, trousers splashed with all manner of ordure. He wore fingerless mittens on his hands in spite of the warmth of the day, and on his thin, uncut hair was a shiny black stovepipe hat, completely unmarked. It might have left the hatter's shop an hour since.

His lantern-jawed face split in an anticipatory leer, and he squinted up at Pitt.

"Mr. Wigge?" Pitt inquired.

The old man bowed jerkily; it was an affectation of gentility he liked. "Septimus Wigge at your service, sir. 'Ow may I 'elp yer? I got a lovely brass bedstead. I got a dancin' lady in real porcelain."

"I'll come in and take a look." Pitt had a premonition of disappointment. If Clarabelle Mapes had simply been selling off household goods, her own or others', to raise a little money, it was not worth pusuing. And yet the knots had been peculiar, identical to those on that terrible parcel in the churchyard and all the others.

What should he do about Nellie? If he sent her back to Tortoise Lane would she tell Mrs. Mapes what he had asked her, and where she had taken him? He did not hold much hope that she would hold out against Mrs. Mapes's inquisition if she were suspicious. Nellie lived in a cocoon of hunger and fear.

And yet if he kept her with him, what could he do with her? Tortoise Lane was her home—probably all she knew. He had already committed her. She knew about the parcels, and if Clarabelle Mapes had tied those bloody and dreadful ones as well as the innocent one, Nellie's life was imperiled if she returned and told how she had led Pitt to Septimus Wigge. He had to keep her.

"Nellie, come in with me and help me look."

"I daren't, mister." She shook her head. "I got chores. I'll be in trouble if I don't get 'ome in time. Mrs. Mapes'll be that cross wi' me."

"Not if you go back with the money from Mrs. March," he argued. "She's in a hurry for that."

Nellie looked doubtful. She was more afraid of the immediate than the problematical; her imagination did not stretch that far.

Pitt did not have time to argue. She was used to obedience.

"It's an order, Nellie," he said briskly. "You stay with

me. Mrs. Mapes will be angry if her money is delayed."
He turned to the waiting man. "Now, Mr. Wigge, I'll take
a look at these brass beds of yours."

"Very reasonable, sir, very reasonable." Wigge turned
and led the way inside the cellar. It was larger than Pitt
had expected, higher-ceilinged and stretching back into the
recesses of the building. Against one wall there was a
large furnace with a metal door hanging open sending heat
out into the stone spaces, and in spite of the mildness of
the day, its warmth was agreeable under the ground level,
where there was no sunlight.

The old man showed him several fine brass bedsteads, a
few pieces of quite good china, and several other odds and
ends in which Pitt affected to be interested, all the time
peering and searching, finding nothing beyond what might
or might not be stolen goods. But while haggling with him
over a small green glass vase he eventually bought for
Charlotte, he did make a very close observation of Mr.
Septimus Wigge himself. By the time he left, still followed by Nellie, he could have described Mr. Wigge so
closely an artist could have drawn him from the soles of
his appalling boots up to the crown of his immaculate hat,
and every feature of his smirking face.

He took his leave, holding the vase, taking Nellie with
him. He had no choice. He must forget about Sybilla,
whose connection with Clarabelle Mapes he could not
understand and very probably was coincidental and had
nothing to do with her murder. He must go back to the
Bloomsbury churchyard, now that he knew who he was
looking for, and try all the residents and habitués to see if
even one of them could place Septimus Wigge there three
weeks ago. It could be a long task.

First he must find a safe place to leave Nellie, where
Mrs. Mapes would not discover her. It was after two, and
they had not eaten.

"Are you hungry, Nellie?" He asked only out of politeness; from the child's hollow eyes and the sunken,
slack quality of her flesh he knew she was always hungry.

"Yes, mister." She did not sound surprised that he should ask; she obviously believed him sufficiently eccentric to do anything.

"So am I. Let's have luncheon."

"I ain't got nuffin." This time she looked at him anxiously.

"You've been a great help to me, Nellie, I think you've earned luncheon." She was fifteen, quite old enough to understand patronage, and she did not deserve it. She had little enough dignity and he was determined not to seduce that from her. Nor would he question her yet about the house in Tortoise Lane. He knew what it was; he did not need to lead her into betraying it. "I know a very good public house where they'll give us fresh bread and cold meat and pickle and pudding."

She did not yet believe it. "Thank you, mister," she said, her expression unchanged.

The pub he had in mind was only half a mile away, and they walked to it in silence, quite companionable for his part. As soon as he went in, the landlord recognized him. He was a moderately law-abiding citizen, most of the time, and that area of his business which was questionable Pitt left alone. It was to do with game bought from poachers, the occasional avoidance of excise taxes on tobacco and similar goods, and a great deal of judicious blindness. Pitt was concerned with murder.

"Afternoon, Mr. Tibbs," he said cheerfully.

"Afternoon, Mr. Pitt, sir." Tibbs came hurrying towards him, wiping his hands on the sides of his trousers, eager to keep on the right side of the law. "Luncheon for yer, Mr. Pitt, sir? Got a luvly piece o' mutton—or a good Cheshire, or a Double Gloucester? An' me best pickle, Mrs. Tibbs's own, put it up last summer an' it's proper tasty. What'll it be?"

"Mutton, Mr. Tibbs," Pitt replied. "For me and the lady. And a jar of ale each. And then pudding. And Tibbs, there are some very unpleasant people who might come looking for the lady, to do her harm. I'd like you to keep her safe for a while. She's a good little worker, when she's fed. Find her a place out of sight in your kitchens. She can sleep by the stove. It won't be for long, unless you decide to keep her. She'll earn her way.

Tibbs looked doubtfully at Nellie's skinny little body and pinched face. "Wot's she done?" he asked, giving Pitt a narrow look.

"Seen something she shouldn't," Pitt replied immediately.

"All right," Tibbs said reluctantly. "But you'll answer fer anythin' she takes, Mr. Pitt."

"You feed her properly and don't beat her," Pitt agreed, "and I'll answer for her honesty. And if I don't find her here when I come back for her, you'll answer with a lot more than money. Are we understood?"

"It's a favor I'm doin' yer, Mr. Pitt." Tibbs wanted to make sure he was laying up future repayment.

"It is," Pitt conceded. "I don't forget much, Mr. Tibbs— good or bad."

"I'll get yer mutton." Tibbs disappeared, satisfied.

Pitt and Nellie sat down at one of the small tables, he with relief, she gingerly, still confused.

"Why yer talkin' abaht me wiv 'im fer?" she asked, screwing up her face and staring at him, a trace of fear in her eyes.

"Because I'm going to leave you here to work in his kitchen," he answered. "You're not safe in Tortoise Lane till I've finished learning what I have to."

"Mrs. Mapes'll turn me aht!" She was really frightened now. "I'll 'ave nowhere ter go!"

"You can stay here." He leaned forward. "Nellie, you've learned something you shouldn't. I'm a policeman, a rozzer. Do you know what happens to people who know secrets they shouldn't?"

She nodded silently. She knew. They vanished. She had lived fifteen years in St. Giles; she understood the laws of survival very well.

"You a rozzer, honest? You ain't got no cape ner 'elmet, ner one o' them little lights."

"I used to have. Now I only deal with big, important crimes, and I have some of the rozzers with helmets to work for me."

Tibbs brought their food himself: crusty bread, thick slices of cold saddle of mutton and rich, dark pickle, two mugs of ale, and two portions of spotted Dick—steamed pudding thick with currants. Nellie was speechless when a full half of it was placed in front of her. Pitt only hoped she would not be sick with the unaccustomed wealth of it. He might have been wiser to give her shrunken stomach a little at first, but there was no time, and he was hungry himself.

"Eat as much as you want," he said graciously. "But don't feel you have to finish it. There'll be more tonight, and tomorrow."

Nellie simply stared at him.

He collected a constable from the local beat and co-opted him into going from one door to another yet again. All afternoon they worked the areas within five hundred yards of where the hideous parcels had been found—first in the approaches to the Bloomsbury churchyard, then closer to the outskirts of St. Giles, where the later discoveries were made. He had given the constable a precise description of Septimus Wigge, both his person and the clothes he had seen him wearing in his cellar storehouse.

By six o'clock in the evening they met again at the churchyard gate.

"Well?" Pitt asked, although the answer mattered little; he already had what he needed. He had been too impatient, too angry, to be subtle. But in spite of his unusual clumsiness he had found a footman who had been up early returning from an assignation and had seen a scraggy, lantern-jawed old man in a stovepipe hat a hundred yards from the church, hurrying along, pushing a small handcart with one fairly large parcel in it. He had not mentioned it at the time of the torso's discovery because he did not wish to admit being out; it would almost certainly mean his dismissal from his position, and he had thought the old man merely a peddlar, probably with something stolen, to be about at such an hour. It was too early even for costers in from the outlying districts with vegetables, or up from the docks or the river with winkles, eels, or other such delicacies.

But Pitt had bullied him into believing that to hide such knowledge now would make him accomplice to the murder, and that was infinitely worse than losing a position over a bit of flirtation with a housemaid a mile away.

And he had also chanced on a prostitute further toward St. Giles, where one of the gruesome parcels, a leg, had been found. Now that he could describe Septimus Wigge so precisely he knew what to ask, and, after several girls, he came upon one who had seen him with his handcart. She remembered the fine stovepipe hat, its sheen gleaming in the moonlight as he turned the corner. She had noticed it then but not considered the three paper-and-string-wrapped parcels in his cart.

And there had been others—men he would not like to call to a witness stand, but nonetheless all helping to seal the certainty: a squint-eyed little fence who had been keeping an eye open for dealers, a pimp in a knife fight over one of his whores, and a burglar busy star-glazing a window to break into a house.

"Two," the constable answered. He was good at his job and knew the crime, but he had not Pitt's anger and had been more circumspect in his threats. He looked disappointed, feeling he had let down his superior. "Not much use in court. A rat-faced little magsman coming home after a night cheating at cards, and a twelve-year-old snakesman, thin as a wire, on his way to climb in through someone's back windows and let his master in. I know where to find them both again."

"What did they see?" Pitt was not disconcerted; no citizen would be about respectable business at that time of night in St. Giles, except perhaps a priest or a midwife, and the first was little wished for, the second little afforded. God knew how many children died at the moment of birth through dirt and ignorance, and their mothers with them.

"A spindly old man with scruffy hair under a shiny stovepipe hat, wheeling a handcart and hurrying," the constable answered. "The snakesman certainly saw him coming out of the alley where the head was found."

"Good. Then we'll go and arrest Septimus Wigge," Pitt replied decisively.

"But we can't call them to a court!" the constable protested, running a step or two to keep up with him. "No judge in London will take their word."

"Won't need to," Pitt replied. "I don't think Wigge killed the woman, he simply disposed of the parcels. If we arrest him and frighten the living daylights out of him, he'll tell us who did—although I'm pretty sure I know. But I want him to swear it."

The constable understood little of what Pitt was referring to, but he was satisfied if Pitt was. They strode rapidly along the narrow, refuse-strewn streets past sweatshops, tenements, and huddles of collapsing houses. Beggars stood idle or sat in doorways; children labored in endless dreary jobs, picking rags, running errands, stealing from pockets or barrows; women begged, toiled, and drank.

Pitt made only one wrong turn before finding Septimus Wigge's cellar again, with its piles of junk and its furnace. He told the constable to wait out of sight while he made sure the old man was in, and that there was no back way out for him to escape, through a warren of passages heaven knew where.

He walked smartly across the yard and down the steps, keeping as quiet as he could. He came upon the old man going through a box of spoons, his head bent to pore over them, a huge smile on his face.

"Glad to find you in, Mr. Wigge," Pitt said softly, waiting till he was within a yard before he spoke.

Wigge jerked up, startled and amazed until he saw it was a customer. His face ironed out and he smiled with brown, irregular teeth, more missing than present.

"Well, sir, an' wot can I do for yer this time? I got some luvly siller spoons 'ere."

"I daresay, but I don't want them at the moment." He moved to stand between Wigge and the back of the shop; the constable should be at the top of the steps and would prevent escape that way.

"Wotcher want then? I got all kinds o' fings."

"Have you got any brown paper parcels with bits of a woman's body in them?"

Wigge's face went slack, bloodless with terror, so the gray dirt stood out on it in smears. He tried to speak and his voice failed. His throat contracted, his larynx bobbed up and down. He gulped, choked, and gulped again. The smell of sweat was strong in the close, hot air.

"That ain't f-funny!" he said hoarsely, trying desperately to control the panic racing through him. "It ain't f-funny at all!"

"I know," Pitt agreed, "I found one of them. The upper half of the torso, to be precise. Soaked with blood. Did you have a mother, Mr. Wigge?"

Wigge wanted to take offense, but the power did not reach his lips.

"Course I did!" he said wretchedly. "No call f-fer . . . I . . ." He subsided, staring at Pitt in mesmerized horror.

"She had a child," Pitt answered, gripping his skinny shoulder. "That woman whose body you hacked to pieces and dropped around."

"I didn't!" Wigge wriggled under Pitt's hand and his voice rose so high and shrill it was painful to hear. "Swelpme Gawd I didn't! You gotta b'lieve me, I didn't kill 'er!"

"I don't believe you," Pitt lied badly. "If you didn't kill her you wouldn't have cut her up and distributed her round half of London."

"I didn't kill 'er! She were already dead, I swear!" Wigge was so terrified Pitt was afraid he might have a seizure and pass out altogether, even die. He modified his expression to one of dawning interest.

"Come on, Wigge. If she was dead and you didn't kill her, why would you slash her to bits and wrap her up, and put the parcels round in the middle of the night? And don't try to deny that—we've got at least seven people who saw you and will swear to it. Took us a little while, but we've got them now. I can arrest you this minute and take you to Newgate, or Coldbath Fields."

"No!" The little man shrieked and squirmed, glaring up at Pitt with a mixture of fury and impotence. "I'm an old man!—them places'd kill me! There ain't no decent food, an' the jail fever'd kill me, it would."

"Maybe," Pitt said dispassionately. "But they'll probably top you before that. You don't always get jail fever immediately, it's only a few weeks before a hanging."

"Gawd 'elp me, I didn't kill 'er!"

"So why did you cut up the body and get rid of it?" Pitt persisted.

"I didn't!" he squealed. "I didn't cut 'er up! She come that way, I swear ter Gawd!"

"Why did you put her all round Bloomsbury and St. Giles?" Pitt glanced at the furnace. "Why didn't you burn her? You must have known we'd find her. In a churchyard! Really, Wigge. Not very clever."

"Course I knew yer'd find 'er, yer fool!" A shadow of his old contempt came back, quickly erased by the terror crawling in his belly. "But adult bones don't burn away— not even in an 'ole 'ouse afire, let alone a furnace like mine."

Pitt felt sick. "But infant bones do, of course," he said very quietly. He gripped Wigge's shoulder so hard he could feel the scrawny flesh crumple under his hands and the hard, flat old bones grind together underneath, but Wigge was too terrified to scream.

Wigge nodded. "I never took a live one, I swear ter Gawd! I just got rid o' them as 'ad died, poor little things."

"Suffocated. Or starved." Pitt looked at him as one might the germs of some disease.

"I dunno, I just done it fer a favor. I'm innocent!"

"The word's a blasphemy from you." Pitt shook him till his feet lifted off the ground and his boots jittered on the floor. "You knew this wasn't a child! Did you open the parcels to see?"

"No! Stop 'urtin' me! Yer breakin' me bones! Two o' them parcels was all over blood when I went to put 'em in the fire. Fair gave me a turn, it did! Near killed me, wiv me 'eart! 'Twas then I knew as I 'ad ter get rid o' them. Can't bear things like that, and I don't want nuffin ter do wiv 'em, not keepin' 'em 'ere in my furnace for the pigs ter find, if they do me over fer loot. I gets some very good fings in 'ere, I do!" It was a grotesque moment for such perverse pride. "Real gold and siller, sometimes!"

"Sc you didn't want to keep the bones in your furnace," Pitt said viciously. "Very wise. We pigs take nastily to things like that—it needs a lot of explaining. In fact, as much as dumping bits of corpse round Bloomsbury." His grip tightened so hard Wigge practically lifted himself off the ground again by his contortions to free himself without actually fighting back. "Where did they come from?"

"I . . . I, er . . ."

"I'm going to hang somebody for it," Pitt said between his teeth. "If it isn't whoever sent you those parcels, then you'll do."

"I didn't kill 'er! It was Clarabelle Mapes! Swear ter Gawd! Number three; Tortoise Lane. She's a baby farmer. Advertises fer infants to raise, illegitimate and the like. Says as she'll raise 'em as 'er own, if she's paid right fer their keep. Only sometimes they dies. Proper weakly, infants is. I jus' get rid o' the corpuses for 'er. Can't afford no burials. We're poor 'ere in St. Giles, you know that!"

"You'll swear to that, before the judge? Clarabelle Mapes sent you those parcels?"

"Yeah! Yeah! I'll swear. It's Gawd's truth, swelpme it is!"

"Good. I believe you. However, I wouldn't want you

disappearing when I need you. And it's a crime to dispose of a human body, even if it is dead. So I'll take you in charge anyway. Constable!''

The constable appeared down the steps, his face pale, rubbing the sweat off his hands on his trouser legs.

''Yes, Mr. Pitt, sir?''

''Take Mr. Septimus Wigge to the station and charge him with disposing of a corpse illegally, and see that you hold on to him tight. He's a witness against a murderess—probably the murderess of a great many children, although we'll never prove that. Be careful, constable, he's a wriggly little bastard. You'd best cuff him.''

''I will, sir, I certainly will.'' The constable pulled his manacles out from under his coat and fastened them on Wigge's bony wrists. ''Now you come along o' me, an' any trouble an' I'll 'ave ter be rough wiv yer, an we wouldn't want that, now, would we, Mr. Wigge?''

Wigge gave a screech of alarm, and the constable hoisted him up the stairs with marked lack of gentleness, leaving Pitt alone in the cellar. The air suddenly seemed heavy, acrid with the smell of uncounted tiny bodies burning in the hot, gray furnace. He felt overpowered by it, sick.

He collected two more constables from the nearest station, just in case Mrs. Mapes were not alone and should put up some sort of struggle. She was a big woman and, Pitt judged, something of a fighter. It would be foolish to go to Tortoise Lane alone to search that large house, where there might well be male employees or dependents, as well as at least half a dozen girls that he knew of plus an unspecified number of infants.

It was after seven by the time he stood on the sloping pavement again and knocked on the heavy door. One constable was half hidden in an alley, a dozen feet away, another in the street roughly parallel, where Pitt judged the back entrance would open.

He lifted his hand and knocked once, then again. It was several minutes before it opened, at first only a crack. But as the child saw who it was and recognized him from the morning, it swung all the way back. It was the girl he had seen on the stairs with the infants.

"May I see Mrs. Mapes?" He stepped in, then stopped, remembering he must not show his anger or he would betray himself and perhaps lose her. "Please?"

"Yes, sir. Come this way, sir." She turned and walked along the corridor, her feet bare and dirty. "We bin expectin' yer." She did not look back, or notice that the other constable had followed Pitt in and closed the door. At the end of the passage she came to the overfurnished sitting room where Pitt had been in the morning, and knocked tentatively.

"Come!" Mrs. Mapes's voice called loudly. "Wot is it?"

"Mrs. Mapes, ma'am, there's the gennelman wivva money 'ere ter see yer, ma'am."

"Send 'im in!" Her voice softened noticeably. "Send 'im in, girl!"

"Thank you." Pitt moved past the girl into the sitting room, closing the door so Mrs. Mapes would not see the constable pass on his way to the kitchen and the back door to let in his companion. They had orders to search the house.

Mrs. Mapes was in a puce dress stretched tight over her jutting bosom, and her voluminous skirts filled the entire chair with taffeta that rustled every time she breathed. That she corseted her flesh into such a relentlessly feminine shape was a monument to her vanity and her endurance of acute and persistent discomfort. Her fat fingers were bright with rings, and her ears dangled with gold under the black ringlets.

Her face gleamed with delight when she saw Pitt. He noticed there was a tray in a space cleared for it on the sideboard, a decanter of wine, Madeira from the depth of the color, and two glasses, the price of which, if they were as good as they looked, would have fed the entire household for a fortnight on better than the gruel they were getting at the moment.

"Well, Mr. Pitt, sir, you were 'asty an' no mistake," she said with a broad smile. "Makes me think yer was awantin' ter come back. Yer got my money, 'ave yer?"

She was so normal, so guilelessly greedy, he had to force to his mind the memory of the bloody parcels, the fact that she regularly wrapped in paper the corpses of infants taken in trust into her care, and sent them to Septimus Wigge to dispose of in his furnace. How many of them had died of natural causes, how many of starvation and disease brought about by neglect? How many had she actively murdered? He would never know, still less prove. But she was an abomination.

"I've just been to see a friend of yours," he answered, sidestepping the question. "Or perhaps I should say an associate. In business."

"I don't 'ave no associates," she said carefully, some of the glisten dying from her face. "Though there are some as'd like ter be."

"This is one who does favors for you now and then— and no doubt you reward him for it."

"I pays me way," she agreed cautiously. "No time fer them as doesn't. Life ain't like that."

"A Mr. Septimus Wigge."

For a moment she was still as stone. Then she caught her breath and continued as though nothing had affected her. "Well, if I got suffin off 'im as was stolen, I bought it honest. I didn't know the little weasel was bent."

"I wasn't thinking of goods, Mrs. Mapes, so much as services," Pitt said distinctly.

" 'E don't do nobody no service!" Her mouth sloped downwards in disgust.

"He does you a considerable service," he corrected her, still standing, and keeping himself carefully between her and the door. "He only failed you once."

Her fat hands beside her monstrous skirt were clenched,

257

but her eyes were still defiant. She stared up at him, her face heavy.

"He did not burn the body of the woman you sent him wrapped up in the usual parcels, which he expected to be babies who had died in your care. By the time he came to put the parcels in his furnace the blood had soaked through, so he undid one and discovered what it really was. Adult bones don't burn that easily, Mrs. Mapes—not like those of a small child. It takes a very great heat to destroy a human thighbone, or a skull. Wigge knew that, and he didn't want to be left with those in his furnace, so he dropped the parcels as far away from himself as he could carry them alone, in one night. He thought he would be safe, and he very nearly was."

She was pale beneath her rouge, but she had not yet realized just how much he knew. Her body was tight, hard under the straining taffeta, and her hands shook a little, so little he could barely see it.

"If 'e's killed some woman it's nuffin ter do wiv me—an' if 'e says it is, 'e's a liar! You go an' arrest 'im, don't come around 'ere, bullyin' me! You don't look like no naffin' rozzer—usually I can smell 'em. 'E ain't murdered nobody from 'ere, so get on wiv yer business an' leave me alone— 'cept fer Mrs. March's money. I don't suppose yer got that, eh?"

"There is no money."

"You lyin' bastard!" Her voice rose shrilly and she lurched forward out of the chair to stand opposite him, eyes blazing. "Yer lyin' son of a bitch! Yer bleedin' swine!" Her hands came up as if she would strike him, but she recollected herself in time. She was a big woman, vastly heavy, but short; Pitt was a good deal taller than she, and strong. It was not worth the risk. "You lied!" she repeated incredulously.

"That's right," he agreed. "At first I simply wanted to find out what you knew about Mrs. March. Then I saw the parcel on the kitchen table, and recognized the paper and the knots. You wrapped the parcels that the pieces of the body were found in, not Septimus Wigge. He says he got them from you, and we believe him. Clarabelle Mapes, I am arresting you for the murder of the woman whose body was found in the churchyard of St. Mary's in Bloomsbury. And don't be foolish enough to fight me—I have two other constables in the house.''

She stared at him, a succession of emotions in her face; fear, horror, disbelief, and finally, hardening resolution. She was not yet beaten.

''Yer right,'' she conceded grudgingly, ''she died 'ere. But it weren't no murder. It were in defense o' meself, an' yer can't 'ardly blame me fer that! A woman's entitled ter save 'erself.'' Her voice grew more confident. ''I'll ignore yer charges against meself an' me work carin' fer infants wot their muvvers can't keep, 'cos they ain't married, or already got more'n they can feed. It's a wicked charge, iggerant of all I do fer 'em.'' She saw the look on Pitt's face and hurried on. ''But I 'ad no choice, or it'd be me lyin' dead on the floor, so help me Gawd. Come at me like a mad thing, she did!'' She looked up at Pitt, first through her lashes, then more boldly.

Pitt waited.

''Wanted one o' the babes. Some women is like that. Lorst one of 'er own an' come 'ere ter get another, like they was new dresses or suffin. Well, o' course I couldn't give 'er one.''

''Why not?'' Pitt asked icily. ''I would have thought you'd be only too pleased to find a good home for an orphan. Save you working yourself to the bone and stinting yourself to care for it anymore!''

She ignored his sarcasm; she could not afford to retaliate, but the anger was there in her eyes, hot and black.

''Them children is in my care, Mr. Pitt! An' she didn't want jus' any one. Oh, no. She wanted a partic'lar one— one as's mother was aht o' means temporary, like, an' jus' 'avin' me care for 'er little girl till she was better placed. An' when this woman goes off 'er 'ead an insists on 'avin' this one babe an' no other, I 'ad ter refuse 'er. Well, she flew at me like a mad thing! I 'ad ter defend meself, or she'da cut me throat!''

"Oh, yes? What with?"

"Wiv a knife, o' course! We was in the kitchen an' she snatched up a carvin' knife orff the table an' went at me. Well, I 'ad ter fight fer me life, an' I did! It was a sort o' haccident she got killed—I merely meant ter save meself, like any person would!"

"So you cut her up and wrapped her in parcels, which you took to Septimus Wigge to burn," Pitt said bitingly. "Why was that? Seems like a lot of unnecessary trouble."

"You got a cruel tongue, Mr. Pitt." She was gaining confidence. "An' a nasty mind. 'Cause I couldn't take the risk o' you bleedin' rozzers not believin' me—just like you don't now. Sort o' proves I was right, don't it?"

"Absolutely, Mrs. Mapes. I don't believe a word of it—except that you probably did stick the kitchen knife into her and killed her. And then carried on with the knife, and maybe a cleaver as well."

"Yer may not believe me, Mr. Pitt." She put her hands on her hips. "But there's nuffin as you can prove. It's my word 'gainst yours, and no court in Lunnon's goin' ter 'ang a woman on the misbelief o' one o' your kind, an' that's a fact."

She was right, and it was a bitter taste to swallow.

"I shall still charge you with disposing of the body," he said flatly. "And you'll go down for a nice stretch for that."

She let out a coarse expletive of denial. " 'Alf the poor doesn't tell the pigs o' every death in places like St. Giles. People's dyin' all the time."

"Then why didn't you simply have her buried, like all these others you're talking about?"

"Because she was knifed, o' course, fool! Wot priest is goin' ter bury a woman as 'as bin knifed? An' she didn't come from St. Giles. She was a stranger 'ere. There'd a' bin questions. But the law's the same—if yer charge me wiv that yer've gotta charge all the others. I reckon when the judge ears 'ow she came at me, an' 'ow terrible sorry I was when she haccidental-like fell on the knife 'erself in the struggle, 'e'll unnerstand why I lorst me 'ead an' got rid of 'er."

"Well, we'll find out, Mrs. Mapes, I promise you," he said bitterly. "Because you'll have your chance to tell him." He raised his voice. "Constable!"

Immediately the door opened and the burlier of the two constables came in. "Yes, sir?"

"Stay here with Mrs. Mapes and see she doesn't leave— for anything. She's a rare one with a knife—has accidents in which people who threaten her end up carved in little bits and dropped in parcels round half of London. So watch yourself."

"Yes, sir." The man's face hardened. He knew St. Giles, and not much surprised him. "I'll take good care of 'er, sir. She'll be 'ere, safe as 'ouses, when yer gets back."

"Good." Pitt went out into the corridor and along to the kitchen. There were five girls sitting round, the other constable in their midst. He stood up as Pitt came in, and the girls did too, out of habit towards adults—not from respect, but from fear.

Pitt wandered in and sat casually on the edge of the big central wooden table, and one by one the girls resumed their seats, huddled together.

"Mrs. Mapes has told me a young woman came here about three weeks ago wanting a baby girl, and became very upset when she couldn't have a particular one. Does anybody remember that?"

Their faces were blank, eyes wide.

"She was nice-looking," he went on, trying to keep the anger out of his voice, the rasping edge of desperation. He had never wanted to convict anyone more than Clarabelle Mapes, and she would escape him if he did not prove murder. The story of self-defense he was almost sure was a complete fiction, but it was not impossible. A jury might believe it. His superiors would know that as much as

Clarabelle herself. She might never even be charged. The thought burned like acid inside him. Seldom had he given in to personal hatred in his work, but this time he could not suppress it. If he was honest with himself, he was no longer trying.

"Please think," he urged. "She was young and quite tall, with fair hair and a pretty skin. She didn't come from round here."

One of the girls nudged the girl next to her, avoiding Pitt's eyes.

"Fanny . . . !" she whispered tentatively.

Fanny looked at the floor.

Pitt knew what troubled her. Had he been a child in Mrs. Mapes's care he would not have dared risk her anger.

"Mrs. Mapes told me she came here," he said gently. "I believe her. But it would help if someone else could remember." He waited.

Fanny twisted her fingers together and breathed deeply. Someone coughed.

"I remember 'er, mister," Fanny said at last. "She came ter the door an' I let 'er in." She shook her head. "She weren't from 'ere—she were all 'andsome and clean. But terrible upset she was when she couldn't 'ave the little girl. Said as she were 'er own, but Mrs. Mapes said she were mad, poor thing."

"What little girl?" Pitt asked. "Do you know which one."

"Yes, mister. I remember 'cos she was real pretty, all fair 'air and such a smile. Called 'er Faith, they did."

Pitt took a deep breath. "What happened to her?" he said so quietly he had to repeat it.

"She were adopted, mister. A lady wiv no children come and took 'er."

"I see. And was this young woman who asked after Faith still upset when she left here?"

"Dunno, mister. None of us saw 'er go."

Pitt tried to make his voice sound casual, gentle, so as

not to frighten her, but he knew the edge was still there. "Did she tell you her name, Fanny?"

Fanny's face remained glazed, her eyes faraway.

Pitt looked at the floor, willing her to remember, clenching his hands inside his pockets where she could not see.

"Prudence," Fanny said clearly. "She said as 'er name were Prudence Wilson. I let 'er in an' told Mrs. Mapes as she was 'ere. Mrs. Mapes sent me back ter aks 'er business."

"And what was her business?" Pitt was buoyed up by a surge of hope, and yet at the same time, giving a name to the hideously used corpse, learning of her loves and hopes, made her death so much deeper an offense.

Fanny shook her head. "I dunno, mister, she wouldn't say, 'cept to Mrs. Mapes."

"And Mrs. Mapes didn't tell you?"

"No."

Pitt stood up. "That's fine. Thank you, Fanny. Stay here and look after the little ones. The constable will stay too."

" 'Oo are yer, mister, an' wot's 'appenin'?" the eldest girl asked with her face screwed up. They were frightened of change; it usually meant the loss of something, the beginning of new struggle.

Pitt would like to have thought this time would be different, but he could not delude himself. They were too young to earn their way in any legal occupation—not that there were many for women except domestic service, for which they had no references; sweatshops barely afforded survival. And without Clarabelle Mapes to connive and cheat monthly money out of desperate women, on the pretense of minding children they were unable to keep themselves, there was no means to support this present group of infants in Tortoise Lane. It would probably mean the workhouse for most of them.

He did not know whether to lie to them and keep fear at bay a little longer, or if that only added to the patronage, the robbery of dignity. In the end cowardice won; he had simply worn out all the emotion he had.

"I'm a policeman, and until I've made a few more calls I don't know for certain what's happening. I've got to discover more about Prudence Wilson. Fanny, did she say where she came from?"

Fanny shook her head. "No."

"Never mind, I'll find out." He went to the door, giving the constable instructions to remain there until he returned or sent relief.

Outside in Tortoise Lane he walked smartly towards Bloomsbury. It was the obvious place to begin. It was a reasonable assumption that Prudence Wilson had walked to the nearest such place as Mrs. Mapes's, that she lived in at her own employment as housemaid or parlormaid, as the police surgeon had suggested.

Therefore Pitt went to the Bloomsbury Police Station, and by ten past eight he was facing a tired and short-tempered sergeant who had been on his feet all day and was so thirsty for a pint of ale he could taste dust in his mouth.

"Yes, sir?" he said without raising his eyes from the enormous ledger in front of him, where he was writing in a careful copperplate hand the details of a charge of vandalizing a fence, brought against a small boy.

"Inspector Pitt, Metropolitan Police," Pitt said formally, to give the man time to correct his attitude accordingly.

"Not 'ere, sir. Don't belong to this station. I've 'eard of 'im, does murders an' the like. Try Bow Street, sir. If they don't 'ave 'im, they maybe know 'oo 'as."

Pitt smiled wearily. This pedestrian misunderstanding had a kind of sanity about it that was vaguely comforting. "I am Inspector Pitt, sergeant," he replied. "And I am here about a murder. I would be obliged for your attention, if you please."

The sergeant blushed a hot pink and stood up smartly, not even wincing as he banged the toe of his boot against the chair leg, aggravating his corns. He faced Pitt with wide eyes, inarticulate with apology.

"I am looking for record of a Miss Prudence Wilson,

264

probably a maid in domestic service, maybe in this area. I am hoping she has been reported missing, about three or four weeks ago. Does the name sound familiar to you?''

"People don't usually report 'ousemaids missin', Mr. Pitt, sir.'' The sergeant shook his head. "Terrible suspicious in their thoughts, people is—and usually right, too. Thinks they's run off wiv some man, an' like as not they 'ave, an' . . .'' He let the sentiment remain unexpressed; it was indiscreet. Personally he wished them luck. His own marriage was a happy one, and he would not willingly have seen anyone bound to a life of service in someone else's house rather than having their own. "But could 'a bin.'' He showed his agreeability by going for the ledger where such things were noted and pulling it out. Dutifully he turned it back four weeks and began to read forward. After six pages he stopped with his finger on an entry. He looked up at Pitt, his eyes surprised and sad.

"Yes, sir, 'ere it is. Young man by the name o' 'Arry Croft came an' says as she was 'is betrothed, an she'd gone ter fetch 'er little girl from someone as was keepin 'er, lookin' after 'er, like, an' never came back. Terrible upset 'e was, sure as somethin' 'ad 'appened to 'er, since they was ter be married and she was real 'appy about it. But o' course we couldn't do nuffin. Young women don't 'ave ter be found by a man they ain't married ter, ain't daughters of, and ain't employed by, not as if they don't want ter. An' we didn't know different as she'd gone off on 'er own with the little girl.''

"No,'' Pitt agreed. It was fair, and even if they had known, by then it was already too late. "No, of course you couldn't.''

The sergeant swallowed. "Is she dead, sir?''

"Yes.''

The sergeant did not take his eyes from Pitt's face. "Was she—was she the body wot was found in—in the parcels, sir?''

"Yes, sergeant.''

The sergeant gulped again. " 'Ave you got the man wot done it, Mr. Pitt?''

"It was a woman, and yes, we've got her. I'm going to charge her now, and take her in."

"I'm off duty any minute now, sir—I'd thank yer dearly if I could come along with yer, sir. Please."

"Certainly. I may need an extra man; she's a big woman, and there are a lot of children to be taken somewhere—I suppose, the workhouse."

"Yes, sir."

By the time they were back in Tortoise Lane it was fifteen minutes to nine. It was still a clear evening, and at this high-summer time of the year there was another hour of daylight and twenty minutes beyond that of fading dusk, while the color slowly ebbed away and the shadows joined themselves together into a solidity broken only by the gas lamps on the main streets and the occasional lantern or candle in St. Giles.

They stopped outside number 3 and Pitt went in without knocking. There was no sense of triumph; he felt only a vindictiveness uncharacteristic of him. He strode along the corridor to Mrs. Mapes's sitting room and threw the door open. The constable was still standing, as uncomfortable as when he had left, and Mrs. Mapes was sitting in her own chair, her taffeta skirt spread round her, her black ringlets shining and a satisfied smile on her mouth.

"Well, Mr. Pitt?" she said boldly. "Wot now, eh?. Yer goin' ter stand 'ere all night?"

"No, none of us are going to be here all night," he replied. "In fact, I doubt if we shall ever be here again. Clarabelle Mapes, I arrest you for the murder of Prudence Wilson when she came to collect her child, whom you had sold."

For an instant she was still prepared to brazen it out.

"Why? Why should I kill 'er on purpose? Don't make no sense!"

"Because she threatened to make your trade public!" he said bitterly. "You've killed too many babies entrusted to

266

you, rather than feed them. You'd go out of business if that was known.''

This time she was shaken; sweat stood out on her upper lip and across her brow. Her skin was suddenly gray as the blood drained from it.

"Right, constable," Pitt commanded. "Bring her along." He turned and went out of the door again and along the passage to the kitchens. "Constable Wyman! I'll send someone to relieve you. Get these children cared for to-night. Tomorrow we'll have to inform the parish authorities."

"You takin' 'er away, sir?"

"Yes—for murder. She'll not be back—"

Suddenly there was a cry from the front of the house, the thud of a body landing heavily, and then yells of outrage. Pitt spun on his heel and charged out.

In the passageway the constable was scrambling to his feet, dusty and with rushes sticking to him, his helmet in his hand, and through the open door were disappearing the coattails of the sergeant.

"She's away!" the constable shouted furiously. "She 'it me!" He ran out with Pitt on his heels and fast overtaking him.

Already twenty yards down Tortoise Lane Clarabelle Mapes was running with surprising fleetness for one so immensely stout. Pitt ignored the sergeant and sprinted as hard as he could after her, scattering into the gutter an old woman with a bundle of rags and a coster returning for his supper. If he lost her now he might never get her back; the warrens and mazes of the London slums could hide a fugitive for years, if they were cunning enough, and had enough to lose by capture.

There was no point in shouting; it would only waste his breath. No one stopped a thief in St. Giles. She was still moving with the speed of terror and even as he watched she turned sharply and disappeared into an open doorway. Had he been ten yards further off he could not have told which one. He charged in after her, knocking into an old man and seeing him collapse with a shower of abuse, but he had no feeling left for anyone but the gross figure of Clarabelle Mapes, black curls flying, taffeta skirts like brilliant overblown sails. He followed her through a room he dimly saw was filled with people bent over a table, ran along a dark passage where his feet echoed, and out into the beer-sour space of a sawdust-strewn taproom.

She swung round and glared at him, her black eyes venomous, and knocked aside a serving girl, sending her sprawling onto the floor, covered in the ale she had been carrying. Pitt was forced to hesitate to avoid falling over her, his feet entangled in her thrusting legs. As it was, he tripped over a stool and all but measured his length, catching hold of the doorframe just in time to steady himself. There was a roar of laughter behind him, and another clatter as the sergeant appeared, buttons undone, helmet askew.

Out of the front door past a knot of idlers, Pitt saw her still running swiftly towards a side alley opposite, no more than a slit in the gray walls between houses. She was going deeper into the labyrinth of sweatshops, gin mills, and tenements, and if he did not catch her soon she would find a hundred natural allies and he would be lucky if he returned at all, let alone having captured her.

At the end of the alley was a flight of steps down into a wide, ill-lit room where women sat sewing by oil lamps. Clarabelle had no care whom she spilled onto the floor, whose shirts she tore or sent flying into the dust, and Pitt could not afford to look either. Outraged cries rang in his ears.

At the far side the door caught him in the chest and checked him for a moment, knocking the breath out of his lungs. But he was too hot in pursuit to care about pain; his mind was filled and possessed with the hunger to capture her, to feel her physically under his hand and to force her to walk ahead of him, hands manacled behind her, drenched in the knowledge she was on the last length of the unalterable journey towards the gallows.

In the areaway three old women shared a bottle of gin, and a child played with two stones.

"Help!" Clarabelle Mapes shouted piercingly. "Stop 'im! 'E's after me!"

But the old women were too rubber-legged and bleary-eyed to respond as she wanted, and Pitt jumped over them without their offering any serious resistance. He was gaining on Clarabelle; another few yards at this pace and he would catch her. His legs were far longer, and he had no skirts to trammel him.

But she was among her own kind now, and she knew the way. The next door was slammed in his face and would not open when he pushed it. He was obliged to hurl his weight against it, bruising his shoulder. It was not till the sergeant caught up with him that they were able to force it together.

The room beyond was dimly lit and packed with humanity of all ages and both sexes; the smell of sweat, stale food, and animal grime caught in his throat.

They ran through, leaping and kicking at sprawled bodies, and out of the far door into a crumbling street so narrow the jettied upper stories almost met. The open drain down the middle was crusted with dry sewage. A score of squat doorways—she might have gone into any one of them. All the doors were closed. There were huddles of people already half asleep or sodden with drink propped up here and there. None of them took the slightest notice of him or the sergeant, except one old man who, watching the situation, yelled encouragement to Pitt, imagining him the fugitive. He threw an empty bottle at the sergeant, which missed him and shattered on the wall behind, sending splinters in an arc ten feet wide.

"Which way did she go?" Pitt shouted furiously. "There's sixpence for anyone who helps me get her."

Two or three stirred, but no one spoke.

He was so angry, so scalded with frustration he would have attacked them even in their stupor if he had thought it would achieve anything at all.

Then another, far brighter thought came to him. He had been only a couple of yards behind Clarabelle when she had gone into the large dormitory. Even with the few moments it had taken to break in the door he should have seen the far door swing, and caught a glimpse of her fuchsia skirt in this frowsy street.

He spun round and charged back into the great room, seizing the first person he could reach, hauling him up by the lapels and glaring at him. "Where did she go?" he said gratingly between his teeth. "If she's still here I'll charge you all with being accessory to murder, do you hear me?"

"She ain't 'ere!" the man squeaked. "Let go o' me, yer bleedin' pig! She's gawn, Gawd 'elp 'er! Fooled yer, yer swine!"

Pitt dropped him and stumbled back to the broken door, the sergeant still on his heels. Out in the alley again there was no sign of her, and the possibility that she had escaped brought him out in a sweat of fury and impotence. He could understand how children wept at their own powerlessness.

He must force himself to think more clearly; anger would solve nothing. She had a flourishing business and considerable possessions in Tortoise Lane. What would he seek to do in her place? Attack! Get rid of the only man who knew her crime. Would Clarabelle think that far? Or would escape be all that mattered now? Was panic greater than cunning?

He remembered the brilliant black eyes and thought not. If he looked vulnerable, offered himself as bait, she would come back to finish him; her instinct was all to attack, to kill.

"Wait!" he said curtly to the sergeant.

"But she's not 'ere!" the sergeant hissed back. "She can't 'ave got far, sir! I'd 'ate something rotten to lose this one! A right wicked woman."

"So would I, sergeant, so would I." Pitt looked up, searching the grimy windows in the flat walls above. It was growing dimmer, closer to true twilight. He had not long. Then he saw it—the pale glimmer of a face behind a window—and then it was gone again.

"Wait here!" he said tersely. "In case I'm wrong." He turned and went in the nearest door, past the inhabitants, up a rickety stairway and along a dim passage. He heard movement at the end and a rustle of taffeta; a fat body squeezing through a narrow way. He knew it was her as if he could smell her. Only a few yards ahead of him she was waiting. What would she have? She had killed Prudence Wilson with a knife, and carved up her body as if it had been a side of meat.

He moved after her quietly now, walking on the sides of his feet; even so, the boards were rotten and betrayed him. He heard her ahead—or was it her? Was she crouched behind some half concealed door, waiting, all the weight of her thick body balanced to thrust the knife into his flesh, deep, to the heart?

Without realizing it he had stopped. Fear was tingling sharp, his throat tight, tongue dry. He could not stay here. He could hear someone further and further ahead of him, going on upwards.

Unwilling, pulse racing, he crept forward, one hand outstretched to touch the wall and feel its solid surface. He came to another flight of stairs, even narrower than the last, and knew she was close above him. He could feel her presence like a prickle on his skin; he even thought he could hear her breath wheezing somewhere in the gloom.

Then suddenly there was a thud, a cry of anger, and her footsteps at the top of the stepladder above him. He started up and saw for a moment her bulk bent over the square of yellow light at the top, where the attic opened out. She was half in shadow, but he could still see the shining eyes, the curls loose like bedsprings, the sweat gleaming on her skin. He almost had her. He was forewarned, expecting a knife. She moved back, as if she were afraid of him, startled to find him so close.

He could make the last four steps easily, in two strides,

and be beside her before she had time to strike. If he moved to one side as soon as he was through that square—

Then with horror paralyzing him quite literally, leaving him frozen on the step, he remembered the secret of these old warrens—and deliberately let go the rail and fell backwards down to the floor, bruising and battering himself, just as the trapdoor came down with its spearsharp embedded blades slicing the air where he had been the instant before, followed by her shrill scream of laughter.

He scrambled to his feet, blood surging through him, pain forgotten, and swarmed up the stairs, striking his hand between the blades and shooting the trap open. He fell up and out of the hole onto the attic floor only a yard away from where she crouched. Before she had time even to register shock he hit her as hard as he could with his clenched fist—and all the stored up anger, the pain and loss of her victims—and she rolled over and lay senseless. He did not give a damn about the difficulty of getting her down, or even whether his superiors would charge him with breaking her jaw. He had Clarabelle Mapes, and he was satisfied.

13

It was late the following morning when Pitt returned to Cardington Crescent. The euphoria of capturing Clarabelle Mapes had vanished, and in the dull, warm daylight he remembered that he had gone to Tortoise Lane to find out what Sybilla March had wanted there. And he had learned nothing. No amount of questioning was going to get anything more from Clarabelle, and none of the children had ever seen a lady like Sybilla.

The butler let him in and he asked that Charlotte be sent for. He was permitted to wait in the morning room. It was oppressive, curtains half drawn, pictures draped with black, black crêpe fluttering in unlikely places like cobwebs stained with soot.

Charlotte came in, dressed in exquisitely fashionable lavender; it flickered through his mind that it was a gown of Aunt Vespasia's altered a little at the bosom to fit Charlotte. Vespasia never wore black, even for death.

Charlotte was pale; there were smudges of tiredness under her eyes. But her face lit up with pleasure as she saw him, and he found it extraordinarily good. In a sense deeper than walls or possessions, wherever she was, he would be at home.

"Oh, Thomas, I'm so glad you've come," she said immediately. "Everything is getting worse. We are looking at each other with terrible thoughts in our eyes and strings of words we want to mean, and can't." She turned

273

and closed the door behind her and stood leaning against it, staring at him, biting her lips, her hands clenched tightly. "It isn't Tassie. I've discovered what she does at night, where she goes and gets splashed with blood."

A monstrous anger welled up inside him, sharp as a dagger, because it was principally fear, not only for her but for himself, fear of losing all that was most precious to him, all the deep, warm safety that supported every other courage and dream he held.

"You what?" he shouted involuntarily.

She closed her eyes, her face tight. "Don't shout, Thomas."

He strode forward and took her by the arm, pulling her away from the door and around to face him in the center of the room. He was hurting her and he knew it.

"You what?" he repeated fiercely. The very fact that she had remained by the door instead of coming to him and kissing him, that she had not replied with any righteous anger of her own, meant that she was conscious of her guilt. "You followed her!" he accused with certainty.

Her eyes opened wide and there was no apology in them.

"I had to find out where she went," she explained. "And it was perfectly all right—she goes to help deliver babies! A lot of poor women, or unmarried women—girls—can't afford a midwife. That's why so many die. Thomas, it's a wonderful thing she's doing, and the people love her."

He was too angry at the idiotic risk she had taken to be relieved that Tassie's conduct was so innocent, where he had feared such horror. Without realizing it he was shaking Charlotte.

"You followed her to some woman's home, alone, at night?" He was still shouting. "You . . . you fool! You imbecile! She could have taken you anywhere! What if she had been responsible for the woman whose body was found in bloody pieces in Bloomsbury? You might have been the next one!" He was so furious he could have slapped her, as one does a beloved child who has just escaped falling under the carriage wheels. In the rush of relief one dares to imagine all the possible dangers so narrowly missed. Memory of Clarabelle Mapes and the appalling labyrinth he had so lately left were stronger in him than this comfortable, civilized house. "You stupid, irresponsible woman! Do I have to lock you up before I can leave the house safely and be sure you'll behave yourself like an adult?"

What had begun as guilt in her was now overridden by a sense of injury. He was being unjust and she was correspondingly angry in her own right. "You are hurting me," she said coldly.

"You deserve to be thrashed!" he retaliated without altering his grip in the slightest.

She answered by kicking him sharply in the shins with the toe of her boot. He was so surprised he let go of her with a gasp and she stepped back smartly.

"Don't you dare treat me like a child, Thomas Pitt!" she said furiously. "I am not one of your dainty ladies who do nothing all day and can be ordered to their rooms whenever you don't like what they say. Emily is my sister, and she's not going to be hanged for killing George if there is anything at all that I can do to help it. Tassie is in love with Mungo Hare, Beamish's curate—he helps her with the deliveries—and she is going to marry him."

He clung to the only other example of male reason and dominion he could think of.

"Her father won't let her. He'll never allow it."

"Oh, yes, he will!" she retorted. "I've promised him you won't tell anyone about his affair with Sybilla if he agrees, and if he doesn't I shall make thoroughly sure all Society knows of it in detail. He'll give Tassie his blessing, I assure you."

"Do you?" He was incensed. "You take a great deal for granted! And what if I don't choose to honor this promise you gave so freely on my behalf?"

She hesitated, swallowing hard, then met his eyes. "Then

Tassie will not be able to marry the man she loves, because he is not socially suitable and has no money," she said bluntly. "She'll remain single and live here in bondage to that selfish old woman, keeping her company till she dies, and then doing the same for her father. Either that or she'll have to marry someone she doesn't love."

She did not need to add that that was what might well have happened to her, had her father not been of a more amenable disposition than Eustace, and had her mother not pleaded her cause with force. Pitt was aware of it, and the knowledge robbed him of the justification he wanted. She had done exactly what he would have wished; it was the fact that he had been preempted that enraged him, not the act. But to say so aloud would be ridiculous—in fact, the complaint was ridiculous.

He chose to change the subject entirely, and play his best card. "I have solved the murder of the corpse in the Bloomsbury churchyard," he said instead. "And captured the murderess, after a chase, with enough evidence to hang her."

Charlotte was impressed, and she let her amazement and admiration show in her face. "I didn't think that would be possible," she said honestly. "How did you do it?"

He sat down sideways on the arm of one of the hide chairs. He was stiff after the bruising he had taken chasing Clarabelle Mapes, and he was surprisingly sore.

"It was a woman who kept a baby farm."

She frowned. "A what?"

"A baby farm." He hated having to tell her of such things, but she had chosen to know. "A woman takes out discreet advertisements saying that she loves children and will be happy to care for any infant whose mother, due to circumstances of ill health or other commitment, is unable to care for it herself. Often they add that sickly children are particularly welcomed and will be nursed as if their own. A small financial provision is required, of course, for necessities."

Charlotte was puzzled. "There must be many women

only too glad to avail themselves of such a service. It sounds like a charitable thing to do. Why do you say it with such disgust? Too many women have to work and can't care for their children, especially if they are in domestic service, and the child is illegitimate—'' She stopped. "Why?"

"Because most of them, like Clarabelle Mapes, take the fee from their mothers and then let the sickly ones starve—or actually murder them—rather than spend money on caring for them. The strong or pretty ones they sell." He saw her face. "I'm sorry. You did ask."

"Why the Bloomsbury murder?" she asked after a moment's silence. "Was she the mother of one of the children who was murdered, and discovered the truth?"

"One who was sold."

"Oh." She sat down without moving for several minutes, and he did not touch her. Then at last he put out one hand gently. "Why did you go there?" she asked at last.

"The address was in Sybilla's book."

She was startled. "The baby farm? But that's ridiculous. Why?"

"I don't know. I never found out. I presume Sybilla found it for a servant, one of her own maids or a friend's. I can't imagine any of her own circle wanting such a service. Even if they had an illegitimate child, they would find some other provision; a relative in the country, a family retainer in retirement with a daughter."

"I suppose it was a maid," Charlotte agreed. "Or else she knew the woman for some other reason. Poor Sybilla."

"It doesn't help me any further towards finding out who killed her, or why."

"You asked the woman, of course?"

He gave a sharp, guttural little laugh. "You didn't see Clarabelle Mapes, or you wouldn't ask."

"Have you no idea who killed George?" She faced him, eyes dark with anxiety, fear heavy at the back of them. He realized again how tired she was, how very troubled.

He touched her cheek gently, slowly. "No, my love, not much. There are only William, Eustace, Jack Radley, and Emily left; unless it was the old woman, which I would dearly like to think, but I know of no reason she would. I can't even imagine one—and believe me, I've tried."

"You include Emily!"

He closed his eyes, opening them slowly, unhappily. "I have to."

There was no point in arguing; she knew it to be true. A knock on the door saved her from the necessity of replying.

"Come in," Pitt said reluctantly.

It was Stripe, looking apologetic and holding a note in his hand.

"Sorry, Mr. Pitt, sir. The police surgeon sent this for you. It don't make no sense."

"Give it to me." Pitt reached out and grabbed it, opening the single sheet and reading.

"What is it?" Charlotte demanded. "What does it say?"

"She was strangled," he replied quietly, his voice dropping. "By her hair, quick and hard. Very effective." He saw Charlotte shiver and, out of the corner of his eye, saw Stripe bite his lip. "But she wasn't carrying a child," he finished.

Charlotte was stunned. "Are you sure?"

"Of course I'm sure!" he said irritably. "Don't be idiotic. This is from the surgeon who did the postmortem. You can hardly mistake such a thing!"

Charlotte screwed up her face as if she had been physically hurt, and bent her head into her hands. "Poor Sybilla. She must have miscarried, and she dared not tell anyone. How she must have hated Eustace going on and on about how marvelous it was she was going to give William an heir after all this time. No wonder she looked at him with such loathing. And that dreadful old woman haranguing about family! Oh, God, what wounds we inflict on people!"

Pitt looked at Stripe, who was obviously embarrassed at

278

such an intimate subject and hurt by the pity he felt but only half understood. He realized this was a whole sea of pain he did not comprehend.

"Thank you," Pitt nodded. "I don't think it helps us, and I see no reason to tell the family. It will only cause unnecessary distress. Let her keep her secret."

"Yes, sir." Stripe withdrew, something like relief in his face.

Charlotte looked up and smiled. She did not need to praise him; he knew it was there in all the unsaid words between them.

Luncheon was as miserable as breakfast had been, and Emily sat at the dining room table more in defiance than. because of any delusion that it would be more endurable than eating alone in her room. An additional incentive was the growing conviction that the ring was tightening round her, and unless she could find her own escape she was going to be charged with murder.

Charlotte had told her about following Tassie and discovering the secret of her midnight excursions and the blood on her dress. A difficult delivery could be a very messy affair; the afterbirth could look, in the glare of lamplight, like the gore of a butchery. And no wonder Tassie had worn such a look of calm delight! She had witnessed the beginning of a new life, the last act in the creation of a human being. Could anything at all be further from the madness of which they had suspected her?

Thomas had been here this morning, had spoken to Charlotte and left again, without explanation or, apparently, any further investigation. Although, to be fair to him, Emily could think of nothing else for him to ask.

She looked round the table at them from under her lashes, so no one would notice, while she pushed a lump of boiled chicken round her plate. Tassie was sober, but there was a glow of happiness inside her that no awareness of others' distress could extinguish. Emily found most of her could honestly be pleased for her; only a tiny core, one she would willingly have quenched, was sharp with envy. Then she felt an unclouded sense of relief that there was no reason on earth to suspect Tassie of any kind of guilt, either in George's death or Sybilla's. Emily had never wanted to think there was; it was a necessity forced on her by Charlotte's extraordinary account of the episode on the stairs. Now that was explained in a way better than she could have dreamed.

At the foot of the table, with its snowfield of a cloth and fine Georgian silver, but flowerless in spite of the blaze in the garden, the old woman sat, dour-faced, in black, her fish-blue eyes staring straight ahead of her. Presumably she had not been told either about Tassie's intention of marrying the curate or of Eustace's capitulation in allowing her, still less of his reason. And most assuredly she had not learned of Tassie's midnight excursions. If she had, there would be far more in her present mood than a cold dislike and, perhaps, at the back of that chill expression and the petty angers, a suffocated fear. After all, it was someone in this house who had murdered twice. Even Lavinia March could not pretend to herself it was a foreign force invading her home; it was something within—a part of them.

But she seemed to remain alone in whatever mourning she suffered; it had not driven her to any softening of heart, any understanding of the fear in anyone else. Emily was aware somewhere in the back of her mind that that was perhaps the greatest tragedy of all, far beyond the need to receive pity—the inability to feel it. And yet she could not evoke in herself compassion for those who gave none themselves.

She would dearly have liked to believe the old woman responsible for murder, but she could think of no reason why she should be, nor any evidence whatsoever which suggested that she was. Mrs. March was the only one in the house whose guilt would cause Emily no unhappiness at all. She racked her brain to find anything to support it, and failed.

As if conscious of her thoughts, the old woman looked up from her plate and gazed at her icily. "I imagine after the funeral tomorrow you will be returning to your own house, Emily," she said with lifted eyebrows. "Presumably the police will equally easily be able to find you there—although most else seems to be beyond them!"

"Yes, certainly I shall," Emily answered tartly. "It is only for the convenience of the police that I have stayed here so long—and to show some family solidarity. There is no need for the rest of Society to know how little we find each other's company agreeable, or seem able to offer each other any comfort." She took a sip of her wine. "Although I don't know why you think the police are unable to solve the murders." She used the ugly word deliberately and was pleased to see the old woman wince with distaste. "They undoubtedly know a great deal that they have not chosen to tell you. They will hardly confide in us. After all, it is one of us whom they will arrest."

"Really!" Eustace said angrily. "Remember yourself, Emily! That kind of remark is quite unnecessary."

"Of course it is one of us, you fool!" the old woman snapped at him, her hand shaking so hard her wine slopped over the rim of her glass and ran down onto the cloth. "It is Emily herself, and if you do not know that you are the only one here who doesn't!"

"You are talking nonsense, Grandmama." William spoke for the first time since they had come into the dining room. In fact, as far as either Emily or Charlotte could recall, he had not spoken at breakfast either. He looked ghostlike, as if Sybilla's death had taken all his own vitality as well. Charlotte had said earlier that she was afraid he might collapse at the funeral, so gaunt did he seem.

The old woman swung round on him, opening her mouth, but then she registered the expression on his face and closed it again.

"I, for one, don't know that it was Emily," he went on. "The motive of jealousy you credit to her might equally well do for me, although in fact it doesn't. The affair was trivial at best, and over with anyway, which both Emily and I knew. You may not have, but then it was none of your business.'' He stopped and took a sip from his glass of water; his voice was rough, as though his throat ached. ''And the other motive you imagine for her, that of an infatuation with Jack; while quite believable—she would certainly not be his first conquest—''

''William!'' Eustace shouted, banging his hand flat on the table to make as much noise as possible and sending the silver and crockery jumping. ''This conversation is in the worst possible taste. We are all prepared to allow your grief some latitude, but this is beyond bearing!''

William stared back at him with burning contempt, his eyes brilliant, his mouth pinched with violent emotion long held in and hidden.

''Taste is a personal thing, Father. I find many of your conversations as 'distasteful' as anything I have ever said in my life. I frequently find your hypocrisy quite as obscene as all the vulgar picture postcards of naked women. They, at least, are honest.''

Eustace gasped, but was not quick enough to stem the tide of anger. He was aware of Charlotte next to him, because she had pushed out her foot under the table to kick him fairly sharply on the ankle. The ridiculous scene under Sybilla's bed was not allowed to fade for a moment from his memory. He clenched his teeth and remained silent.

''But as a motive it is hardly worth murder,'' William went on. ''She could perfectly well have had Jack as well, if she had wanted him—and there is no evidence that she did. Whereas, on the contrary, if he had wanted her—or to be more accurate, George's money, which she inherits— then he had an excellent reason for murdering George.''

Emily sat rigid, acutely aware of Jack Radley beside her, conscious that he had stiffened in his seat. But was it guilt, or embarrassment, or simply fear? Innocent people were hanged sometimes. Emily herself was afraid; why should not he be?

But William was not finished. ''Personally,'' he went

on, "I favor Father. He had excellent reasons, which just in case he is innocent, I shall not discuss."

There was total silence round the table, Vespasia set down her knife and fork, touching her napkin delicately to her mouth once and lying it aside. She looked at William and then down at the tablecloth, but she said nothing.

Eustace was pale and Charlotte could see his fists were clenched in his lap. The veins stood out on his neck till she feared his collar would strangle him, but he also did not speak.

Tassie hid her face. Mrs. March was scarlet, but for some reason afraid to break the silence. Perhaps nothing she dared say was adequate to her outrage.

Jack Radley looked wretched and acutely embarrassed, the only time Charlotte had seen his composure completely shattered. Although she was perfectly aware how likely it was that he was guilty—not only of double murder but of the most callous abuse of a woman's emotions, and that he had fully intended to abuse them further—still she liked him better for seeing him at a loss. It gave him a reality beneath the charming smile and the marvelous eyes.

Emily stared straight ahead of her.

In the end it was the footman with the next course who broke the silence, and the meal proceeded with a saddle of mutton no one tasted and a trivial conversation no one could have recalled a moment after it was spoken.

After the dessert Emily excused herself and retired to the rustic seat in the garden, not because it was a pleasant day—indeed it was overcast and seemed very likely to rain—but because she felt it her best chance of being alone, and there was no one whose company she desired.

Tomorrow was Sybilla's funeral; she stayed because she wished to attend it. Now that Sybilla was dead, all Emily's hatred of her had vanished. The ridiculous affair with George had receded to a far different proportion of importance. He had regretted it. He had been robbed of the chance to undo it, so she would wipe it out for him, cherishing all the other memories that were good. They had shared a great deal; if she allowed Sybilla to rob her of all those things, then she was a fool, and she deserved to lose them.

She had not seen Charlotte alone since Pitt called that morning, except for an instant as they came through the hall towards the dining room. But that had been enough to learn that he still had little idea who had murdered George, or why. Presumably it was the same person who had then killed Sybilla. She must have known something which the killer could not afford her ever to tell.

That did not exclude anyone. Sybilla was a clever and observant woman. She may have understood some word or act that had eluded the rest of them, or even been told something by George.

What could George have known? Emily sat hunched up in the damp, rising wind, pulling her shawl round her and raking through every possibility her mind could imagine, from the absurd to the horrific. At the end she was still left with Jack Radley, and her own clumsy complicity, or else William's rather wild attempt to blame Eustace—and she was obliged to admit she believed that born more of hatred than sense.

She did not hear Jack Radley approach, and only when he was almost above her did she realize he was there. He was the last person she wanted to speak to at all, still less be alone with. She pulled her shawl even tighter round her and shivered.

"I was just thinking of going inside," she said hastily. "It is not very pleasant. I wouldn't be surprised if it rains."

"It won't rain yet." He sat down beside her, refusing to accept dismissal. "But it is cold." He slipped off his jacket and put it gently round her shoulders; it was still warm from his own body. She thought his hand lingered a moment longer than necessity required.

She opened her mouth to protest but did not, unsure that she would not be making herself ridiculous. After all, they were in clear view of the house, and she had no reason to wish herself back there. Luncheon had been ghastly, and no one would believe she wanted to pursue its conversations. And he had removed from her the excuse of being cold.

He interrupted her train of thought. "Emily, have the police any idea who killed George yet? Or were you just defying the old woman?"

Why was he asking? She wanted to be free to like him; she felt a happiness in his company like sunlight through a garden door at the end of a long passage. Yet she was terribly afraid it was deceptive.

"I don't know," she said truthfully. "I didn't see Thomas this morning, and I only spoke to Charlotte for a moment as we came in to luncheon. I have no idea." She forced herself to face him; it was just a fraction better than imagining his eyes.

His expression was full of concern. Was it for her or for himself?

"What did Eustace mean?" he said urgently. "Emily, for heaven's sake think! I know it wasn't me, and I refuse to believe it was you. It has to be one of them! Let me help you, please. Try to think. Tell me what William meant."

Emily sat paralyzed. He looked so earnest, but he had lived by his charm for years; he was a superb actor when it was in his own interest. And this could be a matter of survival. If he had killed George they would hang him. The fact that she liked him did not cloud reason. Some extremely virtuous people could also be extremely boring, and admire them as one might, one shrank from their company. And the cruelest people could be very funny—until the essential ugliness showed through.

He was still talking, his eyes on her face. Could she look at him and keep the balance to disbelieve? She had always had sense, far more sense than Charlotte. And she was a better actress, more skilled in masking her own feelings.

She met his gaze squarely. "I don't know. I think he just hates Eustace and would like it to be him."

"That leaves only old Mrs. March," he said very quietly. "Unless you think it was Tassie, or Great-aunt Vespasia. Which you don't."

She knew what he was thinking now—it took only one step in reasoning, an inevitable step. It was Jack or Emily herself. She knew she had not murdered George and Sybilla, but she was growing increasingly afraid he had. Worse than that, she feared he still intended to court her.

He took her hands. He was not rough, but he was far stronger than she, and he did not mean to let go.

"Emily, for heaven's sake think! There is something in the March family that we don't know, something dangerous or shameful enough to cause murder, and if we don't find out what it is, you or I may very well be hanged for it instead!"

Half of her wanted to scream at him to be quiet, but she knew it was true. Giving way to hysterics now would be stupid and destructive—perhaps even fatal. Charlotte had got nowhere, except to discover Tassie's secret, which as it turned out was irrelevant. Emily would have to save herself. If Jack Radley were innocent, together they might discover something. If he were guilty and she played along with him, perhaps she would trick him into betraying something, however small. It could be survival.

"You are quite right," she said seriously. "We must think. I shall tell you everything I know, then you will tell me. Between us we may finally deduce the truth."

He smiled very slightly, not quite believing her.

She made an effort to deny the fear she felt—not only the great and overshadowing knowledge of danger from the law and the enduring judgment of Society, but the inner loneliness and the belying warmth he offered, which it would be so easy to accept. If only the poisonous suspicion in her mind could be crushed. She had to force herself to remember that he was still the most likely murderer. The thought hurt even more than she expected.

"Tassie goes out at night alone, to help deliver babies in the slums," she said rather abruptly.

If she hoped to startle him she succeeded magnificently. He stared at her while emotions teemed across his face: incredulity, fear, admiration, and lastly, pure delight.

"That's superb! But how in God's name do you know?"

"Charlotte followed her."

He cringed, letting his breath out between his teeth in a little hiss and shutting his eyes.

"I know," she said quietly. "I expect Thomas was furious."

"Furious!" his voice rose. "Isn't that something of an understatement?"

Immediately she was defensive. "Well, if she hadn't, we'd still be thinking it was Tassie! Charlotte saw her coming upstairs in the middle of the night with bloodstains on her hands and dress! What else should she do? Let it remain a mystery? She knows I didn't murder anyone—"

"Emily!" He caught her hands.

"—and if we don't find who it is, I could be arrested and imprisoned—"

"Emily! Stop it!"

"—and tried, and hanged!" she finished harshly. She was shaking in spite of the closeness of him, and the strength of his hands holding hers. "People have been hanged wrongly before." Memories, stories teemed in her mind. "Charlotte knows that, and so do I!" It was a relief to put it into words, to drag the real terror out of the darkness at the back of her mind and share it with him.

"I know," he said quietly. "But it is not going to happen to you. Charlotte won't let it—neither will I. It has to be someone in this house. Vespasia has the courage, if she thought such a thing were necessary. But she would never have killed George, and I don't think she would have had the physical strength to kill Sybilla—not the way it was done. Sybilla was a young, healthy woman. . . ." He hesitated, remembering.

"I know," she said without pulling her hands away

from him. "And Aunt Vespasia is not young, and not strong anymore."

He smiled bleakly. "I wish I could think of a reason why old Mrs. March would have done it," he said with feeling. "She's twice Vespasia's weight. She'd have the power."

Emily looked at their locked hands. "But why would she?" she said hopelessly, anger and frustration welling up inside her. "There'd have to be a reason."

"I don't know," he admitted. "Unless George knew something about her."

"Like what?"

He shook his head. "Something about the Marches? She's choked up with family pride. I'm damned if I know why. They've plenty of money, but no breeding at all. It comes from trade." Then he laughed at himself. "Not that I wouldn't be glad of a little of it! My mother was a de Bohun, traces her family back to the Conquest. But you can't even buy a good meal with that, let alone run a house."

A wild series of thoughts clashed and jostled in her mind. Had he killed George hoping to marry her for the Ashworth money? But then, what about Tassie? Any man with sense would have chosen that marriage; it was infinitely safer, and his for the asking—or he must have thought so. He didn't know about Mungo Hare. Or did he? Was he really so astounded by the news of Tassie's midnight expeditions as he pretended to be? If Charlotte had followed her, so could he—at least, as far as seeing the young curate and realizing Tassie would never marry anyone else. Or perhaps Tassie had even told him herself? She was honest enough. She might have chosen not to delude him with false hope—not of love, but of money.

Emily shivered. She wanted to look at him—surely she had some ability of judgment left. And yet she also dreaded what she would see, and what she would reveal of herself. But as long as it remained undone it would crowd out all other thought from her mind. It was like vertigo, standing at the edge of a high balcony with the compulsive desire to look down, feeling the void pulling at you.

She looked up quickly and found his eyes worried, serious; she could see no deceit in them at all. It solved nothing. To find ugliness there might have freed her, let her believe the worst of him and kill the hope that—that what?

She refused to put it into words. It was too soon. But the thought stayed at the edge of her mind, something to move towards, beckoning her like a warm room at the end of a winter journey.

"Emily?"

She recalled her attention. They had been talking about the old woman. "She might have done something scandalous in her youth," she offered. "Or maybe her husband did. Perhaps we should learn more of how the Marches got all their money—it could be something that would put an end to any idea of a peerage. Perhaps George knew of it. After all, it was her—" She swallowed. "Her medicine that was the poison."

Memory of death came back sharp and cold, physically painful, and the tears stung in her eyes. She found she was clinging to his hand so hard she must be hurting him, but he did not pull away. Instead he put his arm round her and held her, touching her hair with his lips, whispering words that had no meaning, but whose gentleness she felt with an ease that made weeping not an ache but a release from pain, an undoing of the hard, frightened knots inside her.

She realized that she wanted the solution to the crime almost as much for him as for herself. She longed with an intense need to know that he was untouched, unmarked by it.

Charlotte also was happy to be alone, and spent some time in the dressing room which was her bedroom, repeating in her mind all that she had learned since the first news of George's death right up to Pitt's departure this morning.

It was half past three when she went downstairs with the small spark of an idea she wanted to disbelieve. It was ugly and sad, and yet it answered all the contradictions.

She was in the withdrawing room, almost at the curtains which half covered the French doors to the conservatory, when she heard the voices.

"How dare you say such a thing in front of everyone!" It was Eustace, loud and angry. His broad back was to the doors and beyond him she could just see the sunlight on William's flaming hair. "I can forgive you a lot in your bereavement," Eustace went on. "But that insinuation was appalling. You as good as said I was guilty of murder!"

"You were perfectly happy to see Emily blamed—or Jack," William pointed out.

"That's entirely different. They are not part of us."

"For God's sake, what has that got to do with it?" William demanded furiously.

"It has everything to do with it!" Eustace was growing angrier, and there was an ugly note in his voice, as if the dark and unrefined mass of inner thoughts were too close to the frail surface of manners that overlaid them. "You betrayed the family in front of strangers! You suggested there was something secret and shameful which you knew and others didn't. Have you no conception what a meddling and inquisitive busybody that Pitt woman is? The dirty-minded little chit will never rest until she either uncovers or invents something to fit your wild ramblings. God knows what scandal she'll start!"

William moved back a step; his face was twisted with pain and contempt. "She'll have to be very dirty-minded indeed to get to the depths of your soul, if that is not too grand a word for it. Perhaps *belly* would be more apposite?"

"There's nothing wrong with a man having stomach," Eustace said with answering scorn. "I sometimes think if you had more stomach and fewer airy-fairy ideas you'd be more of a man! You mince around dabbling in paints and dreaming of sunsets like a lovesick girl. Where's your courage? Where's your heart, your manliness?"

William did not answer. Beyond Eustace, standing with his back to her, Charlotte could see the white, almost deathlike look on William's face, and she could feel pain in the air like the hot settling of condensation on the lily leaves and the vines.

"Great God!" Eustace shouted with unutterable disgust. "No wonder Sybilla took to flirting with George Ashworth! At least he had something in his trousers besides his legs!"

William winced with revulsion so acute Charlotte thought for a moment he had actually been struck. She was so offended for him herself that she felt sick; her hands were clammy and hurt with the strength of her clenched fists. Yet she still stood transfixed, listening, with a terrible foresight.

William's answer when it came was quiet, heavy with irony.

"And you expect me to be discreet for you in front of Mrs. Pitt? Father, you have no sense of the ridiculous—indeed the grotesque."

"Is it grotesque to expect a little responsibility from you?" Eustace shouted. "Family loyalty? You owe us that, William."

"I owe you nothing but my existence!" William said gratingly between his teeth. "And that was only because you wanted a son for your own vanity's sake, it was nothing to do with me. You want to continue your name. A perpetuation of little Eustace Marches all down through eternity, that's your idea of being immortal. With you it would be the flesh! Not an idea, not a creation, but an endless reproduction of bodies!"

"Ha!" Eustace said explosively, with overpowering derision. "Well, I missed my chance with you, didn't I? In twelve years of marriage you couldn't beget a child till now. And it's too late! If you'd played about less with paints and more in the bedroom, perhaps you'd have been more of a man, and none of this damn tragedy would have happened. George and Sybilla would be alive, and we wouldn't have the police in the house."

The conservatory was motionless; it seemed even the water did not drip.

Charlotte realized the tragic truth. The explanation was clear, like the hard, white daylight of early morning, showing every weakness, every flaw and pain. Without taking time to think or weigh any consequence she seized a china vase off the nearest small table and smashed it on the parquet floor, sending the pieces shivering noisily across the wide surface. Then she turned and ran back across the withdrawing room, through the dining room, and out into the hallway to where the telephone instrument was installed.

She picked it up and clicked the lever urgently. She was not used to it and was unsure exactly how it worked. Her ears were straining to catch the sound of Eustace coming after her.

There was a woman's voice coming through the speaker at her ear.

"Yes!" she said quickly. "I want the police station—I want to speak to Inspector Pitt. Please!"

"Do you want the local police station, ma'am?" the voice asked calmly.

"Yes! Yes, please!"

"Hold the line, please."

It seemed an age of clicking and buzzing, during which she was acutely aware of the dining room door behind her and every tiny creak of boards or whisper which could be a door opening wider or the softness of a shoe on carpet. At last she heard a man's voice at the other end of the line.

"Yes, ma'am. I'm sorry, Inspector Pitt ain't here. Can I give 'im a message when 'e comes in? Or can somebody else 'elp you?"

It had not occurred to her that he might not be there. She felt helpless, cut off.

"You there, miss?" The voice sounded anxious.

"Where is he?" She was beginning to panic. It was stupid, and yet she did not seem to be able to help herself.

"I can't rightly tell you that, miss, but 'e left about ten minutes ago in a cab. Can I 'elp you?"

"No." She had been so sure she could reach him, the thought of having to manage alone was worse now. "No, thank you." And with stiff fingers, shivering, she replaced the instrument in its hook.

She had no proof anyhow, only the certainty within her own mind. But now that she knew, there would be ways. The police surgeon . . . That was what Sybilla had gone to Clarabelle Mapes for: not to get rid of a baby, but to buy the one William could never give her, to silence the nagging, cruel tongues of the family, the condescension and the demand to satisfy the thoughtless, insatiable, dynastic vanity.

Charlotte was sick with grief for her, her aloneness, her need, the hopeless sense of rejection. No wonder she had had affairs, had turned to George. Was that what George had died for? Not because he had made love to her, or stolen her affections, but because in a moment's foolishness, from a need to justify herself, she had betrayed to generous, indiscreet George the secret too agonizing to be spoken even in the mind—let alone aloud for others to know, to pity, to make obscene and humiliating jokes over. There would always be the nudges and the jeers, the brazen manhood exhibited with a snigger. To men like Eustace virility was more than a physical act—it was proof of his existence, of potency and value in all of life.

And William had loved Sybilla—that Charlotte knew from far more than the words in the letters from the vanity case—with a love worth infinitely more than Eustace's narrow, physical mind could climb to. But in that one instance of weakness she had threatened his belief in himself, the respect every man must have to survive—not inwardly, where he had learned to bear it, but in Society, and, worst of all, among his family. Eustace was so close to the truth already, cruel and thrusting, intruding, like a rape of the spirit. What would he do if he knew? Forever pry at it till there was no dignity left, nothing unviolated by the constant remarks, the prurient, mocking eyes, the knowledge of superiority.

And so Sybilla had died, too, strangled by her own, beautiful hair before she could betray him again, perhaps to Jack.

The bought child William might have accepted, even understood, perhaps more easily than one conceived to another man. But he could never have accepted the shame.

Charlotte was still standing in the hallway wondering what to do. Both Eustace and William must have seen her; she had smashed the vase precisely so they should know she was there and stop that terrible hurting. Did they know how much she had overheard? Or were they so caught up in wounding each other that her momentary interruption was incidental, to be forgotten as soon as she left?

Without knowing what she intended other than perhaps to stop Eustace, she began back towards the dining room, past its gleaming, sunlit table, through the double doors to the withdrawing room, all smooth greenness and pale satins reflecting the light, and back to the entrance to the conservatory. There was silence now, and no sign of Eustace or William. The French doors were open wider, and the smell of damp earth came into the withdrawing room.

She stepped through them slowly onto the walk between the vines. She need not have come; there was nothing for her to do, except wait until she could find Pitt and tell him. If it were not for Emily and the fear that would hang over her forever, she would be tempted not to say anything. She did not feel any desire to be an instrument of justice, no sense of satisfaction or resolved anger.

The camellia bush was covered with flawless blooms, perfect rosettes. She did not like them. The canna lilies were better; irregular, assymetrical. The condensation dripped heavily into the pool. Someone should have opened the windows, even though it was a dull day.

She came to the space cleared at the end, where William had his studio, and stopped abruptly. She wanted to weep, but she was too tired and too cold inside.

There were two easels set up. On one was the finished painting of the April garden full of subtle loveliness, dreams, and sudden cruelty. The other was a portrait of Sybilla, realistic, without flattery, and yet with such a tenderness it laid open a beauty in her few had perceived so clearly in life.

In front of them, crumpled rather awkwardly on the stone floor, William lay, the palette knife having slipped from his hand, the blade of it scarlet, only inches away from the wound in his throat. With an artist's knowledge of anatomy he had sliced the vein in one clean movement. He had understood the smashed vase perfectly and saved her the last ghastly confrontation.

She stood staring at him. She wanted to bend and lay him straighter—as if it could make any difference now—but she knew that she must not touch anything. She remained there, silent, hearing the water trickling on the leaves and the sound of a flower head dropping, petals rotted.

At last she turned and walked slowly under the vines, back through the French windows, and saw Eustace coming in from the dining room. With a violence that startled her, the long path up to the tragedy stood out clearly in her mind; the years of demanding, expecting, the subtle cruelties. Her fury exploded.

"William is dead," she said harshly. "I'm sorry. I really am sorry. I liked him—probably far more than you ever did." She looked at his shocked face, the open mouth and pallid skin, without any gentleness. "He killed himself," she went on. "There was nothing else left for him, except arrest and hanging." She found her voice was choking as she said it. She let all her scalding emotions pour out at Eustace.

"I—I don't know what you mean!" he said helplessly. "Dead? Why? What happened?" He moved towards her, floundering a little. "Don't just stand there, do something! Help him! He can't be dead!"

She blocked his way. "He is," she repeated. "Don't

you understand yet, you stupid, blind man?'' She could feel the thickness tightening her throat. She wanted him to know the maiming he had caused, absorb it into itself and become one with it.

He stared at her as if she had struck him. ''Killed himself!'' he repeated foolishly. ''You are hysterical—he can't have!''

''He has. Don't you know why?'' She was shivering.

''Me! How could I know?'' His face was ashen, the first pain of belief beginning to show in his eyes.

''Because it was you who drove him to it.'' She spoke more quietly now, as if he were an obstinate child. ''Trying to make him into something he wasn't—couldn't be— and ignoring all that he was. You with your obsession with family, your pride, your vulgarity, your—'' She stopped, not wanting to expose William to his contempt, even now.

He was bewildered. ''I don't understand. . . .''

She closed her eyes, feeling helpless.

''No. No, I suppose you don't. But maybe you will one day.''

He sat down on the nearest chair, huddled as if his legs had failed him, still looking up at her.

''William?'' he repeated very quietly. ''William killed George? And Sybilla—he killed Sybilla?''

Now the tears burned in her eyes. She saw Vespasia in the dining room doorway, white as the wall behind her, and beyond, gentle and untidy, the figure of Pitt.

She made her decision. ''He thought there was an affair,'' she said slowly to everyone, the words difficult, the lie catching on her tongue. ''He was wrong—but it was too late then.''

Eustace was staring at them with the beginnings of comprehension, a glimmer of what she was doing, and even why. It was a world he had not imagined, and he was frightened by his own crassness.

In the doorway Pitt put his arm round Vespasia, supporting her, but he looked over her shoulder at Charlotte. He smiled, his face blurred with pity.

"That's right," he said deliberately. "There's nothing more for us to do now."

"Thank you," Charlotte whispered. "Thank you, Thomas."

ABOUT THE AUTHOR

ANNE PERRY is the author of seven previous Victorian mysteries featuring Inspector Pitt and his wife Charlotte: RUTLAND PLACE, RESURRECTION ROW, PARAGON WALK, CALLANDER SQUARE, THE CATER STREET HANGMAN, BLUEGATE FIELDS, and DEATH IN THE DEVIL'S ACRE. Anne Perry lives in Suffolk, England.